APR -- 2022

1908 00393 9741

W9-BYZ-195

DISCARD

THOMAS FORD MEMORIAL LIBRARY
800 CHESTNUT
WESTERN SPRINGS, IL 60558

ALL

THE

BEST

LIARS

ALL THE BEST LIARS

AMELIA KAHANEY

FLATIRON
BOOKS
NEW YORK

This is a work of fiction. All of the characters, organizations, and events portrayed in this novel are either products of the author's imagination or are used fictitiously.

ALL THE BEST LIARS. Copyright © 2022 by Alloy Entertainment LLC and Amelia Kahaney. All rights reserved. Printed in the United States of America. For information, address Flatiron Books, 120 Broadway, New York, NY 10271.

Designed by Jen Edwards

www.flatironbooks.com

Library of Congress Cataloging-in-Publication Data

Names: Kahaney, Amelia, author.
Title: All the best liars / Amelia Kahaney.
Description: First edition. | New York : Flatiron Books, 2022.
Identifiers: LCCN 2021043959 | ISBN 9781250312709 (hardcover) |
    ISBN 9781250312716 (ebook)
Subjects: CYAC: Friendship Fiction. | Secrets—Fiction. |
    High schools—Fiction. | Schools—Fiction. | LCGFT: Novels.
Classification: LCC PZ7.K12243 Al 2022 | DDC [Fic]—dc23
LC record available at https://lccn.loc.gov/2021043959

Our books may be purchased in bulk for promotional, educational, or business use. Please contact your local bookseller or the Macmillan Corporate and Premium Sales Department at 1-800-221-7945, extension 5442, or by email at MacmillanSpecialMarkets@macmillan.com.

First Edition: 2022

10 9 8 7 6 5 4 3 2 1

For Ezra

Like any girl, I pulled myself into shreds to test the rumor that something with blood like mine could be halved and still whole.

—Franny Choi, from "Worm Moon" in "Perihelion: A History of Touch"

ALL

THE

BEST

LIARS

PROLOGUE

Tic-tac-toe, three girls in a row. Nine years old and inseparable: Sydney, Rain, and Brianna. Friends for life, or so they think. They squat in Syd's driveway, dusty feet sandaled against the flame-hot concrete, heads bent to study the thing Rain trapped under the jelly jar. It's an electric blue beetle the size of a thumb, a tropical shock against the putty of the desert with bits of gold at the legs.

"How pretty," breathes Syd. She's a freckled shrimp, her nose and shoulders incessantly peeling, new pink skin always emerging underneath the old. She squints at the bug's aquamarine shell and thinks longingly of the swimming pools behind all the big houses down the highway in Palm Springs. "So tropical."

It is 102 degrees at 8 PM, the brutal sun just now starting to dip behind the ring of boulder-studded mountains that circle the desert cities. A pocketknife-sized gray lizard darts out of the shade of the antelope brush that lines their street, blinks at the girls, then reconsiders and retreats. The girls ignore the phlegmy whine of Brie's hated pit bull mix, Spanky, who rubs his flank along the chain-link fence and kicks up dust in her bald yard three houses over.

Rain sits back on her heels and gives the other two a one-eyed squint. Her teeth crowd her mouth in a way that pushes out her lips so from one angle she looks a little like a horse and from another, even though she's just turned ten, she looks like someone out of the tattered old September *Vogue* the girls all share. Rain's limbs are long and deeply sun-browned, her arms awkward branches sprouting from a sagging red tube top, her wild snarl of hair flung over half her face. "Pretty, but in a scary way," Rain pronounces. All of Rain's thoughts she shares confidently, convincingly, as if they're Great Truths the girls all need to hear.

"Look at the antennas," says Brie. She scrapes the jar slowly over the cracks of Syd's driveway, forcing the beetle to move, too. Then she lowers her face close to the jar, her own white-tipped lashes almost touching it. "She's got Betty Boop lashes." And indeed the beetle does, three swoopy black points on each side.

Brie is dressed weird, wearing one of the ugly old-fashioned dresses with a big bow on the chest that her dad keeps cluelessly buying her, but the other two girls don't say anything about it. Hard enough to live with a dad like Ed, they figure, and there's no point in making Brie even more self-conscious.

"We should let it go," Syd says. She can hear her mother moving around in the house, a pot banging onto the stove for mac 'n' cheese. But when she lifts the jar, the beetle doesn't move. It's frozen, the shiniest emerald on the gray concrete, surrounded by the browns and beiges of the high desert, the junked cars, and the beat-up aluminum siding of their crappy neighborhood. A thing too jeweled, too audacious, to exist here among them.

"It's dead," Rain declares, voice flat. She waits a beat. "I'm going to keep it."

Rain's long fingers scoop the bug up, cradle it like something precious. The other girls want it, too, but nobody fights her. Rain always gets her way. The other two swallow their longing until it dissolves into something else, a kind of not-caring that helps make being second and third easier. It's been that way between them for a long time, even after everything starts to fall apart. Until everything shifts and a new hierarchy stacks up.

What the three of them will remember most about their time

together in the dead-dog hills of Termico, California, is brightness and heat and the feeling of being trapped in it, confined under the dome of an invisible glass. Because the desert is a place where you bide your time, trapped and roasting, skittering uselessly until you grow listless. It's a place you're supposed to retire to, a climate for those who have already lived their lives, dreams long since given up. Anyone young—anyone with any sense—would want to leave.

And eventually, all of them will. But it won't happen the way they want it to. One will do it by dying, another by lying, a third by taking the fall.

Rain pinches the beetle between her fingers and stands up, her knees coated in dust. "Dumb bug," she says to it, a smirk alighting then vanishing from her brazen mouth. The metallic blue of the dead bug's armor glows in her hand. "You should have dug your way out."

PART I
SYDNEY

MAY

1

You think you know when you've hit bottom, when things have gotten complicated and sad in a way you'll never be able to fix. But the truth is, you don't have any idea how much worse it can get.

By the time I had drifted most of the way down, washed up on a Monday morning in the last seat of the lurching yellow school bus with the aftertaste of vomit still on my tongue, my life had blown apart so completely that I couldn't see the shape of it anymore. I was friendless, abandoned, dumped, humiliated. More alone than I'd ever been.

It was the ass-end of senior year, far too late in the life cycle of high school to assume any of what was broken could be fixed before all of us scattered forever. All I had to do was get through two more weeks of classes. Soon, so soon, high school and all the people in it would be a memory I could spend the rest of my life repressing. Starting with last night.

As the bus sighed to life, flashes of the party glimmered, bright sparkles of shame that died away as quickly as they flared to life. Pieces of the night were already missing. Things I would never get back. All I had were a few garbled moments glimpsed through smeared glass: The pills I took, the drinks I swallowed, the rage I felt stumbling out of that enormous house. The hurt on Rain's crumpled face. Rain, who always believed I was good. Who never knew the petty, sour girl I'd let myself become.

But why had I been so furious? And what had I said to hurt her so? I remembered only snatches of the fight we'd had. The feel of screaming at each other in that big dim bedroom. How it had been cathartic and terrible all at once.

I closed my eyes and tried to remember, groping for the details of the fight. But like a word you can't quite think of until hours after you need it, it was just out of reach. My memory skipped from the kerosene burn of whatever I'd swigged in the party's packed kitchen to the sting of gravel against my skin. The ice-cold desert that had almost swallowed me up. Spider, my brother, cursing low under his breath on the way home. Blood dripping down my forearms, staining the car's upholstery.

It was almost a coherent narrative.

Almost, but not quite.

Rocketing down the mountain toward school, all I knew for sure was that I was alone, ashamed, a rube. Abandoned in the end even by my brother, who had vanished somewhere in the night. That morning before six, I'd staggered to his room, opened his door to tell him how drug-sick I was, to guilt him into driving me to school . . . but his bed was empty and the car was gone.

Now I curled into my and Rain's old seat, the seat we'd been sitting in since elementary school. Last one on the left, best seat in the house. You had your pick when you got on first. We were always first on and last off, coming, as we did, from the farthest away. Termico was such a tiny dot on the map that we didn't have our own schools. So down the mountain we went, into Palm Springs or Palm Desert, where the hotels were, the expensive houses with their swimming pools, the malls, the movie theaters, and the schools.

My index finger traced the ballpoint graffiti we had drawn on the seat in front of us some years back. Hearts, teardrops, Celtic knots, stylized versions of our names. *Syd & Rain 4eva*, I'd written in sixth grade, or was it seventh? God, did it feel true.

What was that expression? *We plan and God laughs?*

Miss Roberta pulled the bus over for its next stop and the door hissed open. A pack of freshmen and sophomores whose names I didn't know got on, along with two junior boys, Kenny Alvarez and Grant Matthews, who lived in a world of role-playing games so complex and all-encompassing that it was like they existed on some other planet.

I turned up my headphones and looked out the window at the sunbaked hills that stretched out past the highway, their brown softness like the curved backs of giant sleeping cats. Skrillex filled my ears—anxious, unromantic zombie tracks. The sun was already strong enough at 7:35 AM to make the fingerprinted glass hot to the touch. I touched it anyway, wanting to feel the singe of it.

Two more weeks of school and one lonely summer before I could leave this place behind. In the fall I would head to Miami University, which sounded like beaches and volleyball but was actually a midsize college in Oxford, Ohio, where my aunt, Debbie, lived. Miami had given me the best financial aid package out of all the places I applied. Mom was so relieved when I agreed to live in Debbie's spare room after the college promised twenty hours of work study on top of the tuition waiver. "Your future is all decided now!" Mom had declared. It may have been the most depressing thing she'd ever said to me.

But Miami may as well have been in Florida for how badly I longed for it as a vacation from what life here had become. Ohio felt far enough away for me to become a different person. No more ghosts of former friends. No more sweaty afternoons pressed up against a boy who only disappointed me. Debbie's condo's guest room overlooked a scrap-metal yard and a Kroger, and beyond that a gray slice of a river. There, it would just be me, my bitten-down fingernails, and my lonely dreams.

Maybe that was the lesson of all this. That life was only manageable if you lived it alone.

Last night proved how capable I was of hurting people I loved. I shuddered, still groping for details that refused to come. Whatever I'd said, it was bad. Bad enough that I'd spent all night apologizing and Rain still wasn't answering me. I scrolled through all my texts to her.

1:41 AM: I'm sorry. I didn't mean what I said.

2:04 AM: Please write back & tell me you're ok.

2:47 AM: Tell me you hate me. Tell me you'll never forgive me. Just say something.

5:20 AM: Have you really given up on us entirely? Aren't I allowed to be upset, just this once?

I'd always been the reliable, unflappable one. The girl who measured her words out carefully, who thought before she spoke. Or, I used to be. This horrible year had changed me enough that some days, I didn't quite recognize myself.

I tried again: Still waiting. Hello?

I watched the screen, looking for the three dots to prove Rain was at least getting my texts, even if she refused to reply. None appeared.

When the bus finally pulled into the parking lot of Valley Sands High, I forced myself up on shaking legs. I didn't bother to look out the bus window when we parked, so when I shuffled down the stairs and saw hundreds of kids clustered in the front courtyard, I lost my breath with the shock of it. In the desert, people don't usually hang around outside after March or April. But today, even though it was already 95 degrees outside, most of the school was out front. Everyone was weirdly quiet, staring down at their phones or talking in low, somber voices. Lots of kids were crying.

The sour nervousness in my stomach bubbled into full-blown nausea.

Something bad had happened.

I dug my phone from my pocket again and stared at the blank screen. An old reflex from back when it would twitch with missives from Rain a hundred times a day. Nobody had texted me any news. But really, who would?

I heard the word *she,* the word *fire,* again and again as I plunged forward through the heat and smells of high school bodies packed tightly together—the fruit-scented body sprays, the bad cologne, the reek of sports equipment, the makeup and socks and hair gel and the waft of flavored nicotine vapor—until it felt like all of it was in my mouth, an indelible taste I would never get out.

The rubber band snap of missing Rain twanged in my throat. Even with her not speaking to me, I wanted her here. Rain would know what to do, how to deal. She always did.

I pushed through to the center of the courtyard, where the crowd had opened up to make space for Charlotte Yu, a junior from my AP Spanish class who was crying into a microphone held by a woman from News 4. A few feet away, a cameraman filmed them both.

"I just can't. It's awful. I can't even believe how awful this is," Charlotte sputtered, a track set on repeat.

I strained to hear, remembering last year when Jordy Stewart got hit by a delivery truck while he was skateboarding behind the Rite Aid. The senselessness of it, how you knew that it could have been your sibling, your best friend, even you. How it could have been any of us.

"Brie Walsh was the sweetest girl," Charlotte said.

I stopped breathing.

Brie Walsh *was?*

Brie Walsh was?

I had misheard, obviously. A trick played by my subconscious. Because it was true I had wished harm on Brie. Had done so as recently as last night.

"Tell me more about Brianna Walsh," the reporter urged. "What was she like?"

I blinked hard. When I opened my eyes again, everything was tinted a hospital gray, as if the sky had a shade pulled over it.

Terrifying, was what Charlotte wouldn't say. *She owned all of us, and she kept score.*

"She was beautiful and smart and everyone here . . . like, all of us, we looked up to her. She was really nice. Like, a really good person. She was the student body president, ran track, got good grades . . ."

Normally this kind of sucking up would make me laugh, but now I felt all the color drain from my face. Brie had taken everything from me: best friend, boyfriend, sanity, joy. I'd spent so much time this year wishing she would somehow disappear. But I never wished her dead. Would I? *Had I?*

You two deserve each other.

I shook my head in a futile attempt to erase the memory. The last thing I had said to her last night—the last thing I remembered saying—couldn't be the last thing I would ever say to her. Life didn't work that way. In real life, Brie was the winner and I was the loser. She'd made that so clear. And it was never the winners who died tragically.

Still on camera, Charlotte broke down, covering her face with her hands. "I just can't believe this is happening."

I turned in a slow circle, conscious of all of us, hundreds of us in the broiling courtyard thinking of Brie Walsh all at once. It didn't seem possible that she wasn't a part of it. She had always been at the center of things, a front-runner in the marathon that was high school, a popular paradox—churchgoing binge drinker, a self-proclaimed virgin who, somewhere around age thirteen, had shape-shifted from a bland wisp of insecurity into someone people idolized, were afraid of, or both. She was a powerful vortex of blue eyes and track-toned muscle, vanilla-scented everything, white-white Stan Smiths and matching whitestripped teeth, laughter that singled out and mocked you for any reason at all, a machine gun that you prayed would not focus its laser eye beam on you. Or at least not for very long.

It would have killed her to know she was missing this.

Desperate for more information, I backtracked through the crowd until I spotted Anya Patel sitting alone on a bench, staring straight ahead, her eyes unfocused and smeared with old eyeliner, her fingers twisting the nameplate necklace she often wore. She still had a couple of sequins adhered to her cheeks from the party last night, and her purple bangs puffed out around her face in all directions. She looked as wrecked as I felt.

"What's going on?" The plastic of the bench seat burned the backs of my thighs when I sat down beside her. "What happened to Brie?"

Anya looked at me the way people look at their parents when they've said something preposterously out of touch. She'd been in Brie's inner circle as long as anyone, even if she'd managed to be nicer to me these past couple of months than the rest of her crew.

"You didn't hear?" She took a deep breath, looked skyward, then back at me. I held my breath, terrified to learn what she was about to tell me. "There was a fire at Brie's house last night. Her dad was out of town, I guess. But . . ." She searched my eyes and grabbed my hand. Ice shot through my veins and suddenly I couldn't bear for her to say it. *Never mind,* I wanted to say, *don't tell me.* "Brie didn't make it out."

I looked down at my hand in hers. It had begun to shake. "Are you sure?" I asked, though I knew she was. This many people didn't mourn over a mistake.

Anya nodded. "It's so horrible. I—I don't understand how it can be real."

I reached out to hug her and muttered *I'm so sorry,* and then before I knew what I was doing I was up on my feet again, pushing through the crowd.

As I moved through the packed courtyard, my mind filled with images of little-girl Brie with her starched dresses and white-blond frizz, walking solemnly to her father's car or braiding the manes of her My Little Ponies, her face serious, her blue eyes always reflecting a lost blankness. Then big Brie, rich bitch Brie in her fancy new house, her brassy highlights and immaculate crop tops, Brie downing vodka crans until she came alive, that dead-eyed lostness having morphed into something so powerful, so magnetic and mean that you could get swept away in it if you weren't careful. Or lose your best friend to the riptide.

Rain. My thoughts careened wildly. She must have been beside herself. No wonder she wasn't answering my texts. I craned my neck and began to search for her, but then I realized there was no way Rain would be here right now. Rain skipped school if she had a hangnail. No way would she come here today and let people see her cry. She wouldn't be able to watch people talk about her behind their hands, couldn't endure their pity.

I texted her again, frantic this time. My hands shook so badly I nearly dropped the phone.

I just heard. I'm so sorry. Are you with someone? You shouldn't be alone right now.

I paused, checked to see if she was reading, but there was no indication she was. I wrote again:

Please tell me where you are. I'll come to you. Forget last night. None of that matters now.

The morning bell began its shrill buzz. There would be an assembly convened, just like when Jordy died. Grief counselors in peasant skirts and dangly earrings, their faces somber behind Principal Stokes as she made a speech.

I turned in a circle as bodies swarmed past me, students filtering inside much more quietly than usual. A few seniors and juniors, the ones I'd gone to elementary with, nodded in my direction, remembering, maybe, that I'd been close to Brie once. Candice Lombardi, who had been friendly to me last night at her stepbrother's party, broke away from the girls she was walking with and beelined toward me, her eyes and nose red. She smiled in a way I thought was sympathetic, touched my shoulder as she walked past, then paused for just an instant to whisper in my ear: "Happy now?"

Her smile twisted into something else, nostrils flared, before she breezed by, leaving me to shatter into pieces right there in the courtyard. The words pinballed around in my head: *happy now happy now happy now.* I pushed through the throngs of students toward the gaping maw of the school entrance, the low-slung beige building like an army barrack that offered no real shelter. I shoved my hands into my pockets and kept them fisted so they wouldn't shake. A buzzing in my skull grew louder: like cicadas, like leaf blowers, like jackhammers.

I slid into my chair in homeroom just as the final bell sounded, aware without looking that Chase's desk was empty three rows over from mine, a sore spot rubbed raw. As Mrs. Centowicz stumbled through a consoling speech, I crumbled into dust again, nobody to anyone. I stared straight ahead for the rest of homeroom, trying not to think. Wishing, like always, that everything was the way it used to be.

Wishing, like always, for Rain.

2

After a two-hour-long assembly where grief counselors smiled nervously behind Principal Stokes while she urged us to *let it out, we are here to listen, this is a terrible tragedy and it's hard for any of us to understand how these things can happen to good people, to our own Brianna Walsh, who was such a beautiful light in our community,* the rest of the day passed behind that gray curtain of disbelief and horror. I was plagued by thoughts of Brie's lungs filling with smoke, visions of her reaching for the door, grasping the knob, the unknown fact of whether flame licked her skin.

Every half hour, I fired off another text to Rain and heard nothing back.

I spent lunch and my free period in the ceramics room, where I'd been going ever since things had ended with Chase. I sat at a table in the back of the room, an untouched slice of cafeteria pizza congealing in front of me as I stared into space and willed Rain to respond to one of my texts. A few other misfits sat scattered around the room at other tables, everyone granting one another the courtesy of pretending we were alone.

Eventually, Mr. Day, the ancient ceramics teacher, shuffled over.

"A hell of a thing," he said. Then he opened his old tortoise hands to present me with a tiny coil pot I'd glazed weeks ago and forgotten about. "You take care of this, take it home and put it on a shelf." He pressed it into my palm, where it fit just right. "Won't make anything better, but it's something to focus on."

When the bus dropped me off at the corner of Mount Olive Road and Clay Street, it was 106 degrees outside. I walked through the thick heat past the other prefabs—Brie's old one, which had never rented out again, marked by the rusted car parked in the driveway that had appeared a year or two after she and her dad had left here, and Rain's old one, which stood empty since her mom still held the lease and hadn't bothered to find a new tenant. A clump of tangled wind chimes swung wildly from a corner of the porch above a line of plastic pots that held the withered remnants of long-dead mums.

Joan never could keep anything growing, but now she didn't need to. In their new house, she had a gardener for such things. "They don't let you get away with mess here," she'd said to me just after they moved, waving her usual Newport Light in an absurd cigarette holder like she had not only moved into an upscale neighborhood but also time-warped back to the 1940s. "They ring your bell and recite the rules if your lawn isn't the right color."

In my living room, the blinds were drawn tight against the heat. The AC unit shook and rattled, working as hard as it could to get the room to stay at 76, the lowest Mom would let us set it to. Spider must have turned it on. Mom was at work like always, though she'd called me around noon to check on me after she heard the news.

I pulled the front door shut behind me and let my eyes adjust to the darkness. With the exaggerated care of someone who now expected everything to crumble and be destroyed by unexpected forces, I placed the coil pot on our waist-high bookshelf, right in front of Heart Attack Gary's stack of Area 51 alien invasion books Mom still insisted on keeping as a shrine to the great man's hobbies. I could hear the water running in the bathroom.

I took off my backpack and lay down in a heap on the couch. A loose spring poked into my tailbone but I stayed still, too exhausted to readjust. Everything, all our furniture and this prefab house with walls just slightly thicker than cardboard, had been Mom's boyfriend Gary's once. He died of a heart attack eleven years ago when I was six and Spider was eight. Since he had no family anyone could find, we got it all. Gary had been nice enough when he wasn't building up a head of steam about aliens and crop circles. It was Rain who'd christened him Heart Attack Gary during one of the long afternoons Mom would spend holed up in her room "lying down," which meant crying, when me and Rain would scrounge for hot sauce packets from Panchitos in the junk drawer in the kitchen and squirt them on white bread we'd eat while baking in the sun on the plastic chairs in Rain's dead-grass yard.

Once Mom came out of mourning, she began talking about replacing the couch. She'd been talking about it for ten years now. If I ever had any money, the first thing I planned to do was buy Mom a new couch. Now though, the sharp spring in my tailbone felt like a punishment I deserved. I pulled a pillow on top of me and hugged it, wanting to cry but unable to, dehydrated and wrung out from all the tears I'd already spilled today and the hours I'd spent retching into the toilet bowl last night.

The faucets squeaked in the bathroom and soon my brother's heavy step bumped down the hall.

"I'm home," I yelled.

He grunted in acknowledgment. I wondered if he knew about Brie yet or if I'd have to break the news. I assumed he'd only just now woken up after returning from wherever he'd disappeared to in the wee hours of the morning.

I turned onto my side, our coffee table now at eye level. Even this reminded me of Rain. I ran a finger over the rough wood pulp exposed in one corner where the laminate had peeled off, remembering when Rain had scratched a tiny cursive word there with a ballpoint pen: *nadir*. Meaning "lowest point a person can reach" or "rock bottom." Apt for our living room in Termico, the second-shabbiest town in the desert cities region. We were big on that word for a while, somewhere around middle school. Or, she was. If I closed my eyes, I could almost see Rain sitting cross-legged right here in her cutoffs, her long, tanned legs folded under her, picking at the tabletop with one hand and flipping the remote control relentlessly with the other, as if she could find something perfect for us if only she were more aggressive with the buttons.

It was a perfect word for today, *nadir*. If I were any lower, I'd be subterranean.

Rain had practically lived here before she'd moved down the mountain. The space was still so infused with her, though she hadn't been here in months. It was Brie who had died, but it felt like Rain was the one I was mourning.

Spider walked into the living room with a towel around his shoulders. He wore black basketball shorts and a stained white T-shirt with a big pot leaf on it. The belly I still wasn't used to strained against the fabric.

"Where were you this morning?"

"Hello to you, too," my brother said. "I was here. Who do you think drove you home after you passed out?"

I remembered Spider dragging me to the car, yelling at me to stay awake. I knew he'd driven me home. It was later that he'd disappeared.

"I looked for you. You weren't in your room." After a round of puking, I'd staggered to his room to blame him for it. His bed was just a tumble of sheets, a lone FUCK THE POLICE baseball cap resting on his pillow in the golden light of dawn.

"Oh, really? You weren't all that observant last night, from what I remember." He grinned the way he always did when someone else messed up worse than he had. Like *gotcha, now you've sunk to my level.* "You probably just didn't see me."

I shook my head a little, doubting my sanity. "No, I'm sure I would have seen you. Your car wasn't here." I'd looked outside his window where the Fiesta should have been. "Why are you lying to me?" It came out sounding like more of a comment than a question. Spider didn't answer. He'd already moved on to rummaging in the fridge, apparently done with the subject of his whereabouts. I decided to let it go, knowing there was something far more important I had to tell him now.

"Spi. Something terrible happened."

"I had the news on earlier." He'd piled a bunch of food on the counter and paused now to look at me. "You okay?"

"I mean . . . no. Not at all."

Neither of us said anything for a minute. I imagined he was searching for the right thoughtful words to console me.

"I can't believe the bitch kicked it," he said at last.

"Don't call her that." I twisted away from the poking couch spring and buried my face in the corduroy. When I squeezed my eyes shut I saw Brie's heart-shaped face, her flashing teeth, the dimple on her right cheek Rain used to poke when we were little.

"Sorry. I can't believe the *demon spawn* kicked it."

"Jesus, Spider." A thin blade of pain sliced my skull from my left eye through to the nape of my neck. "It's not a joke. Whatever we thought of her, she didn't deserve to *die*."

"Okay, yeah, obviously." Spider opened a pack of tortillas and broke three eggs into a bowl. He sniffed a container of week-old rice. In a minute, he had oil heating in a pan and had tossed in the rice and an alarming amount of Cholula. Cooking, if you could call it that, was something he'd learned at Pine Grove, the state prison in Northern California he'd been in for the past ten months before getting released early on good behavior. "But . . . how does someone sleep through a fire?"

I made a sound in the back of my throat and stared up at the ceiling, unable to fathom it. Home less than twenty-four hours, Spider at nineteen was different from the brother I knew when we he was sentenced—not exactly mature or adult, but definitely not the wild goofball I grew up with. He was quieter now. And also kind of a stranger, with a whole life I knew nothing about, including a new set of disappointments that were just starting to float to the surface. A bitterness sometimes crept into his conversation now, peeking out unexpectedly and then receding behind jokes or apathy. "Especially her," he continued. "I've never known Brianna Walsh not to look out for number one."

"What's that supposed to mean?" I studied my brother as he broke up the rice in the pan with a wooden spoon. I hadn't heard Spider voice a strong opinion about anyone almost ever. At most, he'd pass judgment on one of his beloved Lakers players or defend his creepy friend Whit whenever Mom called him a bad influence, but he'd certainly never voiced opinions about my friends before. Or my former friends. A moment from the party last night came to me then, one of the few that floated up from the abyss—Spider and Anya Patel embracing like the oldest, dearest friends. "What's with you and those girls? When have you hung out with Brie Walsh since she left the neighborhood?"

"Around the way, you know." Spider shot me a fake smile, the kind with lots of teeth and dead eyes. The oil began to hiss in the pan; he bludgeoned the rice a few more times and dumped the eggs in. "Just here and there."

"Around the way?" Was this prison talk? I sat up ramrod straight on the couch now, my eyes narrowed. There was something he wasn't telling me. "So you two were friends?"

"Forget it, okay?" His smile dissolved into a sharp, unreadable look. "She's gone now. I'm just processing, same as you. Thinking about karma. Jail makes you philosophical, you know."

Spider stirred his rice while I thought about karma.

"Wonder how old Ed's doing," he said.

I shuddered. I hadn't thought much about Brie's dad. The news said he was out of town when it happened.

"Bet he's a mess."

I nodded and tried to imagine the guilt of knowing your only child died in a fire after you'd left her all alone to fend for herself, but I couldn't. It was too awful. Again my thoughts ping-ponged back to Rain. She must be watching the coverage. Automatically, my fingers fired off another text.

> Where are you? I'm worried about you. Tell me you're getting these.

I stared at my phone screen, but of course there was no indication she'd seen anything I sent. Just . . . nothing.

"Want some? I call it hangover surprise." My brother held up the frying pan so I could see the glistening orange slop he'd created. "You look like you could use it."

A spicy whiff of it reached me, and my stomach lurched. "No thanks."

When Spider dumped his food onto a plate, I forced myself off the couch. I walked down the hall and paused in the doorway of my room, piles of clothes everywhere, my desk a disorganized heap of papers and books.

I took a deep breath in for two, out for four, the way my anxiety app suggested. Then I dialed Rain's number. It went straight to her voice mail.

"You've almost reached Rain Santangelo." That familiar voice. Bored, cynical, full of gravel. "Leave a message if you must."

"Hi. It's me." I stopped, unsure how to do this. Of course she knew it was me. How long had it been since I'd called Rain instead of texted? "Call me, okay? As soon as you can. Don't—don't shut me out. I know you're angry. But please. I can't do this alone. And you can't either. Or, you shouldn't. Okay, bye."

Idiot, I whispered. For all that was missing in my memory of last night and for my inability to get through to her now.

I leaned against the hallway wall and pressed my forehead into the wood paneling hard enough to leave an indentation. I needed to go see her. Apologize in person. To grieve with her, even if Brie wasn't my best friend or a friend at all. I still felt her loss. It was all I could think about.

In the living room, my brother belched.

When I closed the door to my room, the question he asked echoed in my head: How *does* a person sleep through a fire?

3

Spider wasn't a paragon of usefulness or assertiveness, or even of basic hygiene or simple communication skills, but he had always been an amazing driver. And being fresh out of Pine Grove, he had nothing to do and nowhere to go. This meant that for the first time in years, he was willing—even eager—to hang out with me.

So when I asked him to drive me to Rain's because I was scared to go alone, I braced to hear the old Spider say *no fucking way*, but the new Spider was surprisingly willing. "Just gotta drop a deuce and check in with my probation officer," he said. "Give me a couple hours."

"Gross." I grimaced, but in truth I'd missed having my disgusting brother around to keep things real. Maybe if Spider hadn't been locked up, these past few months might have been a little less annihilating.

By eight, we were gunning the Fiesta down Mount Olive Road, sputtering our way to Rain's. Unfortunately, Spider remembered that this was also the way to Brie's house. "Let's swing by," he suggested. "Just to see."

I shot him a horrified look he didn't notice. "No way."

"Come on," he wheedled. "Five minutes. Don't you want to see what the hell happened there?"

A sick part of me did, but the rest of me really, really didn't.

I groaned, already knowing he'd take us there no matter what I said. I tucked my knees into my T-shirt and pulled myself into a ball with my feet under me on the car seat. Out the window was the sunset-hued unwinding of the road, the brush along the edges whizzing by in the pink light. Every few minutes a meaty June bug or moth splattered against the windshield, its wet insides fanning out, obscene, black as blood.

"Burned alive." Spider ran a hand over his stubbly jowls and winced. "Got to be the worst way to go."

"Please let's not." I was starting to think I could smell the fire even now, even up here on the mountain still, which was impossible. "I can't handle it."

Spider shook his head. "Be brave, dude. It'll be good for you to see it. For, like . . ." He searched for the word. "Closure."

"Fine, Spi." What good was it to fight with him when he was clearly driving us there either way?

The closer we got, the more I thought about Brie. Faint edges of new memories began to emerge from the jumbled wreckage of last night. The ugly words we spat, all that had built up since our friendship ended so many years ago.

This is how you treat your best friend? Brie had sneered. I couldn't remember what she was responding to, only that I'd hurt Rain and Brie had leapt to defend her. *You've been a judgmental bitch ever since we were little.* The self-assurance she'd tossed this off with stung me now like a slap. The ease with which she could speak such hateful words, the way she seemed so sure they were true.

Spider turned the radio up as we entered the valley, the road lined on either side now with peach and beige developments, all terra-cotta roofs and wacky 1960s topiaries.

I tried to picture the fire. Brie's giant room on the top floor with its own bathroom. Her bed in the center of the room. Her royal purple bedspread, her gold pillows. The fairy lights she'd strung up around it. The purple wingback chairs, the sheepskin rug. Had she smelled the smoke? Had she tried to run and just not made it downstairs? Was she too incapacitated to even try? "Do you think she tried to get out and something happened? Like the floor collapsed or something?"

"Something like that." Spider nodded. "Act-of-god stuff."

Spider turned onto a familiar road. I didn't ask him how he knew the way to Brie's place. I wasn't sure I wanted to know.

"Left," I croaked to Spider, though it seemed he already knew. A single cop car was parked at the top of Brie's long cul-de-sac, each large house in the development topped with Spanish tile and painted one of three different shades of tan.

I thought about the last time I was here. How humiliating it had been, Brie smirking, having caught me snooping where I wasn't wanted, loving how mortified I was when Chase showed up and made it all ten times worse. The memory was so vivid even now, after everything. *Go back to Termico,* she'd said that night. She knew exactly how deep it cut, since people used to say that to all three of us.

The smell of fire filled the car. Smoke, burnt plastic, and something sweet under it. *Burnt flesh?* I shuddered with the thought and tried not to breathe.

Spider's jaw tightened as we pulled up to the house. Two more police cars were parked along the sidewalk, one of them blocking the driveway. Burnt spots dotted the lawn, as if someone had spraypainted black dashes on it in the shape of roof shingles. Yellow tape stretched across the front yard.

Only one large corner of the house stood untouched by the fire. The walls sloped away from it, scorched and black, melted glass where a window once was, jagged drywall splayed out in all directions. The roof yawned open, stinking and black, in a permanent scream.

Two blue-uniformed officers stood in the driveway talking to a middle-aged woman in jogging clothes. She gesticulated with one hand and held a squirming Pomeranian in the other.

"Nope," Spider said. He turned the wheel hard and we scraped into a U-turn. "Let's go around the back."

Spider had hated cops as long as I could remember. I couldn't blame him. I would too, if I liked breaking laws. Especially now, with a felony on his record, he had to be careful.

I nodded, drawn to the house in spite of myself. Now that I'd seen this monstrous wreck of it, I wasn't ready to look away. "Go back up the hill and around to the next cul-de-sac. There's a door in the back fence past the pool." Whatever was left of the pool.

Soon he'd made a series of turns on the subdivision streets, each with an ornate name like Sagewillow Springs and Acacia Lane. We pulled up alongside a canyon where the brush downwind of the fire was coated white with ash. Across the street stood the fence around Brie's backyard, which sloped upward to afford a view of what was left of the house. We sat a minute gaping at it. "Okay," Spider said. "We came, we saw. It's definitely fucked up."

"Give me five minutes," I said, surprising myself. "I want to get closer."

I told myself I needed to know what had happened in that house for Rain's sake, so that when I told her about it she could start to heal from the shock. But really, a part of me just didn't want to leave without understanding how Brie's last moments were spent. Something about the severity of the house's damage wasn't making sense. How had an ordinary house on an ordinary street lost its roof and half its sides before the firemen got there? How had Brie not gotten out in time?

"Okay, Inspector Gadget," Spider said, his eyebrows raised like he didn't think I had it in me. "Just don't take too long. And don't let any cops see you."

The gate's latch opened easily. In the yard, the reek of fire and burnt plastic and that horrible, sickly-sweet smell was enough to choke on. I lifted my collar up over my nose and crossed the threshold, drawn in by the smoldering maw of the house, or maybe by death itself.

The water in the pool was black, its surface dotted with floating clumps of char. Ashes like grapefruit peels drifted through the air and dissolved in sludgy puddles on the lawn. Trying not to gag as the smell intensified, I picked my way past the lawn's puddles.

I moved closer to the house and dared to take the stairs to the deck, miraculously still standing on its beams, until I stood where the kitchen's sliding glass door had been. It lay on the deck now, curled into itself, shattered but held together by some kind of coating. Yellow police tape had been affixed to the open space where the door once was.

Facing the kitchen, I could see the blackened insides of the house, blasted with ash, charred and soaked, unrecognizable. A melted-down hunk of metal, maybe a microwave, floated in what was left of the kitchen. The fridge and oven stood dented, filthy, and wet, relatively unscathed compared to everything else. Past the kitchen, the couch was burnt down to wood planks, shards of metal, black springs. Drywall studs poked out in all directions where walls once were. The house's bones were exposed, everything emitting noxious smells of fire and flood. It was like a bomb had gone off. Like the house itself was the bomb.

I stood stock-still, trying to understand. *How does a house explode?*

I thought of Ed, always so orderly, a former military man. His red-scrubbed face, his shaved hair, not a thing about him out of place other than the pockmarks on his cheeks from ancient acne. Everything had always been so tightly controlled in their old house in Termico: hospital corners on Brie's bed, never a dish left in the sink. He'd ironed and starched their dishtowels, hung them from the oven handle like flags.

I pictured Brie in her giant upstairs room, lighting one of those scented candles she liked. All it would take was for one of them to catch on something. Smoke filling the room, Brie passed out after the party, her long hair splayed on the pillow, a curtain igniting.

I reached out to touch the edge of the police tape that was the only thing separating me from the inside of the house, then ducked beneath it.

Inside, clear baggies with notes written in black marker and burnt things inside them were taped to the one intact wall. Evidence. The stove still had a single pot on it, overturned on the electric burners. A yellow Post-it note was stuck next to it with numbers and letters on it. A spill of blackened sauce with circles swimming in it was pooled next to the pot and I recognized the ketchup-on-Cheerios texture of SpaghettiOs. Brie loved SpaghettiOs when we were little. Behind the stove, miraculously unharmed, hung a single crocheted red pot holder with *Walsh* sewn into it. On the kitchen island surrounded by a puddle of murky water stood a bottle of Kahlúa, mostly empty, and two glasses, as if someone had set up a tableau of normalcy in the destroyed house. One of the glasses had lipstick smeared on the rim. All of it was marked with yellow Post-it notes. I stood there, mesmerized by the glasses, until I forced myself to push onward, drawn in by a morbid need to see just a little more.

In the living room, one of the walls had been blasted clean through. A picture frame lay in burnt pieces on the soaked carpet. The flat-screen TV that once hung on the wall was now half-melted, the screen shattered, and dangling from its cord into a pool of water. I kept moving toward the stairs and tried to ignore the way my flip-flops sank into the carpet, the slime of it creeping between my toes. That sweet smell—burnt flesh, singed hair?—filled my mouth and nose, even with my shirt still covering half my face. I nearly tripped over what was left of the coffee table. On top of it was a binder I recognized as Brie's AP Calc notes, pink with a clear plastic cover. A single photograph was stuck inside the cover of it, Brie and her posse, all of them duckfacing, holding red Solo cops. Anya in the corner, cracking up. Deirdre's eyes were shut but somehow Brie has seen fit to print this one out. These were the girls Rain had hated passionately, much more passionately than I ever did, until everything changed. This must have been taken at one of the parties we would never have been invited to, until that changed, too. Another evidence baggie with a Post-it inside it was taped to the binder.

I dragged myself slowly up the stairs, the smell intensifying as I reached the second-floor landing and began to climb the second staircase to Brie's attic room. What was left of the blackened doorway had yellow tape stretched across it marked CRIME SCENE. *You shouldn't be here,* that tape said. And yet I couldn't make myself turn to leave.

I drew closer, careful not to lean on the police tape. Two-thirds of the room was missing its roof. It was here that the house opened itself to sky. Above me, a crow flew past. The room was a horror of black char, spiderwebs of broken glass glittering everywhere, melted hunks of plastic and metal where furniture once was. In one corner, Brie's desk curled around its metal legs, warped and twisted. A bulletin board above the desk had burnt entirely, leaving a black square on the wall. A laptop lay open on the floor, its screen blistered, its keys like wads of spit-out gum.

But the bed was the worst of it.

It was something out of a horror movie. Post-it notes and caution tape marked off the bed area as evidence. The bed was hardly a bed at all anymore, just a black rectangle of cinders atop a burnt metal frame. No mattress left except in the very center, where a few remnants of batting clung to the frame in charred tufts of cotton. *Was this was where the body was found?*

Shaking all over, I stifled a scream and ran back down the stairs . . . smack into a police officer.

"Oh!" Reeling, I took a step back.

The cop was skinny, with a dusting of acne on his cheeks and a bobbing Adam's apple above his starched collar. He had the tentative air of a new kid on the first day of school.

"This is a crime scene." He frowned. "Nobody's allowed up here."

"I—I'm sorry. I just wanted to see. I knew her." I looked at the soaked carpet under my flip-flops and wondered if I'd committed a crime.

"What's your name?" the officer asked, moving closer.

"I . . . Brie was a close friend," I tried, hoping he wouldn't press me. It was true, once. My throat tightened with tears and I willed a few to fall. "I didn't believe what they were saying. I just wanted to see for myself."

"Well, uh." He peered down the stairs toward the kitchen, as if hoping someone would rescue him from this conversation. "The body's at the morgue."

"Oh." We stood there staring at each other for another minute. It seemed he wasn't going to move from his spot on the stairs and let me pass. "And her dad?"

I pictured Ed throwing chicken bones to Spanky, the dog he used to keep tied to a stake in their yard, even when it was way too hot for an animal to be outside. The way his scalp beneath his crew cut would turn purple when he didn't like something Brie was doing, back when we were little.

"He's— Miss, I'm not at liberty to divulge information about the case. You are in an active crime scene. This is evidence you are stepping in." He pointed at my ash-smeared feet.

I nodded and looked at his chest. Just below his badge, his name: J. Duff.

"You need to leave."

"Of course. Sorry." I let him lead me down the stairs and out the front door.

Outside in the driveway, the woman with the Pomeranian had gone and the night air was thick and foul, as though it had been coughed out by the devil himself. A wave of dizziness hit me when I passed the spot where Brie had stood the night we'd argued here. Staggering away, I imagined myself as Brie lying in bed, the flames licking my hair, singeing my lashes, my arms, blistering my feet and calves, my lungs filling inescapably with smoke—the panic was so visceral that for a second I felt like I was actually suffocating.

I gulped lungfuls of air to remind myself that I was here, alive, outside. That it hadn't happened to me. I thought of the awful things I must have said to her last night and wondered if Brie left this earth with my words still echoing in her head.

I didn't turn around until I got to the end of the cul-de-sac, past eight or nine other houses with tidy gravel-and-cacti front yards. Just before I made the turn that would take me back to Spider, I risked one last peek at the house, my eyes drawn up to where Brie must have drawn her final breaths, to the glass shards twinkling where her windows once were.

And in the driveway below, J. Duff stood stock-still, watching me.

4

"That smell," Spider said when I shut the car door. "It's on you, bad."

"I saw her bed," I said. "It was completely—"

I couldn't get the words out, but it didn't matter. Spider seemed to understand without my saying that it had been bad.

"Anyone see you?"

"A cop. Young guy. I didn't give him my name."

Spider made a growling sound of disapproval and squeezed the steering wheel.

As we drove, I stared at the spot ahead of the car where the headlights met the black hole of the night. Along the edge of the road, a jackrabbit flitted between the gray brush, tail quivering, eyes silver in the glare.

"Was the kitchen as burnt as the upstairs?"

I opened my mouth to say *sure it was,* but it wasn't. The kitchen, from what I saw, had fared better than the upper floors. "No. Upstairs was the worst of it."

"Strange." Spider looked over at me, then back at the road. "Fires usually start in kitchens."

In ten minutes, I'd directed Spider onto Amatista Way and we drove down it slowly, its privet hedges and tall iron gates surrounding the huge properties, some built in the mission style, others big modern stucco-and-glass cubes.

"Nice neighborhood they found here," Spider said under his breath, taking in the giant houses. This area was a few steps up from Brie's. Maybe more than a few.

"Mm-hmm," I said, remembering when I felt the same awe as Spider. "Hers is the next house on the right."

"Jesus." Spider pulled the Fiesta into the driveway and craned his neck to take it all in. "Seriously?"

I nodded. Joan and Rain's house looked as imposing as it always did. The glassy white rectangle sat on a corner lot, cool as a tomb, with vertical blinds that clicked against one another like ice cubes. It had come furnished, everything matching and pristine, as if the house had frozen in 1961, with all those low couches and orbital lamps people loved in the desert cities. Everything was "mid-century," Joan had informed me repeatedly, except the kitchen, which was spanking new and glossy white, and the bathrooms, which had puzzlingly futuristic faucets and Japanese toilets that Joan liked to crow "make it so your shit don't stink."

I pictured Rain in her bathroom now, leaning back against the tub and staring up at the skylight, the indigo circle of night sky providing no answers.

In the driveway Spider left the car running, AC on. "You don't want me to come in, do you?"

I shook my head. "She may be in bad shape. I won't be long."

The Santangelos' massive white door was so wide and tall I felt like Alice after she'd shrunk down to nothing in Wonderland. Nerves bubbled in my abdomen after I rang the bell. How would Rain be? Angry at me? In need of a hug and silence? Whatever greeted me, I knew she needed a friend right now. No matter how awful our fight had been, grief was stronger than all of that.

I waited a long time on the mat after I rang the bell. Finally, just as I was considering walking back to the car, the door opened. It was Joan in her silk kimono, teal cranes against a black background. Her red hair was frayed and frizzing and she looked like she hadn't slept. Her eyes were pink and puffy. Immediately, she pulled me into a tight hug. I breathed in her smell of cigarettes and Trésor and let my tears flow along with hers. Her thin back shook as she cried.

"That poor girl," Joan said. "This is a horror, Sydney. I still can't believe it."

"I know," I whispered, remembering that it wasn't just Rain who would be grieving for Brie. Joan must have spent plenty of time with her recently, too. And of course all those years when we were little.

We embraced for a long time. Finally, Joan took a shuddering breath and led me inside. "How is Rainey doing? I haven't seen her yet."

"I . . . I thought she was here. I came to see her," I explained, pulling the front door shut behind me.

Joan searched my face, her eyes wide.

"She's ignoring my calls. I was hoping she was with you." Her voice had grown small. She pressed her lips flat together and squeezed her eyes shut.

I shook my head, not sure what to say. "I've been texting her but she's . . . we had a fight last night and she hasn't really been responding."

Joan grabbed my hand. "That makes two of us."

A leaden feeling settled in my chest.

"We . . . we fought the other day, stupid stuff, just a disagreement about money." Joan's gaze moved around the living room, not landing on anything. I noted the crumpled tissues scattered amid half-full water glasses on the coffee table. This part of the house was usually spotless, but not today. "She and I were kind of cooling off in our own worlds last night, and this morning I just figured she went to school."

I wasn't about to add to Joan's worry by telling her Rain hadn't gone to school today.

"But then when I finally went into her room," Joan continued, nervously straightening a pile of mail on a console table, "her bed didn't look like she'd slept there. I've been checking in, but you know Rainey. Stubborn as a cat up a tree."

Joan let loose a nervous laugh and I felt sick inside.

"I guess she'll come home when she's ready," I said.

"I'll try my sister," Joan said, sounding doubtful. "See if she went there."

"I'm sure everything's fine," I said. "She's someplace safe. Maybe she's in a hotel somewhere."

"You think? Ordering room service while we worry?" Joan smiled hopefully.

I nodded, wanting it to be true.

"Could you just let me know when you hear from her?" Joan squeezed both of my hands in hers as if to say we were bound together in this.

"Of course. And you, too."

Joan took a deep breath and let it out slowly. "I just hope she's not doing anything stupid."

Silence hung in the air between us, the possibilities infinite. I gave Joan a final hug.

"I'll check in soon. My brother's in the car waiting for me." Suddenly I wanted to get away from there and from Joan, who only wanted me to convince her that Rain was all right when the truth was that the last time I saw Rain, she was upset enough to be capable of absolutely anything.

In bed that night, I texted Rain three more times. The message bubbles piled up on top of all the others, unread.

I saw your mom. She's worried about you. So am I.
I went to Brie's house. Like something out of a horror movie.
Where are you?

I sat up in bed and bent back a few blinds to peer out my window. I almost expected to see Rain out there, slouched against that shiny car of hers, long legs kicking at the gravel, restless as always, waiting for me. But all I saw was Clay Street, empty and potholed, and the Espositos' two dented garbage cans at the curb.

Just tell me where you are and I'll leave you alone.

I typed the words into my phone but didn't send them. Instead, I threw my phone across the room.

There was no point sending anything real. She wasn't even reading my messages. For all I knew, she'd tossed her phone altogether and was hibernating in her grief, no tech necessary.

In the next room, Mom's mattress squeaked as she turned over in bed. Down the hall, Spider's TV blared the theme music to *Law & Order: SVU*. I burrowed deeper under my covers and told myself Rain would have to reemerge soon and when she did, we'd come together over this, rekindle all that had been lost. Maybe tomorrow. Maybe by then she would have had enough of hiding and come home.

As I finally closed my eyes to begin a fitful night of sweaty half-sleep plagued by the kind of nightmares that don't end when you wake up, all I knew was this: Brie was dead and Rain was gone.

5

The next morning at school, four police cars were parked end to end in the bus loading zone. When I walked into homeroom, several heads swiveled my way. Lucy Phillips leaned over to her boyfriend, Aidan Sanchez, and whispered something that turned Aidan's ears red.

When Chase walked in just after the bell, I felt the ghost of that old flip-flop my stomach used to do for him. It was weaker now, deflated of hope or energy, but it was still enough to notice. His eyes found mine before he sat down and I flashed him a tentative smile. He nodded and smiled back and I was grateful he was here, even if things were still weird. Even if things would never not be weird between us again.

Five minutes after homeroom began, Anya Patel, Deirdre Wilson, and Candice Lombardi were called over the loudspeaker to report to the bio lab. I watched Anya stand and stuff her books back into her bag, her brow knit with worry. Some people started to whisper questions and Anya narrowed her eyes. "How should I know what it's about?" she muttered before darting out of the room with her backpack still half-unzipped, her black ponytail swishing. When she left, the room grew louder and rumors started to fly.

"Arson," Mark Fox said. "They think it was arson."

"I heard Brie's dad went ballistic yesterday when the police questioned him," said Lizzy Rafferty, whose mother was a public defender.

"I heard he threw a chair," Lucy said.

"Is he a suspect?" Mark asked so only those closest to him could hear. He and Brie went out for a few months sophomore year. "Or did they just accuse him of being an asshole?"

I sat up straighter. It was news to me that so many people knew enough about Ed to say these things.

"Guys, please. I can't handle this right now." Min Shen was curled around her desk, her head on her crossed arms as if she didn't have the strength to even sit up. She had bags under her eyes and wore sweatpants and a Stanford T-shirt several sizes too big. She looked as bad as I felt. I pictured her walking through the Stanford campus next fall clutching her premed books—all those palm trees, all that prestige, but it wouldn't change the past, her friend dead by fire. "He just lost his child. Give him a break."

"He doesn't deserve one," someone muttered softly behind me. I turned to see it was Robin Rodriguez, who I remembered went to the same church as Brie and Ed back when Brie still went to church. "He's a drunk and a creep."

The others nodded, weirdly chastened by the truth. *What did you see?* I wondered. *What did she tell you?*

Robin made eye contact with me, then blushed and looked down at her notebook.

Ten minutes later, the loudspeaker cut in again and the school secretary called Min Shen and Rain Santangelo to report to the bio lab.

Min groaned and slid out of her seat while I texted Rain.

> Where are you?? They just called your name over the loudspeaker. I think the police are here at school asking questions.

The minutes passed the way last night's nightmares had: with agonizing slowness and the sense that something I couldn't fully identify was just outside my vision, coming for me. Like I was walking down a sidewalk made of glue while being pursued by a faceless figure, a knife glinting in their gloved hand.

When the bell finally rang, signaling the end of homeroom, it took me by surprise. "Hey," a voice above me said. I looked up to find Chase staring down at me with a worried expression. "You okay?"

"I can't reach Rain," I said miserably. "She never went home after the party."

"Shit." Chase frowned. "That's not good."

I stood up, my desk between us now.

"I miss you," he said quietly. "I was really glad we talked the other night."

He'd been at the party, too, that much I remembered. We'd made a tentative peace there. "Are you doing okay . . . with all of this awfulness?"

He sighed and opened his mouth to say something when the PA system crackled to life again.

"Sydney Green, please report to the bio lab."

I stared at Chase helplessly, my eyes wide.

But I wasn't her friend.

"I'm sure they're talking to everyone," Chase said. "I can walk you there."

"That's okay." I grabbed my bag, my heart suddenly racing. "I'm good."

Truce or no, Chase wasn't my boyfriend anymore.

Just outside the bio lab, a man stood waiting. He was very large, perfectly bald, and wore gray business slacks, a white shirt, and a navy blue tie. A pair of rimless glasses pinched the skin on the bridge of his nose.

"Sydney Green?" His bland smile showed his top and bottom teeth.

"Yes." My voice was the tiniest squeak.

"I'm Detective Schiff, but you can call me Bill." I nodded as he ushered me inside. *You have nothing to hide,* I told myself silently. This was just a formality, like Chase said.

In the classroom, a petite woman in a gray business suit sat on a stool in front of Mr. Perry's frog dissection poster. She wore her dark, crispy curls shaped into a neat bob and red lipstick that looked freshly applied. Bill motioned to a desk in the front row for me to sit in. "And this is Detective Garcia, but you can call her Arlene."

"Hi, Sydney." Arlene stood up and greeted me with a firm handshake, frowning at me sympathetically. "Heck of a terrible week everyone's having, huh?"

"Yeah," I managed. The clock on the wall said 9:20, but the day already felt like it had been going on forever.

"We just have a few quick questions for you." Arlene slid into the desk next to mine and scooted it so that she faced me. Bill walked to the window and turned his back on us to study the view of the parking lot. "Shall we get started?"

"Okay." I placed my hands palms down on the desk and stared at my knuckles. The index finger of my right hand had a two-inch scabbed-over cut I didn't remember getting. I quickly hid it under the desk and felt my face get redder, worrying that somehow it was evidence of something I didn't remember doing. *You're losing it, Sydney. Get it together.* I blinked hard and forced myself to focus on Arlene, composing my face as best I could.

"How well did you know Brianna Walsh?" Arlene asked.

"Not that well." Already it felt like I was lying without wanting to. If you knew a person intimately as a child, didn't you know them well forever? Wasn't it true that I knew Brie as well as I knew my own shadow? "We used to be close when we were little kids, but that was a long time ago."

"What changed?" Arlene asked. "When would you say you got less close to her?" Her voice was gentle and reassuring. She looked young, like maybe she'd only been doing this a few years.

When she became a nightmare. When she decided we were too poor for her. When she formed her posse of mean girls.

"We used to be neighbors, but then her dad bought a car dealership," I said, feeling stupid mentioning it. "And they moved to a different neighborhood. We kind of grew apart in middle school."

"Oh, I remember those days. Girl drama, middle school." Arlene rolled her eyes and laughed and some of her lipstick bled from her lip line onto her front teeth, lurid as blood. My stomach tightened. *Girl drama.*

"It wasn't that dramatic," I mumbled. "For me, at least." I thought about Rain, how furious she'd been at Brie for all those years after Brie left Termico. They were going to want to find Rain, I realized. They would want to know why she didn't show up here today.

"But you'd spent more time again recently with Miss Walsh, right?" Arlene's gaze flicked for the tiniest second toward Bill before returning to me.

I felt heat rising in my face. What had Brie's minions told them?

"I mean, not really." *Not if Brie could help it.*

"Not really?" Arlene leaned her chin on her hand and raised her impeccably groomed eyebrows. "Do we have that wrong?"

"Just at parties a few times. That kind of thing." I heard myself evading, not exactly lying but not really answering the question.

Bill's shoes squeaked on the linoleum. He was beside me now. "We understand you were with her at a party two nights ago at Candice Lombardi's house." He pulled a small spiral-bound notepad from his shirt pocket. "And a few other gatherings in the past few months as well. Is that right?"

I nodded noncommittally.

"Just do your best to walk us through the night of the party, Sydney." Arlene put a ballpoint pen against her own spiral notebook.

"I'll just take notes, if that's okay with you. In case I hear anything useful."

You won't. I smiled and tried not to look miserable.

"Well, Candice has a new half brother because her mom recently remarried." I paused and looked out the window at a blue van exiting the parking lot.

Arlene nodded, coaxing me along. "Right, we know about Brad. We hear he threw himself a big twenty-first birthday party, parents out of town, all of that. Just tell us your experience there, if you don't mind. Who did you go with?"

"My brother."

"And what's his name?" Arlene studied me calmly. I got the feeling she already knew the answers to all of these questions.

"Justin. But everyone calls him Spider."

Bill and Arlene looked at each other again. They must have already known that Spider was newly sprung from Pine Grove. They probably even knew what he was arrested for. My stomach twisted with worry for Spider—had he violated his parole by going to the party?

"Anyway, Spider wanted to go, because he hadn't done anything fun in a while. . . ." *Because he was in jail,* I didn't add. Bill and Arlene nodded. They weren't writing any of this down. "I didn't want to go, actually. But I went to keep him company." *Because he made me.*

"What did you want to do instead?" Bill asked. He'd begun to pace at the front of the room, back and forth in front of the dissection charts.

Avoid all human contact. Nurse my hurts. Avoid ex-friends. Stalk my ex-boyfriend online. "Homework."

"Sunday night." Arlene clucked her tongue. "Weird night for a party."

We all nodded solemnly in agreement. Dumb Brad, with his dumb birthday.

"And what time did you arrive?" asked Bill. The frog on Mr. Perry's poster was splayed out behind him with all its froggy organs on display.

"Maybe around nine?"

Arlene leaned in. "Walk us through it, Sydney. Did you see Brianna there?"

"Eventually," I said. *Once I was completely shit-faced.* I almost laughed at the thought of saying this out loud. "It was crowded."

"Seems like everyone showed up. One of those end-of-the-year kind of deals," Arlene said.

I nodded. "Right. But I did see her, briefly."

"Did the two of you get into it?" Bill whirled around mid-pace.

"Get into it?" I said, inwardly cursing my hot face. "Um, I'm not sure what you mean."

Except I was sure. Positive. A lot was missing but a few details had stuck, shards of intact memories clinging to the broken window of that night. *So high and mighty, Sydney. So eager to see the worst in people,* she'd said to me. I could see Brie perfectly, her hair dyed to match Rain's. Dressed like Rain. Her face flushed with alcohol and fury. *I tried to tell her what a hypocrite you were. Now she can see for herself.* That smug smile covering up how angry she was, the dimple in her left cheek popping inward like the Gerber baby, her indifferent ice-blue gaze.

"We've heard there was tension between the two of you." Bill flipped through his notebook. "Between the two of you and Miss . . . Santangelo," Bill said. "May as well tell us about it. Could help in our investigation."

I sat silently, racking my brain for how to explain the "tension," to make it seem normal. Because it *was* normal. Wasn't it? Didn't people grow apart all the time? It definitely had nothing to do with the fire. But I didn't know how to explain that I couldn't fully remember the details of that night, and the parts I could remember weren't going to be easy for them to understand.

"Come on, hon," Arlene said. She started to put her hand on mine but I pulled away. "We've all been there, fighting over a *boy*."

I nodded, stalling for time. Everything with Brie had started long before any fight over a boy. After Ed bought the car dealership, he and Brie packed up Spanky and moved out of Termico and Brie was suddenly too good for me and Rain. She had all different clothes, not just new, but much tighter and shorter—the overly formal clothes Ed used to buy her had vanished—and within a few months, she had befriended the popular group of girls we'd hated since fourth grade and stopped talking to us, the grubby remainders from her old life.

She's a rich girl now, Rain had eye-rolled at the time. *We probably embarrass her.*

There was no way I could have guessed that years later, Rain would make a similar descent into the valley, into an even nicer house than Brie's. Even when Rain got her new car and her closet full of three-hundred-dollar jeans, I was naïve enough not to see Brie as a threat.

This was when I still thought Rain didn't care about money. Now I knew everyone did, whether they wanted to or not. Even Rain—who had been so generous at first, who always acted like money was the stupidest, most trivial thing—had changed into an entirely new person because of it.

"We weren't fighting about a boy." I groped at the right words to explain, to show them I wasn't some dumb girl in a snit over some dude. I felt my face glow hotter, the shame of having my personal life exposed to these two strangers spreading itself through my body. "It wasn't a big deal. It was a misunderstanding." *Or several misunderstandings.*

"Tell us everything, okay, hon?" Arlene said.

So I told them. Not about how Brie started to do everything more like the way Rain did. Not about how Brie drove a wedge between me and my best friend that hurt so much I had to stay away.

Instead, I told them the barest details about Chase, describing him as someone I'd been close to for a while in the middle of senior year. Someone I no longer had much to do with. And I told them that Rain and Brie had become close friends again, and that I didn't see either one of them much these days.

"Anyway, I saw Brie and Rain at the party, and Chase. But I can't imagine any of this is helpful to your . . ." Again I groped for the words. "Investigation."

"Was Brianna happy to see you?" Bill asked. He was facing the wall, studying Mr. Perry's cow's eye poster. I wished I could disappear into the melancholy blue of the poor creature's iris.

Look at me when I'm talking to you. A new, alarming memory emerged: The last time I'd touched Brie, I'd grabbed her chin, squeezed it hard, pushed her face up to look at me so roughly I could have snapped her neck.

"I'm not sure. I guess not." It was dawning on me that this line of questioning wasn't actually all that friendly.

"Why not, hon?"

I coughed, looked out the window. Anywhere but at Bill. "I don't know. She wanted to be alone with Rain, probably."

"We heard you kept pretty close tabs on the two of them."

"That's not true at all." But they hadn't pulled this out of thin air. Others had told them this. People they interviewed today in this room. People they clearly believed. Did anyone *not* keep tabs on one another, with practically every movement broadcast on our phones? Every class filled with the people we tried not to care about, every mouth full of gossip?

"If anything, I'd been avoiding them." My voice was thick with indignation. The desk, the classroom, the detectives staring at me, their faces composed and frighteningly neutral—all of it felt like a cage. And the door was closing.

"Okay, Sydney. I guess we have that wrong." Arlene was writing

furiously in her little notebook in beautiful, neat cursive, the kind
my grandma had. I looked at the words but they just swam there,
upside-down loops and curls that didn't make sense. "We heard
you were kind of upset at the party."

Sweat bloomed under my arms. The right answer was spinning,
ungraspable amid all I wasn't telling them, like the answer to a
test I hadn't studied for, something just out of reach. "I only saw
Brie and Rain for a few minutes," I took pains to assure them. A
half-truth.

"So nobody was upset that night?" Arlene pressed me. Had she
caught something in my voice or my expression? I almost laughed
at the ridiculousness of it all. I flashed on Rain's face that night, the
look of disgust she'd directed at me. A look she used to reserve for
anyone, everyone else. Never me. Never me until that night.

And Brie, had she been angry? I recalled her screaming at me as
I ran away.

Why yes, now that you mention it, everyone was quite upset. We
hated one another in that bedroom more than we ever had before,
all three of us split apart at last. "Not that I remember." I stared at
my hands on the desk and heard blood thrum in my ears.

"Who left first?"

"I did."

"So you don't know how long the two girls stayed at the party
that night, then?"

I shook my head. Finally, something I was certain of.

"We have several people saying you left upset, Miss Green." Bill
again. The bad cop.

"I wasn't feeling well." *I was shit-faced, officer. I'd taken prison
pills, many shots.* I bit the inside of my cheek until I tasted blood.

"We heard Ms. Santangelo left looking upset, too. Do you know
why that might be?"

"I wouldn't know. Like I said, I barely saw her that night." Lies,

lies, lies. They tumbled out so naturally. I marveled at the speed I was able to come up with them.

"Those two, Rain Santangelo and Brianna Walsh, they were pretty tight this year then?" Arlene asked.

I nodded. "I guess."

"Didn't it hurt your feelings to lose your best friend?" Bill said, his words so precise and personal I almost lost my breath.

"Look, I was only at the party because my brother wanted—"

"And this is Justin Green, correct?"

"Yes." *The felon. You know the one. The others surely told you all about him.*

"We may want his contact information. We'll let you know if we do."

A charged silence opened up in the room, Bill's words still echoing in my head. A moment later, the bell rang. I'd been here for an entire class period.

"That'll do for now." Bill pushed his tiny glasses up his nose and flashed me a flat smile that made the hairs on the back of my neck stand up. "We'll be in touch. We know how to find you." Though he'd said it mildly, it sounded like a threat.

"I'm sure the fire was an accident," I blurted as Arlene walked me to the door. "Nobody wanted to harm Brie."

"We hope not, hon." Arlene handed me her business card. "If you remember anything else, why don't you give me a ring?"

As I stuffed the card into my backpack pocket, my phone buzzed with a text. Suddenly I felt more on display than ever, the girl with the felon brother who'd left upset, who'd lost her best friend to a dead girl.

Stop it, I told myself as Arlene waved me out the door. *You did nothing wrong.*

I walked as quickly as possible away from there, feeling their eyes on my back. Around the corner in the crowded hallway, I leaned up against a wall of lockers and took out my phone. I was shocked to see a text from Rain, her first communication since the party.

I'll be back in a few days. Need a little more time to process this alone. As for the police, fuck 'em.

The police will be looking for you, I typed in frustration. It was easy to be cavalier about cops when you hadn't just spent forty-five minutes answering questions. They think we had something to do with the fire. Someone told them I was "keeping tabs" on you and Brie. You need to tell them the truth.

Miraculously, she replied right away.

Don't worry. I'll never tell them what we did.

A surge of confusion and adrenaline rocked through me. *What we did?* What the hell did that mean? Instantly, my hands began to shake. I pressed my cheek to the cold metal of the lockers and smashed the keyboard with my thumbs, making so many typos I had to redo it twice.

WTF are you talking about??

I stared down at the phone, baffled, furious, waiting. What had we done?

But Rain didn't write back.

PART II
RAIN

DECEMBER
FIVE MONTHS BEFORE THE FIRE

6

Ms. Malinowski, the guidance counselor, paced the front of the room in her clog sandals, a messy stack of neon pink flyers clutched in her arms. It wasn't yet 8:30, but she was already flashing one of those manic high-beam smiles, the kind teacher-types use when they're about to launch into a speech about our exciting futures.

Homeroom with Mr. Bergstrom was usually a chill affair with Bergie at his desk up front, his bald spot gleaming as he bent over his desk to read a thick book about Lyndon Johnson and count his days to retirement. But today, Bergie perched on a stool in the corner and joined the rest of us in enduring Ms. Malinowski's quivering excitement.

"The time has come in your academic journey, my friends, to finalize your applications."

And so it began, the passing out of flyers. It was December of senior year and everyone had gotten intense about college. And if they weren't, Ms. Malinowski was determined to make them start.

Shielded from Ms. M's view behind the big brown puff of Matt Richardson's hair, I slouched deeper into my seat in the back row and shut my eyes. My morning had been aggravating. Joan had hogged the bathroom getting ready for her Monday lunch shift at the casino, stalking around in her pantyhose and one of her red fake-silk work shirts that always, even right after she washed them in the bathtub, Febrezed them, and hung them outside, smelled like old fryer grease. Mondays were never the greatest for Joan, what with the lunch shift and how beneath her it was—"twelve years there and they still have the gall to put this on my schedule" had been the refrain for as long as I could remember—but today there was her added panic about our dying sixteen-year-old Oldsmobile Caprice.

"Three times last week it wouldn't start," Joan bitched, her voice an engine that kept up a low growl while she stood at the bathroom mirror and swiped blush in the hollows of her cheeks. "Much more of this and that little prick will fire me."

We were barely staying afloat as it was. If Joan got fired, we might lose the house. "We'll be out on our asses as fast as you can say *Ted's shriveled ballsack*," my mother said between coats of mascara.

Other than his shriveled nether regions, all I knew about Joan's new boss, Ted, was that he was twenty-eight, a redhead with premature hair loss, and that he was a demon sent by management to torment her. Layoffs were happening at the casino lately anyway, so Joan being late could be just enough to tip the scales.

I left the bathroom and then the house with Joan still in mid-rant, relieved to escape into the canned-corn reek of the school bus with Syd, who spent the forty-five-minute ride finishing a physics lab. I didn't mind. It gave me time to start thinking about the cheapest way to get a new used car.

I was still pondering it in homeroom, until Ms. Malinowski's breathless speech made it impossible.

"And so, my friends. We have arrived at the moment you've been preparing for all these years," Ms. M was saying. "Your future is barreling toward you like a runaway train."

When the class began to laugh, she caught herself and rephrased.

"Or, more like a bullet train! Those fast ones they have in Japan. Very much on track. You know what I mean. It's all going to come down to how you approach the next two months. And to that end . . ." She smiled like she was presenting us with the sorcerer's stone. "I would like to encourage you all to come to the workshops I'm holding all week for those of you applying to four-year colleges. We will talk personal essays, safeties, Cal States, UCs, Ivies, and everything in between. Questions?"

The front half of the room erupted. This was where the AP kids sat. The ones with résumés and fancy summer programs and trendy clothes they bought with their parents' credit cards. The same kids who'd been raising their hands for participation points since we were eight years old.

Matt Richardson turned and dumped a pile of flyers on my desk. I took one, then passed the stack to Amber Usdall and rolled my eyes. Amber walked on her toes and fluttered her hands and didn't speak much, so you never knew quite what was going on with her. But she smiled in my direction so I felt we were enduring this together.

I thought of the wall behind the jacaranda tree, the spot at the very back of the courtyard under the lip of the metal shade canopy I escaped to whenever being in class felt like too much. It called to me now. A morning high, an escape from the endless, exhausting work of being worried about or pointedly ignored by the teachers. A break from being Rain Santangelo: loser, poor, hot, rude, disruptive, maybe (in the minds of some of the bigger jackasses here) a little slow. Definitely "unmotivated." God, I couldn't wait to stop hearing that word.

On the wall, I was free. Not falling behind the class, not struggling to stay awake. Not getting a C or a D on a pop quiz. On the wall, I was present, accounted for, but checked out of the details, thank you very much. I could look down at the whole beige maze of the school and then drift above it, blissfully apart.

Up in the front of the room, Ms. M asked for volunteers to read. I slumped lower in my seat and felt the others in the back of the classroom shifting, too. Me and Amber Usdall and Matt and his skater boys and Juan and Ramon, who mostly kept to themselves.

Deirdre Wilson asked a complicated question about early action. I decided to turn my flyer into an origami crane. I folded and licked the paper and it tasted like childhood, like the ones I'd made with Syd when we were eleven. Our crane phase. The summer of sixth grade, we'd made five hundred. If Syd were here, she would be listening. She would write down the details in her planner. She would diligently attend Ms. M's meetings. I . . . I would make a crane.

After she'd answered everyone's questions, Ms. M departed. "See you soon, scholars. Anyone applying to four-year programs should sign up for a strategy session on the sheet outside my office."

And then we were back to homeroom, with ten more minutes to sit through before the bell.

"Why can't they just do this during class?" Deirdre whipped around in her seat to address her friends. She kept clicking her pen over and over. I wanted to flick it out of her hand. "Like, aren't we all applying to four-year colleges?"

"No, weirdo, not everyone," good old Brie Walsh, three seats up and one over, corrected her. Brie was always correcting her girls.

"Almost everyone," Deirdre muttered, blushing from her adorable pixie chin all the way up under her platinum baby bangs. "It's only the whole point of high school."

"You think *Juan* is applying to Berkeley? To Cal State?" Brie hissed loud enough for all of us to hear. "Hardly."

Juan turned at the sound of his name. Blinked. Didn't respond. Dude had a cross dripping the blood of Christ tattooed on his forearm. He knew how not to get involved in uninteresting matters.

That's your role model, I told myself. *Be like Juan.*

"That's racist," Deirdre whispered, and I saw Brie narrow her eyes. *Good for you, D. Being brave today.*

I'd gone the entire semester without saying a word to Brie or her biddies in our unfortunate homeroom pairing. We had no other classes together, just homeroom for twenty-five minutes. One little sip of battery acid to start the day.

I had been quietly courteous. I had smiled, even nodded once. I hadn't rocked the boat. And I wasn't going to start now.

Up front next to Deirdre, Candice turned back around and lifted the long caramel curtain of her hair up from one shoulder to the other, twisting it out of her way. There was a look on her face I didn't like, like a cat about to pounce. "What about you, Amber? Are you hoping for a UC?"

Brie tittered, shook her head like Candice was incorrigible. An excellent mean girl, that Candice. A phrase of Joan's popped into my head: *Born on third and thought she hit a triple.* Deirdre turned around again from the front row to try to hone in on the joke.

Amber shook her head.

"Cal State?" Candice wore a fake openmouthed smile, eyebrows raised as if Amber was going to answer her. As if she deserved an answer from this girl who'd done nothing to no one. I closed my eyes and pressed my lips together, not trusting myself to say anything that wouldn't make it worse for Amber. I rubbed calming circles at my temples. There were seven more minutes before the bell. I could outlast this if I just stayed out of it.

But Candice wasn't letting up. "Decisions, decisions, right?"

I opened my eyes and my focus inadvertently landed on Brie. She covered her mouth in a pantomime of horror, but I knew she was laughing under her hand. Fury beat in my chest. Fury and disgust, with myself most of all, for still allowing her to get under my skin after all these years.

"Worry about yourself," I said, unable not to take the bait. I spoke to Candice, but it was really to Brie. Brie looked to me and I held her laser-beam gaze. Without all her makeup, I knew, she had blond-tipped lashes and blond eyebrows, but every day she covered all of it up, just like she covered up her past. "Leave her alone."

"So Raindrop," Brie purred, revealing the dimple in her right cheek. "Where do *you* want to go to college?"

Raindrop had been her dad's childhood name for me, a name that didn't suit and never had. A name she used to be embarrassed about when he said it.

"Wherever all of you aren't going."

"Solid plan." She whipped around to face the front again. I could see the red blotches on the back of her neck forming as she took a prissy sip of her iced coffee. "Have fun at College of the Desert."

Joke's on you, I thought. I wasn't going to College of the Desert, or any community college. In five months, I would be done with school forever. I would drive down to LA and see what work I could get. Some days I pictured myself hammering sets or carrying equipment, a wrench or a walkie-talkie stuck in my back pocket. I liked the idea of being on a crew. I was good with my hands and didn't mind working hard. Maybe I could find a few grizzled old guys who did set building and get them to train me. Anything where I could keep moving, earning from my own sweat. Away from the scrambling parade of overachievers heading off to college, away from girls like the ones in this room. Let them have their internships, their careers, all the stupid stuff they went to expensive summer programs to learn. I would be in Hollywood, would be a part of all of it. And if not, I'd get a waitressing job like Joan.

"Amber will go to USC with me, won't you, Amber?" Brie turned back around to regard Amber once again. "Or should we try for Berkeley? What should our reach be?"

Amber sat back, as if to pull herself as far away from Brie as she could while still sitting in her desk. Candice emitted an ugly laugh.

That was the true end of me being like Juan.

I stood up and grabbed my bag, only vaguely aware of what I was about to do.

I strode up the aisle and veered to my right, my face burning. *Oops.* I bumped Brie's desk hard with my hip and kept walking. I heard Brie shriek, the top of her half-full venti iced mocha hitting the floor, the skittering of ice, the splash of liquid, the smack of her binder and books hitting the ground.

On my way past the front row, I plucked the pen mid-click from Deirdre's hand.

"Miss Santangelo, that's a detention." Bergie sighed before I reached the door. "You're better than this."

"Okey dokey, Mr. B." I smiled tightly. For me, detention was as familiar as breathing.

The class was in an uproar now, filled with the sounds of teenagers in a room where something interesting has finally happened.

When I reached the door I turned to peek. Brie's loose-leaf paper had come detached from its metal rings and spilled out around her, sopping up some of the coffee. The maniacally perfect handwriting of her color-coded notes bloomed into illegible inkblots. She squatted in the soggy mess, trying to salvage her schoolwork. Her face had gone a deep scarlet.

Amber stared at me, still as a statue. I winked at her. People like us needed to stick together. Her face didn't change at all but her fingers tapped faster along the edge of her desk. It was enough.

Halfway out the door, I couldn't help sneaking one last look at Brie. Nostrils flared, her eyes blazing bullets aimed straight for me.

Satisfactory. More than satisfactory. She deserved all of this and more. It was time she got what was coming to her.

7

When Syd's hand encircled my ankle and shook me awake, I'd already been lying on top of the wall for two whole periods. First alone, then later with Matt Richardson, who'd shared his weed pen and affable silence. Now Matt was gone, probably in search of food since by the sound of things the lunch period was well under way. I rubbed at a line of dried saliva at the side of my mouth and croaked a hello.

"What did you do to her?" Syd asked from below, her face dappled in leaf-shaped shadows. I sat up, took a deep breath, stretched. The air smelled like curly fries.

"Nothing." I slid off the wall. "Why, did she seem mad?"

Syd had four or five periods with Brie. Both of them were in every AP class the school offered.

"Um, *yeah*." Syd raised an eyebrow. "Take a look. She's got you in her sights right now." Syd jabbed a thumb across the courtyard. Reluctantly, I let myself locate the Band-Aid-colored picnic table where Brie and her girls always sat surrounded by the popular crowd, all perfect sneakers and expensive backpacks and people filming one another with their phones.

Brie sat on top of her table with her bare legs crisscrossed, Ray-Bans lowered to the end of her nose, her lips squeezed sphincter-tight. Anya Patel talked in her ear at her side, but Brie was staring right at us. At me. *Ugh.*

This place was so predictable. Brie and her girls were so tiresome. Half the time I wanted to shout at them: *Get a real problem!*

"Let's bail," I muttered. I grabbed my bag and linked arms with Syd.

"I take it you ruined her notes?" Syd and I headed toward the soccer fields, where this time of year we could still lie in the grass and eat our packed lunches, or rather I would eat one of the PB&Js Syd diligently packed and dig around in my backpack for change to buy us chips and a soda to share from the field vending machines.

"I knocked over her Starbucks," I said. "She deserved it. They were being absolute witches to Amber Usdall."

Syd sighed, unsurprised. "Nobody's off limits to them."

"I just . . . I snapped. And now I have detention."

"I haven't seen her this mad in years," Syd said. "Remember how her chest used to turn red and blotchy whenever she got upset?"

I nodded.

"It was like that all of history class. And she was extra nasty to Deirdre and Min."

"That's worth a detention, I guess."

We walked down the hall of the science building until we reached the rear doors, propped open today to the sports fields. I spent the rest of the walk catching up on a string of texts from Joan, each one worse than the next.

Car didn't start again.

Had to tow it to the mechanic and take an Uber to work. That's $50 out the window.

Mechanic says it will cost more to replace the engine than the car is worth. How much cash did you save over the summer?

Ted's up my ass deeper than a tapeworm.

"Then she has a string of crying/angry/crying/angry emojis and then, for some reason, two mermaids and the dancing woman." I showed Syd.

"Shit," Syd said. We plopped down on the grass next to the soccer field, the nearest people a group of freshman boys hunched over their phones fifty feet away. "You guys need a new car fast."

"Yep," I muttered as I typed a quick text back suggesting Joan borrow Rusty's car if he wasn't working today. Rusty dealt blackjack at the casino and had helped Joan get her job there. He was her best friend and the closest person we had to family out here.

The last vestiges of fuzziness from Matt's weed had worn off and left a dull roar of anxiety in its place. Syd tossed me a smashed PB&J but I wasn't hungry. Joan was terrible with money. I had close to twelve hundred dollars saved from my summer job at the blowout bar before they fired me. I knew from counting out the wad of cold bills Joan insisted on storing in a Folgers Coffee can in the freezer ("because robbers never steal the frozen food," she'd once explained, proudly tapping her forehead) that she had a little over three thousand dollars in savings these days.

"We'll look at Craigslist," I said, shrugging like it was no big deal even though I knew I was out of my depth. I trusted Joan even less to get it done.

Syd grabbed my hand and squeezed. "It'll work out. Something always comes through." Syd, always reasonable, always steady and calm. Everything me and Joan weren't. Her eyes were full of sympathy. *How am I going to manage without you?* I thought, and not for the first time. I had been thinking it more and more as senior year ticked by and we came closer to the end of everything, the inevitable moment when Syd would go away to college and I would go . . . wherever I would go.

"Don't leave me for Peoria," I whispered. It had become our running joke this year, because Syd was applying to random colleges where she thought she could get scholarships and I could never remember where they all were. I lumped all of them into a place called Peoria, which sounded Midwestern to my never-left-California ear. "I can't handle life without you."

"But they love me in Peoria," Syd said back, part of our familiar routine. She scratched her cheek. "About the car, though. You guys'll find something. You just need an in with someone."

I nodded and pretended to mull over all my connections. Too bad we were more of an "out" family. No ins to speak of.

"Um, Rain?" Syd frowned. "There is one person. But you'd kind of have to maybe . . ."

"What?"

"Make up with Brie."

I blinked at Syd a minute, the sun bouncing off the mirrored sunglasses I'd bought us both at the swap meet last month. My reflection in them was a mass of unkempt frizz, a tiny speck of a face underneath.

"Not likely," I breathed as Syd's words clicked and I pictured Angry Ed. The man did own a Nissan dealership.

"Right." Syd's mouth was full of sandwich. "Whatever, just do it anyway. She doesn't need to be involved."

I groaned. "Gross." I squeezed my eyes shut, not wanting to even picture it. "You know Joan will jump on this. She'll trot out her feminine wiles, try to flirt her way into a deal."

"Hey, whatever works," Syd said gently.

I shook my head and sighed. Like always, Syd was right. I groaned, already composing the text to Joan in my head. I hated being broke, but not because I wanted to buy things. It was the low-grade panic of small emergencies that I hated most, the feeling that at any moment our lives could be upended by something as stupid as a car engine. And even more than that, I hated that these small emergencies meant having to be beholden to the Eds and Bries of the world.

· · ·

After detention ended at 4:45, Joan was waiting for me out front, Rusty's purple Corolla humming. I slid into the passenger seat and sneezed, silently cursing my mother's usual cloud of perfume. "What's with the outfit?" I asked, though I already knew.

"Thought you'd like it." Joan fluffed up the knot in her neck scarf, the cherry on top of her version of business casual.

"I do, actually." She had on a black blazer and black slacks and a violet shell. Her scarf was printed with multicolored dots. My mother looked . . . jaunty. Confident. Much better than her usual too-short, too-tight dress-to-impress garb, loosely based on the philosophy "God gave me boobs and legs *for a reason*." She must have wanted to look professional today. Like a woman with a desk job, someone who was good for car payments.

"So what should our strategy be?" I stared out the window as we chugged down Ramon Road toward the "mile of cars" out past the mall. The sky was already turning a pinkish purple and the cars ahead of us twinkled in the yellow softness of the early winter evening.

"You're looking at it," Joan said, gesturing toward herself, head held high, her pile of red curls banana-clipped tight at her crown. "Rusty says they always have something they want to offload, something that's not moving that they give away for a song to make their quotas. We lean on that, how easy we are, that we'll take anything as long as it's cheap, and how we were neighborly for all those years."

"Hopefully he'll remember," I muttered. I wasn't sure how pickled in alcohol Ed's brain was by now.

"Of course he will. He'll remember how many sleepovers we had and how many meals we gave little Brianna when Ellen got sick."

I looked at my mother, impressed that her tabulations of favors done and owed could stretch so far back in time. I struggled with remembering anything so deep in our shared history with the Walshes, but then I was only six when Brie's mom died. All I remembered of

Ellen Walsh was a bird-thin woman with dark hollows in her cheeks who lay in their darkened living room wearing a Padres baseball cap, the TV running soaps, *Divorce Court,* and *Jerry Springer* all day long in front of her. Every day before *The Young and the Restless,* little Brie would race home from wherever we were playing to sit on the floor leaned up against the couch to watch "their show" while her mother stroked her white-blond hair.

Joan used to say Ellen died slow and then all at once, all of it quiet and graceful and calm, almost like she didn't want to inconvenience anyone. What I always heard when my mother said that was that Ed wasn't going to be inconvenienced by tending to his wife on her deathbed. And that was all you needed to know about a guy like Ed. Out for himself, pissed off at whoever dared to get in the way of that.

"And if he doesn't?" I said.

Joan shrugged. "We tried. His loss."

Joan put on lipstick, checked her teeth. At last, we set off through the Walsh Nissan car lot. By now it was quarter past five and the place was deserted, bright lights spilling from the all-glass showroom in the center of the lot like a spaceship. The hot drag of the Santa Ana covered my forearms in prickly gooseflesh and I tried to shake off my nerves, to stand up straighter and form my mouth into something resembling a smile.

Inside, we were greeted by a big empty room full of cars and piped-in Bruno Mars.

"There he is."

I followed Joan's gaze to the back of the room. Through a glass partition, our old neighbor sagged in a rumpled dress shirt behind a huge desk, the glare from a computer monitor bouncing off his glasses. He hadn't changed much. Same military-style buzz cut, same pockmarked cheeks. How balls-to-the-wall ambitious, all-energy Brie could be related to this dejected heap of a man I could hardly begin to imagine, except that I knew the meanness they had in common. The Ed I knew was an irritable smudge of a man who sometimes yelled at his daughter loud enough so that we could hear it from across the street and two houses over.

"Come on baby. You let me do the talking, okay?" Joan threaded her elbow through mine the way her own mom, Judy, liked to do. The Santangelo women leaned on one another, none of us ever finding men particularly reliable as support. We may have had our issues in private but in public, and today especially, it was us against the world.

"Fine. Just don't come on too strong," I whispered. "Let him think he came up with the idea of giving us a deal."

Joan snorted. "Look who's a master negotiator all of a sudden!"

I shot her a glare she didn't see. We'd been burned too many times by her overconfidence, her too-much-ness. It was why I knew we'd always live in a prefab home with cardboard-thin walls and maxed-out credit cards. My mother had always relied on magical thinking and her looks to get her by, and she didn't appreciate my tendency to burst those flimsy bubbles.

"Well hello, hello!" came Ed's familiar salesman voice, the one we used to hear when he was making business calls while pacing his front yard. "Some familiar faces I didn't expect to see!"

He was up from behind his desk now, heavier around the middle since I'd last seen him and with red maps of broken capillaries around his nostrils, the kind that Joan said meant someone was a real alcoholic. His skin had a sallow cast under the dealership lights but his eyes were bright with recognition.

"The Santangelo women, more beautiful than ever." Ed's open-mouthed smile was wolfish and somehow sleazy. Suddenly this seemed like a terrible idea. "To what do I owe this honor?"

"Wow, Ed. I'm impressed you even remember us." Joan chuckled. She yanked down the lapels of her blazer and patted her curls in their French twist. "It's been a long time."

Ed opened his arms wide and went in for an awkward hug. "Bring 'er here, Raindrop." Ed gestured with his arms still around my mother. *Gross.* He let go of Joan and crushed me in his arms, squeezing too tight and too close, the acrid chemical smell of him the same as ever. I wriggled away as soon as I could. "Hi, Ed."

My mother explained to him that our car was on its last legs.

Ed nodded. "You came to the right place. You looking to finance something new?"

Our awkward, smiling silence must have communicated something. "Or a used model?" he finally added.

"Yeah, something affordable," Joan said.

"We can do that." Ed was in full salesman mode but couldn't stop leering at Joan, his eyes ping-ponging up and down. "Let's head out to the lot."

We followed him out of the showroom past rows of SUVs to the used models, the Versas, Sentras, and Altimas that looked a little less sleek and current, though no less shiny than the new stuff inside.

"Any of these will last you years. Most of 'em have under 20,000 miles," Ed said, stopping every few cars to wipe a smudge or straighten a mirror.

I looked at the prices. We didn't have $12,000. We didn't have $9,000. Joan asked a million questions about mileage and reliability and nodded enthusiastically at all of Ed's answers, as if we could actually pay the sticker prices on any of these.

Finally, I got tired of it. "Um, can you show us something . . . cheaper?"

"I have a few in the $8K range." Ed scratched at something blooming on his neck, a scaly rash the width of a thumb.

I shot a look at Joan. She stared straight ahead, frozen. So much for her negotiating skills.

"Got anything even cheaper than that?" I asked after a beat of silence.

Ed blinked at me and then at Joan. "I'm sure we can do the financing, get you all fixed up with a teeny-tiny monthly payment."

"My credit's not exactly great, Ed," Joan said quietly. "I was thinking closer to $4,000. Somewhere in that neighborhood, anyway. We just need something that runs." Joan laughed a little and Ed laughed with her. It broke the tension.

"Well, Joanie." *Joanie?* "That's a little lower than what I'm able to do."

All three of us stood there a minute. The sun hovered large and twinkling just above the mountains. Magic hour, Syd would have called it, when everything turned pink and orange before the night rushed in. I looked at my mother, thinking we would leave soon. For a second she looked beautiful, so regal and proud that my breath caught in my throat. She was staring at Ed, her brain working an angle.

"I think if you really want to, you can do whatever you want." She touched Ed's bare forearm just below his rolled-up shirtsleeve. "You're the boss. Your name is up there on the sign." Her hand rested on his arm, the hair on it reddish. I looked away, unable to watch.

"I can knock a few thousand off, maybe get you to seven." His voice was softer now, a little whisper intruding on his chipper salesguy shtick.

"Seven's not going to work," Joan said quietly. She stepped closer to him. "How is Brianna? I haven't seen her in so long. She must be so grown up by now. I remember she used to sleep ov—"

"Yeah, Brianna's fine," Ed said. He was looking at Joan more intently now. "You know, we could talk more about this over dinner. Just the adults," he said softly. He winked at me and I felt my stomach bubble up, a queasy panic rising.

Don't do it, I willed my mother. *Don't let this man near you.* I considered faking sick to make the moment end and get us out of here.

"I don't think so, Ed." Joan surprised me here. I had been afraid she was going to say yes. "I'm not . . . I can't do that." Her hand lifted off his arm as if she'd been touching something unclean and only just now registered it.

"Sure you can." Ed stepped closer to her. I couldn't believe this was happening in front of me. "We can catch up. Been a long time, Joanie."

My mother's expression, composed and cordial until now, closed up like a clam. Her face went blank but she kept a neutral mask on the way women do when they don't to want to make things any more awkward, when they just want to get away from awful men with minimal drama. "Can we work something out now, because if not—"

"At our dinner." Ed waggled his eyebrows and it was all I could do not to gag. "We can work it out over a bottle of wine."

"Well, thanks anyway, then."

"Come *on*." Ed was following us now, Joan's arm back in mine as she teetered toward Rusty's Corolla. "You should really take me up on this. A woman like you—"

"A woman like me?" Joan stopped. Didn't turn around to look at him, just stopped.

"You're not going to find a better offer anywhere else," Ed said, his voice raised now that we were walking away from him. "Not on a car and frankly not on a man, honey. Not at your age."

I actually gasped at this. The apple didn't fall far from the tree. The father was just as hateful as the daughter. Worse, actually. My hands formed fists. Joan put her hand on my shoulder to stop me saying whatever I was going to say and I clamped my mouth shut.

"Fuck off, Ed." Still walking, Joan turned back just enough to toss the words off primly so that he could hear. She pulled my arm into hers again and we set off. I couldn't resist turning back and glaring at him. Face beet red, hands on his hips. A lump of a person who didn't deserve the wasted breath.

Then my mother stopped, turned fully around. "You know, I

was just thinking, thank god Ellen isn't alive to see what you've become."

"She always thought you were a tease," he smirked back. "Guess she had your number."

"Leave us alone," I said, pulling Joan along now. We just had another couple of rows of cars to get through before we reached Rusty's. I was so busy replaying Ed's piggishness in my head, I didn't notice the car pulling into the spot a few feet ahead of us, didn't register the driver's side door opening, the varsity track star legs extending out until she stood smack in front of me.

"What are you doing here?" Brie said.

"Nope." I shook my head, frantic, barely breathing now. I pulled my mother along, willing us not to break our stride. "Not today."

"Hi, Brianna, aren't you looking so lovely and grown-up?" Joan said. "See you around, sweetie," she added as I practically pushed her into Rusty's car.

The last I saw of Brie in the lot, her mouth had fallen open, her hands had found her hips. She was a younger, prettier image of her father.

"How dare he?" I said in the car, finding my voice only after Joan peeled out of the lot and had picked up speed on Sunrise Highway. "How fucking *dare* he. Disgusting enough that he asked you out and basically wanted you to prostitute yourself for a car deal, but then to insult you like that?"

We sat in brooding silence for a while and Joan turned the car off the highway onto Mount Olive Road. Joan zipped the car up the mountain in the darkening twilight and I watched the coin of the sun drop behind the black zigzags of even larger mountains miles west. I imagined Ed similarly vanishing. Just disappearing into the earth with a quick pull, a godlike hand yanking him into the ground. A tug, and *poof.*

Someone could make it happen. Someone should. Maybe it would even be me.

PART III
SYD

DECEMBER
FIVE MONTHS BEFORE THE FIRE

8

"How does she think she can just . . . *get away with this?*"

Rain released a plume of pot smoke into the cold winter sky and the question hung there almost visibly. We were lying on our backs, two points of a five-pointed human star, on the bleached-out tennis court behind the boarded-up Super 8 off the highway. It was where we'd been going since we'd discovered it junior year, whenever we could borrow a car or bum a ride.

On one side of the fenced-in court stood the adobe motel, abandoned and taken over by rattlesnakes and a family of red-eyed possums. On the other side was the hotel's drained pool, a deep oval that attracted skater boys from all over the desert cities. The sound of skateboard wheels scraping the empty swimming pool was soothing, like the ocean-waves setting on Mom's noise machine.

I'd learned to skate during long weekends at my grandma's house in Hemet when me and Spider were little. Grandma Rose didn't believe in TV and insisted that if Spider was going to escape her slipcovered living room and head to the skate park at the end of her block, he had to take eight-year-old me with him. Tonight I'd skated for about a half hour—just some easy back-and-forths in the bowl of the pool—before crunching my ankle on a botched ollie and limping over to the tennis courts to sit with Rain.

Rain passed the joint to Matt Richardson, who was next to

her in our heads-in, feet-out star formation. Next was Squirrel, christened that years ago because he'd always been the tiniest boy in school until eleventh grade when he finally grew, then Chase McAllister, then me.

"Someone should remind her . . ." Rain trailed off. I could almost feel her buzzing with her usual hard conviction. I knew if I turned to look, her black eyes would blaze with it and she'd convince me of her rightness and then I too would be furious at Brie Walsh for daring to throw a huge party and inviting seemingly everyone in school but us. But I didn't look, because I didn't want to be mad that night.

"Remind her of what?" someone said after a long silence.

It was nine o'clock and I was hopelessly stoned, shivering in my sweatshirt and conscious of Chase's tiniest movements next to me, his heavy jaw and sweetly beaked nose in profile, the way his long-lashed eyelids opened and closed as he stared up at the swirl of the Milky Way. I wondered if the stars looked to him like they did to me, pulsing and undulating in the moonless blackness of the desert sky.

I heard the rumble of skateboard wheels on concrete, a faraway boy's voice saying "Sweet, dude," the clatter of an overturned board against the concrete, an animal skittering in the ruined motel, and the frantic orchestra of crickets in the creosote. But Rain didn't elaborate.

Brie hadn't been our friend in years. Who cared that she didn't want us at the stupid party she was throwing? I didn't see the point of getting upset, even if the invite had been beamed to everyone's feed except ours. I assumed it meant she'd blocked us at some point, and if she had, it was because of her own weird issues with her past. Whatever Brie's grudge was with me and Rain, I'd long since given up trying to unravel it or make things right. Brie and I had most of our classes together and we were cordial, surface-level classmates. No more, no less, and that was fine with me. Just because we'd spent years together as little kids knocking around

Termico, creating elaborate animal soap operas with plastic figurines from the dollar store and tiny "staging areas" we constructed from sticks and old coffee cans, didn't mean we needed to somehow keep up a meaningful relationship now. That was the difference between us—Rain was always trying to get back what had been lost, to piece together scraps of old hurts into a quilt she could wrap around herself. I was happy enough to take Brie for who she was to me now: a buzzing mosquito, irritating but unimportant.

"I'm killing it," Matt said, audibly holding the smoke inside his lungs before releasing it. He sat up, breaking our formation. The rest of us remained glued to the peeling surface of the tennis court. Tonight Rain had been full of bitter lightning about so many things—her mom, their car woes, moving to LA, the pointlessness of college—but it was only when Matt brought up the party that she'd become agitated.

I rolled over onto my side, tearing my gaze away from Chase. Rain held a strand of her blue-black hair like a pen between her fingers and swept it across the air as if writing a flamboyant letter or conducting a song that only she could hear.

"Remind her of what? That we exist?" I asked. Though suddenly I didn't want her to say it. It had been the kind of week where it felt like whatever Rain said would lead us somewhere bad. "Let's forget about it. We don't even want to go, anyway."

I said *we* because I still thought we wanted the same things. Because for the twelve years I'd known Rain, we almost always had.

Rain curled her body toward me, grabbed my arm, and rested her cheek on the inside of my elbow, her eyes narrowed to slits. Sometimes Rain's intensity was like a laser in a Marvel movie—when it landed on you, you couldn't move. You were drawn toward her, despite your best efforts to resist. With her smeared black eyeliner, her wide lips pursed, her angular features alive with the power of her own rightness, she was so striking that I almost flinched.

If she'd ever cared about her appearance in any way that mattered,

I might have been jealous. If she'd ever acted like a single one of all the guys she'd hung out with pleased her, I might have been jealous. Instead her looks and the attention she received for them seemed to anger, exhaust, or annoy her, depending on the day. The older we became, the more protective I'd grown of Rain. Because the closer we stepped toward our futures, the less equipped she seemed to be to handle everything that came her way. Me, the world ignored. Her, it noticed. Even when she didn't want it to.

"Remind her she's not better than us," Rain breathed, her words meant only for me. She smiled bitterly. "And that we aren't to be fucked with."

"Well . . ." I trailed off, unsure of what she meant. I searched Rain's face, but all I saw was an inscrutable stoned glare.

"You want to crash it?"

"Not exactly." She paused, then gestured toward the boys. "They could help us."

They would, too. Whatever she asked, they would do. Most any boy was like that around her. She didn't even realize it.

In the past couple of months, I'd started to notice Chase. Had these little pangs about him when I watched him skate, warm feelings that I mostly ignored. Boys usually didn't pay much attention to me, but lately I'd noticed he had been. Whenever I spoke, it felt like he was listening intently.

"You're all invited to this party?" Rain loomed over us now, hands on her hips.

The boys grunted their version of *yeah*. With their shredded sneakers and utilitarian clothes, their ability practically to fly, their marble-mouthed quietness that was almost monk-like, guys like Squirrel and Chase and Matt moved between circles with no concern for social politics. At Valley Sands, skaters were the only class of human that seemed to be exempted from popularity rankings of any kind. They were respected by kids at every level, from every corner of the school.

"Even Squirrel?"

"Dude, I'm right here." Squirrel sat up and glared. "Yeah, I saw the invite. I'm in the panopticon, too."

Rain nodded. Her nostrils flared.

If anything, Rain had done it to herself by never bothering to fake care about the things the girls who ran things cared about. We were poor, they were rich, and Rain wasn't able to pretend like she cared about the purses, drill team, summer enrichment, college tours, or any of it. She found these things ridiculous, and they— not just Brie, but all of Brie's friends—they sensed it. It wouldn't matter, maybe, if Rain wasn't also the most beautiful girl in school. If you turned heads the way she did, you needed to make yourself unthreatening, and Rain couldn't. Or didn't care to.

"How is it?" My ruminations were interrupted by Chase's voice to my right. I turned and was surprised to see him looking right at me, waiting for me to answer.

The spotlight of his attention made my insides twist. Also, I wasn't sure what "it" was.

"Your ankle," he said, reading my mind. "How's it doing?"

"I think it's a little better." I bent my right knee and we both peered at my ankle as I flexed and unflexed my foot, self-conscious about Chase examining my pale leg, my beat-up Vans.

"Here," he sat up. On his knees now, he pressed on either side of my ankle. "Bend it this way?" He moved my foot to the right, then to the left. "Does that kill, or just hurt a little?"

My ankle hurt a little, but with Chase so close I barely noticed the pain.

"Just a little." His fingers were still on my ankle. I sat up on my elbows and felt my breathing go shallow. "Think I'll ever walk again?"

A smile flashed across his face, the gap between his front teeth winking. "Probably. If not, you can always get a leg transplant."

My laugh spilled out into the night, loud enough that the others heard. I felt the shift of their attention, their eyes on us. Chase must have, too. Carefully, he placed my leg back down on the tennis court and shot me a sideways smile.

"We should pull a prank." Rain stood up. "On the skank."

"Mastermind smoked too much dank," Chase rhymed so only I could hear, the joke reserved just for me. I laughed quietly, not wanting to break the spell. I moved imperceptibly closer to him and focused on the sensation of his breath on my hair. Not daring to look, I grazed his arm with mine as if by accident.

I had just turned seventeen the week before. I hadn't kissed any-one in over a year, and then it had been a random guy in a Jamba Juice shirt at an all-ages show. Nobody who mattered. I had come to accept that I wasn't someone boys saw the way they saw Rain. At least not the current version of me. But oh, how I liked the feel of Chase's eyes on me now.

"Her pool," Rain was saying above me. She was braless, her long, narrow torso covered by a tight turtleneck sweater (child's size me-dium, I knew for a fact, because it had once been mine) and home-distressed saggy-baggy Walmart jeans cut off at the knee that, on her and only her, looked stylish. "We should fill it with something gross. Make it unusable."

"Mini Baby Ruth bars. Yellow dye," said Chase.

"Don't encourage her!" I whispered, impressed that he had a prank at the ready. I dared to rest my pinkie finger on his palm for the slightest second before removing it. Like a sea anemone at the aquarium, his hand responded and folded around my finger for a quick squeeze.

"Yes." Rain whirled around, looming over us, her hair wild and in her eyes. She was all lips and long limbs and tension, the usual boredom in her sandpaper voice lifted to reveal excitement. "Chase, you're not the moron I thought you were."

Then something surprising happened. Chase threaded three of his calloused fingers—the middle, pinkie, and ring finger—through mine. My breath caught and I closed my eyes. I would go along with whatever awfulness they decided on. I would have set the school on fire if it meant Chase's fingers would continue to warm the corner of my palm.

"I'm gonna go skate," Matt Richardson said, wandering away. Squirrel wordlessly got up and followed him, like they sensed it was time for Chase and me to have a second. We were still on our backs, faces pointed at the sky, listening to the boys rolling toward the drained pool. I didn't—couldn't—breathe.

"You're good, you know," Chase whispered while Rain paced and plotted. It sounded to me like *I see you.* "You should skate more."

"You think?" I began to let my hand slip more fully over his, wondering what we were doing. But then Rain stalked back toward us and I pulled my hand away, wanting whatever was happening to be my secret for now.

"I just got this." She squatted next to me, holding her phone in front of my face so I could read what was there. "She's had too much wine, I'm sure. Probably nothing." But underneath the blasé words, Rain sounded scared.

I sat up, my fingers still vibrating with the magic they'd found moments before. On Rain's screen was a text from Joan.

COME HOME NOW 911 911 911

"I should never have taught her 911 for emergency texts," Rain grumbled from the backseat as Chase's ancient blue Cabriolet chugged toward the turnoff. "She'll never use it properly."

I willed myself to snap out of the boy-inflected dreaminess I still felt. Joan could be sweet and fun, but when she drank too much she grew grandiose and bitter and would go on about how moving here with Rain's dad (Enzo Santangelo, who vanished when Rain was two, took off in the night like a true coward, good riddance, etc.) was the worst decision she'd ever made. Sometimes Joan's drama could last hours and Rain would come sleep in my bed just to get away from it.

"We'll go and calm her down." I glanced at Chase. He was focused on driving, but he turned and flashed me that half-smile again, nodding supportively. So this was how it might feel to ride in a car with a boyfriend.

"Whoa." Chase saw it first when we pulled onto Clay Street.

"Jesus fucking Christ," Rain groaned. Their couch, dining room table, dining chairs, a dresser, some magazines, bookshelves, and assorted Santangelo knickknacks were piled outside in front of their house. And there was Joan, wrapped in her kimono, dousing the whole pile with a can of lighter fluid. "Stop the car."

After Rain and I jumped out, I turned back and stuck my head in the open passenger window. "No need to stay. It'll be better if you're not here for this," I said, not knowing what "this" was but knowing it could be embarrassing for Rain.

"You sure?" Chase looked unconvinced.

I nodded. "My place is right across the street, I can get my mom if I need."

"Okay. Text if you need anything. Do you have my number?"

"I . . . No." My stomach kicked as he punched it into my phone. He smiled, handed me the phone back, then started the car and backed away.

"Baby, we did it!" Joan was cackling between squirts from the lighter fluid can. Rain dove for it and pulled it from her mother's hands.

"You have lost your mind," Rain growled, her expression ferocious. I worried she might hit her mother. "You've ruined the fucking couch!"

"It doesn't matter!" Joan's hair stuck out in all directions. She came at us cackling, her arms spread so wide that her robe came undone. There was only a pair of flower-printed panties and a beige bra between her skin and me when she wrapped me in a tight hug.

"We did it, we did it." Joan's wine-breath wasn't unfamiliar to me—I'd grown up with it. The best thing was to play along until we could convince her she wanted to go inside with us.

"Did what, Joan?" I said, trying to steer her onto the porch.

"We hit the big one." Her words were crisp, not slurred. She stood up straight and wrapped her robe more tightly around herself, then reached into one of her pockets and pulled out a book of matches.

"I'll have to have her committed," Rain cried. She held up an ancient *Vogue* that must have been in the living room when Joan purged it. It was dripping with lighter fluid. "Don't you dare!" she shouted at her mother, shaking the magazine at her. "You're going to burn the house down!"

"Take it, Rainey." Joan whirled around to face Rain and shoved the matchbook at her. "Light the match."

"No fucking way." Rain stepped back like Joan had offered her poison.

"Come on. We've been saying it for years," Joan said. "How we just want to take a match to all this cheap, ugly furniture. *Now we can.*"

"Why, because you're drunk and lost your mind?"

"No, babydoll. Because we're *rich.*" Joan pulled the matches from Rain's hand and ran toward the pile in the front yard. She struck a match and tossed it, but it didn't ignite like in the movies. It was slower. Quieter. Like a campfire.

I went around to the side of the house to get the hose. Desert fires could spread fast. It was reckless and very illegal to light one in the middle of a dirt yard on Clay Street, surrounded by all our homes that were definitely flammable.

"Baby, we did it," Joan was saying, cradling Rain's face in her thin pink hands. "It finally happened. I always knew it would, and it did."

"You don't mean . . ." A slow dawn of understanding passed over Rain's face. "No way. Impossible."

From where I was with the hose I could still hear them. I watched Joan reach into her bra and carefully unfold a tiny slip of paper she'd stashed there.

I stepped closer. The Mega Millions logo was at the top. "36–24–37–61–93–16," she read. Joan had been playing Mega Millions forever. She bought one every workday at the Mobil before the turnoff on her way home. Part of her winding-down ritual, she always said. I watched the fire catch on the couch's arm, the back of the couch, a pile of old mail. The flames were spreading in every direction, but I had the hose ready. I still didn't believe her, not then.

"I checked it on the Internet. I'd fallen asleep for the broadcast but then I woke up and said hell, may as well check. I started screaming when I realized. It's *us,* baby. This time it's *us.*"

"Mom, if you're wrong about this . . ." Rain trailed off. "Give it to me. Let me check."

"They picked my numbers. They finally picked my numbers. I triple-checked it. Six-point-four million, baby. Not their biggest payout, but big enough for us!"

The flames rose up on the back of the couch and on the seat cushions, catching the magazines piled on it. All those *People*s and *Us Weekly*s Joan had saved on her bookshelves, kept unwrinkled and orderly as if they were valuable, like they were a set of encyclopedias.

I took the hose to the couch, spraying it down and down until the fire went out.

Rain had gone inside and Joan had followed her, the fire forgotten. I stayed outside alone, breathing in the lighter fluid and fire and burnt-cheap-furniture smell. I could see them through the yellowed lace curtains, hugging in the empty room, turning in a kind of waltz-like circle. Rain's face atop her mother's shoulder looked different than I'd ever seen it before, like something had cracked open for her, lit her up. It was an expression you only saw on TV during Christmas commercials or on *Ellen* when she presented someone with a big cardboard check.

My best friend who once told me she only had two settings— pissed off and neutral—was crying happy tears.

I stood there a long time watching them, feeling for the first time that my presence inside wouldn't be entirely welcome. The magic that had graced them tonight was theirs alone. I knew enough not to try to join; it would only make things awkward.

When I'd fully hosed down the fire so that all that was left was a waterlogged heap of half-burnt furniture, Joan was pacing and gesturing as if planning their future. I turned away from their living room window and headed through the scrubby lawn to my own dark house with our three trash cans pressed neatly against the aluminium side wall, our front porch covered in AstroTurf. It looked shabbier than ever. I closed the front door behind me and breathed in the musty silence of home.

Our house had become kind of a bummer ever since Spider had been arrested last year. Just a quiet place where Mom and me made microwave popcorn and frozen pizza and tried to pass the time together, mostly with the TV on. I thought of waking Mom up, crawling into her bed like I would when I was little, but that wouldn't begin to fix the creeping dread just starting to set up camp in the back of my mind.

For now, I would shower off the smell of the lighter fluid and try to prepare myself for how quickly Rain's life was about to change.

It didn't hit me then how much my life was about to change, too.

9

"You kids *sure* you want to eat here?" The restaurant's hostess, a tan, trim blonde in a chambray button-down and black pants, looked us over skeptically. I could feel her taking in our flip-flops and ripped sneakers, our ages, the way we didn't belong in this place. To be fair, she was right. Most of us were definitely *not* sure we wanted to eat here. Rain had sprung it on us the first morning back at school after winter break that she was taking us out to a late lunch and that it wasn't optional. "You'd better be hungry by the time the last bell rings," she'd said, looking like she was biting back a smile. "Or else."

We'd spent winter break together mostly at my house, opting for a nachos and horror-movie marathon on New Year's Eve just like we'd done the past few years. Rain was quieter and more spaced-out than usual, still processing the fact that the lottery win had actually happened, I guessed. She changed the subject each time I brought it up, though, preferring to complain about Joan's whirlwind of manic plan-making now that she'd quit her job.

The money finally arrived on January second, just two days before we returned to school. Looking at Rain beside me now in the restaurant entryway, I wondered if she was becoming a little bit manic herself. She shot the hostess her flattest, fakest smile, the one she could throw like a dart at a target. "Can I talk to you privately for a sec?"

The hostess shrugged and they moved toward the bar, all mahogany and shiny glass and leather. Walking into that room, Rain looked both out of place and too good for it at the same time.

"Didn't know Rain had a secret passion for golf," Chase said, standing close to me at the hostess station and peering past my head at the miles of deep-green hills rolling out alongside the hotel, the color shocking amid the brown of the desert. He started humming the tune to that song "Money, Money, Money."

"The hell are we doing here?" Matt Richardson grumbled. He'd been grumbling ever since Rain had ordered him to drive us all here in his minivan. She'd refused to tell him where she was taking us, crowing, "Let yourself be surprised for once in your stupid life!" every time he asked. She'd had to pry the keys out of his hand when it was time to hand them to the valet. "This is so weird."

Squirrel snorted in agreement, busy dipping into a huge crystal bowl and methodically filling every one of his pockets with cream-colored matchboxes stamped with the Ritz-Carlton logo in thin black letters.

Rain came back rolling her eyes. *All good,* she mouthed to me before scooping a handful of matchboxes into her bag.

"Your table is ready!" the hostess announced behind her, pulling a stack of enormous leather-bound menus from her station. Silently, awkwardly, we all followed her. The only other people at the Ritz-Carlton Rancho Mirage State Fare Bar & Kitchen at 3:45 were two red-faced men who looked about seventy and a middle-aged couple in a back booth, both wearing all-white outfits that I suspected had something to do with tennis. The hostess led us through open glass double doors and onto the patio, the brilliant green of the golf course sweeping out for miles behind us. We sat on wicker-backed chairs around a big round table set with a brocade tablecloth and tons of oversized silverware. I picked up a soup spoon and looked at my upside-down reflection in it while everyone sat. Chase was on my left, Rain to my right.

"I told her to pick the best things off the menu. And I reminded her teenage boys are pigs," Rain announced. She sat back, threaded her fingers together behind her head and shut her eyes. She looked like someone pretending to be at peace.

"Also, I paid up front," Rain said more quietly, just to me. "That shut her up."

"I didn't know you could do that at a restaurant like this," I said.

"It's disgusting how nice she became once she saw a roll of cash." Rain glowered in her seat and was about to say more when the waiter appeared.

"Hello hello, how are we today?" asked a man in the same chambray shirt and black pants the hostess wore. "I'm Mark. I'll be your server today. I think we're all set for the food order for now"—he winked at Rain—"but how about drinks? Soda?"

"Cokes for everyone please, Mark," Rain said, her voice upbeat again. "And whatever else they want," she added quickly, gesturing to us. The boys all shrugged and a minute later a different waiter was whisking our wineglasses away and placing tall glasses of Coke with lemon down on the tablecloth for each of us.

"Nice life you've got here," Chase said, sipping his Coke. "And way to convince the hostess you're legit."

I snuck a peek at Chase's profile, his heavy jaw and tumble of brown curls. I memorized the arc of his eyelashes, admired the way his eyes opened and closed. Yes, everyone blinked, but the way he did it was . . . better. More interesting.

"I came here once with Joan when I was like ten. She was here to apply for a job," Rain said, twisting around in her seat to check that the waiter wasn't hovering. "It was the fanciest place I'd ever seen. Figured we may as well try it."

"It's perfect." I smiled at Rain, wanting to see her bask in her good fortune. I remembered the time several years ago when Joan needed a job, when things were really tight and they were on food stamps. And now look, here Rain was ordering seven-dollar Cokes and a lunch that definitely cost more than our monthly grocery bill. I marveled at how unexpectedly enchanted the universe could occasionally be. How Rain's life was going to take off in a million unexpected ways. Even though change could be scary to think about, in that moment I was happy for her.

Rain dug through the huge tote bag she'd brought and fished out a full-size bottle of Jack Daniels. "I brought us something else."

"Rain," I hissed, eyeing the patio doors in case Mark came back. Beyond the fact that we could get caught and kicked out, Rain and hard liquor wasn't my favorite combination.

Barely looking around to make sure she was unseen by the restaurant staff, Rain went around to each of our glasses and poured a hefty glug of the Jack into each of them. "Born to bartend." She smirked. Back at her own seat, she dumped half her Coke into an empty glass and filled the rest of it up with the Jack. "Unlimited supply for everyone but Matt."

This wasn't going to end well, I thought, but I did my best to swallow my misgivings along with a few cautious sips of my drink.

Down below us, the golf course was dotted with men in polo shirts and caps, caddies carrying bags of clubs, a few golf carts. Up from the lush green hills floated the sounds of crows cawing in the rustling trees. Underneath the breeze and the birds I could almost hear it: the confident, steady hum of money.

Next to me, Chase's knee found mine and stayed pressed against it. My stomach tickled with his presence. I tried to focus on the jokes Matt and Squirrel were making about the beef carpaccio and tuna tartare on the menu, but my mind had already gone a little fuzzy. I took a few more gulps of my drink, trying to steady myself. Before too long, Chase's chair had moved closer to mine. After a few minutes, he leaned in and spoke softly so that only I could hear.

"She's good at this rich-person thing." Chase smiled, that gap between his front teeth winking. My laugh spilled out high and loud, whether from my nervousness around Chase or from the Jack and Coke, I couldn't quite tell.

When the waiter had to bring reinforcements to help unload the three massive trays of food, Rain let out a low whistle. "Wow, Mark. You're amazing. Can I have another Coke, too, when you get a chance?" she said a little too loudly.

I checked her glass. It was already completely drained. *Fuck*, I thought.

"Dude." Chase let out a low whistle when the table was full of food. "Like, *thank you*. I mean, damn."

"To all of you." Rain held up her Coke, magically replaced that very second by yet another server in a chambray shirt. "To be cheesy for a minute, I guess I want to say thank you for being my friends. I know it hasn't been easy."

"Yes, it has," I said. It was the easiest thing I'd ever done.

"You're sweet to say that, Squid. I love you best in the world and I always will and I'll die when you go off to Peoria and leave me here. Now"—Rain laughed merrily, that same manic high-pitched squeal I'd been noticing all week—"let's eat our feelings."

We feasted on sashimi, duck spring rolls, sliders, tri-tip, and about six other things I'd never heard of or seen before. Rain ate a few fries and added another hefty pour of Jack Daniels to her glass. "Easy there," I said, trying to keep my voice light. "Pace yourself."

She nodded but rolled her eyes and gulped, telling me without saying it that I was annoying her. Annoying or not, she knew as well as I did that two months ago—the last time I'd seen her drink hard liquor—she'd gotten blackout drunk and puked in my bed. I wasn't going to bring it up, but I didn't want a repeat of the experience again today either.

Everyone ate quietly for a while and then we began to rate dishes in order of our favorites. Squirrel said he didn't know raw meat was considered a delicacy. "Like, they don't even cook it and it's twenty-eight dollars."

Chase and I agreed we liked the spring rolls and the steak best. There was a salad none of us touched; the giant pile of truffle fries we replenished twice. I felt the buzz of the Jack and Coke flit through me and it made me lean closer to Chase, then rest my head on Rain's shoulder.

Rain wasn't eating, though. She continued to mix herself drinks, pouring an even larger amount of Jack into her glass each time, humming to herself.

"Eat, woman!" I said, more assertive now. "I don't want to carry you out of here!"

"Oh no?" Rain turned on me, her eyes flashing. "Are you calling me a drunk?"

"Okay, okay. But you ordered all this food, you should eat it," I said, placating, pleading. Our group already stuck out in this place—I wasn't about to make an even bigger scene.

"Mark!" Rain stood up then, shouting for the waiter.

Uh-oh. She was definitely trashed.

"Where is Mark?" Rain cried even as I tried to shush her.

Instantly, he appeared. "Yes, love, what can I do for you?" He smiled but he also looked a little wary.

"Dessert!" she yelped, still standing. "One of everything. Big tip, Mark. I love you and I'm going to show you how much, I promise." She moved toward him, arms open. Oh no. Her hands were on him then, pulling him in for a hug. Mark looked panicked, his hands and arms trying to convey *not hugging* even as she pulled him tight.

I jumped up, pulled her off him. "Come on, we're still eating. You need to eat or no dessert for you," I tried to joke. "Seriously," I hissed in her ear. "Eat something. You're shit-faced."

"Okay, *Miss Perfect*," Rain said. I watched her put fries in her mouth, chew them. Chase shifted in his seat next to me. "Want to just cancel the dessert and get her out of here?" he asked me. "Or I can get it to go."

"Thanks. Great idea." If I wasn't already sure about Chase, I liked him even more at that moment for knowing the right thing to do.

"He likes you," Rain slurred. "But nobody's good enough for my Squidney. *Nobody.*"

"Okay, settle down now," I said, feeding her another truffle fry, the pile of them oily and cold now. "We're going to eat dessert on the golf course," I whispered. "We'll have to sneak it, okay?"

Rain loved sneaking things, bending rules. Telling her something was illicit or not allowed was all it took to get her excited about it.

"Great idea." She smiled. Her eyes closed again.

Once Chase had gotten the desserts to go, Mark visibly relieved to be getting rid of us, I grabbed Rain's bag and pulled her by the elbow around the side of the restaurant and up to the golf course, where there was a bank of spiky conifers and a little man-made stream. We hiked up it until we came to a set of fake boulders we could sit on in the mild sunshine, only 75 degrees and even a bit of a breeze.

Rain was all worked up about how over-the-top this place was, how it was destroying the environment, squandering our water. "And just think of all the evil men who've plotted horrible things on golf courses like this. This is like the epicenter of toxic masculinity," she said.

Matt Richardson nodded, calmly sucking on his vape pen.

"Uh, women's golf is a thing, I'm pretty sure," Squirrel said.

"Not what I'm talking about," Rain snapped, and then she was off and running down the hill.

"Damn it," I muttered before I got up to run after her. By the time I reached her, she'd taken a flag out of one of the greens and was trying to snap the flagpole in half.

"You're going to get us kicked out," I said. I wrenched the flag-pole away from her and stuck it back in the ground, hoping I'd picked the right spot. Then I started pulling her back up the hill toward the shade of some trees where we could take cover from whoever monitored this place.

"Whatever. You know who would just love it if we did? That hostess. Smug bitch."

"Okay," I said, exasperated, my hands on Rain's back as I pushed her back to where the group was sitting. "So let's not give her the satisfaction."

Eventually, I finally got Rain settled back on the boulders on the edge of the course. I took a seat between her and Chase again as Rain continued naming all the evil men who'd played golf, pausing only to take a puff from Matt's pen. "Sure you want that right now?" I asked her.

She glared at me and took another hit. "Don't you start judging me, too," Rain snapped and flashed me a hurt look.

I'm trying to help you, I wanted to say, but in the state she was in I knew she wouldn't get it. Instead I gave up and closed my eyes, the shadows of the branches from the trees above and the soft sun streaming through them. I tried to forget about Rain for a minute and let myself enjoy the warmth of Chase's hand finding mine.

"I'm never going to change, guys," Rain said a few minutes later, talking a mile a minute. "I'm always going to be just the way I am today. Rich or poor, I'll still be the same asshole I've always been."

"Not me," Chase said. "I plan to become a new asshole every few years, just to mix it up."

I snorted at that, trying to enjoy the banter between the two of them even as I was annoyed about having to take care of the hot mess she'd become today.

Maybe Rain was right, maybe all the good things we had would stay just as they were. But I didn't think so. Things were already changing.

As if to prove me right, Rain muttered a quiet "uh-oh," then rose, swaying like a newborn calf on shaky legs, walked a few feet down the hill, and delicately vomited all over the soft green grass.

PART IV

RAIN

JANUARY

FOUR MONTHS BEFORE THE FIRE

10

Exhausted and woozy, I sat on the floor of the dressing room of Urban Outfitters and stared at the mess I'd made, the "yes" and the "no" piles both requiring energy I suddenly couldn't find. I'd woken up at noon feeling like a dried-out husk, headachy and still nauseous after my antics the day before on the golf course and then my second and even more mortifying bout of vomiting out the window of Matt's van.

I picked up a sweater I couldn't decide on and moved it from the "no" to the "yes" pile. How badly had I embarrassed everyone? I would apologize to Syd later, when she got out of school. She'd tried to stop me from drinking so much, I remembered, and I hadn't been very nice about it.

Rather than face school four hours late, I'd driven Joan's new car (her first post-lottery purchase, a black Range Rover Rusty insisted was perfect for "the new Joan") to the Rancho Mirage Urban Outfitters, a store Syd and I had been to several times but had only ever bought clearance-sale accessories from. It wasn't so much that I wanted new clothes, it was that I was tired. Tired of being treated like a dirtbag, tired of looking like someone who didn't belong. Deep down I didn't think clothes could change that, but if I was going to try to be less angry, less of a mess, maybe changing my outsides would help a little.

Maybe with better clothes, people wouldn't see whatever they'd always seen in me. And if I could buy my way into looking legitimate, then I could turn myself into someone hostesses trusted belonged in the restaurant, someone teachers didn't write off, someone who could actually be nice and polite and easygoing, which Joan said we had to be now since we were rich. "We're not going to become those rich assholes we've spent our lives hating." She'd been saying that all week.

"How are we doing in there?" The condescending voice of the twentysomething salesclerk with cotton-candy-pink hair floated around the fitting room door. She was back to check up on me for the third time. "Do we need any size exchanges? Can I put anything back for you?"

I edged closer to the door and unlocked it so it swung open.

Pinky looked down at me, her pierced nose wrinkled. "Are you okay?"

"I have to hang all this stuff I'm not taking back up." I waved at the heap of garments on one end of the bench.

The girl frowned. "You're taking all that?" She gestured at the other pile. It was pretty big. Maybe thirty items altogether. Certainly more than I'd ever bought at one time. Maybe more than most people bought at once, but what did I know about how people with money shopped?

"Yeah."

She raised an eyebrow. "Lucky you."

Yeah, lucky me. Except right now I felt like death. I needed more coffee, some food. And I needed Pinky to not judge me.

"I can check you out. Don't worry about the rest, we'll hang it."

"Great." I gathered up my bag and my yes pile and followed her to the register, relieved to be one of only a handful of people in the store. It felt a little gross, buying all this. Like I was showing off somehow. Pinky probably hated me. *It doesn't matter what she thinks,* I reminded myself, but I didn't believe that, not really. I still cared a lot more than I wanted to about what everyone thought of me. Random salesgirls, people at school, Syd—all of them. So far, money hadn't changed that.

While Pinky swiped tags through the UPC reader, I moved from one foot to the other and chewed my lip while the number on the screen grew and grew. I checked my wallet inside my bag. It bulged with cash. Joan had handed me three thousand dollars a few days ago and said, "Just enjoy how this feels for a little while, baby." It did feel good, but everything came with a catch. Paying for lunch felt great yesterday, but the hostess's suspicion felt horrible. As if she knew I'd been nothing, had been trash, and would always be trash. And now, the salesgirl paused in her tabulations to blink at me, her head tilted like she was assessing who I was. *Yep, trash,* I almost blurted.

"Um, this is going to come to over a thousand dollars." She leaned in, adjusted her knotted scarf headband, and widened her eyes. "Sure you've got enough?"

Ugh. Just like at the restaurant, I had that same feeling of being under suspicion, not up to a stranger's standards. Humiliating. Confirming what I knew deep down to be true: Something about me would always appear less-than, no matter how much money I spent.

"Uhh." I stalled, wondering if I should just pull out my money like I did with the hostess, hating how desperate I felt, or just give up, tell her she'd found me out, and run out of here and leave all the clothes behind.

"That's kind of rude, isn't it?" a familiar voice said behind me.

"Excuse me?" Pinky blinked. "I was only checking as a courtesy. Sometimes girls have to put stuff back. We've all been there." She smiled and shrugged as if to say she was in on it with me, not against me.

"Would you ever ask a man if they had the money? Or an older woman? It's sexist and ageist to assume."

"Okaaay," Pinky said, suddenly ultra-absorbed in the checkout process and clearly done with the conversation.

I knew that voice. I turned around. There Brie stood in her usual crop top, showing off that assertively tan, rock-hard midsection that said, *You can only dream of being this confident.* She smiled at me, almost bashful. "I needed a mental health day. Guess we both did."

"Hi." I swallowed down how weird this was, even as my face burned to have been caught here by her.

She gave me a little wave, her fingers wiggling. "Can I watch her fold your stuff? I want to see what you got."

I nodded curtly, hoping this little exchange didn't mean I owed Brie something now. The last thing I wanted was to be in her debt. We stood there together in silence while Pinky folded. Most of what I'd bought didn't look like much off the hangers, but Brie managed to remark on a few things anyway.

Finally, Pinky rang me up, colder now and not really speaking to either me or Brie. I handed over $1,300 in cash, not daring to look at how Brie was reacting to that. I was about to say a fast goodbye and hustle away when Brie motioned to the exit. "Shall we?"

Shall we what *exactly?* I thought as we walked out of there like two girls who didn't hate each other. It had to be some kind of trick, Brie working some angle I hadn't figured out yet.

Outside, standing awkwardly with Brie in the sunshine and the canned pop music of the spotless mall, I decided two could play at this nicey-nice act, at least until I figured out what she was up to. "Thanks, for back there. I was ready to just leave," I said. "I might have, if you hadn't showed up."

Brie shrugged. "It was gross. It's happened to me before. People acting like I don't have a right to be someplace."

"Really?" Somehow, I couldn't imagine that. Ever since she'd left Termico and remade herself, Brie had oozed confidence and power.

"Everyone treats girls like shit." Brie dug in her bag and took out a pack of gum. She handed me a piece without asking if I wanted one and then took a piece for herself. Annoyingly, it was exactly what I needed since my mouth tasted like an old sock. "Especially when we're young. Never let them talk down to you," she said, taking on the bizarre tone of an empowerment influencer or big sister. "Remember, they're probably just jealous and hate their jobs."

Who *they* were, I didn't really know. *I don't need your advice,* I wanted to say. "Well, thanks," I said instead, thinking this might be the moment we said our goodbyes and life returned to normal.

"Anyway, I got her back for you." Brie pulled something out of her purse and grinned. It was a blue satin slip dress, price tags still on.

"You took that?" I pulled Brie farther from the window of the store where Pinky couldn't see her. I flashed on a memory from way back when we were nine or ten and we used to get a ride down the mountain to the nearest strip mall. The three of us would hang out in Longs Drugs for hours, deciding how to spend the few dollars we'd scraped together, what kind of candy we would buy, trying on makeup we couldn't afford. Syd had caught Brie slipping mascara and lip gloss into the waistband of her underwear more than once.

Brie shrugged. "I feel like she deserved it, don't you?"

"I guess. I didn't realize you still did that after . . . all this time." Meaning *after you left us, after you became someone else.* I never stole. I had too much pride to prove the shopkeepers right for always watching me, always assuming I would.

"Guess you can take the girl out of Termico, but you can't take Termico out of the girl." Brie stuffed the dress back in her bag and dug around for something else. "We're both still the same as we always were, don't you think? Even though things have . . . changed."

"I guess, yeah." I looked at her hard, still wary of a setup. Weren't we *not at all* the same girls we once were? Hadn't that been the whole problem between the two of us? I didn't know what Brie was doing, why she was being so syrupy-sweet all of a sudden, but I'd had enough pretending for one day.

3 1308 00393 9741

I pulled out my phone and feigned surprise at the time. "Shoot, I gotta go," I said, backing away now. "Nice to . . . see you." I couldn't decide if this was a lie or the truth.

"Enjoy your new wardrobe." Brie gave me a goodbye wave, her face already reverting to her usual mask of boredom.

"See you around," I said awkwardly, but she had taken out her phone and begun some high-speed texting. Walking to Joan's car, I tried to imagine the catty texts she might be sending her girls about what had just happened, what she could be calling me behind my back.

I threw the bags into the trunk of the car and inhaled the smell of hot leather, turning things over in my head. I looked back at Brie once last time, but she was already gone, our moment of connection a strange desert mirage that had already disappeared.

11

At school a week later, I was camped out in the bathroom by the science labs on a little half-hidden window ledge just wide enough for me to curl up into and disappear from view. I scrolled through my feed, trying to decide where I wanted to go for the remainder of the day now that I'd decided to cut. Algebra II was a drag, and even though I sort of liked history with Mrs. Kim, I hadn't done the homework and there would probably be a quiz. According to my philosophy of senior year, which was to do the bare minimum I needed to do for Joan to watch me graduate, it made sense for me to bag out early.

Maybe I'd just go home and put on *Law & Order* and start to pack up my room. Joan had been looking at rental houses for a couple weeks now. Any day she would take me to see her top three, she said, and then we would pull the trigger and move down the mountain.

So I was tucked away in that corner of the school bathroom, squinting through another round of texted house photos from Joan—a blurry kitchen island, a half-covered pool and what looked like an outdoor fireplace made out of broken bottles—when I heard someone slam into a stall and take series of quick, gasping breaths that sounded like an asthma attack. I waited for the pop-and-suck sound of an inhaler, but none came. Instead, the gasping got worse.

I looked up at the ceiling, hoping someone would come in so I wouldn't have to deal with it. I was the worst person at this kind of thing, maybe the least nurturing person I knew. I let a minute tick by but no one came. I could still hear the girl's labored breathing. Nobody else was going to save me—I had to be a good Samaritan and help her myself.

I swallowed a groan, pushed my feet back into my flip-flops, and scooted off the ledge.

"Hey." I stood in front of the stall door and knocked. "You okay? I can walk you to the nurse. They have tons of spare inhalers there. . . ." I knew this from Matt Richardson, who, considering his asthma, should not smoke as often as he did.

Everything went quiet in the stall. I bent to peek under, saw unmistakable bright-white Stan Smiths and perfect low white socks, each with a faint yellow stripe at the top, and then the whittled ankles and legs of the Valley Sands track team's second-best female two-hundred-meter hurdles competitor. How I even knew this stat, I had no idea. Brianna Walsh's accomplishments were known to us all, apparently, whether we cared about them or not.

I'd seen Brie a few times since we'd talked in the mall a week ago. She'd even given me a slight nod in homeroom that morning, but we hadn't talked again. I was just contemplating leaving when the toilet flushed and she opened the door. "Oh."

"Hi." A wan smile, her mascara smeared in the pits of her eyes, her lids puffy. "Small panic attack," she said, embarrassed. "I'm fine now."

I looked her over. She was pale, maybe even a little green, her expression moving from sorrow to shame and back again. "You don't seem fine."

Blinking at me, her eyes welled up with tears again. She took a shaky breath, brushed past me to the sinks, and washed her face. "Just something I do sometimes." Again, the pained smile. "Now you know."

"Is it any fun?" Weird question, but that's what came out.

"Ha. Oh, extremely." She dried her face with a paper towel and I studied her in the mirror. We were almost the same height now. When we were little, I was always a head taller, but she'd just about caught up. "I failed a quiz."

There had to be more to it than that. "And?" I prompted her, waiting for the bad part.

"It's going to bring down my average."

"Don't you get straight As?" I asked gently. Wasn't she famous for it? Track star, student government, top of the class—one little quiz couldn't matter all that much for someone like her.

"Yeah. But only because I have to."

I cocked my head, trying to keep the mocking expression I felt flitting around my face from betraying how ridiculous this sounded to me. "Have to?"

She looked at me and almost winced. I didn't know if it was because she was embarrassed or because she thought I was stupid for not getting it. "Because of college. I have to get in somewhere Ed thinks is worth paying for."

I'd dreamt about Ed after the disaster at the car lot. Nightmare Ed was driving me and Joan down a stick-straight highway until he veered off the road. We bumped along the desert floor, careening way too fast through brush and over rocks. Unable to open the door, unable even to use my arms, I'd resorted to screaming. Even with Joan clawing at him and grabbing at the wheel, he had this awful laugh as he drove us straight toward a cliff. *Don't blame me,* Ed chuckled. *I'm just the chauffeur—and this is where gals like the two of you end up.*

"College is the only way I can get away from here," she went on. "That's why I bust my ass for those grades." She raised an eyebrow at me. "I'm not like Syd or Danny Schuster. I really have to work for it."

I thought about her eerily perfect handwriting that was almost like a computer font, all those index cards she was always scribbling, each in different colored ink, the neon Post-it notes she stuck on everything. Syd didn't do any of that—she studied, sure, but she didn't make it into a *system*.

"You'll be fine," I said. "One bad grade isn't the end—"

"It's easy to say that," she interrupted me, "but it's always felt like if I slip up it could be the beginning of the end. Like I'm walking a tightrope, you know? One false move and *poof*, I fall. The whole thing, everything I've been working for, disappears. And then I'm stuck in that house, with my father, forever."

"You really hate him, huh?"

"You know how he is," Brie said quietly. She had folded and wet some paper towels and was now pressing them underneath each eye. "All buttoned up until the booze comes out. And then you never know what you're going to get."

I nodded and could almost see her in her driveway when we were little, sitting in the backseat of Ed's car a few years after Ellen died, Ed in front, the two of them arguing. Her voice tiny and inaudible, his voice audible even through the closed windows. The way he would hit the steering wheel to make his point. I remembered the way she'd sunk down in the backseat, tiny and deflated, before looking out the window at me walking by. How she'd blushed that violent, blotchy red and turned away.

He'd lay into her like that sometimes, as if she was some kind of bad kid, when the truth was that of the three of us she was by far the most obedient, or at least the best at hiding her tiny little-kid crimes. We couldn't hear the words three houses over but we could hear the yelling. A few times, Joan had gone over there with some made-up excuse about borrowing jumper cables or some eggs, just to make it stop. Once or twice, she'd sent Syd and me over. *Just ring the bell and ask if Brie can come play, and that way he'll have to cut it out.*

Looking at her now in the harsh light of the bathroom and see-

ing her white-blond lashes visible around her swollen eyes, something in me softened. She looked so weary, so bone-tired and worn
out. For once, I didn't feel my usual resentment. Instead I saw the
girl who'd lost her mom, the girl dragged in her church clothes
down our dusty street by that pit bull of her father's, holding on to
Spanky's leash for dear life. I saw the girl Brie had been. She suddenly struck me as fragile, much closer to the edge than I'd realized.

"So . . . your plan is to just be perfect. And then whenever you're
not, you have a panic attack?"

"Ha," she said without smiling. "Pretty much."

Brie looked at me in the bathroom mirror now, then regarded
herself. I could see her mask, her tough exterior, already returning
as she studied her own face. She took a deep, shuddering breath
and dug a compact and a tube of mascara out of her bag.

"Do you want to go somewhere? Maybe smoke?" she said.

I was surprised she wanted to go anywhere with me. Though
habit and impulse told me to say no, she seemed so unsteady, like
she truly needed a friend. I would have to do.

"The wall?" I suggested, but she shook her head.

"I know somewhere better."

We walked through the quiet halls, classes in session, and outside past the library, where there was a kind of gardening shed I'd
never noticed. Brie shimmied onto it and I followed her. Attached
to the stucco wall at the back of the library was a metal ladder.
"How many people know about this?" I whispered, thinking with
a stab of envy that it must be a hangout for her friends.

"Nobody. I learned about it from a guy who graduated a year ago
and I've kept it all to myself." Brie began to climb and motioned
for me to follow.

"Nice," I said, surprised she'd shared her secret with me.

The roof was flat and speckled with gravel. In the dead center of
it, someone had spread one of those waterproof picnic blankets out
and weighted it down in each corner with a rock.

"Cool setup." Brie had gone to a lot of trouble to make it nice up here. I'd assumed she never cut class and was never alone, but maybe that wasn't true. After all, she'd been at the mall on a school day last week, and now this. Maybe I didn't know the first thing about her.

"Right?"

We sat down on the blanket. It was as private a place as I'd ever seen at school. Wordlessly, she took a vape pen out of what looked like a tampon case and took a drag from it.

When she offered it to me, I shook my head. I would sit here post–panic attack, but that didn't mean I was going to let my guard down entirely. "Okay," she said, sounding a little wounded. "It's here if you change your mind."

I lay back and stared at the white sky while Brie talked quietly about the things that were stressing her out. College applications, being in a race with a few others for valedictorian. All the home-work, hours and hours of it, the comedown from the ADHD med-ication she bought from kids who had prescriptions. Her voice, that same slightly flat way of speaking she'd had as a girl, filled the air. Up here I didn't hate listening to her, this royalty of Valley Sands High, this shiny, polished princess with her perfectly white sneakers, her ankle bones that seemed too delicate to even hold her up.

"Did those hurt?" I asked, pointing to three cartilage piercings she had near the top of her right ear, all threaded with thin gold hoops. Syd had told me she'd showed these off a few months ago in class and we'd made fun of Brie for trying to be edgy, but now, up here, I kind of liked the look.

"Everything hurts, doesn't it?" Brie patted the hoops as if mak-ing sure they were still there. "All the things we do to look pretty?"

"Not for me." I shrugged. "I don't do much."

"You don't need to." She sighed. "All I ever wanted was to be half as beautiful as you."

"Oh, stop." I rolled up into a seated position. "I don't care about that stuff. I'm nobody and nothing. You're the queen of this place. You're all anyone sees."

"You can afford not to care." She looked away, her voice faraway, back in her own high-stakes world again where she thought she had to be perfect. "I can't."

Before today, I would have scoffed at that. But after what I witnessed in the bathroom, I understood there was more going on with her than what she showed. She was an insecure mess, like all of us. Like me.

We sat up there for a long time until the sky felt like it was vibrating around us, until the bell rang and reminded us where we were and what we were supposed to be doing.

12

Can you get away last period? I'll be on the roof.

Close to a week had passed since Brie and I had smoked on the roof and it felt like the chill between us was finally thawing a little. We'd exchanged a few closed-mouth smiles in homeroom and she'd even said hello to me in the hallway. Syd, who'd been walking me to history at the time, had nearly dropped her books. "Did Brie just say hi to you?" I'd shrugged. For some reason, I hadn't told Syd about hanging out with Brie. Maybe out of embarrassment for crossing enemy lines, or maybe because it felt private, somehow, witnessing Brie coming apart like that. I knew that Brie wouldn't want anyone else to know.

Still, this was the first text she'd ever sent me.

I was debating how to respond—*did* I want to go?—when another text came in.

Brought you something.

I raised an eyebrow, both intrigued and annoyed at how she knew I'd be intrigued. OK, I wrote back, drawn in despite my wariness.

· · ·

That afternoon I bagged out on Spanish and hoisted myself onto the library roof. Brie was sleeping or tanning, stretched out on the picnic blanket stomach-side-down, shoes off, her head resting on her folded arms. I crunched along the roof's gravel until she lifted her head, pulled her hair out of her face, and smiled. "You came."

She sounded grateful and despite everything, I felt flattered. Busy Brie, with her million commitments, had been waiting for me. And here I was, showing up, falling for the hype.

"I told you I would."

"You did, you did." She sat up and shaded her eyes with one hand. "Sit."

I sat.

"Hang on," she muttered, digging through her bag. "It's in here somewhere. Aha." She tossed something black and silky into my lap. "Hope it's not too weird to give you this. It didn't look right on me, but I realized last night it's perfect for you."

I held it up and examined it. A halter top. It felt expensive, like it might be real silk. I loved it. I glanced at her from behind my sunglasses. Were Brie and I *friends* now? Had hell officially frozen over?

"It was too long for me. I wish I was as tall as you," she was saying now as she rummaged through her bag again. "You're like a walking hanger."

"With my tiny boobs, you mean?" I rolled my eyes. "Trust me, it's not that fun."

"But you can wear anything," Brie said. "And now you can afford to buy whatever you want. I mean, how cool is that?"

"Well, you know what that feels like." It wasn't like Brie didn't have money. She drove a sports car and always had the latest tech, the newest clothes.

A shadow passed across Brie's face for a moment. "Trust me, it's not the same."

I shrugged, feeling awkward about the lottery all over again, even though I should have been used to the strangeness of other people knowing about it by now. People at school who had never spoken two words to me before had been high-fiving me and asking me about it ever since Joan and I had gone to receive that giant cardboard check.

She smoothed the fabric of the halter top in my lap. "Try it on."

"Here?" I looked around. It was very private on the roof, other than Brie sitting there blinking at me. Nobody from below could possibly see us where we sat.

"I'll turn around," she said. And then she did. While I changed, she took out her pen.

I took my shirt off and wriggled into the halter as fast as I could. Without seeing it in the mirror, I could tell it fit perfectly. Like it had been sewn just for me.

"I knew it," Brie said, taking a puff from her pen and passing it to me. Today, I accepted it and took a small drag. "It's perfect on you."

Had we moved from faking nice to actually *being* nice? "Thanks," I said. It was exactly my taste, but dressier than the clothes I usually wore. "But are you sure you don't want to keep it? It's kind of . . . upscale, and I don't exactly have anyplace to wear it to."

"You will," she said.

"I will?"

"Your life's changing. You'll see," she said.

I mulled this over. When we moved into Joan's top choice, I would be living in an embarrassingly big rental house soon. Still, it wasn't like my life was going to completely change. Was it?

"I remember when we left Termico," Brie said as if she'd read my mind. "I thought everything would stay the same. Same life, different house, you know? But it wasn't."

"Same annoying parents, though," I joked, immediately wishing I hadn't, given what she'd told me about Ed. I passed the pen back to her.

"Unfortunately." Brie's eyes met mine and then she looked back at the shirt.

The weed was hitting me, making me notice little things—the feel of the warm wind on my bare shoulders, the dips and furrows in Brie's voice, the way she sounded just like she used to when we were little. "This stuff is strong."

"I know." Brie closed her eyes, blew the smoke upward, and grinned. "It took me a while to get used to it. Had to find a new source after Spider went away."

I blinked. "Spider was your dealer?"

"Wasn't he everyone's?" That clueless innocence was always something that bugged me about Brie, as if we were all the same, with the same advantages. But today it didn't bother me. Today it just seemed naïve.

I wouldn't know, I wanted to say. *I've never been able to waste money on drugs.* Until now, I realized. "Not mine," I said simply.

"Anyway, Whit's been good. He's kind of a psycho but he's been dependable."

Whit had been Spider's friend for years. He had greasy blond hair, messed-up teeth, and clothes that were a little too filthy and ripped. I knew he worked as a line cook at Denny's but maybe he made extra money selling drugs to Brie and her friends. He lived nearby, even deeper up in the Termico hills than we did, and he'd invited me and Syd over to hang out the few times we'd seen him since Spider left. We'd always said no, never even pausing to see what the other one thought about it since he'd always struck both of us as seriously off. *Dependable* wasn't a word I would have expected to describe him.

I was going to ask Brie more about Whit, but then the bell rang. A second later, my phone chimed with a text from Syd.

What are you up to?

I smiled, still stoned, imagining what she would say if I told her I was smoking pot on the school roof with Brie Walsh. "Syd'll be shocked we're together," I said, showing Brie the text.

But a wary look came over Brie's face. "Don't tell her."

"Okaay," I said, blinking. "Why not?"

"It'll only upset her. You know what she's like."

Here we go, I thought, my eyes rolling behind my sunglasses. The old, jealous, chip-on-her-shoulder Brie was rearing her ugly head again. She never understood Syd the way I had, even when we were little. She always took Syd's reserve and natural shyness personally. "Come on. She'll be fine."

"How's she been handling the whole lottery thing?" Brie put her legs out in front of her and bent into a deep stretch. She could reach all the way around the heels of her feet with her legs straight. If college didn't work out, I thought, she could start a YouTube yoga channel.

"Fine. Great," I said, wondering if it was true as soon as I said it. I still hadn't told Syd we'd settled on a place, a big white stucco box in Palm Springs. I felt a surge of joy and then a shudder of mortification whenever I pictured it, but every time I tried to tell Syd, I held back. Whether to protect her from having to think about us not being on the same block anymore or to protect myself from the weirdness of having to talk about it, I didn't know. I just knew that it would be awkward, the first concrete proof that things were changing.

"Well, good," Brie said, but she sounded doubtful. "I just remember when I moved away and we had a little more money than before, things changed a lot. It didn't go down so easy with everyone."

Meaning us. Me and Syd. "Yeah," I said. "But I never thought it was the money or your move that came between us."

"Don't be naïve." Brie snorted. "Money changes everything. People get jealous. You should be careful, Rain. Syd acts chill, but mark my words, she'll drop you like you guys dropped me."

"I don't think so," I said, narrowing my eyes at Brie. "And that's not exactly how I remember it happening."

Maybe that was how she explained all of it to herself when she ditched us all those years ago, that we were jealous and that somehow it was *us* who had pulled away from *her* when in fact the opposite was true.

But Brie might have it partway right about Syd, even if I didn't want to admit it. Things were changing. It might get messy. Why else hadn't I told Syd when I'd gone with Joan to look at houses on Sunday? And why else couldn't I bring myself to tell her about what had happened with Brie last week? I hadn't even told Syd about what Ed had said to my mom at the car lot.

Brie adjusted her sunglasses. "Whatever. Don't say I didn't warn you."

I shrugged like it didn't matter. Maybe it didn't, after all this time. Had it truly all been a misunderstanding? Had Brie truly thought we'd been the ones to ditch her? I felt all the anger I'd held on to over being left behind start to recede and, in its place, a weird new curiosity.

"I missed you when I left, you know," Brie said quietly. "I know you never believed it, but I did."

"I missed you too," I said simply. "You were my friend."

"I still am," Brie said. "Or, I could be."

I bit my lip, nodding to myself.

About to do a bunch of errands with Joan, I wrote back to Syd. I swallowed down my guilt about lying and put my phone away.

Lying back on the blanket now, Brie looked like the quiet, serious girl with the penumbra of white-blond frizz that I remembered from Termico. The girl who had once led us into the canyon out past the creepy shack all three of us were scared of to a pool of stagnant water she'd found in some tire tracks. Syd and I had shrieked when she brought us close enough to see that it was full of tadpoles.

"Let's raise them," Brie had said, already pulling out three Ziploc bags from her pocket. "We'll build habitats for them up near our houses, ones that won't dry out." Clutching the sealed bag of tadpoles she handed me, I didn't feel worthy of the responsibility. This was around the time my schoolwork had taken a nosedive and the school had begun to bring Joan in for meetings where all my teachers looked concerned. "I don't trust myself to keep anything alive," I'd whispered. "I'll just mess it up."

"*I* trust you." Brie had looked into my eyes and frowned, exuding that steely willpower she was just starting to develop. "You're Rain Santangelo and you can do anything you put your mind to."

What would it be like to let all the ugliness between us go? To have this whirlwind of power and poise in my corner again? How peaceful would it feel to just stop hating her? Could my new life, with everything supposedly about to change, include a new relationship with Brie?

"I'm open to friendship," I said cautiously. "I mean, that sounds good."

"Cool," she said, like it was done, like years of history had been erased.

And just like that, I was back inside Brie Walsh's world. A place I hadn't visited for years, but I remembered I once loved.

PART V
SYDNEY

MARCH
TWO MONTHS BEFORE THE FIRE

13

Can't come tonight after all. Sorry 2 cancel again, promise
I'll make it up to u soon! Unpacking and other BS w/ Joan.

I stared out the window of the Shell station at a woman in a PG&E
uniform pumping gas into a white pickup truck, her face lit pink in
the glow of sunset. Tonight was the second time Rain had canceled
on me this week. I took a breath and held it as I wrote back, a spasm
of hurt twanging in my chest like an off note from a plucked guitar.

Don't worry about it. See you at school.

Rain hadn't been in school much this week either, but whatever.
I slipped my phone in my pocket and turned my attention back
to work. "Pump three." The PG&E woman stood before me now
with two packs of strawberry Mentos in her hand. "And these."
I rang her up and slid her change across the counter.
Growing pains, I told myself. That's all this new distance between
us was. Rain being preoccupied lately was totally understandable.
She'd just moved into her new house last weekend. Unpacking and
settling in must have been exhausting. If she couldn't pick me up
from work tonight like we'd planned, then I'd see her soon. But
even as I told myself all this, the hurt still reverberated.

While the Santangelos unpacked and settled into their new life down the mountain, I was doing my usual—juggling homework with working the register at the Shell station on the highway about a mile down the mountain between home and school.

Even before Rain and Joan officially moved, it felt like she'd started keeping a little more space between us. Ever since Joan had cashed the lottery check, Rain had been busier. With what, I couldn't quite tell. Maybe she was worried I'd be upset or something, but I wasn't. I just missed my friend.

She had promised—unrealistically, I thought, but she'd insisted—she was going to drive me to and from school every day as soon as she got a car, but she hadn't bought one yet. Or if she had, I didn't know about it.

"Chamomile or mint, Sydney?" My boss, Rafid, had come in from the back office for one of his hourly tea fill-ups and it made him happy when I assented to join him for a cup.

"I'm feeling adventurous today." I smiled. "How about green?"

"Wild girl." He pulled out a bag for each of us from the tea caddy at the coffee station and began busying himself with filling our plastic Shell-logoed to-go cups, each of which he'd carefully Sharpie'd months ago with our names.

Rafid was pretty okay. I'd been working for him since I was fifteen, and he was sort of a friend by now, as much as a fifty-eight-year-old man could be. When our shifts overlapped, he mostly left me to my thoughts or complained about his son, Amir, busy partying and possibly on his way to failing out of USC, judging by what Rafid saw when he paid the balance each month on Amir's Mastercard. I knew Rafid respected me at least a little bit, because that fall he'd started to ask for my advice on the matter.

"Two in the morning, three in the morning, he is eating out," Rafid had been saying every few weeks lately. "Filling up the gas tank at five in the morning, and I know Amir does not wake up at four AM. He is up all night doing god knows what, and yelling at him changes nothing."

I always suggested the same two things: taking away Amir's credit card cold turkey or making him pay it off each month himself. I made sure to shrug so it didn't seem like I was judging, to which Rafid would nod and mournfully sip his tea with lemon.

Tonight, though, our conversation turned to Rain and Joan. Like the rest of the world, Rafid had heard the news. Even if he'd missed the broadcast of them accepting their check, everyone in Termico was still talking about the single mom who'd hit the numbers at the Mobil down the highway.

Rafid knew Rain, of course. She'd been hanging out with me at the Shell station since I got the job, waiting for me to get off a shift or just keeping me company when she was too antsy to hang out at home. We had spent several hours last summer trying to get Rafid to hire her after she lost her job at the blowout bar, but he said it was out of the question. I never knew if he was scared of her, or if he didn't trust her, or both. Most people who didn't know Rain had the wrong idea about her. She didn't know how to talk to adults, how to just be quiet and pleasant. It was like her personality sat too close to the surface, and she had no tricks for containing her every emotion and opinion, no method of smoothing herself over.

"If only the ticket had come from the Shell." Having delivered my tea to me at the register, Rafid sighed and rubbed the white stubble on his cheeks. "Business would be booming. We're probably losing business now, people visiting the Mobil to lookyloo. Unless these Mega Millions devotees feel that lightning cannot strike twice?" He looked at me eagerly.

"Maybe." I shrugged. "Hard to say."

I was still struggling to process everything that was happening. Even though Rain said I would have my own room at their new place in Palm Springs, it was hard not to feel a little abandoned.

"They will probably lose it all in short order," Rafid said.

I blinked, affronted by this insinuation on Rain and Joan's behalf.

"I'm worried every a-hole Joan has ever met is gonna crawl up our butts now," Rain had said the last time she'd come over before the move, stabbing a finger at her phone screen. "It says here lottery winners have to deal with a lot of people trying to take the money or, like, swindle it out of them, and that all kinds of people start hassling them, thinking they don't deserve it."

"You two won't let that happen," I'd said at the time.

"Lose six-point-four million dollars? I don't think so," I said to Rafid now.

He sipped his tea. "Half of it goes to taxes. That's three million left for them. You and I, Sydney? We are responsible. We would put it in the bank, let it grow. Meantime, live frugally in a small home."

"Okay," I said, unsure where he was headed or how he could be so certain I would live modestly. Maybe I would. I must have seemed frugal to Rafid when he compared me to Amir, but wasn't that just being broke? Maybe if I had money, I wouldn't be frugal at all.

"But most people, they aren't responsible. They begin to live like the rich, when they're not really rich." Rafid straightened up the Big Grabs as he talked, sorting the barbeque Lay's back into their own separate row away from the sour cream and onion. "The pile of money seems endless at first, but very soon they're down to one-point-five million, and then there are bills and bills, and then— pah!" He clapped his hands on either side of the register so that the coins inside shook against the drawers, startling me. "In a few years, it's over. They are right back where they started. Even if they win ten, twelve, twenty million, this is often what happens. Some wind up poorer than when they began."

"Maybe." I'd be lying if I said something in me didn't find this story comforting. Yes, I wanted Rain and Joan to be rich beyond their wildest dreams. But an ugly part of me that I mostly suppressed wasn't altogether happy for them. It wasn't that I even wanted it to be me, though at moments I'd thought about that, too, and how many problems the money could solve for my family. More often, I just wished it hadn't happened to anyone I knew, so that things could be the same as they always were—me and Rain against the world.

"Warn your friend." Rafid shot me an ominous look. "Her troubles may be just beginning."

"Okay, Rafid," I said. "I'll try."

But there was no way I would say any of this to Rain. They would be fine. Better than fine. Joan might have been eccentric, but she was smart. And so was Rain.

When Rafid took a call on his cell and began to speak in Bengali, I told myself to put the lottery out of my mind.

I spent the next hour cleaning and rotating the candy shelves at the front of the register so the older merchandise was in the front. It was a Thursday night and totally dead, just a trickle of fill-ups at the pumps outside, barely anyone bothering to come in for gum or water or to use the bathroom. I let my thoughts drift to what Mom might do with a sudden windfall. Even with a fraction of it, she could quit her job at Five Fronds and finish the aesthetician program she'd dropped out of when she got pregnant with Spider. Maybe open her own salon. Definitely pay down her credit cards.

It was only starting to sink in for me what the money could mean for Rain. We had always talked about moving to LA, getting jobs as gaffers, whatever those were, or just taking whatever jobs we could get on movie sets while we right-place, right-timed Hollywood and found our niche. Rain was going to try it right after high school, and I'd said I would join her for summers when I was off from college, where I planned to study something sensible, something that would get me a reliable job.

Even though I'd always loved Rain's Hollywood talk, I knew

I couldn't afford to wing it through life. I was the one who had to pull our family out of our paycheck-to-paycheck existence. Now more than ever, with Spider in jail, it was on me to not mess up. This was why I'd focused so hard on school, researched colleges that might give me money, asked Aunt Debbie if I could live in her spare room in Oxford, Ohio, if I got into Miami.

But Rain had never had a backup plan. All through high school, I'd been quietly assuming she'd end up going to College of the Desert and living with Joan while she figured out her life, but now she could actually try to live in LA because her money wouldn't run out in a week or a month. Not even in six months.

That was what money gave you. The ability to take a chance, to ride out a dream and see what happened.

I was lost in my thoughts and vacuuming the shelves with Rafid's Dustbuster when the door dinged open behind me. I looked up into the convex safety mirror behind the register and saw Chase come inside, car keys swinging around his index finger.

I turned off the vacuum, stood up, and felt my face turn hot. *Don't be desperate, dork,* I ordered myself.

"Hey." Good. I sounded close to normal, if a little too excited. I'd managed not to speak too loudly or softly or fall over. Rafid didn't make me wear a uniform, but he did insist on a black cap with the Shell logo. So now Chase was seeing me in my Shell cap. Mortifying.

"Oh, hey." The gap between his front teeth flashed. I wondered how it would feel to touch it. He cleared his throat for what seemed like a long time. Was he nervous? "You're here."

"I am."

And then he was next to me, both of us on the customer side of the counter. I had the urge to offer him something. A bag of chips, some candy. Stuff near expiration that I'd always been able to slip to Rain without Rafid noticing. But it seemed like that would be weird, in this context. Nobody from school ever came all the way up here, unless they lived in Termico. That's what made this job bearable—no one to make fun of me in my Shell cap. And yet here Chase was.

"It's . . . good to see you," Chase said. Was he blushing? I could have sworn he was. We'd hung out with the group for a while now, but this was a step further. This was the first time I'd been alone with him.

"So, just passing through on your way to Death Valley?" I joked, hoping to break the tension.

"Ha-ha." He swallowed and his Adam's apple bobbed up and down. "I came to check in. I'm glad I found you."

"Check in?" I repeated dumbly.

"You said you worked here on Tuesdays and Thursdays, but I didn't know what time so I took a guess." He grinned.

"You have a good memory."

"So," Chase said. "How are you?" His gray sweatshirt was frayed at the cuffs but it looked clean and warm. He pulled his hands out of his pockets and rocked back on his heels. I took in the scraped fingers on one hand, his ripped-up suede sneakers, the small scar above his eyebrow. All markers of a life of skating. Falling and getting back up again while learning to fly. His body was battered and bruised, sturdy and warm. Like somewhere I wanted to live.

"How am I?" I cleared my throat, hating how stupid I sounded. I realized I was holding a bunch of bags of Skittles and I stuffed them back where they belonged, second shelf down on the right, and turned to face him again. "I'm . . . good?"

"You definitely sound like you're sure about that." That crooked smile. Dear god.

"I, um." I coughed. "No, really, I'm great." My best friend was pulling away from me literally and figuratively and I was wearing a dorky hat in front of a boy who made me nervous as hell, but other than that, I was peachy.

"I was worried." Chase paused, grabbed a bag of peanut M&M's, and began to throw it from hand to hand.

"Worried?" He worried about me?

"You guys haven't been coming to the Super 8." He tossed the bag and twirled around 360 degrees to catch it.

I felt myself begin to blush again. Then the thought of him noticing it made me blush harder.

"It's been a weird few weeks. And I've had to cover some shifts. But I'll be back there soon."

"Good."

Good?

"You miss us?" I asked, trying to make it sound like a joke.

"I miss *you.*"

Me, not Rain. Not a matched set like always, not unpredictable Rain and her boring sidekick.

He tried for another fancy maneuver with the M&M's, tossing them under his leg, and the bag fell on the floor. He scooped it up and grinned. I tried to ignore the way my stomach flipped over, the way my hands wanted to flutter up to my hair and fix it, though it was tucked up under the awful Shell hat. I laughed at my own awkwardness, and Chase laughed a little, too.

"It'd be fun to skate again with you sometime, Sydney Green." That sparkle in his eyes. What was it about someone saying your whole name, first and last, that made a person turn to mush?

"Yeah, that would be fun. I'm not that good, though."

"Sure you are. You're great."

We talked for a little longer, about nothing really. School. The people we knew. A new movie Chase wanted to see over the weekend. College. Then he paid for the bag of M&M's and left, mumbling, "See you at school," to which I answered, "Not if I see you first," and then blushed horribly all over again. I settled in to the last two hours of my shift with a tickly feeling in my guts, just thinking about this person who'd appeared as if by magic. Who'd noticed me. Me, not Rain. Ordinary jeans-and-T-shirt Sydney Green, with the hair that was neither blond nor brown, with a body that was neither short nor tall, with a face that was entirely unremarkable, with regular features, hazel eyes, standard-issue nose and mouth.

But Chase liked what he saw. Liked the way I skated. Listened when I spoke, and wanted to know more about me. He even missed me when I wasn't around.

The rest of the night, it was like a tiny door had opened in my chest and warm honey oozed out, slow and sweet. I imagined putting my hands on Chase's stomach, on his arms. Wondered how his skin would feel against my palms.

I thought about texting Rain and telling her that Chase had come to the Shell. Ordinarily, that's exactly what I would do. But things felt different now. She was too busy for me, apparently. Unpacking, whatever else. Doing new things I couldn't begin to guess at yet because she didn't have time to tell me about them. A little visit from Chase couldn't hold a candle to all that.

But also, I was enjoying that this was mine alone. I'd never had a private life before, something I didn't share with Rain. Once she knew, she would start to pick at it with questions and opinions.

For now, I didn't want anything to spoil how good this felt. I was happy to keep it all mine, to finesse whatever it was into something with potential, the way we formed clay on the wheel in ceramics class, coaxing it with the faintest pressure from our fingers until it found its ideal shape.

14

On Sunday, Rain came roaring up Clay Street at nine in the morning in a black Mini Cooper with a white racing stripe on the hood and honked the horn.

I came outside in sweat shorts and a tank top, my feet wedged into Mom's house slippers, still rubbing sleep from my eyes. "No way."

"It's a maxi Mini." She grinned from the driver's seat. "Or a Mini maxi. I can never remember. You like?"

"Who even *are* you?" I rested a hand on the hood. When I took it away, my fingerprints remained, the only blemish on the car's oil-black surface. I strode to the open driver's-side window and peered down at her. "So . . . no Walsh Nissan for you or Joan, then?"

Rain snorted. "We took our business elsewhere." She put her sunglasses up and checked the state of her eyeliner in the rearview. "But Ed deserves worse than that," she added, narrowing her eyes in the mirror.

"What do you mean?" I knew Ed had refused to bargain with them, but that was all in the past at this point, wasn't it?

"Nothing. Never mind. Come here." Rain beckoned me closer. "Smell my car."

I leaned partway into the car and breathed its new-car smell. The seats were covered in rich tan leather.

"Get in." Rain patted the passenger seat. "Wait, no. On second thought—"

She hopped out and left the door open for me, then ran barefoot around the cracked driveway to the passenger side. She motioned for me to take the driver's seat. "You drive."

"I can't, Rain, it's too new. What if I crash it?"

"Then I'll get another one."

"Oh, okay." I laughed and stood there hesitating, one hand on the hood of the car.

"Would you please just get in? If I have a car and you can't drive it, I don't even want the thing." She frowned at me, impatient or annoyed, I guessed, that I was making this a big deal.

"Fine." Now that we were finally together again, maybe things would start to get back to the way they'd always been. Who was I to say no to her now, especially when she'd come all the way up here? "Let me go get my bag—"

"You don't need it. I'll bring you back later. Come on, get in already. I order you to drive!"

"Okay, Jesus." Rain's excitement was infectious. Anything I'd been upset about earlier evaporated in the sunshine she was giving off.

"There's the girl I love!" Rain threw her head back and cackled.

Driving that car down the mountain away from Termico with Rain by my side, Beyoncé blasting from the car speakers, I could almost feel the benevolent hand of destiny that had reached out and lifted her up—maybe it was lifting me up, too, because she was mine.

We chugged south in the valley, Rain directing me using Waze since she still didn't know her way around down here. I turned to look at Rain at a stoplight. She wore a new top, a silky black halter that fit her perfectly. She had so many new clothes lately, but this was a little more formal than her usual T-shirts.

"You look great," I said. "You dressed up to buy the car, didn't you?"

Rain nodded. "You noticed."

"Love the shirt," I said. I pressed the gas pedal and scooted around a minivan that was making a left.

"Actually." Rain paused for a weirdly long time, then cleared her throat. "Brie picked this out."

"What?" For a second, I was sure I'd misheard.

"I ran into her at the mall a couple weeks ago and then we kind of . . . ended up hanging out at school." Rain shrugged and looked a little sheepish, as if the years she'd spent railing against Brie had just been a funny little mistake. "She's actually been nice."

There was that old horse-kick in my stomach, a sensation of having arrived late to a party full of strangers, everyone laughing at a joke I hadn't heard. I focused on the road, not wanting to look at her. Had Brie already seen Rain's new car? Her new house?

"So you two are friends now? Wow, I guess I missed the memo." Instantly I wished I hadn't said it. I felt Rain's eyes on me, could feel her assessing how I was handling this. She probably wondered if I was jealous or hurt. Well, I was both. Why had Rain kept this from me? Did she think I was so pathetically attached to her that I couldn't handle her mending fences with Brie?

"Maybe. Is that allowed?" She asked it lightly, in the tone of a harmless joke, but the question still stung.

"I mean . . ." Would it have been *allowed* if I had gone behind her back and starting hanging out with Brie? How would Rain have handled that? "Of course."

I took a deep breath and told myself to drop it, not wanting to ruin our first drive together in her new car, our first time together in what felt like ages even though it had really only been a week.

But I couldn't resist picking at the wound a little more. "I'm just surprised."

Rain nodded next to me, considering. "I am, too. Maybe all this time we had her wrong." She put her bare feet up on her new dashboard, one of them right over the vent. "Or maybe she's changed.

She's acting really . . . *human* lately. It's like the old Brie is back, the one we used to like."

"Well, that's good," I said warily. Rain had always been more attached to hating Brie than I was. She'd always been looking for ways Brie had wronged us. And now, it seemed, Rain was going to be the first to re-embrace her. Maybe this was all part of Rain's tendency to see everything in extremes. In her book, people were either perfect or awful, never anywhere in between. I suspected Brie, like everyone else, was somewhere in the middle, and I wasn't interested in exploring her more deeply than that. We were graduating soon. I didn't need new friends. I just wanted to hang on to the ones I already had.

I peeked at Rain. She wore that dazed, dreamy smile again. Nothing was going to permeate her good mood, I realized. And why should it? She'd literally won the lottery.

Let Rain have her good mood, I told myself. It didn't matter if she and Brie stopped hating each other.

I could even pretend to be happy about it. "I'm glad you guys buried the hatchet," I said.

I turned up the music and let the thudding bass of Juice WRLD wash over us. "I love this car for you." I grinned and squeezed Rain's hand and she squeezed back. I hoped that meant we'd reached the end of talking about Brie Walsh.

The house, when we got there, was a trick of the eye, a giant flat-roofed rectangle hoisted on top of a smaller rectangle, the glass-walled living room balanced in thin air above the eco-friendly front yard filled with rocks and spiky desert plants.

"Some old Hollywood director built it," Rain told me as I parked the car in the cactus-lined driveway. "Joan's obsessed with him now. She's threatening to make me watch all of his movies."

I stared up at it in disbelief. It made Brie's house look like a trailer. It made Rain's old house—and mine—look like a milk carton. I thought of what Rafid had said and then shook my head a little to put it out of my mind. *You're happy for them,* I reminded myself.

"This is beautiful," I breathed.

"You don't think it's a little creepy?" Rain asked. She peered up at it with me as if seeing it for the first time.

"Creepy?"

"I don't know," Rain said. "It looks like the house in a bad eighties movie where the girl gets found floating dead in the pool."

"You're always so positive." I laughed. "It's what I love about you."

Inside, Joan wore her same black kimono with the teal cranes. She paired it with gold kitten-heeled slippers I'd never seen before, and she had on big black sunglasses with pink lenses. Her hair was tucked up into a pink turban. She was taking the old Hollywood thing as far as she could stretch it.

"Welcome, baby doll. Welcome to our new home." She pulled me to her briefly, but looked distracted by the two men in movers' braces who stood awkwardly behind her, seemingly awaiting her instructions. "We're just rearranging all this furniture the house came with. Our casa es su casa, okay? Just help yourself to whatever you want. Rainey wants you to pick out a bedroom for when you sleep over. Rainey, don't forget to give Sydney a room," she shouted to Rain, who had already wandered out of the palatial living room.

"On it," Rain shouted from deeper in the house.

"It's beautiful, Joan, congratulations," I said.

"Oh, stop. I know it's a little over the top, but maybe we'll all get used to it soon. This is your place, too, don't forget. You're our family." She gave my hand a squeeze and turned back to the movers, pointing the cherry-red nail of her index finger toward a long leather couch.

I wandered in the direction of Rain, the sun flooding in and making the white walls and white marble floor look like a futuristic version of the afterlife, blank and clean and filled with heavenly light.

"I'm in here," Rain called, and I walked down a hall into the kitchen, where Rain had the French doors of a large fridge open, her hands on her hips. The fridge was immaculate and empty except for six or seven takeout boxes. "We haven't bought normal food yet," Rain said, annoyed. "Joan is useless these days. All we have is left-over sushi from last night and some leftovers even older than that. Oh, and some chocolate mousse thing the real estate agent sent."

I thought with a pang of my kitchen when we were little, how happy it used to make us to eat hot sauce on white bread. We were so far away from that now. I looked at my friend in her new Brie-approved top, her artfully ripped denim shorts that probably cost more than all of my clothes put together. At least her eyeliner was smudged like always and her hair was caught up in its usual uneven pile. I looked down at my own outfit, faded olive-green sweat shorts with a hole at the crotch and a baggy tank top I'd had since I was fourteen.

"I'm not hungry now anyway." I slid onto a tall leather chair that abutted the kitchen's marble island, put my hands on the cool stone, and tried to absorb that this was really where Rain lived now. I tried to feel like I had a right to be here, like I belonged. "This place is amazing."

Just then, Rain's phone buzzed with a text in her pocket.

"It is, I guess," Rain said, distracted now. "Hang on, sorry." She pulled the phone out.

"Oh," she said.

"Who is it?"

"Brie." She flashed me a pained smile. "Sorry, let me just . . ." But she trailed off, already texting, thumbs flying.

"Don't worry about it," I said, swallowing down that sensation of the earth moving under my feet, the rumbling of tectonic plates shifting. They'd hung out once by accident and now they were text-ing? I opened my mouth to ask her if Brie had been here yet, but then I shut it again, thinking of the car, the way tension had flared up between us. Thinking I might not handle it well if she said yes.

Besides, I could text someone special, too.

And as if by magic, my own phone chimed. I hid a smile with my hand when I saw it was Chase.

Super 8 tomorrow?

OK, I wrote back.

Shld I pick you up?

I looked up from my phone, watching Rain deep in communi-cation with Brie in her lavish kitchen, and thought of Chase com-ing to pick me up at my house, the Fiesta in the driveway with the bumper held on with duct tape, our roof with the siding peeling off on one side.

I'll meet you there.

After we polished off the real estate agent's chocolate mousse, Rain took me upstairs.

"I've been sleeping in here since we moved, but something's just been off about it for me." Rain lolled on an unmade king-sized bed in the all-white corner bedroom upstairs. A flat-screen TV was affixed to the wall, the only object that wasn't white or the color of driftwood. "It's the best bedroom in the house after Joan's, techni-cally. We should call it your room."

"Sure," I said hesitantly. It was sweet they wanted to give me a room, but it felt more embarrassing than anything else. It's not like it would ever feel like mine. "I mean, when I sleep here, won't I sleep in your room?"

"Good point," Rain said. "Let me show you the room I want to try out next."

I followed her down the hall to a large, mostly empty room filled with yoga mats and pillows. It looked like whoever had furnished it had intended it to be a meditation space. It was painted a purplish gray and didn't have any furniture in it other than a Buddha statue and a shelf filled with yoga equipment. On the wall was a framed command written in purple calligraphy: BE HERE NOW, it said.

"This one?" I said.

"Yeah. It feels right." Rain shrugged. "I like that it's darker in here. And it's far from Joan."

We dragged in a king-sized mattress from another bedroom and put it on the floor just below a big circular window. We moved most of the yoga stuff out into the hall but left the Buddha statue. Suddenly the emptiness felt like luxury. Like potential.

After we'd moved a sectional couch from yet another bedroom into one corner, we both collapsed for a while in the dimness, watching the occasional shaft of afternoon light peek in whenever the blinds rustled in the breeze of the silent AC.

Rain lay horizontally on her new bed on the floor, and I sprawled out on the couch.

"I guess I'll get used to this," I joked weakly. "Will you?"

"Who knows," Rain sighed, an arm draped over her eyes. "I'll probably freak out one of these days." After a long silence, she asked, "Who were you texting earlier?"

"Chase." We're going to skate tomorrow night, I almost said, but what if she wanted to come? It was only me he'd asked.

"That's not going away, is it?" Rain sounded irritated.

"Who knows," I said, careful not to match her tone even though it bugged me. "Why, do you wish it would?"

"No. I just . . ." Rain sat up, blinked at me through the room's luxurious shadow. "I don't want you to get hurt. Are you sure he's good enough for you?"

My eyes rolled inadvertently. If I'd asked that about any of the boys who'd passed through Rain's life over the past few years, she would have laughed in my face. "I don't know, Rain. Who is, in your expert opinion?"

"None of them. Not a one. Since, yes, we all know I'm the slut with the expert opinion."

"I didn't mean it like that," I said. "Don't twist my words."

"Mmm. Maybe you did, without even realizing. It's okay. I know who I am and what I've done. I'm okay with it. You're different than me, though."

"You want me to be a virgin forever," I snapped, opening up social media and scrolling through picture after picture of happy, attractive peers filtered to perfection. I paused on a picture of Deirdre, Min, and Brie in bikinis and pressed my lips into a tight line, then closed the whole app so as not to have to look at Brie a moment longer. "It gives you some sick pleasure. Like I'm frozen in time."

"Don't be so dramatic." Rain crawled to the end of the mattress and pulled herself onto her feet. "Do what you want. It's just . . ." She looked around, searching for the words. "You've waited all this time. You deserve perfection. A love that blots out the sun." Her eyes grew soft and faraway, a funny smile playing on her face. "You know?"

"Whatever." I softened then, unable to stay mad. "It's not too late for you to have that, either."

Rain rolled her eyes and left the room.

A love that blots out the sun. I leaned back into the folds of the couch and shut my eyes. Maybe I was about to have that with Chase. How could I know until I knew? When I opened my eyes I was met with the strange instructions on the wall again. BE HERE NOW. Good advice, I decided. The future would get here when it got here.

Rain returned with two bulging shopping bags printed with names of stores I'd never heard of. "So, I got some stuff I thought you might like."

Speechless, I started to lay it all out. Sneakers, jeans, sweatshirts, T-shirts. All of it stuff I already wore, just nicer. Just like in those cheesy eighties movies we used to watch, the ones where the girl got some kind of makeover and triggered what Rain had always called the wish-fulfillment montage.

"Rain."

"Don't say you won't take it." Rain looked at me like she was scared. Like she feared the worst. "Don't be mad."

"Of course I'm not mad," I said. "It's just . . . extravagant. I'm not here because of your money." Actually, I was here in spite of how uncomfortable her money was making me.

"I know," Rain said, her yellow-brown eyes finding mine. "Of course not. But you know I'm going to take care of you, right? This is your win, too. We're still going to LA together before you leave for Peoria. Nothing's changed, except now it will be easier to do everything we've always wanted. Who knows, maybe you'll put off college a while and just . . . hang." Rain smiled sweetly, clearly liking the sound of this off-the-cuff new plan she'd come up with.

"But they love me in Peoria," I joked, feeling like maybe we could still have the summer we'd planned on. Maybe nothing would change after all.

It was impossible not to believe Rain. She acted so sure.

Looking down at everything she'd picked out for me, a smile spread across my face and I blinked away a surprise mist of happy tears. "Thank you," I whispered. "This is so nice."

Surely Rain didn't do all this for Brie. We were still fine. More than fine. Money or no money, Rain wasn't going to leave me behind.

15

The sun had dunked low in the sky over the empty pool by the time I arrived. I shivered in the quickly cooling night air and clutched Spider's board under one arm, trying to focus on the *shlush-shlush* of polyurethane wheels on pavement instead of the nervous rush of blood in my ears.

I found Chase metronoming back and forth in the bottom of the pool. He waved when he saw me. A few others looped random arcs around him, all of them miraculously never coming close to crashing into one another. I tried to do that thing boys do with their chin where they jut it out fast and pull it back in as a silent hello, but it felt so awkward that I gave up and waved back. I had never come here without Rain before. She'd always been my security blanket, the sparkly one people noticed so that I could blend into the background. For a second I wondered how it felt for her hanging around someone like Brie, the two of them sharing the spotlight for the world's attention. *Don't think about them now,* I ordered myself. It would only put me in a dark mood. *You have a life of your own.*

Now I worried I looked like I'd tried too hard in my carefully planned-out baggy jeans from Rain's shopping trip (the fit had been eerily perfect) and my battered high-top Converse with a sweatshirt that Spider had left behind when he began his sentence at Pine Grove, a skull with a cartoon pink worm smiling out of one eye socket, the name of a skate brand I knew nothing about tattooed on the worm's neck.

Chase beckoned from his board, a shaggy grin on his face. *Dive in,* that grin said. *Share this with me.*

I hopped onto Spider's board and skated around the outside of the bowl to get my bearings, feeling the cold wind on my face and the cracked pavement unfurling its messages under the soles of my feet. After a few minutes, I set up the board at the edge of the empty pool, my foot on the back of it to keep it from flying over. Usually I brought the board to the bottom of the pool and went from there since I didn't have the guts to drop in from the top. Now I balanced on the lip, having not dropped in vertically in ages. My stomach churned with nerves.

Just let gravity ease you down into it and find the balance, Spider had said when he taught me to skate. *No fear. It's the only way this works.*

Of course he'd had no fear. He was that way about dealing drugs, too. Spider was missing that caveman part of his brain built to scan for predators, the part we now used to obsess about modern-day fears: home intruders, school shooters, failure, humiliation, death by skateboard.

"Yo, make some space," one of the boys in the bowl said in that loose-lipped mumble skaters all seemed to have. "She's gonna do it."

I was. At least I was going to try.

Chase was at the far end of the pool, his eyes on me, confident that I could. But I wasn't doing it to perform for him, I realized. I was doing it for me. To remind myself of what I could do, and that there were things I could do without Rain. This was something she would never be able to buy.

I sucked air hard through my nose and slowly exhaled. Straight ahead past the Super 8 with its reptilian rustlings and burnt-out windows was the dark mountain with its three craggy peaks rearing up against the sky, the bright stain of spent sunlight washed above it like a promise.

No fear.

I pressed my right foot down on the board with just enough tilt off the lip to go vertical. My knees bent, my arms finding the balance, my fingers reaching out to trail the cement wall of the pool, and I was in freefall.

The wind slammed into my eyes as I went back and forth, again and again, up and down the pool's curved edges. When I slowed enough, I heard applause. A couple of boys even whooped.

I didn't fall off that time or the next, but my third time dropping into the bowl I lost my footing and bungled the descent, a massive wipeout that somehow only hurt my tailbone a little. Chase skated by me, around me, side by side. He was a calm presence who wasn't judging or instructing, just there to have fun on the board.

Later, when it grew too dark to see anymore and the others had trickled away to their cars, we sat on the edge of the bowl with our feet dangling into the basin, the mountain now almost invisible against the purple-black sky.

"It's great you came," he said. His skin shone with sweat in the dim light. There was a smell about him, something musky and mineral and very different from anyone else I'd been this close to. "I love watching you skate."

Not *you look good when you skate,* but *I love watching you skate.* I loved how direct this was, how he didn't treat me like an ornament.

"Thanks."

It felt right to lean against his shoulder, to feel our upper arms touching through our sweatshirts, and to wonder what else I might touch eventually, what the rest of him felt like.

"I used to love skating in middle school," I said. "I guess I gave it up when Spider did."

"It must . . . it sucks what happened to him. He's a nice guy, Spider."

I nodded, appreciating the delicate way Chase spoke about my brother, the way he used the present tense. Some people talked about

Spider like he'd died, as if he didn't have his whole life ahead of him as soon as he got out. "At first I was upset about it, but now I think getting busted may have been the best thing that could have happened. Maybe when he's out he'll get his act together, find something he likes to do. Other than drugs, I mean." I snuck a look at Chase. "Maybe it'll turn out to be a blessing in disguise, not to be cheesy about it."

"It's not cheesy at all," Chase said. "My cousin dealt and things just got worse and worse for him. He started using harder and harder stuff. He used to be so smart, and kind of . . . you know those people who seem like they're extra-alive? Like more alive than the rest of us?"

I nodded. Rain floated through my head, the way she laughed louder and raged more angrily than anyone, seemed to make decisions faster and just live harder than everyone else. "Sure," I said.

"Now he lives in a halfway house in Mississippi. His parents flew him home for Thanksgiving last year and he just sat there, barely spoke, his eyes all glassy, like whatever specialness he'd had just got emptied out. He's on methadone now." Chase's voice cracked and it sounded like it meant something to him to tell me this story. I took his hand in mine and didn't even feel nervous about it.

We sat like that awhile, reflecting on Spider, Chase's cousin, the way you can have a light and let it go out. The way people can burn so bright that they flame out early. I wondered if quieter people, those more like us, might be able to carry that flame a little further, let it burn a little brighter later instead of using it all up, and if that was true, if it was worth it.

When he kissed me I was so deep in thought I wasn't even prepared for it. But his lips on mine, his tongue in my mouth and mine in his, and our hands reaching under clothes to find warm skin, all of it felt like something I'd been missing forever without even realizing it.

And then we two were burning brighter, extra-alive, urgent and risky.

"I like your freckles," Chase whispered.

"I like your chin," I whispered back, coming up for air. "And the gap you have between your front teeth." How many nights had I gone to sleep thinking about that gap? I leaned back, touched it with my thumb.

"I like how you're serious when you talk, and how your nose wrinkles when you smile." His voice was a hot whisper in my ear, his hands exploring places that made me feel like I might not be able to form a complete sentence ever again.

"I didn't know my nose . . ." I said, a half-formed thought I couldn't think to finish. We leaned back on the cold cement but all I could feel was warmth, his smooth skin under his T-shirt, the muscles all around his stomach, so much definition from those hours and weeks and years of balance and motion, and there was nothing more to say.

Chase had a blanket in his trunk and he brought it out and we stayed on the edge of the pool for another hour or more, sometimes kissing, sometimes talking. I wasn't nervous anymore. I just wanted him as near to me as possible.

Much later, he walked me in the pitch-black night to the Ford Fiesta. He kissed me long and deep before he enclosed me in the space of the car so that I was alone again, humming in the places bodies do when they've connected with someone they don't want to say goodbye to.

By the time I pulled into my driveway, the Syd who would have been too embarrassed to send a cheeseball text—or any text—to a boy was MIA. The new extra-alive Syd texted right away and didn't care how un-chill it was:

That was fun. I miss you rn.

In a second, he wrote back. No chill either, I thought, smiling.

Again tomorrow? I miss you too. A lot.

Was this what everyone had been doing all the time while I'd been sitting up late studying, stewing in my own juices, daydreaming about a time when someone would notice me for something other than homework copying or being Rain's bestie? All this time, so many kids around me with honey flowing through their veins instead of blood, with secret flushes of desire filling in the gaps between algebra and WWII and their social media feeds, and I was only catching up now.

"Worth waiting for," I said out loud to myself in the car. If this had happened to me any sooner I might have dropped out of school just to chase this feeling. But now there were only a few more months to study through. Even now, grades hardly mattered anymore. My college applications were in. I could devote all my free time to exploring whatever this was with Chase.

Later on, if I squinted, I could still see that naïve girl. She walked into her flimsy house, clutching her phone against her chest like it was a love letter from the eighteenth century. Poor dumb Syd who thought it would go on and on this way, who thought she'd discovered the new shape her life would take.

Have caution, I wanted to yell to her. *Protect your heart. Don't trust this.*

But I couldn't.

The girl brushed her teeth in a haze, slipped naked between her sheets, her mind whirling, replaying the evening, closing her eyes so that she could almost feel Chase's hands still on her, on almost every part of her. She didn't sleep much. When you were this alive, there was no need.

In the dark, in her bed, it was all honey and light. She had no idea what was coming.

16

It wasn't until early April, more than a month after Rain had moved down the mountain, that Brie said more than the most basic hello to me. It was a Friday, and Rain had picked me up for school wearing her usual black jeans and gray shirt—updated, nicer versions, not her old stuff from the H&M sale bins—and a new pair of highlighter-yellow Gucci high-tops I'd admired that morning. I hadn't said I wanted them, more like, "Nice kicks," but nonetheless they were waiting for me in my locker when I went to put my books away after last period. Rain could be unnervingly generous sometimes.

I was lacing up the shoes when I heard Rain's gasp spill into the hallway.

"I love them on you," she said. She was barefoot. She'd literally given me the shoes off her feet. I looked up, about to tell her I was just trying them on, but then I noticed Brie standing there, arm in arm with Rain, elbows linked the way all three of us used to do as little kids when we skipped down the street together in Termico. Brie flashed me a quick tight smile, her face flushed, her eyes covered in mirrored aviators. She was dressed all in white, an eyeleted belly shirt over white shorts. The knot of her belly button stared down at me like a third eye. She was Rain's vivid opposite, salt to Rain's pepper.

"Aren't they amazing, Brianna?" Rain said. *Brianna.* I didn't know why Rain using her full name bugged me so much, but it was all I could do not to roll my eyes.

"Uh-huh."

Rain leaned over and whispered something in Brie's ear that made Brie laugh so hard she gasped for breath and nearly doubled over. When Rain looked back down at me, I noticed her telltale bloodshot eyes. They were obviously both high. There was that dread in the pit of my stomach again, the feeling that was a fixture for me whenever I couldn't find Rain at lunch or when she would text to say she couldn't drive me home or pick me up, each time supplying a vague reason loosely related to Joan that I feared actually had everything to do with Brie.

"So, we're having a little party." This was the first full sentence Brie had said to me outside of a classroom in what seemed like years. Her voice was seasoned with vocal fry these days but was otherwise the same as when we were kids—a little bit flat but with perfect enunciation, always sounding as if she was performing for an invisible audience. I wondered if she still had her My Little Pony dolls hidden away in a closet somewhere, her silky zippered case for the plastic combs that she used to be so fastidious about. "And we want you to come."

Delivered like a royal summons, as if it was an honor they were bestowing upon lowly me. I stood up, feeling stupid with the yellow sneakers on. I forced a smile and searched for a gracious, polite way to make it clear that I'd rather drink bleach.

We want you to come. I wasn't used to Rain being part of any other *we* than us.

"Oh." I had no intention of going. "When?"

"Tonight. A group of us are going to Moon Rocks." Brie smiled knowingly to Rain. "With treats."

"I was just telling Brianna how we've always wanted to go there. Remember the place Spider used to talk about, with all the craters?"

I nodded.

Rain leaned down so her face was next to mine. I could smell the pot smoke in her hair. "Brie has Molly," she whispered, smiling like this was the greatest thing ever.

"Well . . ." I groped for an excuse. "Thanks for the invite, but—"

"No buts. We're going," Rain said, shooting me a look that said *don't screw this up.* I would tell her no later, I decided. After Brie left.

"I can pick you up," Brie said to Rain. "She's on my way," she explained to me, as if I didn't know where Rain's new house was. "That way you can get fucked up and not worry about driving."

"What about you?" Rain asked Brie. Brie obviously wasn't designated-driving material.

"Deirdre will drive my car on the way back." Brie shrugged with the bored assurance of a duchess who knows her handmaidens will do what she tells them. "Her parents drug test her, poor thing."

"We'll wait for you at my house," Rain said to Brie, assuming without my even officially accepting that I'd be there, the ever-reliable friend who shows up when called for.

I watched Brie give Rain a long hug goodbye, astonished at the sight of it. The hostility between them, that hatred that had reliably bounced between them since seventh grade, had been replaced with a charge I couldn't identify.

That was when I changed my mind about going. Not because I wanted to spend time with Brie and her friends but because, however pathetic it was, I didn't like the two of them hanging out without me.

"Those shoes look better on you," Rain said after Brie left. "Keep 'em."

They didn't, and I shook my head no. "So, you two are planning parties together now?" I stared at the ground, trying not to let on how upset it had made me, knowing it was stupid to feel that way.

"Aw, don't be jealous." Her fingers snaked up my arm. Her black eyes were bloodshot, lids heavy, mouth curled in a stoned half-smile.

"I'm not." I bent over and began unlacing the shoes. "I just, I guess I don't get it. You and Brie."

"We're just doing . . . what's that thing from history?" Rain's long body twirled, arms up in the air, chipped black nail polish on her fingers that she pinched above her head like she could pull the word out of the sky.

"Covert ops?" I said.

"When countries are, like, worn down from fighting. When they hold out the olive branch or whatever. Remember, I got it wrong on the final junior year?"

"Détente." We'd discussed it again last week in Mr. Merton's WWII unit. The easing of tensions between historical enemies. England and France. The U.S. and Russia. Brie and Rain.

"Yeah, that. She's had a very fucked-up time with her dad, you know. I think if she wasn't so strong he would have broken her."

"I mean, that's obviously awful, and Ed is an asshole . . . but all these years you seemed to have your reasons for hating her," I reminded Rain, a needy tone I didn't like catching in my voice. "Back in winter you wanted to fill her pool with yellow dye and chocolate bars."

"That was an angrier me." Rain opened her locker, grabbed a distressed-but-brand-new black leather bag from inside, and started riffling through it. "Maybe the lottery thing made me more open or something. Less of a bitch. Anyway, you're the one who didn't want to us to prank her, remember?"

Yep, good old reliable Sydney. I rolled my eyes and handed Rain her shoes with such force that she stumbled back against her locker.

"Jesus, Syd. That hurt." Rain rubbed her tailbone.

"I don't need Gucci shoes," I said, hearing condescension in my voice but unable to stop myself. "And frankly, neither do you."

"Jesus, judge much?" Rain straightened up and scowled at me. "What, are you keeping a tally of my purchases?"

"Listen, do what you want, but just because you have six hundred dollars doesn't mean you should spend it on sneakers. Is your mom actually cool with that?"

"Don't worry about our spending habits, okay? We're fine. Your shitty vibes are ruining my high." Rain began to yank the shoes back onto her own feet. "Let's not say anything else we don't mean, okay? I'll see you tonight."

"Fine." I walked down the hall, already regretting saying anything about the stupid shoes. What was going on between us was so much bigger than shoes, and it was none of my business how Rain spent her money.

I was always trying to save everyone from their worst instincts. Who was going to save me from my own?

That night, Brie and Deirdre picked us up from Rain's. We drove into the hills, Deirdre already at the wheel, the Lorde song blasting from the car speakers, the melancholy lyrics matching my mood with absolute precision.

This dream isn't feeling sweet / we're reeling through the midnight streets / And I've never felt more alone / it feels so scary getting old.

Brie's bare feet were propped on the dashboard, her toes as cute and compact as her little red Nissan with the spoiler on the back. I sat glowering in the backseat next to Rain, who put the window all the way down and gulped the cold night air.

Brie unwrapped a square of tinfoil the size of a quarter and passed it back to Rain, then handed me a bottle of water, her expression eager in a way I hadn't seen since we were little.

"Everybody ready to feel amazing?" Brie shouted above the music.

Rain dug two caplets filled with beige powder from the foil and handed me one. "I don't know," I stalled. This was way out of my comfort zone, especially with this crowd. "I need to think about it."

"It's totally safe. They use it in therapy now, like, doctors recommend it." Rain popped hers in her mouth and swallowed it down.

"Don't force her." Brie turned back around and studied me, a smug smile passing over her face as if I'd done exactly what she'd predicted. "You should only do it if and when you're ready, Sydney."

"Thanks. That's really big of you," I muttered, knowing she couldn't really hear me over the music.

When I put the pill in my shirt pocket, Rain shrugged and turned back to the wind rushing through her open window. I pulled out my phone and texted Chase: On my way.

OK I'll be there soon.

I smiled and put my phone away. At least the night wasn't going to be all bad.

If Rain noticed me smiling at my phone, she didn't say a thing about it. Probably too busy thinking about her détente with Brie. I turned away and spent the rest of the ride silently looking out my window while the others chatted.

To get to Moon Rocks, we walked single file along a narrow path in the sandy canyon, rocks and scrub on either side of us. Branches with wispy leaves waved in a dry wind that smelled like sage and campfires. As we walked, lizards darted beneath the bushes. I was last, stuck behind Deirdre, doing my best to light our way with the only flashlight I could find at home, a yellow plastic one that wasn't bright enough. Brie and Rain moved up ahead, their voices low and rushed, already in a private world with the Molly, the space between the two of them and us widening until I could hardly see them in the blackening night. Deirdre ambled slowly down the path carrying two bottles of vodka, and though I wanted to keep close to Rain, maneuvering around her would look desperate.

The darkness of the desert was nearly total under the tiny sliver of moon, and by the time we reached a campfire with fifteen or so kids gathered around it, I'd lost sight of Rain and Brie altogether.

I knew all of these people, of course. This was the core of elite-level girls and the usual boys they hung around with, most of them on sports teams, all of them probably going to good colleges their parents could afford next year.

Nobody seemed surprised to see Rain or me. Maybe because by then, the drugs seemed to be hitting many of them. "This fire is so *real*," I heard Min whisper. Justin Klein ran his hands atop Candice's head over and over like she was a golden retriever, remarking on how soft her hair was.

When Deirdre passed me a pipe, I took a long hit from it and tried to relax, though I wondered where Brie and Rain had gone. I thought about texting Chase again but figured he'd find me soon enough.

Feeling conspicuous, I wandered out past the campfire to the sandstone rock formations. The rocks were pocked with deep, otherworldly craters the size of bathtubs, many filled with initials carved into the sandstone. I spotted a few skaters and some other quieter, less sporty boys. These were Chase's people. I squinted, trying to see if I could find his shape in the darkness, but he wasn't here yet.

Back at the campfire, Min, Deirdre, Anya, and Candice stood with their arms around each other's shoulders, all of them swaying slightly as if dancing, only there was no music.

"The sky is so beautiful," Candice said.

"The world just goes along spinning on its axis but none of us will ever feel it, can you believe that?" Min was saying, her breath coming in short little puffs. I looked at Deirdre, knowing she was sober. She stayed silent and stared at the campfire, periodically running a hand over her platinum bangs. The other girls were far away from that kind of self-consciousness. It must have been a relief for them, these girls who were so used to being seen and studied by the others, us mere mortals, us troll-like non-popular people.

I moved slowly between clumps of kids around the campfire, wanting to be near Rain, but I couldn't find her. The night grew darker and a cool breeze swept across the desert floor. I pressed closer to the campfire, though I wasn't cold. A bottle of Goldschläger was passed around. When it reached me I tipped it back, two big glugs of fire in my throat.

"Hey." Chase's voice found me in the darkness. I hadn't seen him arrive. I wondered how many of these sorts of parties he'd wound up at over the years, and how close he was to this group. I wanted to believe he was outside of it like I was, but maybe he wasn't.

"Hey." I drifted toward him in the shadows, away from the corona of light around the campfire. He wrapped his arms around me right away, pulling me close. My forehead pressed the crook of his chin right there in public, like we were a couple. I touched my lips to the soft skin near his Adam's apple, a kiss so light and quick that he may not have even felt it.

"Whoa, it's so strong." Rain's voice reached me from back behind a scrim of trees about twenty feet away. She sounded scared.

I tensed and stepped back, away from Chase.

"I'll be right back, just want to check on Rain," I mumbled.

"Okay," Chase said. "I'll be here."

I edged around the rocks and through the trees toward a clearing I hadn't noticed earlier. Brie and Rain were on the outer edge of it where the forest reared back up, huddled near a stand of acacia trees. Rain was rocking back and forth on her toes and looking at the sky, and Brie stood like a sentinel on the path, guarding her. "The stars," Rain said, her breath coming in quick bursts. "They're *moving*."

"She's fine." Brie smiled when I approached. She moved between Rain and me and crossed her arms, her body a wall blocking my path. "We're going to look at the stars. *Alone.*"

"I just want to check on her." I tried to push past Brie, but she grabbed me by the shoulders, her grip surprisingly strong.

"I *said* I've got it." Though she was smiling, her eyes carried a warning.

"You're not her keeper," I said, willing myself to remain calm, to not start yelling.

"Okay, weirdo." Brie rolled her eyes. "I know how to help her right now. Go have fun with Chase."

Ignoring how strange it was that she knew about me and Chase, I was about to sidestep Brie, to start running if I had to, but then Rain turned to face me. Looking into my eyes with a rapturous, manic expression across her face, Rain opened her mouth.

I'm here, I was about to say. I took a step closer.

But when Rain called out, the name she said wasn't mine. "Brianna friggin' Walsh! Come back here, star-girl." She threw her head back, her sharp chin pointing up at the treetops, her hands beckoning Brie closer. "Did you know we're all, like, *made* of stardust? Isn't that beautiful?"

I blinked, stunned.

"See?" Brie's satisfied smirk said it all. "We're fine here."

I backed away, my hands shaking with that same unnameable fear I couldn't explain. Was it a fear of Rain leaving me, or a fear of Brie herself? I couldn't quite tell.

By the time I reached Chase again, I'd composed myself, turned my fear into disgust with Brie, and with Rain. Rain was on a different planet, on the moon, with her newest, oldest friend. *Fuck you both,* I thought. *I have a new friend, too.*

It was easy, when I got back to where I'd left Chase, to smile and ask him if he wanted to go somewhere alone.

He'd brought the blanket from his car and lined a crater with it

so we could lie down inside and look up at the stars. Barely noticing the cool night air, I took off his shirt and ran my hands across
his chest, observed his body in the moonlight, licked the salty skin
of his chest. I straddled him in my jeans, feeling what I did to him,
his quiet groan of pleasure when I moved. I unzipped my sweatshirt, unbuttoned my shirt and leaned back, arched my back until
he sat up, his hands all over me, cupping my breasts like they were
holy relics, his lips everywhere. Impersonating a more confident
girl, I laughed when he took my shirt off, helped him unhook my
bra. There was a power in sex, a language between our bodies I was
only just starting to learn.

Let her have her new, stupid, control-freak friends, I thought as I
sucked Chase's tongue into my mouth, his hands everywhere, our
skin all starlight and salt and dust, all goosefleshed and tingling. *I
have my own my own private world now, too.*

We whispered to each other in that crater, hours of talking and
not-talking, our silences easy, our explorations fervent.

At some point in the moonlight Chase pulled away from me, his
face serious. "Sydney, I really . . ."

Really what? I looked into his eyes, fell into his gaze, and waited
out the silence. His hand went to my cheek, a gesture that was so
tender I had to shut my eyes to fully experience it.

"I've wanted this for a really long time. With you. I . . . I'm
really into you. I think about you all the time."

Words caught in my throat. *Same,* I wanted to say. *Literally all
the time.* Instead, I just whispered, "Me, too," and kissed him deep
and long.

Whatever this was, I was a thousand percent in.

Much later, after so much kissing and grinding that my lips felt
chafed and my body felt bruised and sore, I would wonder where the
Molly trippers had gone off to. Why I didn't see them again when we
left, though I had looked around, had checked the clearing.

At 1 AM, I texted Rain to check in and heard nothing back. Finally at 2 AM I wrote had a rly great night with Chase. almost sex. Can't wait to tell you about it.

Normally Rain checked her phone constantly, but I heard nothing back, not that night before I finally passed out in my bed at 2:30 wearing Chase's sweatshirt, and not the next morning either.

I didn't hear from Rain until midafternoon.

Amazing night!

I stared at my phone, assuming she would write again with questions. But a few minutes later, her next text was just as vapid.

Did u have fun?

I texted a thumbs-up and hit send.

What happened to u? lost track of where u went

A bitter laugh escaped me. Rain was so wrapped up in her new world with Brie that she hadn't even bothered to read what I'd written.

Told you already, I wrote, then deleted. Reading comp? I wrote, and then deleted. Lost track of you and Brie too, but I figured it was intentional, I wrote and deleted again. I texted a mermaid emoji instead and threw my phone across the room. Rain wasn't the only one who could serve radio silence. She wasn't the only one who could stop caring.

17

Sorry, just woke up. Can u take the bus?

I yanked a T-shirt over my head, shoved my feet into my shoes, grabbed my bag, and raced to the bus stop just before it pulled away. Boarding the bus, adrenaline and anger hummed inside me. It hadn't been me who'd insisted it was a good idea to drive up the mountain to get me for school every day. Rain had only managed to pick me up a few times last week, too. Clearly I was more of a burden to her than she'd anticipated. But if Rain couldn't do it anymore, it would have been nice to give me a little more notice.

Let's not do the mornings anymore, I wrote back once I'd plunked myself down on the bus seat. I braced myself for a fight, certain she'd insist that this wouldn't happen again.

So when she didn't write back, it stung a little.

Whatever. It didn't matter, I told myself. But something was starting to harden inside me when it came to Rain. This was just one more stick in the bonfire. Nobody had thrown the match in yet, but combustion still felt like it was coming.

I spent all of lunch and my free period in the library finishing an AP history paper and scrolling through social media, zooming in on pictures Brie had tagged Rain in from the weekend, the two of them grinning wildly in the craters, the two of them looking bleary but filtered the next day in front of plates of pancakes and bacon. Brie had hashtagged this one with #worthit and #reunitedandit-feelssogood.

I zoomed in on Rain's smile, the look in her eyes that said *best time ever.* I clenched and unclenched my jaw, opened and closed the app dozens of times. Then I zoomed in on Brie and tried to see past the filters and makeup to whatever lived inside her. I zoomed so close she turned to pixels, blurred to invisibility. I liked her better like that—gone. Blended out of existence until she was just a wash of flat color on a screen. If only it were so easy to erase her in reality.

Eventually I shut the app, disgusted with myself.

You busy after school? I wrote Chase. Want to drive me home?

There. I smiled. This way I got to spend more time with Chase, and Rain could devote her afternoon to her beloved Brie.

At the end of the day on my way to the parking lot, Chase nearly crashed into me on his skateboard.

"Hey." He grinned, jumping off the board at the last second and scooping it under one arm. "You're a fast walker."

"Hey." I smiled. Grabbed his hand.

As I walked with Chase to his car, I continued the conversation in my head that I'd had weeks ago with Rain when she'd suggested he wasn't good enough for me. *He is more than good enough for me,* I said to her now, defending him to her but really to myself. The playful way he knocked into me when we walked side by side. The way he pulled me to him. His hand in mine. How good he was at making me feel alive. The way he nodded and almost closed his eyes when I told a story, like he was listening extra hard. How he remembered little details, like the name of my dad—Ben—who I hadn't seen since I was seven.

"That was fun, the other night," he said, my hand in his.

"Mm-hmm." I took a deep breath and smelled jasmine and car exhaust and tried not to look around the parking lot for Brie's crowd, or for Rain.

When we reached his car, he jogged around the front of it to open the passenger door for me.

"I've never seen anyone do that outside of the movies," I said.

"Is that a good thing?" He looked sheepish.

I laughed. "I mean, I like movies."

It was so easy to be with Chase. Easy to sit beside him in his car and talk about nothing much. Easy, when we pulled off the highway onto the main road in Termico, to nod my head when he suggested pulling the car into the parking lot behind the Vons. So very easy to kiss him and kiss him until the skin around my lips was raw.

Easy to lie down in his backseat and make out until our sweaty skin stuck to the vinyl.

He dropped me off at the Shell station and I spent my five-hour shift in an enjoyable daze, loopy from my car activities with Chase. Rafid was there for the first half of my shift and I *mm-hmm*ed him as he told me about the latest credit card bills from Amir, about the cruise to Alaska he was planning with his wife and her parents, how much his mother-in-law wanted to see the glaciers, the way they were the pale blue of heaven itself, how he'd been Google Earthing them at home at night and had to admit they were relaxing to contemplate.

"Glaciers," I said. "Got to get 'em while they're cold."

Rafid raised an eyebrow.

"You know, because of global warming?"

But even contemplating the melting polar ice cap couldn't bring me too low this afternoon. I cranked up cheesy pop songs once Rafid left and contemplated making a playlist to share with Chase. Twice I pulled out my phone to text Rain, just to write something stupid like *too soon to officially call it blotting out the sun?* But both times I deleted it, feeling that things were so off between us right now that I couldn't open up to her about this.

But I was patient. I could wait. As soon as she woke up from her own little love affair with Brie, we'd get back to the way things had always been.

The next morning, I was surprised to get a 7 AM text from Rain.

On my way.

I smiled, happy to see I mattered to her again.

In the car, she put on Taylor Swift—a very un-Rain selection but I didn't say anything about it. We didn't talk about Moon Rocks or the fact that we'd barely talked since then. "How are things with Chase?" she asked.

"Pretty great," I admitted. "We've been hanging out a lot."

"Aw." She smiled and goosed me in my side. "That's so cute."

We settled into easy banter, Rain telling me about Joan having shattered a glass container of scented bath oil in their kitchen so now everything they ate tasted a little like gardenias, and me telling Rain about how whenever I'd seen Chase look into a mirror, he unconsciously made a kind of tough-guy face that made him look sort of constipated.

I almost thought things were returning to normal, but then she turned the wrong way down Rio Rancho Boulevard on our way back down the mountain.

"What are you doing?" I asked, but part of me knew. This was the way to Brie's.

"Brianna's car is in the shop," Rain said. "I told her I'd get her."

Taylor Swift warbled on as we drove, Rain speeding and singing along off-key.

You like this song? I wanted to ask. *Because you used to hate her.* But I knew better than to get into all the tiny ways Rain was changing.

As with everything lately, I was certain this too must have come from Brie.

When Brie ran out of her house, she was in darker clothes than I'd seen her wear before—a simple black tank with gray ripped jeans and harness boots, the kind of clothes Rain wore. But the most striking thing was her hair.

"What do you think?" Rain murmured to me in the front seat while Brie darted down her driveway. "We did it yesterday."

"Wow," I said, using all of my willpower keep my voice neutral and my eyes from rolling. The word *we* she'd tossed off so casually felt like a billboard-sized announcement that they'd hung out again without me. "Big change."

Brie's blond highlights weren't just gone. Her hair was now dyed a deep mahogany. It wasn't quite as messy as Rain's, but it was definitely trying to be. Annoyingly, it looked great with her pale blue eyes. In fact, I conceded, deflated by the realization, Brie looked better than ever.

She also looked a lot like Rain.

"You look like twins." I felt a sourness spreading out from my stomach, bile filling my throat.

"Hey," Brie said, bending to smile at Rain through the driver's-side window, pointedly ignoring that I was in the car, too. The cross at her clavicle glittered in the sun. "Still like it?"

"I love it. So does Syd," Rain said. "Right?"

"Yeah. A whole new you," I said, straining under the effort of my false smile.

"Uh, Sydney, love?" *Love?* Brie stuck out her lower lip in an exaggerated pout, the kind of thing I'd seen her friends do with their boyfriends when they wanted something. "I was really hoping to have shotgun, actually. Just this once? Because the backseat is murder on the hair with the way *this one*"—she jabbed a thumb in Rain's direction—"likes to keep the windows down. And I'm insecure, you know? Because it's so new? I want it to look good at school." She patted her hair and looked at me with false contrition.

"Seriously?" I waited for her to say she was kidding. I turned to Rain in the silence, but Rain just shrugged.

"Just humor her," Rain said quietly. "It's her first time not being blond, like, ever."

"Fine." I got out of the front and wedged myself into the back.

"So, tonight! Candice is bringing something fun," Brie chirped as Rain reversed out of the driveway.

What fresh hell was this? Another party I wasn't invited to? Abandoning my dignity, I leaned toward the front seat to listen, not wanting to miss a word.

"Excellent. I want to keep it small. Just like ten or fifteen people. Joan is in Lake Tahoe, but I need the place to not get wrecked or she'll end me."

"Totally, totally." Brie nodded. Joan must be visiting her sister, Marsha. I peeked at Rain's reflection in the rearview. She seemed a million miles away, distracted and kind of loopy, like the addition of Brie to the car had injected extra oxygen into the atmosphere. Had Rain bought into the myth of Brie Walsh? Did she think she was special somehow, now that she'd gained the approval of the self-appointed queen of the twelfth grade? Or was it just that every facet of her life was new and more exciting than she'd ever expected it to be? I studied Rain's profile but I suddenly felt so distant from her that I couldn't begin to figure out what she was thinking. We used to joke that we had ESP when it came to what the other one thought. Not anymore.

"And Ryan is bringing tequila," Brie went on, oblivious.

"Cool, cool," Rain said, barely listening. "Squid, you'll come early, right? To the pre-party?" Her eyes met mine in the rearview. I glared at her.

Screw you, I wanted to say. *Were you even going to tell me?* What was happening to Rain? Who was she now?

"I doubt it," I said. "I didn't know—"

"I told you about it," Rain snapped. "I could have sworn I did." Her eyes narrowed at me in the rearview like I was the one betraying her.

"Nope." I looked away. "You didn't."

"Don't fight, ladies. There'll be a million more parties," Brie said, looking bored and combing her fingers through her new hair.

I met Rain's eyes again in the rearview. I thought I saw pleading there. I hoped I did. And I definitely didn't want to leave it up to Brie, who clearly didn't want me there. The last thing I wanted to do was go, but if I didn't, I worried I would lose what little of Rain I still had left.

"I'm covering someone's shift tonight," I said after a pointed silence. "But maybe I'll swing by after."

I tried to sound casual, like it was nothing to me. Like everything wasn't crashing into ruins. Like we were the same as ever, two bodies, one brain.

"Yay," Brie said in monotone. "The Termico three, back in action again."

It took everything I had not to fling Brie's book bag that she'd tossed so carelessly beside me right out of the car. I pictured it sailing against the bright sky, and could almost hear the satisfying *thwack* of it landing on the road, the pop of it being run over by a semi.

It was totally out of Chase's way to drive from his house to the gas station and then to Rain's, so I claimed the Fiesta for my own that night to get to the party. Before I left work, I locked the doors and changed clothes in the Shell bathroom. Under the fluorescents, I caught glimpses of my pale body as I wriggled out of my old T-shirt and jeans and into some of the new clothes Rain had bought me. The new shirt was much skimpier than what I normally wore, a camisole kind of thing Rain had insisted on giving me a couple of weeks ago that had to be worn without a bra. Standing on paper towels so that my feet didn't touch the bathroom floor I'd mopped a half hour ago, I pulled on a pair of jeans from Rain that had cost $165 and were full of intentional rips and weird seaming. I stepped into the platform sneakers Rain had gotten me ("in case you need to be a tall bitch sometime"). I was now three inches taller, teetering on the fake self-confidence that came from the clothes.

"Oh, this?" I whispered into the mirror as I applied some of the makeup Rain had bought me. "Just grabbed it off my floor." In truth, I'd hung the jeans up in my closet and made sure none of my other clothes touched them, as if they were a religious artifact or a precious work of art. When I was done applying the so-not-me red lipstick Rain had told me was to be worn with the camisole, I tried to fluff up my hair a little. It was still neither brown nor blond, neither short nor long. My face was still neither pretty nor ugly, my body still neither smokin' nor objectionable. But these clothes were like armor, and armor was what I needed. Because not only was I going to get my friend to remember I existed, but tonight might be the night I would take things further with Chase. My legs and pits were freshly shaved. I had on black underwear with three tiny red silk rosettes along the top seam.

See you soon, I texted Chase from the car. The Fiesta smelled like Mom's Jergens and sweaty shoes, but I'd reapplied deodorant and had the all-new clothes, so I reasoned I could rise above my smelly car and my gas-station weariness. I would get through tonight on sheer willpower, no matter what weirdness Brie might bring to the mix. I plugged my phone into the cigarette lighter and put on Nina Simone's version of "I Put a Spell on You" and willed myself to think more about Chase than about Brie and Rain.

There were a lot more people at Rain's house than I'd expected. Seven or eight of them looked like they were in their twenties, all visible from the living room as they gathered around the white marble kitchen island. A guy with a fauxhawk was cutting limes and paused to gesticulate to a girl facing away from me. The paring knife in his hand glinted in the overhead light.

Jay-Z blasted from the living room's enormous TV, and kids from school sprawled across the low furniture. Min vaped and held, then passed the pen to her boyfriend, Mike. As she blew the vapor out into the room, she waved at me and grinned a baked smile.

They're upstairs, she mouthed, pointing up to the ceiling. I nodded. *Thank you,* I mouthed back. Maybe Brie's girls weren't so awful, I thought. Maybe my hang-ups about them weren't fair.

After a quick loop through the kitchen, where I considered and then decided against a vodka shot, I moved up the stairs. The house pulsed with music. Good thing the neighbors on both sides were people who only came to the desert on weekends from LA. If it hadn't been a Wednesday, someone might have called the cops by now.

Upstairs, the long hallway lined with rooms was dark. At one end of the hall was Joan's room, dark and silent. The throb of music carried me to the opposite end, to Rain's room, where there were candles burning and trap music blasting, but where it was otherwise empty. I heard laughter from the bathroom.

"Hello?" I tapped on the bathroom door. It was already open a crack and would only take a tiny push to open more. Nervousness running through my veins, I figured I would say a quick hi and then go find Chase. I could hear male and female laughter over the music. Brie's was the loudest, sharp and shrill. I heard Rain's throaty cackle. And some boy sounds, quieter, voices deeper. I threw my shoulders back and pushed the door open gently, ready to smile.

On the bathroom counter, a bottle of tequila, several shot glasses. Some cut-up limes. A lit joint. The room reeked of weed. Rain and Brie, two eerily matching brunettes now, stood in the center of the room, facing three boys who sat awkwardly in the dry bathtub. Rain filming, Brie in a shirt the size of a handkerchief, her body bent awkwardly over the tub.

It took less than three seconds to see everything. Brie's mouth on the mouth of the boy in the center of the tub. The three boys' legs draped over the lip of it. Rain chanting, "Shots, shots, shots." Rain's arm outstretched, panning out on her phone. Brie pulling away from the boy and laughing hysterically.

And oh. The boy in the center of the tub. The one holding a lime wedge in his mouth, grinning like an idiot? It was Chase. Of course it was.

"Syd!" He spat out the lime wedge and reached for me. Baked to a crisp. Like all of them, the whole revolting tableau. I didn't want to know what they were doing. I didn't need to know. All I needed to see, I had seen. Had Brie and Rain orchestrated this to show me how easy it was? How meaningless whatever I thought I'd had with Chase actually was?

"Finally!" Chase yelled. "They made me do body shots!"

"Sydney!" Brie pulled me in for a hard hug, her grip surprisingly strong. "What took you so long?" She smiled primly when I pulled back.

Rain continued to film. "The Termico three, back together again," she cheered, as if this was all perfectly normal.

I opened my mouth, shut it. Wanted to grab her phone and drop it in her stupid Japanese toilet.

"We had to entertain him in your absence." Brie's eyes twinkled. Her dimple popped. "You know how boys are. They get so *bored*."

Rain cackled, lit up from the alcohol. "Squid! You look so beautiful. We missed you so much. Especially Chase. It was awful here without you." She moved toward me, folded me in her arms. It was so hard to stay mad at Rain when she seemed so sincere and so out of it at the same time. So unaware of what Brie had just done or how it made me feel. Unlike Rain, Brie knew how easy it was to hurt me.

"Poor you," I managed, my fury dampened slightly.

"We're being so ridiculous with the body shots, I don't know what got into us." As Rain filled the air with her words, Brie grabbed her hand, threaded her fingers through Rain's, and pulled her close. She looked right at me when she did it, as if silently saying *mine*. Chase pulled himself out of the bathtub, sensing, maybe, that I wasn't as cool with this as he'd thought.

"Have a shot," he slurred. For the first time in weeks, he wasn't attractive to me. He leaned in and hugged me, picked me up a little, spun me around.

This was the moment. I could be a cool girl, find some measure of calm and act like everything was fine, like this happened to me every day and it was *nothing, obviously just stupid fun, and anyway we aren't exclusive* . . . or I could be my uptight, naïve self and bolt. I took a breath, turned around, and saw Brie and Rain looking at something on Brie's feed and cracking up.

If I left now, they wouldn't even care. But Chase would.

I stood there in the bathroom, found my face in the mirror. In the red lipstick and this skanky camisole I looked garish and childish at the same time, like a child playing a vulgar game of dress-up. The cool girl had left the building and only my true self remained. I wasn't even cool enough to turn on my heel and storm out in righteous, dignified fury. Instead, I did the most cowardly thing imaginable and made a stupid excuse.

"I left something in my car," I said to Chase, looking him right in the face and even managing to smile. "Be right back."

And then I charged out, careful not to wipe away the tears that were starting to well up lest someone see me do it.

Instead of going straight to the car and driving away like I wanted to, I pushed through the crowded kitchen into the backyard where the pool glowed, the Jacuzzi floating like a UFO just above it in one corner. Maybe Chase would come and find me. Maybe Rain would. Maybe if I ignored my instincts and took a minute alone to calm down, somehow the night would turn around and I wouldn't feel so humiliated.

I carefully pulled the platform sneakers off, sat down beside the Jacuzzi, and rolled up the $165 pair of jeans.

When my feet slid into the warm water, I heard a voice. "Needed a break from those two, did you?"

It was Anya, all alone on an outdoor couch inside the canvas cabana tucked in the side of the pool's patio. Her face was lit up by the glow of her phone screen.

"I guess," I said, not wanting to share anything personal with any of Brie's people. "They've had a lot to drink."

"Haven't we all." Anya sighed, scooting down to the end of the couch and joining me beside the Jacuzzi. "I mean, except you, right? You've always been so *virtuous.*"

She smiled at me in a way that made me think she meant it as a compliment, as if she wished she hadn't always made the choices she made.

"I drink sometimes," I said, not wanting her to think of me as a total prude. "I'm not as virtuous as you might think."

"I should drink less," she mused, having gone back to her scrolling. Without looking up from her phone, she went on. "I hear you have a man now? Getting those needs met." Anya laughed at her own turn of phrase, proud of herself, I guessed, for sounding so adult. "You should be careful, though."

"What? Why?"

Anya continued swiping through photo after photo on her phone. "Oh god, I shouldn't do this." She looked up, swiveled her head to make sure nobody else was in earshot, and carefully set her phone down. Then she let out a big sigh. "But fuck it. I'm sick of mean people."

Don't take the bait, I told myself. *Don't ask. You don't want to know.*

Anya let a silence open up. The steam rising off the Jacuzzi swirled around us like mist, and aside from the thump of the music leaking out of the house, it felt as if we were the only two people within miles. After the long silence stretched on even longer, I couldn't help myself.

"If you're going to tell me something, just say it, okay?" I said quietly.

Anya blinked at me. "Maybe you already know. Maybe you're cool with this. I wouldn't be, but to each her own." She glanced back up at the house again before continuing.

Oh, I'm not cool with anything, I wanted to say. Instead I nodded, hoping she would continue, too afraid to say a word in case it came out strangled.

"Brie and Chase hooked up a couple weeks ago," Anya whispered. "*After* you two got together."

Her words landed like a punch. It took me a second to even be able to respond.

"How do you know?" I asked, trying to sound bored, to save face, to keep the freaking-out sound out of my voice even though inside I was shattered, disgraced.

"We all know." Anya shrugged. "I've been there, girl. We've all been there. Boys are stupid. They always say they didn't know it was, like, *a relationship,* that you didn't tell them the rules." She sighed bitterly. "I just . . . I would've wanted to know, if it were me."

I opened my mouth with no idea what to say to her. "Thanks," I finally said.

She slipped her feet out of the Jacuzzi. "Talk to him about it," Anya said. "Tell him you're serious about the relationship and that you don't do hookups. Maybe he'll get it." She shrugged.

I let out a sharp *ha* and felt my face grow warm. Anya made it sound so easy, but I would never do that. I'd already ended it with Chase, the second she'd told me. There wasn't a single way he could've hurt me more than this.

"See you around, Sydney. Don't let Brie get to you. She's been a total bitch to us, too, ever since she and Rain . . ." She waved her hand to signify their new closeness, and I realized this new pecking order must be destabilizing to more people than just me.

I managed to wave weakly, my eyes stinging with humiliation as she stalked back across the patio into the thudding force field of bass that surrounded Rain's house.

As soon as she'd gone, I grabbed my sneakers and socks and hurried barefoot around the side of the house, nearly tripping over a cactus in my haste to get out of there before Chase found me, if he was even looking. Why would he, though? There was no need for sloppy seconds when the first and ideal course stood before him. Why would he ever choose me when he could choose Brie?

I wasn't going to wait around for the answer.

As I opened the car door, I felt the buzz of my phone. A text from Rain.

Where are u? Is everything ok?

Fuck you, and fuck him. I didn't need their false pity. I tossed the shoes in the backseat and started the car.

Not feeling well, I wrote before I took off. Stomach bug maybe. Gotta bail.

I deleted every one of Chase's texts as soon as they came in. Eventually, he stopped writing. I tossed and turned all night, drifting in and out of sleep and replaying the most humiliating thing Anya had said. *We all know.* Did Rain know and keep this from me? Was everyone pitying me behind my back?

Rain didn't write back until 2 AM, and then it was just to say feel better. At least she was honest about how much I mattered to her.

Alone in my bed, I tried to imagine what she and Brie had done with the rest of their night once they'd let my absence roll off their backs. Maybe Brie was puking by now, maybe she'd fallen into the pool or fallen down Rain's stairs, I thought, my chest surging with pathetic hope. Maybe one of the partygoers had damaged Rain's new house and now something was broken that couldn't be fixed. Maybe at this very moment Rain was freaking out, scared of what Joan would do to her when she got home. For the rest of the night, I tossed in and out of fitful dreams set at the party, each one leading to a new scenario where Rain or Brie was suffering. But in the cold light of morning, I knew I was the only one in pain.

18

By 6 PM the following day, after spending the afternoon nursing a Big Gulp of Diet Coke and deleting Chase's regular stream of texts one by one without reading them, it felt righteous and appropriate to smash my molars against a couple of past-their-prime Charleston Chews, the very worst candy bar Rafid carried.

As I ate, I looked out into the darkening evening from inside the fluorescent-lit Shell kiosk. I could see my own reflection there, a pale, smudged face with puffy eyes, a girl stupid enough to think she had something close to a boyfriend when what she really had was a fuck buddy, a friend with benefits. It was all the same to Chase—he could trade one warm girl-body for another.

Are you sure he's good enough for you? Rain had said. Had it been right around then that Brie and Chase hooked up, or even earlier? Had Rain known the whole time and been trying to signal me without telling me?

And why had Brie done it, I wondered? Chase wasn't her usual football- or swim-team type. Had she wanted to sample what I had suddenly deemed worthwhile, a dessert left on the table that I'd tasted and liked enough that she wanted to have a bite? Was it to show me that he would be with anyone who let him? To teach me some kind of cynical lesson that boys are scum, that they *only think with their dicks,* something Rain had been saying since we were thirteen? Or was it just to take what was mine?

Outside, the sky blazed into a pink sunset and a distant rumble of thunder rippled through the glass door of the Shell. A mother pumped gas while her two kids fought over the windshield squeegee. Behind them I saw something we almost never saw out here—a flash of lightning above the mountains. I felt heavy and wistful the way I always did just before a storm, wishing I could retrace all the steps that had led me here. A few minutes later, a louder crack of thunder sounded above Rafid's easy listening radio station and the sky opened up.

Fucking perfect. I had no car tonight. Just my stupid skateboard. My phone buzzed. Chase again. This time I decided to read it.

Want a ride home?

A horrible phrase Rain had uttered years ago floated through my mind, something she'd said after a senior football player, Jordan Curtis, went all out with her, flowers, dinner at a nice restaurant, stuff we'd only seen on TV shows. It had ended just a few weeks later and she'd muttered something so appalling it had rattled around in my head ever since: *He just wanted to get his dick wet.*

The rain drummed on the Shell station's tin roof above the pumps, funneling down in a waterfall at one corner, a massive puddle quickly forming on the cement in front of pump four.

Chase probably thought he'd say something sweet in the car, figure out whatever had been causing me to ignore his texts, and work it all out. That we'd park outside Rain's empty prefab and get a little closer to full-on sex.

Let him drive me home, I thought, my hands balling into fists. Let him come in here all smiles, freshly showered. I would make sure he'd never come back. I sent a reply:

OK. Pick me up in an hour.

The closing tasks were always the same, but tonight I performed each task with a rage-filled precision. I dumped out all the coffee and scrubbed the carafes. Tossed all the hot dogs and nachos from their warming trays and cleaned out all the components with a soaked rag. I counted the till twice, making sure every dollar and five and twenty in the drawer faced the same way. I wiped down all surfaces, making everything gleam and reek of the industrial yellow cleaning fluid Rafid stocked.

Alongside my tasks, I sipped at two tall boys of Coors Light (on special that day) that I paid for with cash, having made change for myself as if a customer had bought it. The beer filled my empty stomach but did nothing to coat the white-hot singe of humiliation burning in my chest.

I wiped every handle of every freezer, every doorknob, every counter. I swept every corner, every inch of the store until my armpits were damp with exertion. I whipped my sweatshirt off and mopped in just my tank top. Even with the AC blasting and the storm outside, I was on fire. By the time Chase pulled up next to the station door, the place was spotlessly clean.

I set the alarm, locked the doors, and nearly fell running through the puddles to Chase's car. "Thanks for the ride." I slammed the door shut and stared straight ahead, the lights from oncoming traffic whooshing past us in the dark, the storm turning shapes and colors into a Van Gogh painting.

"You smell like beer," he said. He pulled the car out of the Shell and drove up the highway through the pouring rain.

"Had to mop up a spill in there," I said, amazed at how easy it was to lie to him now.

"You haven't been . . . reachable lately." Chase looked at me for a second before turning his eyes back to the road.

"Well." I leaned against the passenger seat door and shot a look at him, appreciating his profile yet again despite everything. What was it about that mussed pile of dark hair that made me want to play with it? His long lashes, cheekbones bouncing moonlight off them. I wanted to inhale him, even now. Too bad I hated him. "That's because I don't think this is working out."

Chase slowed down, looked at me, smiling, waiting for the joke. I stared back at him.

"What?"

"Just . . . what I said. It's not working out." I had my dignity. I wasn't going to spell it out for him.

"Why not?" I could see his mouth working, his jaw pulsing as he drove.

"You know why." I stared out the window, willing the hot tears that had gathered at the edges of my eyes not to fall. They fell anyway.

His mouth fell open then and he nodded. "Because of that stupid thing with Brie?"

I blinked, shocked he just came right out and said it. I stared straight ahead. "Yeah, because of that," I said bitterly.

"That didn't mean anything. I'd just . . . we were . . . It was dumb. It was nothing. But Syd, I—"

"If you really like someone, you should show it in your actions," I whispered, wiping tears from the corners of my eyes, cursing myself for crying in front of him. "I'm sorry if that's, like, not obvious, if we didn't define whatever—" I waved my hands around to encompass us both, "Whatever this is. I just—I'm not up to it. I'm an all-or-nothing person. You're either my all, or you're my nothing." The whole car felt close, claustrophobic. My stomach clenched and I worried for a moment that I would be sick, whether from a spasm of carsickness or the two beers or the pain of ending things. I opened the window a little, felt raindrops hitting my forehead.

"So that's it, I'm nothing?" Chase frowned. "I think you're over—"

"Just so you know, she laughs at boys like you. She probably did it just to show me she could. That she could do whatever she wanted, get whatever she wanted. Which was cruel of her, yes, but she was right. You'll just take whoever comes your way. We're all the same to you. I see that now."

"Real nice, Syd." We were almost at my house. Chase shook his head like he couldn't believe this was happening. "That's not true at all. I care about you."

"You care about sex, you mean."

Chase flinched and shot me a wounded look. "This is such bull-shit," he muttered.

"It really is," I said. I looked out the window and tried to concentrate on a turkey vulture arcing over the desert sky so as not to break down any further.

"I don't know who hurt you or why you think I'm such a piece of shit, but I would think it's pretty fucking obvious that I care about you. I came all this way—"

"To my dogshit neighborhood, you mean? So you could get some?"

"Jesus. That's not what I said." Chase hit his steering wheel hard and I flashed on Heart Attack Gary yelling at my mother in a supermarket parking lot the year before he died. He'd gotten so worked up he'd taken a little chip out of the car window with his watch. "You need to calm down."

"Please don't tell me or any girl to *calm down*."

Chase emitted a sound that was somewhere between a sigh and a groan. "I can't say anything right tonight, can I? Let's talk about this later when we're both calmer. You're blowing this way out of proportion."

"I guess I'm not as relaxed as you thought, then, so good thing we're ending this then. Win-win." I glared at him, my heart breaking but my resolve firm.

"That's not what I want." Chase gritted his teeth as he turned onto my street.

I hated him then, his sighing and eye-rolling, as if I was the most high-maintenance, unreasonable freak. The car was humid in the storm. I could hear my own breathing. The rain pounded on the roof and slid in sheets down the windshield. I stared ahead of me at the peeling Sk8Mafia sticker on his dashboard, wanting to look anywhere but at him.

Chase took a deep breath. He was almost to my house. "Can we just, can we sit here a minute and start over?"

"Thanks for the ride," I managed as I unbuckled my seat belt.

"Come on," he said, pulling up alongside my house now. Some rain had snuck in through the crack at the top of my window. I smeared it across the glass, like I was wiping all of this—everything with Chase—away. "Don't go. This is stupid."

"Not to me," I said. And then I sprang out of the seat and into the storm, running through mud and puddles until I reached my porch.

"Syd." I turned around. He'd gotten out of his car. Was standing there in the pouring rain, getting soaked.

"Why are you still here?" I cried. "Just go away!" My face contorted with hurt, my hair plastered to my face, I must have looked deranged to him. Good, I thought. The meaner I was, the sooner he would leave and the easier this would be.

He stared hard at me and shook his head a little like he couldn't quite believe this was real. Then he got back into his car and backed out.

I held it together as he backed out of the driveway. It was only after I couldn't see the car anymore that I let myself break down.

Tears falling freely, I let myself in, ran to the bathroom to peel off my soaked clothes. I stood under the hottest shower I could stand, let out one last sob, and then I was done crying. I stayed in the shower until the hot water ran out. After chugging water from the bathroom sink, I went to bed wrapped in my towel, too numb and wrung out to bother putting anything on.

I thought how much better off I would be spending the rest of the school year alone.

My grades were already slipping, with all the time I'd wasted with Chase. Without Rain or Chase weighing me down, I would become a machine. I would study harder, bring my academic work back up to the perfection I knew I was capable of. Brie and Chase could have each other, and Rain, too, and all of Brie's stupid friends.

I was perfectly fine all by myself. Alone, I wouldn't go around wearing ridiculous clothes that didn't suit me. Alone, I was invincible.

Inside my crumpled jeans, my phone buzzed. When I dug it out, I saw Rain had texted.

Chase said to check in. U ok?

I lay back in bed and stared at the ceiling, annoyed that he'd communicated with Rain so quickly. Certain they'd stay close after all this, which meant Brie would stay in his orbit, too. The light fixture on my ceiling flickered and I spotted the shadows of dead bugs gathered in the glass fixture that covered the bulb. Everything and everyone around me was contaminated, infested with threats I'd never noticed until now.

I'm fine, I wrote. Going to sleep.

She didn't write back.

19

A three-day weekend and then four school days passed where I barely left my room except to work at the Shell station. I wondered if this was what it felt like for Rain when she skipped school. The world kept on spinning, it turned out, whether you showed your face to it or not.

Chase stopped texting after only two days of me not responding. *Easy come, easy go,* I thought, disgusted with myself for thinking what we had was deeper than that, and even more disgusted by my disappointment that he'd given up on me so quickly. Even though I had no plans to forgive him, shouldn't he have tried harder? Rain continued texting but her words felt cloying, fake-sweet and shallow.

U OK? Chase says ur mad @him?

I'm fine. Just wasn't feeling it, I wrote. I was ashamed to tell her the truth, that she'd been right about him not being good enough. And I definitely didn't want her confronting Brie about what had happened between Brie and Chase. The two of them discussing my hurt feelings was more humiliation than I could bear.

She replied with a string of question marks.

Really, I'm fine. I'm actually just sick right now. Flu, ugh.

The old Rain would have seen through this right away, would have dropped what she was doing and driven over, but Rain as she was today took me at my word. She didn't drop by, didn't even try to call. Her easy acceptance of my lies felt like more of a betrayal than what Chase had done. Either Rain could no longer read between the lines with me, could no longer sense when something was off . . . or she could, but didn't care enough to bother figuring out the truth. Both possibilities hurt.

Every day there was another check-in from her, saccharine and rushed.

Hey girl. u srsly still sick? LMK when you're up to talking.
Chase still seems bummed—what happened extly?

You really don't know? I typed but deleted at least three times. If she'd known that Brie and Chase had hooked up, she was a horrible friend. If she didn't know, well, that was better, but somehow this made me angry, too, like she was totally oblivious to anything that might matter to me.

Instead of just asking her and then explaining, every day I waited a couple of hours to respond and then put her off, kept things light. But inside, I was stewing. In my room, I'd become a one-person FBI surveillance unit, monitoring social media for Chase, and for Rain. My fingers flew across photos and videos, my eyes scanning everything, all corners of everyone's feed until they grew dry and exhausted. Here and there, a piece of Chase's shoulder, his shoe, Rain and Brie off to one side of someone's stupid dance video, someone else's story. Rain tagged in group shots of glossy girls holding Solo cups, girls duckfacing, girls dressed up, girls busted or filtered or flirty or sporty. Wherever the eye of a camera was in Brie's group, Rain seemed to be captured. Rain and Brie tongues-out on a rooftop somewhere, the blurred brown of Palm Springs behind them.

It was clear Rain's orbit extended far beyond me all of a sudden.

That she'd been absorbed fully into Brie's world. While my life was on pause, she'd continued expanding her life with her new friends.

I lay in bed, fingers twitching, searching vicariously in all places and at all times, every sighting like a stab in my gut confirming exactly what I wanted to confirm—that Rain didn't need me anymore, that Chase wasn't who I'd thought he was.

What are they doing right now, right now, right now? The question popped into my head at all hours, irresistible, unstoppable.

On the fifth day I skipped school, Mom put her hand on my forehead while I drank chamomile tea at the kitchen table. I didn't bother to remind her that I wasn't sick, only brokenhearted. She frowned, chewed her lip. I felt guilty, looking at Mom's tired, worried face. The weight of her one reliable child falling apart was probably more than she knew what to do with. It was bad enough that Spider had flamed out so spectacularly, but now I was laid up with an illness no amount of Chicken & Stars soup or tea could fix, an existential sadness that left me hollow and tired.

"You don't think it's mono making you so worn out, honey? Maybe we should take you to urgent care."

"No," I said. "I told you, I just needed a break."

A break. From love, from friendship, from the human race.

Mom studied me as she ran her hands through her hair to gather it up in the high ponytail she always looped into a bun before her shift. "You know, you can talk to me, tell me anything."

"I know," I said.

She nodded and looked the faintest bit relieved. "What if I called Rain and asked her to come over?"

Mom knew the barest basics of what had happened: that Chase and I had broken up, that Rain wasn't here to mend my heartbreak. The old Rain would've been over in a second. The old Rain was such a fixture here that she didn't even knock.

"I'm actually fine on my own," I said, hating how defensive it sounded. "We just . . . we're growing apart right now. It happens."

I stood up from the table and headed to my room, wishing I could feel as blasé about it as I sounded.

"Maybe just check in with her today," Mom called behind me. "She might cheer you up."

"'Kay." I closed my bedroom door behind me knowing I wasn't going to reach out. I was tired of always being the bigger person, the one who could rise above high school drama. In my heart, I felt small. Small, petty, and bitter.

I let the hours pass. Lying in bed, I listened to Mom leave for work, heard her car start, and had another day of total aloneness to wallow in. I flitted in and out of YouTube wormholes, scrolled through social media for the millionth time, but posting slowed during class hours. I finally settled into a reality show about ski instructors, marathoning episode after episode on my ancient laptop until blazing late-afternoon sun snuck into my room through the broken slats of my blinds.

The ski instructors constantly slept with one another's boyfriends and girlfriends, their powder-white parkaed worlds destabilized and restabilized every few episodes. It was all so stupid and so like life. Human connection and destruction, again and again until we died.

When the afternoon light turned pinker and I realized I had a headache from not enough food and too many videos, I hobbled out to the kitchen and nuked a burrito from the freezer. I ate it with my phone in my hand, my thumb betraying me yet again.

#quietnightin, Brie had written. #selfcare, she'd written. #old-friendsarethebestfriends, she'd written, and fury leapt into my throat. In the picture, filtered and polished, she and Rain were neck up and sharing a chaise lounge, Brie's deck and house blurred in the background, the pink skies and big cottony clouds of the evening reflected in their sunglasses. Their heads were angled close, the strands of their long hair blending together into one dark, shining mass. She'd tagged Rain, obviously. But even though he wasn't in the picture, she'd also tagged Chase.

I nearly choked on my burrito.

When Mom pulled in an hour later, I was dressed and ready. I'd plowed through a bag of congealed candy corn I'd found in the back of the cupboard and my chest pounded with sugar and purpose. What the hell were the three of them doing? Was Chase officially with Brie now? How could he stand her? How could Rain stand by and watch it?

I needed to see. To understand how Brie had managed to replace me so fully for both of them. Once I'd seen it, maybe I would figure out how to undo it.

Brie wasn't the only one who could ruin things.

I parked a block away and walked, my Converses silent on the spotless sidewalk outside Brie's house. It was dark now, a little after 9 PM. Brie's house blazed with light and I drifted closer along a row of hedges, drawn inexorably to what would hurt me. Me and the ski instructors, we were no different.

Through the window, Brie's living room was empty except for a black leather bag slumped on a loveseat. Rain's bag. I edged around the side of the house where there was a wooden fence. Quietly, like the home invader I now was, I reached up and unlatched the side gate. After nearly tripping on a tangled-up hose, I crept toward the sloping backyard, keeping myself pressed along the side of the raised deck. If I bent low, I had enough coverage to see what was happening on the deck through the slats and could even see a few feet into the kitchen.

A cheesy Katy Perry song played on someone's phone and the deck shook with footsteps. I pressed myself lower and peered through the slats.

". . . kind of paranoid. You're nothing like that," Brie said. Was she talking about me?

I heard the flick of a lighter, the slurp of a bong. "Couldn't be if

I tried," Rain said, sucking in at the same time. No, Rain wouldn't have said that if they'd been discussing me.

"She's a one-hundred-percent original," Brie sang, either a song I didn't recognize or she'd made up a tune to go with her flattery. God, was she kissing Rain's ass. Maybe that was why they were so close now. Who wouldn't like their nemesis to turn around and start calling them the greatest thing since sliced bread? All that was missing in their little party was Chase. Had I imagined the tagging? Or had it not meant what I assumed it had?

Rain began singing along with Katy Perry. I was astonished she knew the words, something about not saying goodbye, something about it not being the end of the world.

Yes it is, I thought, having already said goodbye and wishing I hadn't.

"Hang on, let me check on the food," Brie said.

I pressed my hands against the weathered wood of the deck and slipped underneath it. I was so close to Rain now, just underneath her. I reached up and touched where the wood sagged, just two inches of plank between my fingers and the sole of her shoe, and miles between who we were to each other now. I could hear her above me, still humming along with the song.

Why had I come? What had I hoped to get out of this? What was I doing here, invading their space? Did I actually think Chase would be here, that the three of them would somehow, what, sit around and hang out and . . . talk about me? I should be so lucky to know they cared enough to discuss me. The truth of it was so much worse than that. I'd snuck in and witnessed the most hurtful thing of all, the fact of Rain and Brie's ordinary, boring friendship. No boys needed. And nobody was thinking about me in the least.

It was time for me to go. Spying on them felt too pathetic, even for me. I backed out from underneath the deck, back into the night along the side of Brie's yard.

I unlatched the gate again, taking care to creep out as quietly as I'd come, and tried not to let myself dwell on the sad reality of what I'd witnessed—that I'd been successfully replaced, forgotten, discarded. That there was a new, more exciting person that better fit the shape of Rain's richer, more exciting life.

I was threading my way in the dark when a stick snapped a few feet ahead, the sound close enough to make me jump.

"Sorry, did I scare you?"

Shit. Brie stepped out of the shadows and began to laugh. Somehow, this was more humiliating than yelling at me. My snooping wasn't even a threat or a bother, just a funny, stupid nonevent.

"Oh my god, you little stalker." She giggled. "I didn't think you had this in you."

"I don't," I sputtered. "I'm not . . ." There was no way to get out of this with my dignity intact. None. "I'm sorry, I just . . ."

"You missed your friend," Brie said simply. Her eyes were still glassy from laughing, but that was about the long and short of it. I did miss my friend. I missed my life.

"You're still such a child, it's kind of sweet," Brie breathed, stepping closer to me.

My chest thumped with how unfair it all was.

And then it tumbled out, not anything I'd planned to say aloud, the words a sharp whisper. "I'd rather be a child than a whore."

"Okay, weirdo." Infuriatingly, she smiled, her perfect teeth glittering in the moonlight. "You can't hurt me with slut shaming."

With two hands she pushed my hair out of my face, tucked it tenderly behind my ears in a creepily maternal way, the way a parent would do to a five-year-old. "Rain was right, you really are a judgmental little prude."

"Don't touch me." I ducked away from her hands, my heart pounding in my ears, my worst fears about Rain and Brie confirmed now.

Brie smirked. "Don't spy on me, bitch. Go back to Termico." And then she moved closer and shoved me with both hands, hard enough so that I nearly fell. I pushed past her and ran toward the driveway, blinking in the rush of headlights just as a car pulled in. Ed, I thought. I started to run, but then Chase's voice pierced the darkness.

"Syd, wait."

Oh god. My eyes found his and I quickly looked away, panicked now, horrified that he'd seen me show up here, uninvited and pathetic. I kept on running, my heart in my throat, my whole body vibrating with shame.

"Where are you going? I want to talk to you!" he shouted, but a second later I'd reached the car. I opened the door and started the engine with shaking hands. When I looked back, Brie was bent over the driver's side of Chase's car, her face inches from Chase's. She was shaking her head and gesturing as if to say *stay away from that one, she's a mess.*

It wasn't until I'd peeled out in the Fiesta that I stopped to wonder about Chase's words. If he wanted to talk to me so much, why would he go to Brie's?

Fuck it, I told myself. *Doesn't matter.* Let the three of them have one another. This judgmental little prude was done with them. A cold surrender wrapped itself around me like a straitjacket as I pulled out of Brie's subdivision and into the flow of cars, a speck among thousands, heading I didn't know where but doing it alone, ashamed, and beaten.

PART VI
RAIN

APRIL
TWO WEEKS BEFORE THE FIRE

20

It wasn't that I hadn't noticed that a month had gone by with Syd hiding from me. It was more that suddenly school involved non-stop socializing and I was actually accepted, actually ranked as a human being by everyone who I'd once thought looked down on me. I had a newfound confidence, a new feeling of not exactly belonging, but not hating everyone and everything anymore. And it was all thanks to Brie, who I had misjudged, who I hadn't seen was hurting just as much as I was. Now I was almost . . . happy. And I resented—yes, resented!—Syd for begrudging me that happiness. Resented her for judging the fact that I was growing, changing, stretching my wings. *People branch out!* I wanted to yell at her. But I couldn't pin her down long enough to do it.

I'd tried so hard to bring her with me. To integrate her. At the beginning I had always been there with open arms, always tried to drag her out to every party. But each day, she'd pulled further and further away until there was a week where she basically disappeared. I saw disgust and judgment in every half-assed text she'd sent back when I was still trying, as if it was a huge inconvenience to communicate with me. Still, I didn't want to call her on it, didn't want to push her further than she was willing to be pushed. Didn't want to get into a whole big thing about Brie and the lottery and how I'd changed.

Growing pains, I'd told myself. Things would be all right again soon.

But then when Syd returned to school, she practically ran from me. I saw her see me across the courtyard and when I waved, when I shouted, "Syd! Finally!" she'd looked away. When I jumped up to run after her, she'd wound her way through the crowd and vanished into thin air. What was I supposed to think, except that she was avoiding me? That she was judging me for my every action, every choice, the same way she had with the stupid Gucci sneakers I'd tried to give her? That she thought whatever I spent my time doing now was stupid, gross, ridiculous?

Over the next few weeks I tried a new approach and hung back. I reached out less, looked for her less. I figured eventually she'd crack or I would, and we would put whatever this deep freeze was behind us. Meanwhile, for the first time in a long time, I was having actual fun. *Sorry you hate me so much for this,* I would think, spotting Syd glowering across the courtyard while a group of swim team boys practiced sea shanties. I would put on a big smile and wave her over, but she turned away as usual. *You'd like it here,* I wanted to say. I would text her later, I decided. This had gone on long enough.

But when I texted and asked if we could talk, she didn't bother to reply.

Fine. I shrugged, swallowing down the hurt. *Be that way.*

Before too long, I even stopped seeing Syd in the halls at school. It had been a couple of weeks since I'd caught so much as a glimpse of her, until, on an unremarkable Tuesday, I was rounding the corner in the hallway near the bio labs with Matt Richardson and we nearly knocked Syd down.

"Oh." She looked at Matt. "Hey." Her smile was more of a wince, and for Matt only. It was as if I was invisible. Or that she wished I was.

"Hey!" I ignored the way she ignored me and opened my arms, intending to give her a hug. "Where have you been?" I asked, wanting to pretend like I hadn't noticed that she literally ran the other way whenever I was near. But she stepped backward and shook her head slightly, her eyes blank and unfocused, looking anywhere but at me. Her Irish milkmaid complexion, normally all rosy cheeks and freckles, had gone pale.

"Gotta get to class," she muttered. "Nice seeing you."

And before I had a chance to say anything more, she was gone, shuffling down the hall, head down, hustling as far away from me as she possibly could.

"What the fuck?" I whispered to Matt, but he just shrugged.

"Is she talking to you about me?" I asked, suddenly angry all over again, that same feeling of being judged slipping like needles under my skin. "Tell me the truth. She hates me now and I don't know why."

Brie had insisted Syd was avoiding me because of the money, that she was jealous about the lottery win and bitter that it wasn't her. That her bitterness made her judgy. All this time, I'd insisted Brie didn't know what she was talking about. That Syd was just going through something. But what if Brie was right? She'd certainly been ready to judge me about the parties, about Brie herself, about the shoes. Those could have been just the tip of the iceberg.

Matt shrugged again. "I never see her anymore. She seems . . . sad?"

"Shit." Suddenly, I felt sick inside. Of course Syd was sad. She'd broken up with Chase and then basically broken up with me. All this time I'd been so mad at her for avoiding me, but what if her anger with me was all depression talking? What if she needed help? Maybe I'd been so busy being mad about the little things that I'd become blind to the big thing. Maybe Syd wasn't okay at all.

"I've been a shitty friend," I said to Matt, not that he cared. I'd been too quick to write Syd off as a problem I didn't feel like solving, too dependent on the tit-for-tat let-her-return-when-she's-ready approach. It was time to force a conversation, unpleasant though it may be for us both.

When the lunch bell rang, I went to the one place I knew she'd be.

The lights were off in the ceramics room and the place smelled like clay and chicken soup. At first glance, it looked empty, until something moved in the corner near the curtained windows. In the back of the room, the thinnest stream of dust-moted light sliced through the shadows and illuminated the top of Syd's head. She sat on a stool at the back table facing the wrong way, her back to me.

"Hi." My heart pounded in my chest as I approached. She didn't respond, and then I noticed the wires of her headphones snaking beneath her hair. As I had done hundreds of times before, I rested my hand lightly on her shoulder. But this time she whirled around, flinching at my touch.

"Sorry, didn't mean to scare you."

"It's fine." She smiled tightly and her eyes wandered to the velvet curtains covering the windows and stayed there. She made no move to take her headphones out. Tinny music I didn't recognize continued to blare in her ears. What had happened to our friendship that she wouldn't—or couldn't—even look at me? That she didn't want to hear me?

I searched her face. "It's been a minute."

She looked at me for a moment and then looked away. Her eyes were puffy. I wondered if she'd been crying or not sleeping enough, or both. "Yeah. It has."

I watched her tug her headphones out at last, switch off her music, and slowly wrap the cord around itself. Her nails were bitten down, her cuticles ragged and chewed.

A silence opened up between us that felt unbridgeable. I cleared my throat.

"I miss you." I reached for Syd's hand. "How have you been?"

She pulled her hand away. "Fine." She blinked hard, her head tilted as if she was trying to figure out what I wanted.

"It feels like I never see you anymore," I said. And though I felt miserable and awkward, I tried to sound upbeat, like *huh, how weird is that?* "I mean around, at school."

Syd let out a sharp staccato laugh that startled me.

"Is it funny?"

"Just that you're only noticing it now. It's been almost a month." She looked away again. I could see her jaw working behind that tight smile she wore.

"I'm not just noticing now, actually," I said.

"Okay." Syd stared out the window. "Just figured you've been busy with your new friends."

I narrowed my eyes at Syd, who was still throwing herself a pity party that had clearly gone uninterrupted since last we'd talked. As if she'd done nothing, not pulled away at all, not made it clear how shallow she thought I'd become. "They could be your friends, too, you know. I always invited you—"

"Just . . . don't." She cut me off. "Is that what you came to say? That I should start hanging out with you and Brie?"

"I didn't come to say anything. I just miss you." That was the truth. I missed the friend I used to have. I owed her enough to tell her that, even if whoever she was right now didn't want to hear it. "Somewhere along the line I felt hurt, and I gave up on us a little bit, and I shouldn't have. That's why I'm here now."

Syd rolled her eyes.

Forcing myself to remain calm, to be better than this stupid fight, I racked my brain for something else we could talk about. "It's April. Spider's getting out soon, right?"

Syd nodded. "Just a couple more weeks."

"That's really great."

Syd pressed her lips together and nodded, staring straight ahead. "Hopefully it'll go okay."

"He's coming to live with you guys at home?"

"Where else would he go?" Syd shot me a puzzled look and rolled a piece of clay around on the table in front of her.

"I was sorry to hear about you and Chase," I said after a beat, trying to get her to open up without pressing her too hard. "I feel like I never got the full story from either of you."

"Oh?" Syd turned away from me but I thought I saw her roll her eyes again.

"Yeah. Though as you know, I never thought he was good enough for you." I smiled, trying for a joke.

"I guess you were right then." Syd stood up and smashed her clay ball onto a big hunk of clay, then started gathering up her books and pens, shoving everything into her backpack like she suddenly remembered someplace she needed to be. "It must feel great, to always be right."

"Can you drop the act for a few minutes? I just want to be there for you."

"Little late for all that," she snapped.

"Because you stopped communicating with me! It's a two-way street, you know. You stopped answering my texts, you've been literally *hiding*, and, like, *running* from me." I grabbed her forearm to try to get her attention, to show her I was here now, that I wanted to work things out. "What if we hang out this afternoon? We could go shopping or something—"

"Are you fucking serious?" Syd snatched her arm away and looked at me like I had three heads. Even in the dark room I could see her face had gone beet red, her eyes wide and flashing.

God, the drama. As if she'd played no part in our newfound distance. At least I was still trying to fix things. I couldn't say the same for her. "Is it such a crime to want to hang out?"

"Just listen to yourself!" Syd backed away, her eyes still wide. Judgment radiated from her, as if I was the stupidest, most evil person who had ever lived.

I moved toward her, suddenly indignant. "I'm being fucking *nice*."

"Listen to who you've become." Syd flung her backpack across her shoulders so hard she staggered from the weight of it. "You can't fix this with shopping. You can't solve everything with money. The old Rain knew that."

The old Rain? Anger flared in my chest. Maybe Brie was right, maybe all of this really was about Syd's jealousy. Seeing her here, now, her face twisted into a mocking smirk, it seemed so clear. "It's not about the goddamned shopping. It's about being together! I'm the same person I always was. Actually, I'm a better person than before. I'm happier now. I *like* going to parties, it turns out. I'm fucking enjoying myself. You're just never around to see it."

"You're so much more far gone than I'd realized. You're like her perfect little project." She was halfway to the door now.

"What are you talking about?"

Syd whirled around. "Or maybe she's *your* project. She's your *twin.* I'm surprised she let you out of her sight long enough for you to come here."

God, it was so much worse than I'd thought. The anger. The envy. Syd's certainty that she was so much better than us, that she had everything all figured out while I was just someone's *project,* a materialistic bitch. And then I said the words I knew would hurt her the most. "You just sound jealous, honestly. I don't need this negativity in my life. Maybe it's for the best we aren't exactly close right now."

Syd's face drained of color but that awful smirk remained. "I agree. It's for the best. Enjoy all your shopping. Enjoy your new best friend. All these years, you prided yourself on being so real and then the second they pay attention to you, you eat it up. I hope someday you'll figure out why you want their approval so much."

Her hand was on the door now. "You're twisting everything," I whispered. "Making it all seem so shallow and stupid. How did we even get here? How can my best friend be so wrong about me?"

"Yeah, what do I know?" Syd's eyes, when she looked back at me once more, were glassy. "I'm just a jealous, judgmental prude."

Before I could respond, she turned and ran out of the room.

21

"Classic Syd." Brie slapped her hand against her chair leg as if adding an audible period. "Better than everyone else." We were on my second-floor balcony overlooking the pool, and Brie was scribbling her color-coded notes on a stack of index cards at the little metal table I'd set out between our chairs, her usual elaborate study system in full swing. While she studied, I'd told her the gist of my and Syd's fight but left the parts that were about her out of it.

I nodded. "She thinks I've become this totally other person. She said I used to know not to try to solve problems with money, something like that."

"Of course money solves problems." Brie looked up from her notes at last. "I mean, objectively, it just does. Money makes everything easier."

I stared out over the pool and listened to the roar of the cicadas. Underneath them was the soft gurgle of the neighbor's landscaped waterfall. From up here, it was hard to argue with that. "I guess that's true."

"You were just trying to connect with an old friend, and she judged you for it. Why do you still care about her, anyway?" Brie stuck a pink pen in her mouth and began to write with a green one. She was only halfway focused on this conversation, halfway on memorizing AP history facts. "She doesn't care about you anymore.

She avoids you. She isn't even happy for you about"—she gestured around her without looking up from her index cards—"all this."

"She was happy for me when it happened," I said, but now I wasn't so sure. I tried to think back to when Joan and I first won the lottery, when things were still good between us. Syd had seemed excited for me . . . but maybe even then something had been off. "Not anymore. Now I wonder if I was an idiot to not have seen it all along."

"You were," Brie said, her pen still moving across her note cards. Leave it to Brie to still be cramming when everyone else was finally relaxing. It wasn't like USC was going to kick her out now, but whatever. "She wasn't happy for me when I left Termico and she isn't happy you did either."

I considered this. "I thought back then that she was sad because she'd miss me. Now I know she's just bitter."

"She's been a shitty friend," Brie said sharply. She shot me an exasperated look. "Someday you'll see it, when you get enough distance."

I nodded. "There's definitely distance now," I muttered. "She made sure of that."

"It's okay to take a break," Brie said. "You don't need that negativity in your life."

I watched Brie's hand move across her index cards and swallowed down a little burst of unease, remembering how I'd used this exact phrase with Syd earlier. Was Syd right that I'd changed? That I was desperate for approval, that I was Brie's *project*? I shook my head, wishing I could just forget about the fight altogether. It was exhausting trying to understand how things had exploded. Exhausting to keep talking to Syd in my head when she clearly wanted nothing to do with me anymore.

No, I decided. These realizations about Syd were my own. So what if Brie agreed with me? I hadn't changed. Couldn't if I tried. I'd been trying and failing to fit into other people's perceptions of who I should be my whole life. If Brie and I both had the thought that Syd was negative, well, that was because she was. "You're right," I said. "Still, it's all so fucking sad. I never expected to have this . . . rift."

"You tried to fix things, and she shit on you." Brie shrugged. "You gave it your best shot."

"I guess, yeah. It was like she wouldn't even give me a chance. Like I'd missed the boat on working things out. Maybe I kind of waited too long to clear the air, but I was caught up in . . ." I didn't want to say *caught up in hanging out with you,* but it was true. It was distracting. All the parties, all the people. I'd never imagined I'd actually enjoy it. But lately Brie's social life was as warm and embracing as Syd was cold and judgmental.

"Syd was caught up in her own life, too. She was all about Chase, couldn't have cared less about you during all that." Brie put her final pen down at last and gathered up her index cards in a neat pile. She pulled her hair out of its bun and began finger-combing the dark strands.

I nodded, mad at Syd all over again now. It took two to wait too long. If she insisted on pulling away from me, why should I be the one to force her to stop? I looked into Brie's eyes and saw someone who got me, someone who'd suffered with her own changes and challenges and come out the other side stronger. Someone I'd gotten so wrong for so long. I marveled that we'd spent all of high school so angry at each other, and about what? The fact that she'd left us? That we'd had one weird summer where we didn't talk, and she'd gone and made new friends and maybe didn't rush to bring us along? Being on the other side of it now, I realized how much I would've resented Brie no matter what she'd done. And now Syd was treating me the same way—in her mind, I'd left Termico and therefore I thought I was too good for her. It was so unfair.

"You know what would take your mind off this? Boba and makeup."

I smiled, remembering how much I enjoyed one of Brie's favorite stress relievers. There was nothing quite like drinking a massive bubble tea in Sephora while she applied a Vegas showgirl's face on top of my own.

"Except, shit, I forgot my wallet." Brie sighed as she followed me back inside.

"No big, I got it." I motioned for Brie to follow me to Joan's room. "You want a couple hundred just to tide you over?"

"Are you sure?" Brie widened her eyes. "I'll pay you back tomorrow."

"Don't worry about it." Brie had treated me more times than I could count. In Joan's room, I kept the lights off. Joan was out to dinner with Rusty and his boyfriend, Ricardo. She treated every Tuesday since they both had Wednesdays off. They had a long list of restaurants they were working their way through and Rusty's new favorite joke was that Joan was destroying all his hard work at the gym.

"Don't laugh," I said, flipping on the light in Joan's walk-in closet and heading to the top shelf in one corner where Joan kept spare towels and quilts neatly stacked. I reached behind them and pulled out a stack of bills wrapped in yellow paper. Ten thousand.

"Oh my fucking god," Brie breathed. "What. On. Earth."

"I know, it's bad. She needs to get a better spot for it."

"Has she heard of this invention from the sixteenth century where you lock your money up safely in a vault with armed guards and such? They call them banks."

"Joan doesn't trust banks." I rolled my eyes. "She thinks we're on the brink of a worldwide economic collapse and that she needs to keep cash on hand, blah blah blah." It was embarrassing having to explain Joan's theories to Brie. Syd would intrinsically understand all of this.

"Okaaay," Brie said, absorbing this. "Well, since we're here, let me see it."

"See what?"

"When else in my life will I get to see what six million dollars looks like?"

"Oh, it's not six. She gave like half of it to the tax accountant already."

"Three million then."

Suddenly this felt weird. I was already where I shouldn't be, already had showed Brie something Joan had told me not to show anyone else. "Maybe we shouldn't."

"Come on." Brie elbowed me in the side. "Let me see it."

After I'd gotten all the quilts and towels down from the closet, we climbed onto a chair and took a look at the money. It was neatly stacked and wrapped. It smelled as it always did, new and chemical. "So funny how everyone worships this stupid paper," I said to break the silence.

Brie squinted at the pile, her head tilting sideways. "Hey, um, not to be nosy . . ."

"Too late," I joked.

"But that doesn't look like all that much to me."

"What do you mean?" The money took up the entire back wall of the top shelf in one corner. There was tons of it.

"I mean, are you guys counting it regularly? Monitoring your spending?"

"Not really," I admitted. "I mean, I'm not. Some days I do worry about it. . . . Maybe Joan's counting it, but I doubt it."

"She's out to dinner right now, right? And didn't you tell me she's looking into real estate investments? Seems like she could blow through a lot of this, fast."

I pressed my lips together, suddenly feeling protective of Joan. *Of course she's enjoying spending money,* I wanted to say. *Remember what it's like to be poor?* "She's enjoying herself a little, yeah. We both are."

"In a bank, they give you statements. You can see what you're spending. But this way"—Brie raised her eyebrows at the shelf full of money—"nobody will notice until it's too late."

"Oh god, what a horrible thought." I chuckled, but inside I felt uneasy and out of my depth, my chest fluttering with anxiety all of a sudden.

"It happens all the time." Brie grabbed my wrist and gave me an intense look. "Trust me, you don't want to go back to being poor."

I considered this. Maybe Joan *was* going too hog wild. She'd never been great with money before, so why would she start being a financial whiz now? And I'd done plenty of damage already, too. The car, all the clothes . . . just living in a whole new way where I never gave money a second thought anymore except to make sure I was generous with it. "Maybe you're right. You think I should just sneak in and count it all the time?"

Brie shook her head. "I know you love your mom, but you know what she's like. Put it in the bank for her. At least put *some* of it in a bank. You'd be doing her a favor."

"I can't," I said. "It's not my money."

"Right, right. Well, you should put some of it somewhere else then. Someplace safe." Brie sighed and tapped her chin in thought. "In the movies, they always hide money in the air-conditioning vents."

I looked to the top of the closet and studied the vent for a moment. It had four screws. Looked easy enough to bust into with tools and a little patience.

"She might notice if I did something like that." The closet was kind of a mess, but it had a logic to it.

Brie raised an eyebrow. "Would that be so bad? All you'd have done is protect her, help save her from herself. It's not like you'd have spent it."

"I'll think about it." For now, I wanted to put everything back the way it was and just get out of here. Something about looking at all that money sitting naked on the shelf felt wrong, like I'd let loose an intimate family secret.

Which, in a way, I had.

22

"Rainey! Something terrible has happened."

I was in a dead sleep when I felt Joan's hands shake my shoulders. The smell of her post-shower gardenia moisturizer filled the pitch-black of my room.

"What," I groaned. I'd fallen asleep with my phone next to me and pawed it now to check the time: 2:12. Joan hadn't stopped keeping waitress hours. I pushed her hands away. "Get off me! I'm up."

"The money. I went to check it and a lot of it—" My mother's voice broke. Even in the blackness I could tell she was struggling not to cry. "A lot of it is missing."

Shit. Joan was keeping better track of it than I'd thought. It had only been a week since I'd decided to move some of the money.

"I have it. It's fine."

In the darkness, her footsteps moved away from me. I turned over, thinking that was it, that I'd go back to sleep and we'd talk about it tomorrow, but a moment later the room was shot through with blinding overhead light. I covered my head with my pillow but Joan pulled it off.

"Excuse me?" Looming over me, her nostrils flared. Her face shone with serums and other gunk she now slathered onto her skin, but her eyes were red. Her quick-dry turban was askew on her head. I almost laughed at how ridiculous she looked, but bit the insides of my cheeks instead.

I sat up, squinting against the light. "Can we put on the lamp instead? It's so bright—"

"You took the money?" She bent so close to me I could feel her breath on my cheeks. "In what world did you think you could do that?"

"It's fine. I just moved some of it."

"What the hell for? I've been scared to death! I thought we'd been robbed!"

"To save you from yourself." Brie's words came tripping off my tongue before I could even think them through. "Because you aren't careful with money and you're going to spend it all."

I didn't expect the slap. When it came, my cheek stung with pain and I saw stars.

"What the fuck?" If I wasn't awake before, I was awake now. I leapt out of bed. "That really hurt!"

"Good." Joan took a step back but she was breathing hard through her nose as if struggling to keep calm. I sniffed the air and thought I smelled wine.

"Have you been drinking?" I was mad enough now to unleash everything that would hurt my mother.

"*How dare you.* I have done *everything* for you. I have worked myself to the bone to raise you. I have always celebrated you, always defended you. Always believed in you. I have *loved* you . . . and this is how you treat me? You steal from me and say you're *saving me from myself*?"

"Calm down," I said. "I told you, it's not stolen."

Joan's eyes flew open even wider. I stepped away from her, suddenly worried she might hit me again. "Don't you dare tell me to calm down."

"Sorry! Jesus," I muttered.

"Where is it, Rainey?" Joan threw open my closet, started rummaging around. I moved closer to her, intending to pull her out of the closet by her arm, but she whirled around and grabbed my chin in her hands, her eyes wild. "Where is the goddamned money?"

"I don't understand why you're so upset," I said, my voice small and strangled in a way I hated. I tried to wrench my chin free of her but Joan was strong. "Let go of me."

With her face so close to mine, I was positive I smelled the alcohol on her breath. "You stole from me. I gave you access to our funds and you violated my trust and now you are acting like a smug little bitch. That's why I'm upset." She finally let my face go and I stumbled backward against the bed, fury rising in my blood, my whole body shaking with adrenaline now.

"If that's how you feel about me, maybe I should move out." I rubbed my cheek where it still stung. I felt tears forming in the corners of my eyes. My mother had never said anything so nasty and hateful to me before. She'd certainly never hit me. It felt like something fundamental had just broken between us, and like we might not come back from it.

Joan folded her arms across her chest. She looked down at me and shook her head like she couldn't believe what she was seeing. "If you're going to steal from me, maybe you should. Now tell me where the money is."

I pointedly didn't look at the AC vent above my bed. I wasn't going to tell Joan about it if this was how she was going to act. A new avenue was opening up in my mind. I didn't need to wait until graduation. I could take some of the money and drive west right now. I could be free. Why should I hand it all back to my mother to waste it all on wine and shady real estate investments? "Not until you get ahold of yourself."

Joan lunged at me and I rolled across my bed, sprang up, and ran to the other side of the room.

"Get out of my room," I cried, adrenaline pumping through me faster than I could process what I was doing. I grabbed the nearest thing I could find, an empty water glass, and brandished it in front of me. "Now. Or I'm calling the cops."

Joan pulled her kimono tighter around her. "You'd better think long and hard about what kind of a person you plan to be, Rainey. This—" She waved in my direction, her hands circling the air helplessly. "This is not who I raised. You can't be a thief and live here in my house."

On her way out of the room, she slammed the door so hard that the BE HERE NOW print the room had come with fell off the wall, the glass in the frame cracking clean in half. Perfect, I thought, because I was about to be somewhere else.

In a fury, I threw together some clothes and my toothbrush and stuffed everything into a backpack. *My house.* Not our house, but hers alone.

I got in the car and drove barefoot through the night, my chest thrumming, visions of burning down my life shimmering in my mind. Joan had the right idea when she'd thrown everything into that bonfire on our lawn in Termico.

I drove through the dark streets as if saying goodbye to this stupid town, this place that could not contain me. I would make a plan to come back for some money and then I would leave here for real, find somewhere I could disappear, make a new life, forget this suffocating furnace of a town and finally start to breathe. Maybe it would be LA like I'd always planned, but suddenly the whole world seemed possible.

I thought about going to Syd's house, where I'd gone a million times before when Joan was too much for me. But I couldn't go there. Syd hated me. There was only one place left.

At 3 AM I pulled into Brie's cul-de-sac and climbed up the trellis to her little Juliet balcony off her attic room. I'd done it once before. She'd shown me how. Had told me I was always welcome there, that Ed took Ambien and slept like the dead. But I remembered Ed was out of town, some kind of car convention.

I took a deep, shaky breath before I knocked on her window, knowing she'd let me in.

PART VII

SYDNEY

MAY

THE NIGHT OF THE FIRE

23

The second Sunday of May, when it arrived, seemed to have taken forever and no time at all. It had been circled on Mom's kitchen calendar for months, *Spider home!* written in one of my old glitter gel pens, gone over two, three times in her shaky cursive. Written even bigger than the other exciting date at the end of the month— *Sydney's graduation!*

He'd insisted Mom and I shouldn't come pick him up—he took a Greyhound bus the whole way down I-5 and had Whit pick him up from the station in Cathedral City.

Mom was nervous all day. She'd taken the day before off from Four Fronds and had spent the whole day scrubbing the bathroom, dusting in Spider's room, even rearranging the furniture in the living room. The carpet still had its bald spots and the cabinet veneers were still peeling off at the corners, but at least the place was spotless. I watched from the couch as she threw open the yellowed curtains in the kitchen and yanked open the blinds in the living room with a flourish. We normally kept the lights off and the shades drawn in the spring and summer to save money on airconditioning, but not today.

"How does it look, honeybun? Does it look nice?" Mom clasped her hands together and assessed the place.

"It looks really good," I said, trying to smile, wanting to focus on this one small, good thing instead of the angry knot that had lodged itself permanently in my stomach.

"He deserves it." She peered out the window and down the dusty street, waiting for Whit's blue pickup truck.

The cake sat on the counter, frosted and jolly and leaning like a squat Tower of Pisa with coconut sprinkles all over it. Mom had woken up early and made it from a mix.

"Do you think he'll be different?" I took the spatula and scooped some leftover frosting from its bowl, then brought it with me to the couch and took my time licking it off. What I meant was: Will he be damaged?

"We'll find out, won't we?" she said brightly. "I have high hopes."

"You always have high hopes." I smiled. It was what differentiated her from me. Even though my and Spider's dad had left her on her own with nothing, my mother was an optimist. Whereas I had always had to talk myself out of the certainty that something terrible waited just around the corner.

"Little sis, all grown up." Spider stood in the doorway of my room several hours later, his hand snaking in and out of a huge bag of Flamin' Hot Cheetos Mom had bought for his welcome home. His favorite.

I was slumped on my bed, my back pressed up against the wood paneling as I scrolled social media for images of Brie and Rain, an addict looking for my fix. With each new filtered video or image of Brie, malice sliced through me like a blade.

Today there were two pictures. Rain's chipped black nails visible around Brie's shoulders. Another one of her wild mop of hair and a slice of her profile, facing away, an expanse of canyon opening out before her. Brie faced the camera, laughing at something, her dimple popping. Studying these had become the bitter fuel that powered my days.

Earlier today, Matt had posted a sped-up video of Chase on a half-pipe. I'd watched him catch air and slice back down again and again, that easy grace leaving me almost breathless with longing. Each time I felt a stab in my chest, as if grieving someone who had died too young. Soon enough, though, the pain morphed into rage. Rage at myself for having been played, and at Brie for taking everything away from me and making herself so unrepentantly cozy in the life I'd built.

"Is this what being all grown up looks like?" I asked. I glanced up at Spider and closed the app.

"Something's different about you." He moved into my room, sat awkwardly on the far corner of my bed. I noticed how heavy the newly formed slabs of skin looked along his cheeks and neck, how absent of light his eyes were now.

"It's my newfound bitterness."

Spider snorted. "I heard about the lottery. How is Rain the Pain liking all that sweet moolah?"

"I don't really know," I said. "Haven't seen her much lately."

"I hear she's hanging out with Brianna Walsh." Spider examined the inside of the Cheetos bag, not looking at me, but I could tell he was fishing for dirt. "That true?"

"Who told you that?"

"Whit."

I wondered how Whit knew. Had Rain bumped into him somewhere?

"They're best friends," I said simply. It was the first time I'd said it out loud, to anyone. It sounded like such a simple fact, so why did it still hurt me so much?

"Brianna Walsh is bad news," Spider muttered. "Would've thought Rain was smarter than that."

"Same." I shrugged, wishing we could talk about something else.

"So who do you hang with these days?" Spider asked after an awkward minute of silence. "Now that you lost your beloved Rain?"

"You're looking at her." I tried to laugh, but it came out like a bark.

"That's no good."

I shrugged, wishing he would leave so I could get back to my Internet stalking.

"You need to get out there again. Mend the fences, get back into the swing and all that." Spider sucked Cheeto dust off his thumb and forefinger and didn't say more. I'd forgotten what it was like, communicating with him. His slow-drip style of making a point, his way of making you coax everything out of him. "There's a party tonight. I heard about it from Whit."

I tried not to sigh. Spider would understand eventually how much of a recluse I was. I didn't need to bombard him with it all at once.

"In Desert Hot Springs. One of those sick mansions up in the hills. Whit was going to try to get there but he has to work, so he's not sure."

"Cool," I said. "But I'm not interested."

"Oh come *on*." A petulance caught in his voice. "Don't make me beg. We should go."

"You and me?" *No thanks.*

The truth was, I already knew about this particular party. It was at Candice's house. Her mom and stepdad were in Europe and her stepbrother was home from college already and throwing himself a birthday rager. "Brad told me to invite everyone I've ever met," she'd said when we were finishing a soviet propaganda poster for AP history. "I know you never come out, Sydney, but you're more than welcome." She'd looked up then, straight at me, smirked, then looked away.

"I don't really go to parties anymore."

"Screw that," Spider said. "You're coming."

"I'm not." *Crawl away, Spidey. Spin your web somewhere else,* I thought, then immediately felt guilty. He was just as friendless as

I was. He needed me. But this was asking too much. "I'm sorry. I'm just not."

Spider looked at me then like it was the first time he'd seen me, actually seen me, since he'd gotten home.

"It was hard inside, man." He sprawled out in the exact center of my bed and propped his head on a pillow, making it clear he had no intention of leaving anytime soon. He stared up at the ceiling and took a deep breath. "I didn't want to bum you and Mom out, but I went through a lot up there. Just, like, drifting through the days, almost not even caring that I would get out. Depression, I guess. And sometimes I just get so *angry*. My life was ripped out from under me, you know? I was barely an adult. I had just finished high school. And now I have to live with it on my record forever." I watched his fists clench so hard his knuckles turned white. "Like, game over, before my life even got started."

I bit my lip and looked away, thinking of the one awful visit Mom and I had made to Pine Grove. After an hour-long wait inside the most depressing waiting room ever, we sat at a table in the visitation room that an expressionless guard led us to. Next to us was a miserable-looking woman visiting a man with a black eye. They whispered furtively to each other and never smiled. When Spider came out and sat across from us, pale and haunted in his beige jumpsuit, Mom began to cry softly and didn't stop until it was time to leave. All around us, babies and toddlers reached for their fathers or shrank from them, these men who must have felt like strangers. I'd focused on keeping the conversation with Spider going, noting how different he was only four months into his sentence. The dark circles under Spider's eyes, his hair shaved soldier-short, his dopey Great Dane quality vanished now. In high school, his body had seemed too big on him, like he was just a hyper kid playing the part of a grown man, but now at only nineteen he was solid, immovable, suddenly trapped in a tired man's body that moved only with tremendous effort. He spent most of our forty-minute visit eyeing the prison guard who stood in one corner, hand resting on the handle of a Taser as if he was itching to use it.

At the end of the visit, Spider had cleared his throat and said to Mom not to come visit anymore because it was too sad for them both. He didn't want us seeing him this way anymore, he'd said.

My throat had filled with a swallowed sob. My big brother, the wild child, reduced to this. It seemed so very wrong.

Looking at him now, I wondered if he'd ever be able to shake what prison had done to him, if the goofy brother I'd grown up with was gone forever.

"I'm so sorry, Spi. I wish to god you hadn't gotten arrested."

"So, take me out. Show me a good time. I need this." Spider turned on his side and picked little fabric pills off my comforter. "I need to feel like a normal person. With normal people, happy people. That's what's great about a party, right? Happy people?"

I nodded, feeling myself caving.

"It's too weird for me to walk in there alone. With you there, it's like I have a reason to show up." He glanced up at me and my stomach twisted with guilt. I knew I'd been beaten.

"Fine," I said, even though everything in me screamed no. The clock radio on my dresser said 6:18. "We'll get there around nine. But I don't want to make it a late night. I can do an hour, an hour and a half tops. Is that okay?"

"Yup." Spider hoisted himself and his bag of Cheetos off my bed. "Maybe Rain the Pain will be there with her new friends and you'll make peace."

"Oh, they'll definitely be there." I'd have to find a way to skirt the sidelines of the party, to blend in enough so that I didn't see Rain, Brie, or Chase.

If only that had been possible.

24

"I can't go in."

I had just pulled the parking brake on the Fiesta at the end of the long line of cars on a twisty street called Glen View, strung high up on the side of the mountain that rose up behind Brie's neighborhood. We'd driven by her turnoff just a couple of minutes before and I'd cringed, remembering the humiliation of the last time I'd been there.

To the right of the car, just past the inadequate-looking metal guardrail, was a steep drop-off into a black canyon, all creosote and boulders, and then shadowed negative space in the moonless night.

Spider sighed in the passenger seat. "'Course you can."

I shook my head, tightened my hands around the steering wheel, ten and two, as if I might pull the car away at any moment. "You go in, have fun. I'll wait for you here," I said quietly.

"Nope." Spider flipped down the visor mirror, checked his hair, his teeth. "You're coming. Ol' pusherman ain't going in without his little sis."

"Spi." *Don't make me.*

"Sydney."

"I'm . . . I can't. I'm not in a good place."

A mocking little half-smile wiggled at my brother's mouth. There was no point in explaining. My alienation couldn't compete with his. My pain couldn't compete with his. And he'd just shrug it off or laugh if I tried spelling it out.

But then he nodded and pulled something from the pocket of his hoodie. A pill bottle that was a strange shade of green. He unscrewed the cap, grabbed my hand, and shook two pills into my palm. "Chew them up. They'll work faster that way."

"What is it?" They were powdery ovals, faintly yellow.

"It'll relax you. You'll feel like you're flying."

I shot him a skeptical look. "Where'd you get these?"

He passed me the bottle. PINE GROVE DETENTION CENTER was stamped on one side of the bottle along with a bright orange sticker that said CONTROLLED SUBSTANCE. "The doctor up there was loose with the prescription pad," he said. "I have a whole pharmacy at home."

Out the driver's-side window, two girls made their way toward the big white house, heads bent together, laughing at something one of them had said. Their purses swung against their hips, their faces animated with secrets only they could know. I had that once, I thought wistfully.

The headache I'd had off and on for days pulsed as if it were alive, a sinister stab of something bad radiating toward both ears. Missing Rain *hurt,* physically and in every other way.

"Maybe I'll take one," I whispered. "How many do you take, when you take them?"

The girls passed the car now, still laughing. So lucky and they didn't know it.

"Four, five? They're perfectly safe."

My head and my heart ached, a wistful kind of dread washing over me about what was coming, what new hurts might arrive beyond high school, what new disappointments. Maybe tonight didn't have to hurt this much. I chewed up the first pill, gagging at the bitter chalk it left on my tongue. Spider handed me a glass bottle he'd fished out from under his seat, some half-drunk iced tea

I'd bought from the Shell station days ago. I drank it down, silty and sweet.

"Take two. Two is good if you want to fly." He grinned and I realized I had missed that smile more than I'd let myself admit. Spider, my brother. With me forever, through whatever would come.

Already, just having tasted the pill, I felt more relaxed. A little more reckless.

"Okay." I chewed the second one up and finished the tea. "Flying sounds nice."

When we got out of the car, the air was a warm caress, the temperature having dropped by now to a tolerable mid-eighties.

"I'm glad you're home," I said as we walked together toward the house. The thump of trap music swelled into the road for a moment and then went silent again, leaving only the usual racket of crickets and rustling from the canyon.

Spider put his bulky arm around my shoulder, pulled me so I knocked against him and almost fell. "Me, too."

As we walked, I began to feel lighter. A new energy reared up inside me like a jack-in-the-box springing open. In fact, I realized, I was starting to feel downright chatty. "You going to be a respectable member of society now?" Had my words been a little slurry, sticky, or was I imagining it? Had "respectable" sounded like "receptacle," or was I just paranoid?

"Eh." He shrugged theatrically. "Probably not. But you never know, right? Anything could happen." He flashed me a spidery grin, a real one, the first full-blown smile I'd seen from him since he'd walked into the living room earlier today. His jaw was working, eyes narrowed as we passed the threshold of an open security gate, the grassy sweetness of just-mown lawn in our nostrils.

"How about a receptacle member then?" I laughed at my own stupid joke, linked my arm with my brother's. The pills were already working. My sad self was flattening out, my anger and hurt no longer craggy rocks I had to navigate. Tonight began to feel like a smooth surface I could glide across.

"You excited?" he teased as we climbed the gleaming white steps toward the columned porch.

"Not the word I'd use . . ." I trailed off, focusing now on the few kids who rocked like the elderly on rocking chairs placed along the wraparound porch, sucking on beers. I saw Danny Schuster and he waved to me.

"We made it!" he beamed. "Finally getting the hell out of high school!"

I smiled and nodded, grateful to have found a person here who wasn't linked to anyone who hated me. I moved closer to him, my fingers grazing the house's shiny white columns, opening my mouth to say something clever, hoping something would emerge.

But then Candice burst out of the front door, a red Solo cup in each hand. She strode toward Danny and handed him one, and fell into his lap on the rocking chair, her beer lapping over the cup and spilling as she kissed him full on the mouth. The kiss was so flagrant and passionate that I looked away, embarrassed in the face of it. Danny Schuster, who had worn headgear for two solid years in middle school, who raised his hand so often in our AP classes that the teachers joked that he was carrying the lot of us. Danny, who ran cross country, who was whippet-thin and who would happily show you his aerodynamically shaved legs during track season, who made me cringe he was so dorky sometimes, was wrapped in the arms of Candice Lombardi herself, who used to say proudly that she'd only dated first-string varsity football players, who actually lived in this massive house. My god had things changed. Just as I was about to turn away, Candice pulled apart from Danny and grimaced a hello at me.

"We studied together a lot this year," she said simply, flashing a sheepish grin. "Go grab a beer, Sydney. I'm glad you came. It's the end of the year. Everyone's friends now."

"Thanks," I said, and drifted away from her, following Spider as he moved toward the open front door. Candice and Danny. A lid for every pot, as Mom would say. Except mine. My own pot was lidless, cracked or deformed in some way. And inside I was boiling, boiling.

I pushed the black lacquered front door open and stepped through.

25

Inside was a maze of dim, noisy rooms, each one crowded. It looked like the whole school was here—enough bodies to fill Candice's hotel-sized house. The air thudded with screamed conversations on top of an old Nicki Minaj song I'd listened to with Rain a million times.

I followed Spider from room to room, wishing I could just go back to the car.

My brother greeted people here and there, performing those elaborate handshake-high-five combo greetings boys did. I was happy to let Spider soak up the attention since all I wanted was to be invisible here, just floating along quietly on my little prison-pill cloud. Slouching in my hooded tank top sort of worked—a few people waved hello to me, but otherwise I was mostly ignored.

"Oh my god, look who it is!" Anya Patel had recently redone her bangs in a bright magenta and wore tiny stick-on sequins dotted along the ridges of her cheekbones. She grabbed my brother in a bear hug that went on a weirdly long time.

During their endless hug, the Nicki Minaj song ended and something newer and harsher came on that sounded like a list of reasons to kill someone, the singer's voice deep and casually murderous. I danced along, an awkward third wheel in this reunion, my mouth stretched into an involuntary smile, my whole face frozen around it. *Doesn't matter,* I realized. *Nothing matters.* By now, the pills had more than kicked in.

"Hey, babe!" Spider yelled when they finally pulled apart. "Long time no see. Love the hair."

Babe? Love the hair?

"I'm so happy he's back!" Anya shouted in my ear. She pulled me in for a quick, cordial hug and the three of us headed together toward the kitchen with Anya's arm around Spider's shoulders like they were the best of friends. I followed behind them, still smiling like a demented clown, the murder music thumping down my spine.

Anya peeled away in the gleaming kitchen, leaving us at a white-marbled island that had become a well-stocked bar. The pills buzzing inside me, I yelled to my brother over the music. "You're friends with Anya?"

Spider laughed. "I know everyone."

He began mixing drinks and a dizziness washed over me. I breathed in someone's pot smoke, a sickly sweet vapor, so many people around us and not a one I wanted to talk to. Over by the kitchen sink stood the boys' swim team, all shoulders and shaved heads. They shouted "Chug, chug, chug," at a boy in the center, the keg nozzle in his mouth like a medical tube, as if his insides were being pulled out of him and into the metal cylinder below. But that couldn't be right. I blinked, swallowed down the saliva that had filled my mouth. Spider pressed a drink into my hand then, a Solo cup filled with blood.

Or no, it wasn't blood. I looked closer and sniffed at it. Grape juice mixed with alcohol. I drank it fast, lukewarm and horrible though it was, like grape-flavored gasoline. I was so thirsty, thirstier than I'd ever been. It was gone in an instant.

"Well, well. Looks like you learned how to party." Spider took the cup back and mixed another one. I watched the juice slosh into the cup, the splash of clear booze on top, Spider's sure hand with the business of bartending. "Here's another one. You flying yet?"

I shrugged and downed the second drink. It tasted slightly better than the first. I whirled around and felt the air in the kitchen throb with all the energy of the young bodies crammed in together. The music, the loud talking, the swim team still chanting. Maybe I *was* flying. If I closed one eye I could float high up above this crowd, swooping through space like a bat, none of this mattering, none of this real. And then before I even realized it, I was dancing, pin-balling against random shoulders and hips of the tightening crowd.

I threw my head back and the laugh that flew out of me was that of a stranger.

"I think I feel it." I pulled Spider to me, wanting to dance like we did when we were eight and ten, jumping on the sofa, the car-pet hot lava, the *Power Rangers* theme song blaring from the TV, our holey pajamas, the joy and abandon of dancing with my big brother, Mr. Hyperactive, just wilding out.

Why hadn't I wanted to come? I wondered now, grabbing at Spider's wrists with both my hands. This party was the best.

"Okay, let's get you away from the bar a little," he said, half bear-hugging me, half hoisting me so that I bobbed alongside him through the kitchen's gleaming French doors. Outside was a mas-sive flagstone patio, a firepit built into the center of it, flames danc-ing on the faces of dozens of kids around it. Leering faces, laughing faces, stoned and drunk faces. Faces I'd stared at all my life.

Everyone was really good looking, I realized. How had I never noticed that before?

Everything felt riskier out here, quieter and somehow more seri-ous, but also like it couldn't touch me. *So soon,* I felt like shouting, *so soon this will all be over.* So soon, we'd all go our separate ways, become something else. Shed our skins.

Along the sides of the patio were couches filled with boys, two girls grinding together in front of them on a makeshift dance floor, performing a version of sexiness copied from the Internet. A few boys closest to them whooped and hollered. Matt Richardson, who had grown a scraggly beard of late, waved to me from across the patio where he sat on an ottoman packing a pipe with a few skater boys. My heart pounded as I braced myself to see Chase, but he wasn't with them. I waved to Matt, a pang of missing him stabbing me in the chest.

Over by the firepit, Spider had found some more people he knew and was already regaling them with prison stories. "My cellmate stole his own grandmother's life savings," he was saying to three boys whose faces were rapt with attention. Had he been *everyone's* dealer?

I edged back toward the house, suddenly feeling brave and reckless. Chase hadn't been outside, but he was probably here somewhere. Maybe it was time to talk.

Pushing my way back through the kitchen, I felt perfect—unflappable, maybe even invincible. Better than I'd ever felt in my life. Flying like this, I could confront Chase, ask him why I hadn't been enough. Ask him what was wrong with me. Whatever he'd say, I could handle it. Maybe I could even handle talking to Rain, who was around here somewhere, too.

I moved through room after room in that maze of a house, feeling strong and powerful and like everything was funny. I was a little like my brother now, I realized. When you've lost everything, nobody and nothing can hurt you. Spider had reached his nadir, and he was stronger for not allowing it to kill him. Now I was like that, too. There was nothing more that anyone could take from me. Friendless, betrayed, alone—my pain was also my power.

I walked down a long hallway and a song that sounded like *nasty nasty girl* pulsed through the air. I brushed by a group of junior girls, all shiny hair and strong perfume, gossip flying from one of them to the next.

I moved farther down the hall, my head swiveling. *Where are you, Chase McAllister? Where are you, Rain Santangelo? With your new best friend?*

Speeding up, I climbed a set of wildly carpeted stairs, all paisleys and peacock feathers underfoot. Another group of girls moved in sync toward me like a school of fish, this time with Candice herself as its leader. The lady of the manor, back again in the flesh! She was flanked by Deirdre, Anya, and Min. I wobbled toward them, smiling, invincible.

"Hi, Candice," I slurred, someone else's voice where mine should be. "Have you seen Chase?" *I want to tell him what an ass he is.*

"I have," Anya piped up. "I'll take you."

She smiled, put her bare arm around my shoulders and pulled me with her. As we walked down yet another hallway (How big was this house, exactly? Did it just go on forever?), she put a hand on my elbow, leaned in. "Listen, there's something I've been meaning to tell you." She paused and looked around, her cheekbones glittering in the dark. "I think Brie played me about the Chase thing."

"What?" My stomach dropped.

"You and Chase were cute together. I feel bad about it," she said. Her gaze moved from the floor to me. "I just thought you should know. In case, like, you were upset with him about that. I know you guys broke up, so maybe you don't care."

"What do you mean, she played you?"

"I mean, it wasn't just me. She told a few people. But then later she acted shocked that we'd thought it was true. She pretended she was kidding. Who knows, maybe she wanted it to get back to you. She messes with people, you know? Always has. Just like how she messed with your brother. 'Course now it's all Rain, Rain, Rain. She has no time for any of us losers anymore." Anya laughed then, like it was all the biggest joke.

I looked into her gold-flecked eyes and felt a cold sweat slick down my back. Brie lied about hooking up with Chase? We'd broken up over a lie?

I formed my mouth into the semblance of a smile, though I felt like smashing something. Or someone. "Thanks for telling me. It doesn't matter anymore."

"Okay then." Anya let out a breath and smiled at me. "I'm glad. I'm sure you and Chase would've probably broken up anyway, right? I just didn't want it on my conscience anymore. It's the end of the year, clean slate, you know?"

"I get it. Don't worry, clean slate." But not for Brie. Something was almost fitting together in my brain, and I looked at Anya as I groped drunkenly toward it.

What had Spider said about Brie tonight before the party with that bitter tone in his voice? I'd passed right by it then, but now it echoed in my ears like a clue. *Brianna Walsh is bad news. Would've thought Rain was smarter than that.*

I opened my mouth to ask Anya what she'd meant about Brie messing with my brother, but before I got the words out she was pointing me toward a door. A moment later I was inside, sailing into clouds of pot smoke, looking for Chase.

The room was a vast office lined with floor-to-ceiling bookshelves. Candice's parents probably called it the library. Trip-hop skulked from invisible speakers and a few kids played Cards Against Humanity at a big gleaming desk. Others lay on leather couches or sat on the plush carpeting, so thick in this room I could feel my shoes sink into it.

And then Chase appeared right in front of me. *Oh.* That flop of hair in his eyes. The crooked smile. The pink mouth I'd once wanted to live inside. Still did, really.

"Hey." He smiled nervously and led me to a window seat lined with bookshelves. It was a tiny oasis of privacy, a silken pillow laid along the mahogany as if someone had built it for tearful conversations, for secrets to be revealed, for girls to ask *why* of boys who could never really say.

"Hi."

"Hey." He looked at me from under that flop of hair. His pained expression said he was being cautious, and also that he was sad. "You still skating?" His first conversation with me in weeks and this was what he most wanted to know. Or maybe it was all he felt safe talking about.

"Not really." My hand had a mind of its own. It touched his upper arm, the muscle in the tricep just below where his shirtsleeve ended. A part of him I'd loved, still loved. He wore a new shirt, red-and-black plaid. So new I could see the creases where it had been folded. I wanted to cry and also to laugh. Instead I swallowed hard.

"Too bad." Chase said. "You should be."

"I should, you're right." I let my eyes meet his. "Mostly I just study and wait for it to end."

"For what to end?"

God, that had come out sounding morbid. "School. Everything." I shrugged and tried to smile but what I felt seeing him now was a bare sadness, like stepping into an empty room after a party.

I leaned in, whispered in his ear. "What happened to us?"

So near him now, I smelled that Chase smell I'd loved, Old Spice deodorant and Carmex and something that reminded me of the way trees smelled after a rainstorm.

"That's *my* line." He smiled. The way he said it, like it really hurt him, was a knife to my heart.

"I guess it is," I said. I leaned against the window, the cool glass on my cheek, and wondered if I might break it with my skull. What would it feel like to bleed out at this party, to have the last thing I ever saw be Chase's face, his sad eyes? "But you *know*. We both do."

"I don't. I wish I did. I was so into you." The knife to the heart was twisting now, hearing this.

"I think I made a mistake." The cool glass. I put my palm on the window, too. "I may have been confused. Or . . . misled. Someone told me you were hooking up with Brie."

Chase's jaw pulsed. His nostrils flared. "Why would you believe that? You shouldn't have shut me out. I would have proven . . . I would have told you there was nobody else." The look he gave me was so earnest, so vehement, I knew instantly I'd been duped. I'd ruined everything, and for nothing.

"I thought—" I groped for how to explain. "I got some bad information."

"It was nothing. Just stupid body shots. I tried to tell you it was no big deal."

Ah. The knife twisted deeper. What he'd been thinking I was mad about and what I'd been thinking happened were two different things.

"I should have believed you. I should have listened harder."

"You should have."

I shut my eyes for a moment, wishing I could rewind everything to the night he'd driven me home from work. That feeling of flying continued, only now I was experiencing a mild spinning sensation. And flying on a carpet of pain.

"And then you wouldn't take my calls. I must have sent you a hundred texts."

"And then you stopped." I looked at Chase and swallowed hard, determined not to cry.

"You never answered! I thought you wanted me to stop." Chase looked at me like he'd been slapped. "I didn't want to be that guy. I just . . . I guess I figured you'd made up your mind."

"I did." I sighed, furious at myself. Furious at the world. "I'm sorry."

"I'm sorry, too."

"I know." My head had begun to throb again at the base of my skull, back where the migraine had been starting before the party. But it wasn't pain there now, it was a white-hot anger. A rage I'd never felt before or since. The hookup with Brie was so obviously a lie planted like an Easter egg just for me, I saw now, that a child could have figured it out. Brie had banked on me believing it. Had known I was insecure enough to doubt Chase's feelings. And, as predictable as mud after a rainstorm, it had worked. Just like claiming

Rain as her own had worked. All she'd had to do to seal the deal was suggest the stupid body shots, which she no doubt had made sure to get on film in case she needed the footage to mess with me later. Maybe tagging Chase on her feed, inviting him over, was also just to mess with me. Now I knew Chase hadn't showed up there out of infatuation with her. "And I guess Brie invited you to her house, that one night when you were there and I ran off?"

Chase nodded. "She said we should talk about what to do about you, but they didn't really have any ideas. I ended up going home less than an hour later." Chase looked away, embarrassed, maybe, about how hard he'd tried to solve the puzzle I'd left him with.

Chase reached out and stroked my cheek now, tenderly, tenderly. I took his hand and held it for a moment before I stood up. There was no time for tenderness now. Someone had done this to us, had interfered with my life in every conceivable way, had taken everything from me that mattered. And I'd let her. I had made it so easy. And there was no reason to think she hadn't manipulated me away from Rain the same way.

I'd had enough of all of it.

"I need to go find someone," I said. "It was really nice seeing you. I'm so sorry I ruined everything."

My hands shook as I bolted from the room, not daring to look back, not daring to slow down though I heard his voice floating above the trip-hop saying, "Hey, wait."

But I'd waited too long already.

If before I'd felt like flying, now my strength felt superhuman as I flew down the hallway, my body shedding its worn-out old skin of inhibitions and self-control, a new self emerging for a reckoning of old accounts.

I'd been stabbed in the back long enough. It was time for someone else to hurt for once.

26

I made my way downstairs, my heart racing as I looked for Brie.

The party had grown louder, wilder, drunker than before. I picked up a small bottle of brown alcohol from the sticky island in the kitchen and didn't bother to read the label. It was about a quarter full when I tipped the liquid into my mouth, enjoying the punishing fire of it. Someone had left a yellow Bic lighter on the counter and I grabbed it, ran my thumb slow along the wheel until it sparked and I stuck it in my pocket.

The bottle empty now, I wheeled around. The whole room lurched.

I moved through the party until I found Deirdre and Min weaving through one of the living rooms.

"Hey," I yelled over the music to Min.

Her lips curved into a smile, wine-red and glossy as a freshly removed organ. "Hey."

I was nothing to her. A speck, a fly buzzing. We'd had most of our classes together for the past four years and yet she still insisted on pretending she barely knew me. Who had influenced her to do that? I wondered now. How different might everything be without Brianna Walsh and the hexes she had cast?

Fighting the sensation that the room had begun to spin around me, I made myself smile. I needed to get this right. I needed to be brave but meek, assertive but unthreatening. "Have you seen Brie?"

She sipped from her Solo cup and stopped looking around the room for someone better. "She's upstairs with you-know-who." And then she rolled her eyes as if we shared a mutual dislike of the two of them together, Brie and you-know-who.

I couldn't resist poking at this, even though I knew I shouldn't. "You all don't like Rain very much, do you? I thought she was one of you now."

Min leaned in, pulled me closer by my elbow. "You've always had the wrong idea about us. We're fucking nice, Sydney. We like people. We even like *you*. You just always made it so clear you didn't like *us*."

I'd opened my mouth to respond but then Deirdre stepped between us, her pale pixie face blotchy from drinking. I wondered if her parents' drug-testing regimen was over or if it didn't pick up alcohol. "Oh stop it, why don't you?" she snapped at Min. Then, to me: "Min's just jelly because she's been replaced. She lost her best bud to Rain."

I nodded, absorbing it all, backing away as Min hissed something at Deirdre, their internal politics none of my concern. But Deirdre followed me, pulled me toward the base of the stairs where it was just us and a pair of freshman boys slumped over a phone against a wall.

Where is Spider? I remembered to think. Oh well. Somewhere.

"Whatever happened between you guys when you were little . . ." Deirdre widened her green eyes to indicate she'd heard some stuff. "It always bugged Brie. But now she's, like, *obsessed* with Rain. Min's taking it hard. Anya hates her now, too, kind of. They're possessive. And so is Brie. Personally I'm over all of them, you know?" She shrugged and beamed a sweet smile at me.

"Yep. All this is ending now." I nodded again, vaguely searching behind Deirdre for Rain, for Brie, for Spider. Billie Eilish crooned "Bury a Friend" through speakers above us, behind us, inside us. How many people had Brie hurt and manipulated to get what she wanted?

"Check the bedrooms on the top floor. Those are the nicest. I bet they're in there talking shit about the rest of us." Deirdre laughed and rolled her eyes.

"Thanks." I reached out, wanting to give her a hug, but she pulled back. There was still a distance between us that all the pills and alcohol in the world couldn't bridge. "I won't tell Brie what you said. I get it. Really, I do."

Maybe everyone was mourning a lost friend, a missed opportunity, an unlived life. Maybe the end of high school had been a slow-moving train wreck for everyone, and all of us felt in our own ways as if we had been chugging toward a brick wall.

The main thing now was to keep the room from spinning long enough to find Brie and say my piece. It was now or never.

And then I was clumsily climbing the plush-carpeted stairs, my legs heavy, the walls undulating as I walked. The song's macabre chorus poured into me, each question relevant, each question a joke: *Why aren't you scared of me? Why do you care for me? When we all fall asleep, where do we go?*

My eyes were shutters clicking open, clicking closed. *Take two if you want to fly,* Spider had said, but now I was beyond flying. I was rocketing through space, incandescent on a cloud of rage. I pictured Brie in front of me, those blue eyes, that smirk she constantly wore. I imagined screaming obscenities, ripping it off her.

I stumbled around looking for the stairs to the third floor before they finally appeared. The music was quieter here, the conversations of the few people up on the third floor landing less frantic. The house gathered its energies around me as I began to throw open door after door.

You took everything from me, now I'm taking something away from you, I decided I would say. My mind whirred with everything Brie had done to isolate me from Chase and from Rain, all the little digs that had gotten us here. Why had I let her get away with it? Surely she'd manipulated Rain the same way. It was time Rain heard the truth, all of it. It was time Rain understood who her new best friend really was. Maybe then Brie's little game would end. And then what? I wondered. Would all of this start to make some sense? Would Rain and I repair things? Where would the night take the three of us, bound forever somehow, still the same three girls in the sticks of Termico, seething with something we didn't understand, a poison that was still unwinding itself in us even now?

What would I take from Brie, if given the chance? The walls went watery and I was a shark, moving toward the smell of blood.

When I threw the door open to the last bedroom on the right, Rain was seated at a desk in one corner and Brie was lying on a king-sized bed. They both looked up, startled. This was a boy's bedroom, or a man's. Probably it was Brad's. Walls painted navy, almost black. Lacrosse sticks hung on the wall next to a shelf full of trophies, an old map of Portugal hung above the desk.

"You," Rain said. Unsmiling, she jumped up and walked toward me with a guarded expression on her face.

Looking at the two of them so comfortable in their own private world, I almost felt bad about intruding. It would have been easier for everyone if I just slunk away like I always did, tail between my legs. Oh well, not this time.

"Hello, Sydney." Brie sighed, calm and seemingly sober. "I didn't think you came to parties anymore." She smiled tightly and didn't make a move from the bed, not even to lift her head off the comforter. Her dyed-dark hair fanned out in all directions.

"Bummer, right?" I laughed bitterly. "I know you like me best when I'm home alone and out of your way."

"That's not what I meant." Brie snorted and turned onto her side, her head propped on one bent arm. "No need to be a bitch about it—"

"Don't call her that," Rain said to Brie. She hugged me awkwardly, more out of habit than out of any warmth she felt, I guessed. "Have you come to yell at me some more?" she said softly.

"No," I muttered, an ache in my chest at what we'd become. "I'm sorry things got so ugly with us in the ceramics room. That's not—that's never what I wanted."

"Me, too. Obviously." Rain sniffed.

"I have some things to say, actually. To both of you."

"Okay." Rain shot me a nervous look and took a step back. "I still don't know what I did that was so terrible."

You chose her, I didn't say. "I just . . . I need to say some things to Brie and you need to hear them."

"Can we save the drama for another time?" Brie sat up now and yawned. "I'm really not in the mood to rehash—"

"Maybe you could shut up for once." Both girls stared at me. I straightened my spine, growing braver. "For fucking once, I'm doing the talking."

I moved closer to Brie and ignored the way the walls seemed to vibrate slightly with each step I took. "I know you started a rumor to break up me and Chase. You took away the only person I had. And not even for yourself, but just . . ." I waved my hands around uselessly. "For fun, I guess."

Brie blinked at me, the beginnings of the bored smirk I knew from class forming on her face. "People say a lot of shit about me at this school. It's not, like, under my control. I can't help it if you believe every stupid rumor about your boyfriend, Sydney. Or, sorry, ex-boyfriend."

I turned to Rain and gestured to Brie as if to say *this is who you chose.* "I hope you're paying attention. She told people she hooked up with Chase so that it would get back to me."

Rain turned to Brie and blinked hard, as if with clearer vision she could see her for what she was. "Did you really do that?"

"She'll say no, but I know for a fact she did." The walls leaned in closer now, as if the room was listening. When I spoke, I heard the consonants fall off my words, all of them sticking together. *Noforafactshedid.*

"You were sort of desperate to believe it, though, weren't you? Take responsibility for your own poor self-esteem." Brie had her phone out now and scrolled as she talked.

"Why would you do that, though?" Rain asked.

"That's your best friend for you." I waved my hands like a TV lawyer. *Exhibit A, your honor.* "She did it for you. To get closer to you somehow. Maybe I was showing up to too many things, getting in her way."

"Paranoid," Brie said under her breath and rolled her eyes so Rain could see.

Rain looked back and forth between us as if deciding who to trust.

"But it suited you fine, didn't it?" I asked Rain. "You were happy when we broke up." I hadn't thought it through completely, but I wanted her to know she was complicit.

"Why would you say that?" Rain's voice came out strangled and hurt. "I only want good things for you. You're my best friend, too."

Too? The *too* was the most stunning of all. I looked at the ceiling and had to laugh. It was an ugly bark.

"You left me when my life got good," Rain said slowly, her face contorting in a way I didn't understand. Like she was somehow both disappointed and embarrassed. I watched her eyes get glassy. Rain never cried. Never.

"Same as you did to me," Brie chimed in, looking up from her scrolling.

So this was what these two bonded over? Feeling like victims for abandoning me? Absolutely amazing. "I never left either of you. Brie, you disappeared into your new life and left us both behind. And Rain, you disappeared inside Brie's world and didn't even notice I was gone. I was always happy for you. Always. I still am."

"And you show that happiness by avoiding her, judging her, and blaming her for all your problems." Brie eye-rolled.

"Why are you talking right now?" I wheeled on Brie. "This has nothing to do with you."

"Look at yourself for once. So high and mighty, Sydney. So eager to see the worst in people. You come in here shit-faced and rude and just hammer away. This is how you treat your best friend?" Brie pointed to Rain, who was dabbing at her eyes, then went on serving as Rain's attack dog, her voice a battering ram. "You lecture her like she's stupid. You blame her for her good luck. And inside, it's all resentment and self-pity. I tried to tell her what a hypocrite you were. Now she can see for herself."

Rain's face was red when she put up a hand to silence Brie. "You had a funny way of showing how happy you were for me, Syd. I stopped texting you because you literally never responded."

"You stopped responding first! You didn't even care when I told you about my first night with Chase at Moon Rocks. I texted you and you never even replied."

"That never happened," Rain said. "You never told me about that."

"I *did.* I texted you that night. That's the night things . . . got serious with us. You were too busy with Brie to even respond." I turned away from them both and shut my eyes, willing the tears not to fall. I wouldn't give them the satisfaction.

"Jesus, you two. Who cares about a stupid text?" Brie was in full exasperated scold mode now. But her neck had gotten blotchy, big red patches of emotion she couldn't hide.

"She deleted my text," I whispered, suddenly sure of it. I turned to face her. "You did, didn't you?" When I turned back around, the room kept on turning.

Brie shrugged and rolled her eyes but didn't deny it. The truth was written all over her bright red chest.

"You went into my phone and deleted texts from Syd?" Rain's eyes widened. "Seriously?"

"What else did you do to get between us?" I hissed. All these months, manipulated and controlled until I was left totally alone. My hands tingled with how much I hated Brie in that moment. I imagined wrapping my fingers around her splotchy neck, the vision of it felt so real I stepped back, afraid of what I might be capable of doing.

"No offense," Brie said softly to Rain, "but you were a mess that night. You didn't need her needy energy weighing you down." She crossed her arms over her chest as if to say *case closed*.

"See?" I whispered to Rain. "You see who she is? You used to see it. Same girl as ever. She's never changed. You have."

"I thought I'd been wrong about you," Rain said to Brie, sounding unsure.

"Jesus, the drama with you two! I'm your *friend,* Rain. I'm the one who showed you how to handle your new lifestyle. I'm the one who listens to you, who isn't jealous. She stalked us, you know." Brie paused, then went on. "I didn't want to tell you because it was just so sad, but one night I found her outside my house. She was standing there in the dark watching us on the deck."

"That's the night you said Rain called me a judgmental prude," I whispered.

"I never said that." Her eyes wide, Rain backed away from both of us. "I would never say that."

I believed her, but it was too late. The damage had been done. It seemed impossible to undo it now. Why had it been so easy for me to buy the lies Brie had spouted?

"Hello? Can we focus on the fact that she's a creeper? She was literally in my yard!"

As Brie talked, something else was snapping into place for me. *She messes with people, just like she messed with your brother.* I could see Spider in my bed eating Cheetos, the way his face grew stormy when Brie came up. *Brianna Walsh is bad news.*

"Spider was your dealer, wasn't he?" I whispered. I moved toward Brie, my hands shaking. The room had been slowly spinning this whole time but now it sped up. "Before he . . . left."

Rain nodded. "He was."

"You knew?" I grabbed on to the back of the desk chair now in an effort to keep the room still. It was so hot in here. I felt sweat break out under my arms and along my shoulder blades. "You could've told me."

Rain shook her head. "I . . . she only told me that a few weeks ago."

"Your brother was everyone's dealer, if I remember correctly," Brie said. Her voice was choked now and her face grew redder, the blotches on her chest expanding.

"He's out now. Home today. Maybe you heard? He's actually here at this party. Said he wanted to talk to you." I walked closer to the window now, hoping I could open it for some air, my shoes sinking into the plush carpet as the room continued to wobble. Every step was like quicksand. When I looked at Brie, my vision doubled. There were two of her. Or no, one of them was Rain and one was Brie. A matched set, watching me, eyes wide. Only one of them looked panicked, though. Only Brie. "You turned him in, didn't you?"

"Syd, you need to check yourself before you make, like, baseless accusations." Brie's words were halting, like she was groping for the words. Her chest and neck and face were burning.

"Oh my god," Rain whispered. "You did."

Rain and I looked at each other long enough to acknowledge that we both saw the truth. We both knew Brie well enough to spot her grasping at straws.

Brie's mouth twisted shut. Her nostrils flared. "Fine, Jesus. I had no choice. I was going to get suspended, probably even expelled. If it wasn't me turning him in, it would have been someone else."

"Wow." Rain reached over and grabbed my hand. I shook her off and leaned against the wall, pressed on it to make the room stop spinning. My mouth filled with saliva and I swallowed it down, the task of opening the window all but insurmountable now.

"You would've done the same. Both of you." Brie glowered at us.

"No," Rain said. "We wouldn't."

"Don't act like you're some saint." Brie turned on Rain. "You were desperate to drop Syd. The second you got money, you were gone. Just the other day you told me you thought she was jealous."

Aha, finally. The truth came out. At least Brie had the decency to hurt me to my face, which was more than I could say for Rain. "I knew it," I whispered.

"That's because you told me she was!" Rain exploded. "None of what you're saying is true. I can't believe I didn't realize how manipulative you are. You're as awful as your dad."

"And you're as big a train wreck as your mom," Brie snapped.

Rain actually gasped. "I can't believe I ever thought we were friends," she snapped at Brie. "You manipulated me this whole time. You burn down people's lives for fun. Just because you can."

Brie looked from Rain to me and back again. "You two. So sanctimonious. Well, some of us have nobody in our corner but ourselves." Brie's face crumpled momentarily and then re-formed into that mask she wore, that dimpled smile that was really a smirk. I blinked and for a second she was seven again and we were together in the canyon behind our houses, frozen in place, our path blocked by a coiled rattlesnake. Rain and I had both screamed but Brie just stood there watching it, fearless and patient. *Quiet,* she'd ordered. *It won't strike if you just shut up and stay still.*

"One day someone's going to do that to you," I muttered, my words sticking together again. "And you won't even see it coming."

But Brie was locked in a silent communication with Rain, the two staring at each other, Rain radiating disgust, Brie's eyes imploring, her face a rictus of what looked like panic.

Even now, I didn't matter.

Rage bubbled up inside me again, and I let it take over. I lunged at Brie and grabbed her chin in my palm, my fingers and thumb pressing hard into the sides of her cheeks. If she couldn't pay attention to me, I would make her. "Look at me when I'm talking to you." My voice carried a low rumble of violence I hadn't known I was capable of.

"Is that a threat?" Brie wrenched herself away from me. She put her hands on her hips just below the slice of midsection her crop top revealed, but I didn't find her threatening. Not anymore.

I shrugged, done talking. The room spun faster. The edges of my vision blurred black and purple and my stomach began to seize. "Take it however you want. I'm leaving."

"Wait, I'm leaving, too," Rain said as I barreled toward the door. I felt her hand on my arm and snatched it away. Rain saw what I'd needed her to see, but it couldn't erase the past few months. She'd hurt me too much and I'd been alone too long.

I raced from the room and flew down the hallway away from both of them, my head on fire, the boundaries between me and the throbbing house bruise-colored and blurred. I needed to get out of there fast—my body was about to rebel against everything I'd put into it. I couldn't feel my legs or the tears streaming down my face, but I patted my pockets to make sure I still had my keys and phone. The little yellow lighter I'd taken was there, too, bouncing against my thigh. As I clattered down the stairs, desperate to escape this place and find somewhere to expel the poison inside me, all I knew was that the night wasn't through with me yet.

27

"Wake up."

The night was moonless, but it still hurt to open my eyes. I was sprawled on the ground, rocks and sticks poking me through my clothes. The hoots and chirps of the desert and the plasticky *thwip thwip thwip* of insect wings filled my ears. The *whoosh* of cars came and went. Through one cracked eye, I watched bits of refracted headlights move across brush and cacti. Somewhere there was a fire burning. Under the sage and desert dust, I smelled smoke and traces of something acrid and chemical.

A ball of pain in the back of my skull expanded when I tried to sit up. I remembered I had left the party furious, but the details weren't there and I didn't want to know. I wanted only to put my head back down on the ground and go back to sleep. Dust coated my hair. I touched my face and found it smeared with something gritty and wet.

Out of the blackness, two hands grabbed my bare shoulders and pulled. A scream ripped through my throat.

"Christ, quiet down. It's me."

Spider came into view now. He bent over me, a blur, a ghost. Hood up, drawstring tightened so that only the small oval of his face showed. He looked me over like I was a bigger problem than he'd anticipated. I tried to speak, but it didn't come out right. I put a hand on his head, patted it, and gripped his skull in my hand in a gesture of recognition. But then I fell back into the dark. I wished it would take me, wished I could sink back into that void where everything was easy, where nothing was asked of me.

"Come on, wakey wakey." He was shaking me now, pulling me upright. "Sorry about this." Something horrible waggled in my mouth, his dirty dusty finger, and he shoved it down my throat. I was limp as a rag doll. Made of nothing, cotton stuffed where a brain should be. It was all going to come back up. The fight, the truth of having been Brie's marionette dangling on strings. Whatever was in my stomach coming up alongside it, but I wanted to swallow it back down. I moaned a garbled "Leave me alone" and writhed away from my brother, but he wouldn't stop.

Soon, my own sick splashed across my jeans and shoes.

I found syllables when it was over. "Fuck you."

"I know, I know. This isn't my first choice for fun either." He pulled me away from the puddle of vomit and I stumbled, half-walking, half-dragged, through the desert. We staggered toward the shoulder of the road. Now that I was upright I could make out the bass skipping faintly in the air and the tinkle of laughter from the party—we couldn't be too far from Candice's.

"How'd you find me?" I muttered.

He grunted a nonanswer.

And how did I wind up here? I groped at memories: running down the stairs, desperate to get out of that airless, throbbing house. I remembered running, wind whipping my face so that I couldn't cry, thorny brush that scraped my legs and arms. And before that, Rain's face twisted with tears, Brie's blotchy chest, her nostrils flared in anger. But there were so many gaps in between. So much I couldn't account for.

I wanted to sleep. My knees buckled, but Spider hoisted me up by my armpits again and dragged me along.

I closed my eyes just to rest a second as we walked, but he kept shouting at me, a stern, mean tone I'd never heard from him before. "Stay awake."

At one point he slapped my face hard enough to sting. I returned the blow and conked him over the head with a weak fist.

"Keep hitting me," he said. "Make me feel it."

Screw you, I wanted to say. *This is all your fault.* Instead I smacked him a few more times. "Weakling, hit me like you mean it," he ordered.

Eventually we lurched out of the brush and into full view of the Fiesta, hitting each other like we were five and seven again in Mom's backseat.

"I hate you," I managed to slur.

"Sweet," he said. "Hate me all the way home."

After he shoved me into the car and clicked the seat belt around my slumped-over body, I sank into the seat, into the car's bottom, into the road, into the core of the earth, and let sleep take me into its arms again.

PART VIII

BRIE

THE NIGHT OF THE FIRE

28

Lying back down on the California king that Candice's brother dreamed his rich-boy dreams in, I stared at the ceiling, feeling tears slip down my temples and into my hair. Everything was ruined. Nothing was ever free, it seemed. Someone always had to pay.

Syd had careened from the room. Her childish sense of betrayal sent her bolting in horror over big bad Brie and all I'd done to mess with her, and then Rain ran right after her, her orders—*don't follow me, don't call me*—delivered with a deadly glare before she left. The night had undone all the trust I'd gained. I got up off Candice's brother's bed, composed my face into a mask of normalcy, and walked slowly out of the party. On my way out, Candice and Deirdre called my name and waved me onto the living room's dance floor.

Sorry, I mouthed to them, barely caring. *Gotta bail.*

I walked with purpose out to my car, my little red baby, already a reminder of all I had lost.

I plopped down into the driver's seat and rested my forehead on the steering wheel, replaying the terrible night and the empty future it foretold. Underneath my right thigh, something poked at me through my jeans. I reached down and pulled out one of Rain's matchboxes from the Ritz-Carlton. She had an endless supply of them floating around in her big black bag. I slid the box open, struck a match, and watched the flame consume the stick. By the time I shook it out, I knew what I was going to do.

I'd rather die than go back to the way things were now.

My whole body shook with the weight of it. I needed to sit and think a minute, work it out step-by-step. I tucked my hands in my lap and breathed, waiting for the adrenaline to pass through me. Out in the moonless night was the tinkle of laughter, the shouting of boys. Up ahead, a couple sucked face against the side of a car, their bodies grinding, oblivious to everything around them. Must be nice, I thought, to be able to care so much about someone else that you'd be willing to dry hump them in public like that. Everywhere, absolute idiots were carefree, seizing the moment, secure in their bright futures. How nice for them.

I looked back down at my hands. They had stilled. I knew how to do it now. Everything came together like the final steps of a physics proof: the answer shimmering, crystal clear. I started the car, kept my foot on the brake. While the engine sprang to life, I sent a text.

Need a favor. Can you meet me at the spot?

I pulled the car out and took deep breaths—in for four, out for four—as I drove. He'd write back. Always did. Very reliable, considering his line of work. We had an uneasy trust between us. Or if not a trust, a tolerance.

I laughed to myself, squeezed the steering wheel tighter. Felt that numb emptiness that had straitjacketed itself around me the past few months loosening, a new sense of purpose filling me up inside.

I drove onward, a calm sense of inevitability washing over me. I found KPSC, the classical station. Vivaldi was on. *The Four Seasons.* A strange choice for nearly 2 AM but I would take it. I turned it up loud.

As I drove toward the highway, the way to where I was headed as familiar to me as breathing, I slipped in and out of time. The streets were wide black ribbons, empty and smooth. They unfurled in every direction, on and on, each road a different path of escape.

Driving through town, I observed every traffic signal. I put my blinkers on when there was not a soul behind me. *Look how law-abiding,* I marveled. *What a good girl I am and have always been.*

Calmly, so calmly, I waited at each and every stoplight on the 10, plodding through the valley past the strip malls and housing developments. Thousands of empty houses in every shade of avocado, beige, burnt sienna, mustard, and terra-cotta lit up under the halogen streetlamps, all the vacation people cleared out for summer. It was already so hot. Nobody with somewhere else to go would stay here past May if they had any choice. But we were used to it. We'd been roasting all our lives, long enough so that we could stand barefoot on burning concrete and not even scream.

Except tonight. Tonight everything was burning. Tonight would be my scream.

When I turned onto Clay Street at last, the road to my old house, it was the most natural thing in the world. A homecoming.

On the radio, the movement ended. The seasons shifted from fall to winter. The strings came in, the violin. All mournful. Everything dying now.

My phone buzzed in my pocket.

I'm here.

I reached my old block, where I had been so small and meek and vulnerable. Before we moved down the mountain and Rain and Syd stopped calling me and I became someone new, a girl with a core of steel. There was Brie, little mouse, weak and sad, who became the newer, better Brianna, strong and armored and in control, with new clothes and a put-on brashness that made me seem powerful. But

Brie, that little mouse, had never really left me. She was still there, chewing at the wires in the walls. Waiting, always expecting, to be trapped.

And now the mouse would roar.

I slowed the car driving past the old house, empty and abandoned now. Tall grasses grew all around it. Spanky's doghouse was still there, though Spanky was long dead now. The living-room windows were boarded up. Good, I thought. The house where Mommy died, the house where Ed's drinking had flourished, the house where I'd looked in the mirror at six, seven, eight and begun to plot my escape . . . that house was tainted. The Walsh family's unhappiness had probably seeped into the walls. I was glad nobody had moved in there. I kept driving slow down Clay Street.

Two doors down was Sydney's house, a bike on the front porch, her mom's little herb garden full of mint and lavender, wind chimes made of beach glass hung by a window. I remembered her mom's high voice, her perpetually dry hands she was constantly moisturizing, the way she would make a pile of spaghetti and top it with weird food—pepperoni, olives, canned beans, canned peas, whatever had been on sale that week—and how she taught me how to braid my hair in a fishtail.

She'd been nice. Nicer than her daughter. Syd was fine, a good-enough friend back then, but she had always hidden something essential about herself from me. Had always given everything she had to Rain.

I wondered if Syd's mom worried about her after I took Rain from her.

Not that any of it mattered anymore.

I parked as close to the canyon as I could. The rest of the way, I had to walk. The canyon was full of rattlesnakes, so I clapped as I went. Every few feet, clap clap. *If you're fucked up and you know it, clap your hands. Clap clap. If you want to blow your life up, clap your hands. Clap clap.*

Alone in the canyon, I actually laughed, the path narrowing to nothing in places so that I crashed through thornbushes and scraped up my legs. I could still laugh. That's how I knew I was on a righteous path. *Laughter is the beginning of prayer.* Some saint said that.

The air was thick with tiny bugs that bounced off my face, prickers reaching out from brush to claw at me. When I stepped in the ATV tracks imprinted in the valley floor, I aimed a weak beam of cell-phone light past the brush to where I thought the clearing was, squinting through the night until I spotted the little shack that had once been Spider's center of operations. Faint light spilled out from inside.

The door was open, waiting for me.

"Took you long enough." Whit drawled from inside the shack, his surfer's swallow on *long*. He rolled his desk chair across the shack's swept floor, peeked his head out, his pink face scrunched up like a rodent used to the dark, framed by his yellow rat's nest of hair.

I shut my light off and said nothing. I walked toward Whit like a ghost. He would come through with what I needed. I had incriminating evidence on him—he knew my history of putting people away. He wouldn't ask too many questions. And later on, I hoped he wouldn't think too hard about any of it except to realize he was implicated. He'd want to make sure nobody knew a thing.

That nobody knew he was responsible for the death of Brie Walsh.

PART IX
RAIN

THE NIGHT OF THE FIRE

29

At home, I stopped in the kitchen to chug a glass of water and found a note from Joan.

> *Let's talk tomorrow once we've cleared our heads. You need*
> *to give me the $ back.*
> *Love,*
> *Mom*

I never called Joan *Mom.* Not since second grade. I held the note up with my fingertips and sniffed it. It smelled like her moisturizer.

Too late, "Mom," I considered writing back in some sort of goodbye note. The last thing I wanted to do was talk. We'd reached the end of our ability to live here together, so I would do her the favor of clearing my head elsewhere. After our fight yesterday, I'd spent the night at Brie's and all day today, too. But that was over now, and Syd didn't seem all that eager to restart our friendship at this point, either.

I left the note on the counter and took the stairs two at a time. Blood thrummed in my ears and a nervous excitement spread through my limbs at the thought of driving out of the desert and getting away from Joan, the sting of whose slap I could still feel on my cheek if I closed my eyes. Getting away from everyone here who'd let me down, who'd misunderstood or manipulated me. I'd been planning to leave after graduation anyway—leaving now would put me just a little bit ahead of schedule.

I wouldn't take much. A fraction of the lottery money. Fifteen stacks of hundred-dollar bills in their cheery yellow wrappers would be more than enough to start me out on a brand-new life.

I threw a bunch of clothes and shoes and a few toiletries into my old army-issued duffel bag, the one thing I owned that had once belonged to my father. As I packed, I ran through the fight with Syd and Brie in my head.

The way Brie had laughed in my face, had framed me as somehow a bad friend, had acted like all the garbage she'd filled my head with had shown up there on its own. The idiot I was for believing it. Brie had proven herself to be exactly the puppet master we'd always thought her to be. *The second you got money you distanced yourself from Syd.* Had I? Or had she greased the wheels?

I felt a spasm of sadness for everything I'd tried and failed to do, for everything that was ending. A sob gathered in my throat. Even Syd, once my truest friend, thought there was something wrong with me. I was nothing to her now. She'd left me there, had literally run away rather than spend another second with me.

And my own mother had called me a thief. Maybe I was what they'd all thought I was. Gullible, stupid, mean, selfish.

Well, now none of them would have to put up with me anymore. I was going to give myself a clean slate. I would drive off into the sunset and they could all be free.

At last I had the duffel bag packed. It sat on my bed open at one end, just needing to be zipped shut. Next, I dragged the stepladder from the hall closet to my room, then rummaged around in my desk drawer to find the screwdriver I'd used to hide the money.

I pried the metal facing off the vent above my bedroom door. I stuck my hand inside the narrow heating duct that had served so well to hide a portion of Joan's money.

I'd placed a hundred wrapped stacks of bills here last week, each containing $10,000. It still seemed like an absurd number, but that was literally a million dollars. I reached for the perfect stacks now, only halfway paying attention. I thrust my hand deeper into the duct, looking for the bills and finding only metal ventilation walls and air.

The hairs on my arm stood up. "What the fuck?" I whispered.

I pulled out my phone, shone a light into the chasm of the duct, and stretched as far up as I could to peer into the vent with my own two eyes.

There was nothing there. Not a thing.

I blinked back tears and shook my head. *Nononono.*

I nearly broke my neck getting off the stepladder. Every part of me shaking, I tiptoed into Joan's room, past her sleeping body with its Bluetooth eye mask that played Brené Brown audiobooks in her ears all night. Silently, I watched my mother for a minute. Her chest rose and fell, her faint snoring was regular. She'd said in her note that I still needed to give the money back, but maybe she'd gone ahead and found it before going to sleep. Silently, I crept to her closet. The door was open. Once inside, I checked the stash, but it looked the same as it had when I'd left it. Half there, half gone.

I put everything back, my whole body still shaking with adrenaline and panic. I felt like puking, like screaming. And then a calm settled over me. I knew where it was.

There was only one person who could've guessed where I'd stashed it. The person I'd been stupid enough to think was looking out for me.

Back in my room, I texted Brie.

Where is the money??? I know you took it, I typed with shaking hands.

I sat at the edge of my bed staring at the three dots on my phone screen, waiting. Trying not to cry. The dots disappeared and reappeared.

I'm about to call the cops, I wrote after a few minutes.

That got to her.

Come over, she wrote. I'll explain everything.

"Sure you will," I whispered.

I zipped the duffel bag and dragged it down the stairs, heavy as a corpse. Two minutes later I was on my way to Brie's, my hands squeezing the wheel, imagining it was her throat.

PART X

SYDNEY

TWO DAYS AFTER THE FIRE

30

All day and into the evening I waited to hear back from Rain. I checked in with Joan. I checked in with Chase. I even DMed Anya and Deirdre. Nobody had heard from her beyond a few texts saying she would be back soon and not to worry.

By 5 PM I was staring anxiously out my living room window as if Rain's car would roar up the driveway at any moment. I turned her absence over and over in my mind, not finding any rational explanation for how she could let herself stay away for so long. Weren't the police going to wonder where she was? Could that be—here goose bumps broke across my forearms—why she wasn't here? Rain couldn't have had anything to do with the fire, could she?

A memory from the day Rain had bought her car had started to pop up in my head whenever I thought about the fire. I'd made some joke about not getting it at Walsh Nissan and she'd grumbled something about Ed, her eyes narrowed in anger when I'd mentioned him . . . something like *we took our business somewhere else, but Ed deserves worse than that.* What had Ed done to make Rain so angry? Had she been mad enough at Ed for not selling Joan a car that she would have tried to hurt him? Could she have been upset enough that night to hurt both Ed and Brie?

My head spun with all I didn't know, all of the pieces of this that didn't fit together. I scrolled back through my dozens of texts to Rain and looked at what she'd written to me after I'd been interviewed by the cops. Don't worry. I'll never tell them what we did.

But we hadn't done anything. *Had we?*

Pacing the living room while the air conditioner rattled and coughed, I sifted through my memories of the night of the fire for the hundredth time. We'd fought. I knew that much. Then I ran away angry. And then there was a window of time I couldn't seem to account for no matter how hard I tried to zero in on it, a missing piece of the night I tried and tried to remember between leaving Candice's and being shaken awake by Spider. I'd been alone all that time though, mixed up in the desert . . . hadn't I? Rain wasn't with me then, couldn't have been . . . could she? I'd gotten turned around, passed out from the pills, and Spider had found me. And anyway, it had only been a short time that I was out there . . . *hadn't it?* Certainly not enough time to go set a fire.

But there was her text in black and white, taunting me. *I'll never tell them what we did.*

Why would Rain write that, unless somehow she'd pulled me into some stupid idea of hers? Had I been blackout drunk enough to tag along on some ill-conceived plan she had to hurt Ed?

No. I froze in front of Gary's crop circle books. The human mind works so hard to make sense of the inexplicable. We can invent the wildest explanations just so the pieces will fit together in a way that makes sense to us. But there was no way I'd been a part of any fire, even if I couldn't account for exactly what I'd done during that window of time. Was Rain trying to frame me somehow, trying to make me a part of something she'd done? I pushed the thought away, hoping, praying I was being paranoid. It was too awful to contemplate. Rain would never. Could never. Rain was many things, but an arsonist, a *killer?* No. She was not that. And no matter how many pills and shots I swallowed, neither was I.

I was almost, *almost* sure of it.

By nightfall, Mom was at her late shift at Four Fronds and Spider had spent an hour cooking. He made spaghetti with homemade sauce and I managed to eat about six bites of it before I felt sick. It wasn't the food, which was pretty good. It was thoughts of Brie asphyxiating in her bed, of Rain running off to god knew where.

"Worry about your girl, fine." Spider glowered across from me at the table. "But not about Brianna Walsh. She's already making herself at home in hell."

"Don't talk about a dead girl like that," I said coldly. "Even if you didn't like her, that's not okay." *Even if neither of us liked her.*

"It is definitely okay." Spider's eyes flashed. "I'm glad she's dead."

"Spider, Jesus!"

"Who do you think sent me to prison?" Spider stood up, sending the chair flying back behind him so that it thudded against the kitchen counter. He took his empty bowl to the stove and started angrily scooping more spaghetti into it.

My mouth dropped open in surprise, but then it all came back to me in a rush and I realized I already knew. The alcohol and pills and then the shock of Brie's death had blurred it out, but now I remembered: *If it wasn't me turning him in, it would have been someone else.* I clenched my hands into fists and looked up at my brother.

"How'd you find out it was her?" I asked him quietly.

Spider slammed the pasta pot into the sink, still worked up. "There's a lot of shit you don't know about Brie Walsh. She was the connect at school. She farmed out all the product to her druggie friends. They liked study drugs, Molly, all kinds of stuff. It's not like I gave them opioids or anything. And then things got hot for her, the school found something, and she took me down. One of her friends texted me the day she was caught. She didn't get into any trouble, but next thing I knew, I got busted. So yeah, I'm not gonna mourn her, if that's okay with you."

His bowl full of his third helping of spaghetti, he stalked out of the room. A minute later, his bedroom door slammed.

I thought about going after him but a sudden exhaustion kept me glued to my chair. I remembered all the reasons I'd confronted Brie that night, and all the reasons I'd run out of that house. It all came flooding back, the way Anya had shrugged and told on Brie as if it was nothing, water under the bridge, and even then I couldn't see it until she was right in front of me.

I looked behind me down the empty hall and thought about how furious my brother was. How I couldn't find him at five in the morning when I'd stumbled into his room after puking my guts out. But I knew my brother. I knew he wasn't capable of doing something like that. Not even after ten months in prison. No way. He wouldn't. *Would he?*

My phone buzzed with a call that shook me out of my thoughts. An unknown number flashed on my screen.

I picked it up on the second ring, knowing in my heart that Rain was finally back.

"About damn time," I said by way of hello.

"Sydney?" A woman's voice said. Familiar, but I couldn't quite place her.

"Yes?" Crestfallen to hear it wasn't Rain, I had to fight not to sound too annoyed.

"It's Officer Garcia. Arlene. We met at school?"

My heart thudding, I stared up at the stalactites in our popcorn ceiling as if they could help me. "Oh, hi."

"I understand you met my colleague Officer Duff the other night."

"What?"

"Yeah, someone called it in to our tip line. I just confirmed it with him this afternoon. He says he found you on the top floor of the Walsh's house the night after the fire? Would have been—" The line dropped for a second and I missed a few words.

"Hello? You still there?" I asked feebly. I wasn't even going to try to defend going to Brie's house, would not try to explain my reasons for not telling them about it. Anything more I said would dig me deeper into a hole of suspicion. I stared down at the pasta still in front of me on the table, the chunks of ground chuck slick and gruesome in the red sauce, the spaghetti revolting now. I pushed it away in the silence of Arlene's awkward pause and listened to her breathing, suddenly certain she was also listening intently to me, waiting to catch me in more lies or omissions.

"I'm here. I was saying it would have been a good thing to tell us about."

I bit the insides of my cheeks, a wash of fear coming over me now. Who had tipped them off? Who could have seen me enter Brie's house? "Anyway, Bill and I were hoping you could do us a favor and come down to the station tomorrow, maybe after school? We just have a couple more questions for you. Won't take long."

I squeezed my eyes shut and felt my chest flare with heat. It crossed my mind that I might be having a heart attack. Behind my eyes, all I saw was Brie's room at the top of the stairs, the blasted-open roof, the black hole of her bed. And then I could smell the sweet awful scent of that house all over again.

"Okay." If I said no, if I hesitated at all, it would make me look that much more like I had something to hide. *Okay, yes,* I pled my case in my head. *That night I was angry. Maybe even in a rage. But I had nothing to do with that fire, no matter what the police think, no matter how upset I was, no matter how many pill-shaped holes I've got in my memory.*

"No problem," I added weakly.

"Great. And would you be able to bring your brother with you? We'd love to talk to him, too. If not, we can swing by your house—"

Oh no. The thought of Mom seeing more police coming after her son after what we'd already been through was too much to bear. "Sure, I can do that," I said warily, not at all certain that I could deliver Spider to the police station.

"Great. We'll see you tomorrow afternoon."

"Okay. But Arlene? I just . . . I want you to know I had nothing to do with the fire." It came out like a croak, my voice fried and unsure.

"Okay, Sydney. We just want to talk. But you may want to look into a lawyer, just in case."

I stared at my phone in horror. Were they going to put me in an interrogation room? Put Spider in one, too? Was I going to get arrested? What if the anonymous caller had said more, had set traps that I was about to walk right into? I leaned my forehead into my hands and put my phone back to my ear. I squeezed my eyes shut until the edges of my vision started to blur. Desperately, I tried one last time to remember how I'd gotten to the desert where my brother had found me lying in the brush. Again, infuriatingly, my memory refused to cooperate.

"Okay," I whispered. "See you tomorrow."

I hung up without saying goodbye. It was all too much. I couldn't do this alone anymore.

Immediately, I texted Rain with shaking hands.

The cops just called me. They want to talk again tomorrow at the station. They told me to bring Spider and to call a lawyer. Someone told them about me going to Brie's house after the fire. I'm a suspect now for real. I feel like I'm being watched. I'm so scared.

I was shocked a moment later when my phone pinged.

That sucks.

She may as well have given me the middle finger for how much she clearly didn't care.

Wow, I wrote, furious she could be so callous. But then I realized something. The only person who knew I'd gone to Brie's house—

other than Spider, of course—was Rain. Had she called the tip line? Could she really hate me enough to frame me? Had she set the fire, left town, and decided I should take the fall?

She wouldn't. She couldn't. And yet. Where the hell was she? What other reason could she have for staying away this long? What had Ed done that had bothered Rain so much? Or had she simply realized Brie had played her all those months and just . . . snapped?

I wanted to scream, to throw my phone. But what good would that do? Instead, I sent a text I knew I would probably regret.

> My world is falling apart and you're just gone. If I didn't know better, I might think you were running from something.

I watched the three dots appear and disappear, appear and disappear again, as if she was deciding how to respond.

> What do you mean?

Should I back off my accusation here or double down? I bit my lip and tried to thread the needle between the two.

> Just that I would never leave you to get through this alone. Whatever stupid fight we were having, I would come back and I would help you. And the fact that you're not coming back from Peoria or wherever the fuck you are? I'm starting to wonder why.

If she was going to tell the cops horrible things about me, I could do the same. I was about to write this when I saw her reply.

> Peoria?

I rolled my eyes. *Really?* Here she should have written *But they love me in Peoria.* Peoria should have been as familiar to Rain as her own name. No amount of grief or anger could erase it. Rain not remembering our Peoria routine—or pretending not to remember it just to hurt me—almost felt like the cruelest thing she'd done yet. It was part of our friendship's DNA. Had we ever really been friends at all? I was starting to doubt I'd ever actually understood Rain. How could the girl I was closest to in the world pretend not to know me?

?? Yeah don't they love you there?? I prompted her, as if to say, *Oh, now you're going to pretend you don't remember even this?*

After a long pause, she responded.

Okay weirdo. There's no big plot against you. You're being paranoid. I'll be home soon, I told you.

Instantly, my skin was covered in gooseflesh.

The text sat there in its little bubble, shattering everything.

I stared down at my phone and started to scroll through all of her recent texts. Everything was spelled properly. All the periods and commas were where they should be. Nothing was careless. Rain didn't write this way. Couldn't if she tried. And she never called anyone *weirdo.* But someone else did.

How had it taken me this long to notice?

I bit back a scream and typed out a question, even though I already knew the answer.

Who is this??

PART XI

RAIN

THE NIGHT OF THE FIRE

31

Brie's house was dark when I pulled up, every shade drawn tight.

Ed's still away, a new text from Brie said. Front door's open.

I gripped my car keys the way we were taught in eighth grade, the pointy end of three keys threaded through my fisted fingers, so as to be able to use them as a weapon. What was I going to do, beat Brie up? Unlikely, especially considering how I never worked out and she'd been weight training and sprinting since middle school, but it felt better having something to threaten her with.

"Brie?" I called, pushing the front door shut behind me. I kept my right hand with the key-claws behind my back.

"In the kitchen."

She'd lit a candle, one of the Aesop ones she was so proud of shoplifting because they were so expensive. The flame set the kitchen island aglow. Behind it she was mixing White Russians. My favorite.

"When's Ed back?" I muttered, not caring much but feeling nervous enough to bumble my way through small talk. I knew from sleeping over here last night that Ed was at a car convention in Vegas.

"Tomorrow." She looked up from the drinks and smiled brightly. "Listen, thanks for coming. It's not what you think. I would never steal from you."

"I'll be going as soon as I have the money," I said stiffly.

"Rain." Brie sipped her drink and slid the other one across the counter. "I feel like everything got so mixed up at the party. I'm your friend. All this time, I've been looking out for you. Nobody loves you more than I do."

I took the drink and knocked it all back, needing the liquid courage to get through this. "That's why you took the money? Because you're my friend who loves me?"

"I put the money somewhere safe, that's all." Brie looked wounded and maybe also a little panicked.

"It already was somewhere safe."

"Not exactly." Brie took another sip of her drink. "Once Joan found out you'd taken it, that money didn't stand a chance. You were going to have to give it back to her. You told me that, remember?"

I nodded, wishing I could move this along. I couldn't pinpoint why, but the whole house, Brie herself, the candle . . . all of it was giving me the creeps.

"You two would have been broke in a few years, tops. I just didn't want you to be left with nothing. So I just went in and moved it to a different safe place. Somewhere Joan couldn't get to it. I wanted—*want*—all your dreams to come true. I wanted to help you with everything." Brie paused here, looked at me from across the counter like she was letting these words sink in.

Just stop talking, I thought. I breathed out hard through my nostrils to signal that my patience was wearing thin. "And what *are* my dreams, Brie? Since you're my best friend?"

I thought of Syd with a pang, wishing I could call her now. After this was done with, I would go see her, tell her how wrong I'd been to ever get wrapped up with Brie. How stupid I felt that I'd let her manipulate me. I would apologize with everything I had for ever doubting Syd's friendship.

"Let's see . . . going to LA, um, using your money to have an awesome life? I'd been thinking we could share a place, you know. For the summer."

My face must have registered horror at this because she looked up at the ceiling and sighed loudly.

"You're right to want to get out of here," I said after an awkward silence. "Spider's not going to forget what you did you him. Now that he's out, you'd better watch your back."

"What*ever*," Brie snapped, exasperated. "Spider is the last thing I'm worried about right now. I was doing you a favor, why can't you understand that? The only thing worse than being poor is to have had security for a short time and then have it snatched away from you." Brie spread her fingers out on the countertop, her smooth, tanned forearms flexing and relaxing. In the dim light, I could see her eyes were glassy. "Trust me, you don't want that."

"*Trust* you?" For some reason, I had grown inexplicably tired. Brie must have worn me down with all her talking. I yawned, feeling my anger dissipate a little. "Yeah, I don't. That means you broke into my house and took the money to, what, *save* it for me? You're lying. I see it now. You're always lying. Always out for yourself."

She flashed me a tight smile. "I didn't break in. You gave me a key, remember?"

This was true. I had given her a key. It had seemed easier since she was always coming and going and the front door was so far from my room.

"One of my many mistakes." I swallowed another yawn and stood up off the barstool, hoping I looked like I meant business. Enough talk, I wanted my money. "Just give it back and I'll get out of your hair."

When I looked at Brie in the candlelight there were two of her where there should have been one. The shadows flowing out behind her were hazy. The edges of my vision blurred to black. I gripped the countertop by its edge, suddenly feeling like I needed it for support. How strong was the drink she'd given me?

"You okay?" Brie frowned. "You look a little pale. Maybe sit down?" She motioned to the barstool next to me. I reached to pull the stool out and my car keys clattered to the floor.

"I'll get those," Brie said. She helped me onto the seat. I looked into the stupid candle, watched the flame vibrate into two, three flames. Brie was at my side now, standing close. She had begun to talk again, only this time her voice was quieter, deeper, a hypnotic monotone. "I had to take the money, you know. Your mother, god bless her, is a drunk. And she doesn't make good choices. I went through her emails, actually, just for fun one day. She's investing in, like, five properties. She doesn't know what she's doing. I couldn't let her just . . . *evaporate* the money like that. Nothing worse than an idiot who can't manage his—her—money." She paused and chuckled at this, an inside joke with herself. When I looked at her she was staring straight ahead, a blank expression on her face. "Trust me, I would know."

"It's not yours to worry about." My eyelids felt heavy. "Just give it back. I don't know why you would go through my mother's email. That's incredibly fucked up, even for you."

Brie didn't seem to feel the need to address this. It was almost like she didn't hear me, or like I wasn't really talking. "Come on then, let's go upstairs. The money's up there. But . . . you look a little tired."

Now I was struggling to hold my head up. Panic spun through me and cut through my wooziness. Had I been so drunk earlier tonight that the White Russian had pushed me over the edge toward passing out? That didn't seem possible. I'd felt totally sober when I walked in here.

Brie slugged another sip from her glass. The ice cubes hit her teeth. And suddenly I realized.

The drink I'd so stupidly chugged. My favorite. The drink we'd always had together over here. She'd put something in it.

"What the fuck did you do?" My words came out slurred.

Brie's arms were around my shoulders now and she was pulling me off the barstool. I tried to push her away, but my arms were limp and uncooperative. I had no choice but to let her drag me along beside her. My legs flopped under me like they belonged to a marionette.

"Tell me," I demanded.

"Oh, Raindrop." She sighed. I felt her dry lips kiss my cheek. So calm and smooth. The best liar who ever lived. "You're so trusting under all your toughness. I love that about you. Just so you know, my first choice was for both of us to run away, to use the money together."

Panic shimmied through my chest, but I couldn't even manage to scream. Could barely manage to speak. I finally got a word out, wanting to understand, needing to know how bad this was going to be. "But?"

"But once you stopped trusting me, that wasn't going to be an option anymore. Even tonight, I thought maybe I could convince you. Explain to you why you needed me. But that didn't work, so now we're going with plan B."

"Stealing?" I managed. My lips were numb now. We stood in front of the final staircase, the one on the second floor that led to her attic bedroom.

"Something like that." Brie pulled my hair away from my face and tucked it gently behind my shoulder. She leaned in and looked at me close, flashed her class president smile, the one she saved for the stage and for track meets. "Let's get you upstairs to rest."

My breath caught in my throat, poison in my guts. I took a breath to scream but all I heard was a faraway mewling, no louder than a kitten's.

In Brie's room, everything was a hazy purple. She'd lit all her scented candles and shadows danced up the walls. Her desk, her neat piles of index cards fringed with tiny neon Post-its, her tiny, neat handwriting. Her maniacal organization. Her endless work. Brie the bee. Never resting, all these years.

She led me to her bed. "Lie down," she said. "I'll go get the money." But she didn't. She sat next to me on the bed and stayed perfectly still. Sitting there next to her, I could hardly keep my lids open. I felt like a spider being washed down the drain, fighting to stay in the bathtub but getting closer to oblivion with every swirl of water.

And then the edges of things continued to dissolve, everything blurred, the lines between me and the air around me, the line between me and Brie, the line between this world and all that lay beyond it had disappeared.

"Brie," I started. *It doesn't have to be like this,* I tried to say but couldn't, slipping as I was into the space where words didn't exist anymore.

"I'm sorry," she said. "I really am. I wish it didn't have to be this way."

The last thing I saw was Brie's blue gaze, her eyes filled with tears even as she held that perfect smile.

PART XII

BRIE

THE NIGHT OF THE FIRE

32

I cried the whole time. For my mother, mostly. To die when your baby is so young, when your baby's father is Ed, nobody would have chosen that. I always wondered if my mother predicted how it was all going to go, or if she was too busy dying to see that Ed wouldn't raise her girl to be normal. I wondered if somehow she could see all this, all her daughter had tried for, all I'd failed to do.

Not that I believed in an afterlife, or in heaven. As for hell . . . how much worse could it be than actually living?

Still, I was sorry for Mommy that her girl had grown up to be me.

I watched Rain for a while after I'd put her in my bed, my fingers on her wrist registering her pulse. Slow and faint but definitely still alive. I had at least three hours before the six crushed Xanax I'd put in her drink might wear off enough to let her stir. Enough time to finish what I'd started. I lifted her head and fanned her hair across my pillow. She looked so lovely I almost gasped, her wide mouth and long lashes straight out of some Renaissance painting. I kissed her cheek. "Bye, Brie," I whispered, trying it on for size. I would be Rain now, I told her silently. I would do her proud just as soon as I could. My jeans pockets bulged with her keys and wallet and phone. I left my things beside her on the nightstand the way Egyptians put offerings in tombs. She could take Brie's things with her into the afterlife. Maybe they'd be useful there. "I love you," I whispered before I left her. In my own way, I did love her.

Now I crouched in the crawl space under the living room. My hands shook as I swirled the chemicals Whit had given me in an old Nalgene bottle. It was 3:45 in the morning, the last chem lab experiment I would ever complete. I hummed as I worked, the gas mask Whit gave me fogging and unfogging with my breath: *I decided long ago, never to walk in anyone's shadow.* My favorite song when I was little. Cheesy old Whitney. I still loved it. Still believed it. *If I fail, if I succeed, at least I'll live as I believe,* I hit the higher key under my breath and blinked sweat out of my eyes. So many meth houses had exploded in the desert that there was a name for it—a meth demolition. If I did this right, if I didn't mess up and die in the blast, the house would explode fast enough that Rain would feel no pain. And the destruction would be extreme enough that it would take the cops weeks to figure out what had happened. Weeks, or forever.

As the chemicals sat and mingled, I watched the steam on the lenses shrink and grow with my breath and tried not to think of Rain dreaming her drugged dreams in my bed.

At last, the liquid in the Nalgene bottle turned an oily blue. It was time. I'd already transferred my suitcase into Rain's car. In the trunk I'd found a duffel bag she'd packed, so neatly planning to run away from this town just as I now would. Wearing her clothes would make it that much easier to pretend I was her. To use her money to start a life far away from here, away from my father. All I needed was to tie up this one loose end and make sure Rain couldn't sic the police on me. And after that, I would be free.

I found the greatest love of all, I hummed, moving like the ghost I was up the crawl space stairs. I patted my pocket. Rain's matches were there, awaiting the fuse. Poetic. As if in a weird way, she was killing herself.

Just below the stairs to my bedroom, I placed the bottle on the carpet. From a Ziploc bag I took a string I'd presoaked in kerosene, unwound it, let it snake along the carpet, and placed one end of it in the bottle.

Goodbye, Rain. Goodbye, house. Goodbye, everything. Goodbye, mouse.

My hands shook as I fumbled with the matches. *Tzt, tzt.* I broke three in a row scraping them along the striker. *Calm down, mouse,* I said to whatever bit of myself remained.

If the next match lit, I would do it. If it didn't, I'd take my pathetic homemade explosive and leave, just drive and drive and never come back. Rain would wake up and even if she remembered what I'd done, I'd be long gone.

The match blazed to life. *That's it then. Goodbye, beauty.* My hands trembling, my goggles filling with tears, I put the flame to the string and watched it start to travel. Then I ran, silent and quick, my chest about to explode, my head spinning. I bolted out of the house, got into Rain's car, and drove. Behind me, about sixty seconds later, I heard a distinct pop, a single, loud firework.

In the rearview, an explosion of orange. I watched it for a moment, not daring to breathe. Then I hit the gas hard and lurched through the night, gripping the steering wheel with white knuckles and trying to ignore the way my whole body had begun to shake.

If I'd done it right, the house would be destroyed, and Rain along with it. It would be a fire worthy of the action movies my father loved to watch alone in the living room while sipping his beloved Canadian Club, the hero running out in the nick of time, unscathed.

If I'd done it wrong, maybe it didn't matter. I was already gone.

33

The longer I drove, the easier it was to pretend it never happened. The Mini Cooper rolled eastward, smooth and silent on the 10, past the fields of cacti raising their prickled arms to the moon in Joshua Tree and on and on, the highway empty in the early morning darkness. East meant away, a migration toward sunrise along the stick-straight strip of bleached highway on the desert floor. It was so easy I didn't need to consult a map. One highway, all the way to Texas.

As the miles ticked by, my hands gradually stopped their shaking. My breathing returned to normal. Eventually I stopped unconsciously whimpering like a kicked dog. "All the best liars are dead inside," Anya used to joke whenever I lied to a teacher or to my father without batting an eye. Rocketing down the highway in Rain's car, I practiced Rain's laugh. I did her shrug, her half-smile. If I locked up the bad things I'd done in the dark corners of my mind, I could almost become her.

By the time the first fingers of sunrise bled pink across the sky at 4:55 AM, I was crossing the Arizona border. ARIZONA, a big blue sign with a sunset-colored star design announced. THE GRAND CANYON STATE WELCOMES YOU.

"Oh, me?" I said aloud in the car, pressing my hand to my chest in a gesture of feigned modesty. I waved to the sign as if it cared. "I didn't expect a welcome."

I pressed the gas pedal harder, before Arizona could change its mind.

An hour later, I pulled off the highway and ordered Rain's usual, black coffee and hash browns, from the drive-thru at McDonald's. I gazed into the rearview with my sunglasses on as the car inched ahead, my dark hair tumbling around my face. I smiled like Rain would when I paid the cashier. "Thanks," I said, and I could almost believe I was her. I'd been absorbing her mannerisms for so long, maybe I really could wear her like a second skin.

It was only when I lifted my sunglasses and peered into my own eyes that I saw myself again, blank and empty, haunted by what I'd become.

The coffee, when I sipped it, scalded my tongue.

I'd watched Rain type in her passcode enough times that her phone opened for me on my first try. I found a playlist she'd titled "Squid & The Pain" and let the first song wash over me as I turned back onto the 10, one of those guitar-thrashing women they both liked, singing like she couldn't keep the words inside her anymore. I hardly listened to the lyrics but I could hear the power and exasperation in her voice, done with the world's bullshit and ready to kick it all apart. That was so Rain. Come out swinging, go down fighting. Which was why I'd had to make sure she couldn't fight.

Rain's phone sat charging beside me in the cup holder. In an hour or two when people woke up, the texts would start coming thick and fast, one reason I was headed east rather than south to San Ysidro. If I'd driven south, I'd be at the border already. Better to keep this phone working a while longer to sprinkle the bread crumbs of Rain's digital presence.

I'd never been to Texas before, but I'd seen a documentary for AP history about its border towns. In a big enough city, a person could fade right into the hustle-bustle, could disappear without a trace. Or so I hoped.

I drove for hours on the one McDonald's coffee, the hash browns sitting like a brick in my stomach. The highway's canvas of dust and scrub was so desolate between cities, it looked like it could murder me if I even slowed down. I stopped only once more, to gas up, use the bathroom, and buy granola bars and water with cash at a gas station outside of Tucson. On impulse, I bought an Arizona Wildcats baseball cap from a stack at the register and pulled it low on my forehead before I ducked past the security camera and headed out. News of a girl dying in a fire probably wouldn't make it across state lines, but it didn't hurt to be careful.

Back in the car, I parked near the station's air pumps and idled a few minutes with the AC blasting. I chewed a granola bar mechanically, scanned Rain's texts and calls for unknown numbers—police or whatnot—and determined that so far all the calls and texts were from people Rain knew. I started writing to Joan, telling her I needed some time to decompress from our fight and that I'd be home in a few days. Safe and sound, don't worry, I wrote. I'm sorry we fought, I added, remembering Rain's account of the blowout fight they'd had, remembering it was because of me. I love you, I wrote, my stomach twisting with the syrupy sweetness of those words. I couldn't even imagine saying that to Ed, but other people were normal, I assumed. Rain could run off with one million dollars of her mother's money and still love her, couldn't she?

I stared at what I'd typed for a minute before I decided to delete it. It would be better to send this to Joan later, when I would be less distracted and could focus on what she would write back.

There was still so much to do if I was going to pull this off.

My fingers hovered over Syd's final text, the last in a string of five or six.

Where are you?? They just called your name over the loudspeaker. I think the police are here at school asking questions.

I'll be back in a few days. Need a little more time to process this alone, I wrote. I channeled Rain's rebel spirit about the police: As for the police, fuck 'em.

My lips curved into an involuntary smile I tried to suppress. I didn't want to take this much pleasure in fucking with Syd, but it was impossible not to enjoy it just a little. She wrote back right away, sounding even more panicked than before:

> The police will be looking for you. They think we had something to do with the fire. Someone told them I was "keeping tabs" on you and Brie. You need to tell them the truth.

"Poor Sydney, you're really losing your mind over there, aren't you?" I said out loud. "And you were keeping tabs, you little stalker." And then an irresistible idea floated into my head, one that I knew would help me while simultaneously hurting her. I typed out one last text and hit send before I could think too hard about it.

> Don't worry. I'll never tell them what we did.

I sat back and reread my words, savoring the satisfaction of injecting more chaos into Syd's life from so far away. Let her put that in her holier-than-thou pipe and smoke it. Let her squirm and wonder what she did while shit-faced that could possibly have caused her old frenemy Brie to die such a gruesome death. If the cops suspected her and if she doubted herself, all the better for me.

When Syd's next text arrived, I was already pulling Rain's car back onto the highway.

Stuck in El Paso traffic that afternoon, my eyelids kept drifting shut. I pulled off the highway and found a Motel 6 near the airport. At the front desk, I handed over Rain's debit card to the clerk, a ferret-faced man with a single hoop earring whose name tag said FRANK.

"You won't charge this though, right? I can pay cash when I leave?" I asked.

"Yup. We only charge the card on file if there's an outstanding balance," Frank said, directing his words to my chest instead of my face. *Good,* I thought, for once rejoicing in the predictability of men. *Don't memorize my features.*

"There won't be." I smiled.

I pulled the car right up to the door of my room and dragged my suitcase and Rain's duffel bag inside, looking around from under my sunglasses before I closed the door to make sure nobody was watching me. After I pulled the curtains shut tight, I took in the room with its flimsy furniture and Wild West motif and tried to decide where to put the money, neatly packed in five zippered free-gift-with-purchase makeup bags at the bottom of my roller bag. I would sew it into my suitcase lining at some point, when I had the time. For now, I dug the makeup bags from the suitcase and considered the motel safe underneath the TV. "Never trust a motel safe," I remembered Ed saying at a hotel room in Orlando, the very last time I'd joined him at a car convention. "People leave their valuables and forget about them and the motel busts into the safe and keeps the good stuff." I'd been thirteen and he'd promised we'd go to Epcot and Disney World, but—typical Ed—he was so hungover on the last day that he declared we would actually visit neither. Instead, he'd barked when I got upset, I could go to the motel pool.

Ever Daddy's perfect girl, I took the makeup bags and placed them out in the open on the bathroom counter where I couldn't forget them. I wasn't leaving the room anyway, not without the money.

I sat down next to Rain's duffel bag, stared into space, and listened to my stomach growl. I could still smell the chemicals from last night on my clothes.

I peeled everything off me and kicked the pile of clothes into a corner. In the motel bathroom, I stared at myself in the mirror and tried again to smile like Rain—a half-formed dreamy smirk. I held it for a while until it fell off me and my face dissolved back into who I really was: someone who had done the unthinkable. I shook my head. "You're not wanted here," I said to my reflection. I smirked like Rain again, flipped my hair around to make it look more like hers. I would never be Brie again, unless I got caught. For now, I was Rain Santangelo and maybe in the future I'd become someone else. What a relief it was to say goodbye to Brianna Walsh, that striving, desperate thing. That bottomless pit of want.

You'll have to find a way to live with this. I blinked at the mirror. Hadn't Ed said that to me back in December? Back when I still thought all my ass-busting in school was going to pay off with a ticket out of the desert and away from him? I'd applied early action to USC, my absolute first choice, and had been accepted. I'd printed out their emails and gathered the brochures they'd sent to discuss with Ed after he'd eaten the dinner I'd made us, the Costco eggplant Parmesan he liked. USC was pretty expensive, but when I'd applied Ed had shrugged and muttered "may as well go ahead and try." *Anywhere you get in, we'll make it work.* He'd been saying that for years. And though he'd let me down in so many ways, I still believed him about this.

"Actually"—he dabbed marinara sauce from his chin with a napkin—"we need to have a sit-down about you and college." He got up, pulled down his bottle of Canadian Club from the cupboard, and poured what I knew to be a double.

A knot formed in my stomach. Ed was mean when he was sober but he was vicious when he drank. This wasn't how I wanted to do this.

"Another night," I said, on my guard. I felt heat rising on my neck and chest. "Not when you're drinking."

"This conversation requires a drink," my father muttered before he swallowed most of the whiskey. *What a weak man,* I thought, *to admit that.* The knot tightened in my stomach, and part of me knew right then that Ed was about to disappoint me yet again.

When he told me, I laughed. The dealership was in the red. Very much so. It had been twenty-four months since he'd come close to hitting targets. He'd thought he could turn it around, but people just didn't want Nissans right now. The economy, blah blah blah. To bridge the gap, he'd taken out some loans. We'd been living beyond our means for a long time, he said.

"How long?" I asked, taking care to keep my face composed when inside I was filled with revulsion.

"Oh, years." He wiped the back of his hand across his mouth. "It's just not in the cards for us right now, the college thing. Not a rich-kid private school like USC."

I'd stared straight ahead, tried not to panic, tried not to scream. "I could talk to the financial aid office," I whispered. "They might—"

"Doubt we'd qualify on paper. The numbers from the business are a little, uh . . . fudged at the moment." Ed poured more whiskey into his glass and belched softly. He looked at me with glazed, bloodshot eyes and winced. "But I don't have any more rabbits to pull out of my hat," he went on. "Realistically, the dealership is going to fold within the year. We'll probably have to sell the house. You can go to College of the Desert, save the money, work and contribute to the rent wherever we end up and maybe put a little aside. It'll be good for you, give you some life skills. You can transfer in a couple years when I'm on my feet again."

"I didn't work my brains out every day for four years to go to College of the Desert," I said, practically choking on the words. "I'd rather die than stay here next year, honestly."

Just the thought of it made me feel like I might explode.

"You want to assume thirty years of crippling debt, be my guest. I'm not paying a dime for it." Ed shrugged as if he'd just told me they were out of the cookies I liked at the store. "You know, not everyone is spoiled enough to think they can go to any college they want to."

"Not everyone has an irresponsible ass for a dad either," I spat. "Aren't I the lucky one?"

That was when he threw his glass against the wall. *"Ungrateful little snot."* His voice was flat and emotionless, but his face was so red it was practically purple. "Don't talk to your father like that. I've supported you for eighteen years. You can damn well help *me* out for once in your goddamned life."

I stared down at the widening pool of whiskey on the tiles and watched shards of broken glass float toward its edges. Then I ran from the room.

I couldn't be poor again. The thousand pinpricks of shame swallowing down your every material desire as extravagant while the world carried on getting and spending. The grind of always, always wanting. Knowing the world didn't care about you and never would, because without money you were invisible. But by far the worst part of it all, the part that was unbearable, was that being broke would yoke me to the person I most hated and feared in the world. Dear drunk Daddy.

Everything I'd worked for—my whole future as a top student at a good college, at a great law school—felt like a joke now, a handful of stupid dreams as smashed and useless as the highball glass that floated across the kitchen floor.

And then the very next day, as if God herself was laughing at me, I heard Rain Santangelo had won the lottery.

For a week or two, I watched her from afar to see if it was true. As signs of her newfound wealth accumulated—new clothes, a new leather bag that looked beat-up and distressed in the most expensive possible way, a cute new Mini Cooper—I began to construct a plan. With six million dollars, the Santangelos had more money than they knew what to do with. Rain didn't even want to go to college! All I needed to do was find a way to get in, gain Rain's trust, and get access to just a tiny fraction of that money. Maybe I could even convince her to help me out, fund my education. I could offer to pay her back when I became a lawyer. And if not, I could find a way to take some of it off their hands. Even a few thousand would help if we, as dear Daddy kept on telling me, were truly on our way to not having a pot to piss in. Rain and her mother wouldn't even notice if some of it was gone.

And then everything had gone so well. I even started to actually like her again. Rain remembered who I used to be. Not the bad parts that I remembered, but the good things from our childhoods, too. She even remembered my mom.

"She was so pretty." Rain had sighed one night beside me in her big bed on the floor of her room. "Even when she got sick, remember, she still sang? I remember those Cyndi Lauper songs would just float out of her mouth when she was just puttering around, and she sounded better than any singer on the radio."

I'd lain there, eyes shut, overtaken by a memory of my mother, frail as a bird, washing dishes and singing "Time After Time" in her folk singer's voice, the notes high and sweet.

"I haven't thought of that in years," I'd whispered. "I think I'd forgotten all about her voice until now."

"You probably forgot a lot of stuff from when you were that age," Rain said, her face bathed in moonlight just as it had been when we'd had sleepovers as kids, her gaze intense the way it always was. "Trauma and all that."

I turned away then, not wanting her to see my eyes misting over.

My only obstacle turned out to be Rain's loyalty to Sydney, but even that was easier to dismantle than I'd expected. All I'd had to do was plant a few doubts in Rain's mind about Syd, get her to think Syd was jealous of her new money and critical of her new life. After that, Rain was all mine. And she was a generous friend. Generous with her time, her attention, and her money, paying for stuff like it meant nothing to her. It got so that I almost felt bad about it. It had been so easy to borrow a little here and there, to conveniently forget my wallet. She'd been so trusting.

Once I finally found the mother lode it seemed like it was going to be so easy to get Rain to share it with me. I was just waiting for school to wrap up and then we could both get out of here, go off to LA and rent a place together. She could help me pay for college and I could help her grow her fortune.

Either way, I would get away from Ed, start my new life with the help of my best friend. It didn't hurt that we looked alike now, in case I ever needed to pass as her once I talked her into opening a bank account.

I'd never planned on killing her.

I unwrapped the motel soap and tried to push last night back down where it belonged, locked in the recesses of memory with all the other bad things I'd experienced. When the water in the shower was close to scalding, I stepped inside, the cheap curtain curling like molting skin around me until I smoothed it against the side of the tub. I closed my eyes and let the water hit my face.

And then I was back on my staircase, Rain's limp body knocking against me as I pulled her toward my room. I saw that final shocked look on her face when she realized what I'd done, her mouth hanging open, the terror in her eyes as the truth hit. "What's happening?" she'd slurred, but she knew. The Xanax I'd ground up and slipped into her glass didn't let her get the words out, but her eyes registered horror. When she passed out, I knew I was going to go through with it. I could see now that I'd lost Rain's trust, that there was no way I'd ever gain it back. I couldn't risk Rain telling the police. Because she would. Syd would make sure of it, as payback for what I'd done to her and to her brother. She'd jump at the chance to get Rain back on her side, turn her even more against me than she already was. The two of them would gang up on me just like when we were little, paint me as a criminal for "stealing" the money I was only borrowing, send me to prison for as long as they could.

I opened my eyes in the shower and shook the images of Rain

away. The hot water had turned my body lobster red. Even so, I shivered.

"You burn everyone's lives down for sport," Rain had said at the party, full of that same old disgust she'd had for me for so long and then had briefly set aside. Everything I'd worked for, over in an instant.

Now there's an idea, I'd thought when she said that, feeling the brunt of her hatred for me hit with full force. I'd already taken the bold step of moving the money from Rain's predictable hiding place, thinking I would keep it safer from Joan than she could. I was about to tell her I was keeping it safe for her, for us, so that we could move to LA together and set up a new life. I just hadn't found the right way to say it yet. But now that our friendship had imploded, that wasn't going to work. She'd accuse me of stealing it. She'd call the police. I would not only be outed as broke, but as a thief. Now that Rain hated me, I wasn't getting away with anything anymore.

Just another thing you've fucked up, I'd thought that night at Candice's as Rain and Syd raged at me, hating myself. *Another dead end in a lifetime of them.*

When the shower ran cold, I wrapped myself in one of the motel's thin towels and used a second towel to wrap my wet hair. I lay down under the motel sheet in the cool dark, Rain's phone glowing in my hands. Even after scrubbing every part of my body, I could still smell the chemicals on my fingers. I moved the phone farther from my face and tried to breathe through my mouth.

I scanned the headlines from the desert cities. I was all over them. TRAGIC DEATH OF ONE OF VALLEY SANDS' MOST HIGH-ACHIEVING SENIORS. CAUSE OF EXPLOSION STILL UNKNOWN. Brianna Walsh, bright future, distinguished student, top of her class, track star, class president, yada yada. All my résumé points were covered. SHOCK GIVES WAY TO GRIEF AT LOCAL HIGH SCHOOL. COMMUNITY MOURNS STAR ATHLETE FOUND DEAD AFTER A HOUSE FIRE. A detail from that article stuck out: "Edward Walsh rushed home from a

Las Vegas business trip in a state of shock. He'd lost everything that mattered—his beloved daughter and his home—in one explosive and still-unexplained blaze." Work trip? Try *last chance to drink and gamble on the company dime at a car conference.* I kept reading. "'I don't understand how this could have happened. She was my everything,' he said, his voice breaking." *Your everything? Really, Ed?* I wondered what my father was doing right now. Probably sleeping underneath his desk at the office. I'd found him there once before, passed out after one too many nips from the bottle he kept in his desk drawer.

I blinked hard, a tickle of feeling in my chest but nothing more. This was what he got for all those years of drunken screaming. For not being able to show love. For pushing me to be the best and then not supporting me when I was. For ruining my life.

I scanned another article and watched a segment I found from the local news that showed the house smoldering and black behind a perky reporter. I turned it off after a minute—looking at the house and thinking about Rain having been inside it was making my hands shake.

There was nothing in the news yet about foul play. No speculation about the cause of the explosion. Nothing about Rain. At least not yet.

I returned to Sydney's increasingly panicked string of texts, figuring I had to say something. She seemed to think the police wanted to get ahold of Rain. This could have been the truth or just a fabrication to get Rain to come back.

I'll be back in a couple more days, I wrote. Too upset about everything to rush home.

I looked at the motel ceiling, at a water spot in the shape of Alaska that surrounded the ugly light fixture. Rain's work done now, I closed my burning eyes, settled back on the threadbare motel pillowcase, and tried to sleep.

34

By 5 PM the following day, I'd finally ditched Rain's Mini Cooper and swapped it for the cheapest, most nondescript car I could find, a beige 2012 Ford Taurus I bought from a retiree named Elmer who'd advertised on Craigslist. I'd left Rain's car on a side street two blocks from Elmer's house, not wanting to risk selling it to him and leaving a clearer trail for anyone to find Rain, should they come looking. I'd spent the rest of the day avoiding texts from Joan and Syd and plotting out my route through Mexico. I'd managed a few hours of sleep at the motel with the help of two of Whit's Xanax, but I still felt wrecked and wobbly by the time I'd packed up the Taurus with water, food, and all of Rain's worldly belongings.

I flipped through Elmer's radio presets as I snaked along the banks of the Rio Grande toward one of El Paso's border crossings. Across the river, Ciudad Juárez twinkled in the twilight. I squinted out the car window and studied its hills dotted in colorful little houses and just past that, miles of soft brown mountains where a girl could follow a highway due south until she dropped out of sight.

In Mexico, Rain would disappear into the mist like so many troubled girls did. By the time Joan came looking for her, I would make sure she'd be untraceable. There were some little artsy towns in southern Mexico I planned to lie low in for a while. And after that, anything was possible.

There was only one other loose end to tie up before I crossed the border into Ciudad Juárez.

Rain's phone buzzed on the passenger seat as it had all day. I pulled the Taurus over next to a sloping embankment that led down to the river and took a look. More missives from Syd. A long rant about Spider, the cops, how much she needed Rain, blah blah blah. The cops knew she went to Brie's house, she was saying.

I'm a suspect now for real. I feel like I'm being watched. I'm so scared.

I smiled. Everything was going just as I'd hoped, Syd-wise.

That sucks, I typed. I got out of the car and walked down the embankment on a little path cut into the bushes that lined the river, only halfway paying attention. Then Syd finally did what I'd been expecting and asked me if I was running from something.

What do you mean? I wrote, all innocence and stupidity. Syd had always had a brain. I'd studied ten times harder than her all these years, I sensed, and yet we were neck and neck in the class rankings. Funny how it had taken her this long to put two and two together.

When the phone buzzed again, I was standing at the edge of the Rio Grande, the wide brown stillness of the water broken here and there by boats. A few men in waders were still fishing near the shore about a hundred yards away, far enough that I couldn't see their faces and they couldn't see mine. I glanced down at the phone and saw more of the usual freakout and a weird reference to Peoria.

Peoria? I wrote, not thinking too hard about whatever inside joke this was. It didn't matter anyway.

?? Yeah, don't they love you there??

God, Syd was so weird. No wonder she didn't have any friends. I rolled my eyes and typed a quick reply.

Okay weirdo. There's no big plot against you. You're being paranoid. I'll be home soon, I told you.

I stared across the river again and tried to feel brave. A cloud of gnats drifted toward me and I shooed them away before walking a few paces closer to the muck at the water's edge.

Finally, a text pinged back.

Who is this??

Shit. I'd said something wrong. My chest fluttered with nerves, panic running hot through my veins. I thought about writing back, but what could I say that wouldn't make it worse? I couldn't walk it back without knowing what I'd said wrong.

You're fine, I reminded myself. Earlier today, I'd sent two pieces of insurance to the Palm Springs Police Department that would keep them busy with Syd a while longer. I still had plenty of time to disappear.

On rubbery legs, I maneuvered over rocks around the muddy shore. A mile or two downriver was a border crossing lit up with blazing halogens on both sides. Cars inched forward along the bridge in a long, slow-moving line.

I already knew to drive south toward the mountains past Ciudad Juárez once I crossed. I'd memorized the names of the highways I could use. I would pick up a burner phone in Mexico, not that I planned to call anyone. My AP Spanish should work well enough for that.

All along the river, birds were settling in bushes. I heard the rustling of rodents or lizards in the brush behind me, creatures waking up again after a long, hot afternoon. The sky was a deepening violet. Balanced on a boulder, I turned a cautious 360 to make sure I was alone, unseen.

The phone buzzed again and again, but I had no reason to read any more of Syd's texts.

"Sorry, sweetie," I said out loud, two chickadees on a nearby bush the only living creatures close enough to hear. "Rain can't come to the phone right now."

I assumed a pitcher's stance and threw the phone as far as I could. It sailed through the air and made the tiniest, most undramatic plop before the river swallowed it up.

I wanted to hum a song Rain had liked as I headed back along the cut path to the car, but I couldn't think of one. I couldn't even think of a song *I* liked. My mind was totally blank for a blessed minute until I flashed again on the pop of the house exploding, the vision of Rain's body tucked into my bed, flames engulfing her, crawling across her beautiful skin, burning her hair. All night long, even with the two Xanax, I'd woken to these images, my own lungs filling up in nightmares until I sat up with a start.

My arms broke out in gooseflesh even though the evening was warm. And though I kept thinking I heard footsteps behind me on the trail, when I whipped around there wasn't anyone there. I shook my head and trudged back toward the car, toward my hard-won cash, my face streaked with tears I didn't remember crying. I kept on moving, pinching the inside of my forearm to keep myself focused on the task at hand, on this beautiful evening where I was free and rich. This was the beginning of my new life, after all. I'd better start enjoying it.

I pulled myself up straighter and tried to walk the way Rain would, that sidelong slouch she had, that don't-fuck-with-me stare she gave strangers. I would become her so completely that it would be like she was still here among us, one of the living. And it would be like Brie really had died after all.

I'd escaped Spider's vendetta, escaped Rain calling the cops on me, escaped being trapped under Ed's roof.

So why did I still feel so scared?

I slammed the car door shut behind me and sat in the hot car a moment, savoring the warmth. My arms, when I looked down at them, were still covered in gooseflesh.

I pulled out of my parking spot and braced myself for all that lay ahead. A few minutes later, I would join the line of cars inching slowly toward Mexico. "Rain" was officially gone now, no more phantom texts assuring everyone she'd see them soon. Syd would start the wheels turning any minute. She wasn't a total idiot.

"We did it," I said out loud to Brie/Rain as the Taurus joined the end of the line of cars waiting to cross the border. "We're rich. We're free." I curled my lips into a smile and held it so long my cheeks hurt. When I peeked at the rearview mirror to reassure myself, the face I saw there was so grotesque and fake that I had to look away.

PART XIII

SYDNEY

TWO DAYS AFTER THE FIRE

3 5

My head swimming with shock, I retreated into my bed. I clutched my phone to my chest, afraid of Brie writing back and equally afraid she wouldn't.

But then my phone pinged twice, and neither text was from her. The first was from Chase.

Hey, just checking in. Hope you're okay.

Though it was sweet of him, I had never been less okay than I was right now.

The other text was from Joan and it made me want to die.

Any word? I haven't heard from Rain since last night and she wouldn't tell me where she was. I'm filing a missing persons report tomorrow.

My shock morphed into fury. I wanted to break things. Without even thinking about it, I fired off a couple more texts to "Rain."

I KNOW IT'S YOU
MURDERER

PSYCHO

WHAT HAVE YOU DONE???

I sat shaking, hitting the phone against the wall as if that would help, but I got no reply.

And then my anger dissolved into tears. If Brie was off somewhere impersonating Rain, the body in her house could only belong to one person.

I pressed my face into my pillow and wailed, my sobs a series of violent screams.

My best friend. The girl my brother used to refer to as my wife. The funnier, wilder, sharper-edged half of my brain. Gone. Before she'd even begun to live.

"Let's just get in the car and drive and eat tacos and fall asleep on the beach," she used to say after particularly bad days at school, her dark eyes imploring. "We'll build a little fire and sleep on the sand."

I'd always put her off. Always said I didn't have time, that with traffic it would be three hours or more, always promised we'd do it later. Everything was always going to happen later.

All her dreams, up in smoke.

I turned my face to the wall, pressed my fingers to a smiling devil face she drew there in pencil when we were fourteen. I'd drawn an angel next to it, feeling the need for balance. Underneath, Rain had written *Squid's panel of advisors* in her wild scrawl.

But you were my advisor, I thought now. *Only you. You taught me how to live. How will I do it without you?*

When my eyes were swelled to slits and my throat was ripped apart and I had no more tears to cry, I headed to the kitchen. I filled up a glass of water, drank it, then smashed it into the sink, pressing my palm against the wet shards, wanting to transfer some of the pain I felt inside to a place I could manage but feeling nothing. In the bit of moonlight that shone in through the kitchen window, black blood spread from the gash on my palm. I stared numbly as the blood pooled.

Rain had had a long life line, supposedly. A woman selling mangoes at the swap meet read our palms once, had traced the life line on Rain's hand, showing her how pronounced it was. "Good," she had snorted, cracking her gum. "Because all this time I've been thinking I'll probably flame out early."

I stood at the sink and cried a while longer, as if howling into a pit or a cave, until I'd cried so much I'd gone numb.

I washed off the blood, picked the broken glass out of the sink, folded up a stack of paper towels, pressed them to my hand, and taped a makeshift bandage there with masking tape I found in the junk drawer.

In my room, I called Rain's phone again, ready to scream with everything I had.

How could you? I prepared myself to say. *I will never get over this. Not ever.*

But the phone didn't ring at all. It went straight to the same voice mail recording I'd heard for years. Rain's gravelly voice, half serious, half-teasing you for doing something as earnest as leaving a message. *Hi, you've almost reached Rain Santangelo.*

Brie had already gone dark.

"Spider!" I grabbed my brother's meaty upper arm and shook him awake. He was passed out in bed with the TV on, though it wasn't even 8 PM yet. "It wasn't Brie."

He sighed and slowly turned over. He cracked one eye open. "Damn, you look like someone ran you over," he observed. "What wasn't Brie?"

I blinked at him. Willed him to understand.

At last, in the silence between us, something seemed to click.

"The *body*?" he whispered, as if just saying it was somehow part of a crime. "No fucking way."

I nodded.

Spider rubbed his eyes. "Well, who was it, then?"

Again I was weeping, my head in my hands, on the edge of hyperventilating.

Spider sat up in bed now. He pulled me against him, a gentle rock in the turbulence. My crying was almost medical at this point. After a while I looked into his eyes again and I could see him fighting it. "Not Rain," he whispered. "I don't believe it."

"She's missing. Someone's been texting from her phone. I know it's Brie. If Rain were alive, wouldn't she contact someone? Wouldn't she *call*?"

Spider nodded. I saw he believed me. "How'd you figure it out?"

Wordlessly, I handed him my phone. I showed him where Rain's texts ended and the new ones began. I pointed out the differences in style, in spelling. I showed him where Brie missed the running gag between us. Where she gave herself away.

Looking at the conversation, Spider had gone so pale he looked green. He shook his head. "This is so fucked."

I nodded. We sat there for a while, huddled in Spider's bed that smelled like old green beans and weed. Grief expanded to hold both of us in its iron grip. Soon it filled the room. Like love, it turned out grief was infinitely expandable.

"You need to tell the cops." He handed the phone back to me. "Like, *now*."

"What if they don't believe me?"

"They'll test the body. Look at the teeth, the dental records. Maybe they're doing that anyway, I don't know. But until you tell them, every day that goes by is a day Brianna Walsh is closer to getting away with it. She's probably on the run."

I nodded miserably, trying to picture Brie out there somewhere, trying to imagine what was going on in her head. "I still can't believe she'd do this."

"People surprise you," Spider said. "I shared a cell with the nicest guy ever. He lent me books, told me what to say to get the good stuff from the psychiatrist. Come to find out he killed his own grandmother."

I laughed, then felt awful for laughing. My hand covered my mouth as I tried to stuff it back inside. "The guy who stole her life savings? He *killed* her?"

Spider nodded. "People are wild, Sydney. I told you that girl was evil."

I cleared my throat. I had to tell my brother that he was more wrapped up in this than he realized. "I didn't tell you this yet, but earlier tonight, one of the detectives called. She wants me to go in tomorrow after school, to the station."

"Okay, so you'll go sooner." Spider shrugged.

"She wants you to come in, too," I added.

"They think I was involved?" He laughed his new bitter laugh, that resigned chuckle he came home from Pine Grove with that said *life sucks and then you die.*

"I guess. Maybe. I don't know."

"Well, let's inform them of their mistake. Come on, I'll drive you." He lunged out of bed, suddenly full of energy. "No way are you gonna take the fall for a murderer. You're way too soft for prison."

"I can call her first," I remind him. "I have her number."

Spider nodded and opened his bedroom window a little. I could smell the Santa Ana, the dust and sage in the wind. The distant wail of a police siren reached us both, strangely on the nose for a moment like this.

"Spi. What about Joan?" I whispered. The thought of telling her broke my heart all over again. I wiped my face and my eyes felt bruised from all the crying. "Someone's got to tell her."

"First the cops," he said. "So they can find Brie. Rain deserves justice."

I went to my room to dig up Arlene's business card from the front pocket of my backpack where I'd stuffed it. Outside, the siren grew louder.

Deserve. What a concept. As if anyone deserved the way their life spooled out. One girl wins the lottery, another stays poor. One girl dies, the rest of us mourn. Meanwhile, monsters run free. Walking back to Spider's room, I felt all of it rise up inside me, the whole writhing mass of it. The mess of us, our history, me, Brie, and Rain's. Our blown-apart futures. The way the fire destroyed us all.

It only rang once before she answered.

"Detective Garcia," she said by way of hello.

I said nothing, paralyzed. I listened to her breathing on the other end of the line. I was frozen again, terror and grief hammering in my heart. Finally I choked out a greeting. "Hi. It's Sydney Green."

"Oh, hello," she said after a slight pause. I wondered if she'd pushed a button to record me. She was oddly formal now, no more "hi, hon" or trying to be relatable to draw me out. I knew it was because they suspected me now. "What's up?"

"Well," I looked over at Spider, who flashed me the thumbs-up. "I have some new information. It's urgent."

"Okay," Arlene said, drawing out the word like it might not be okay at all. "I'm all ears. But Sydney, you should know that we have some new information, too. We actually need to see you and your brother at the station as soon as possible."

What? What new information could Arlene possibly have?

Outside, I heard two car doors slam in the driveway.

And then there were three very loud knocks at the door.

Never in my life did I expect to ride in the back of a police car with my brother.

"Fucking hilarious," Spider said loud enough for the cops to hear. They hadn't cuffed us. They had been stiff but polite, simply saying the detectives needed to see us both right away and they were here to "escort" us.

"We could have driven ourselves. They didn't need to send these nutsacks out," Spider muttered in the back of the car.

"Shhh," I hissed. "Don't antagonize them. You'll just make this worse."

"They aren't listening to us, believe me," Spider said. "If this was really serious, they'd have done the whole thing, the handcuffs, the Miranda rights. They're trying to soft-shoe us, let us incriminate ourselves."

"Well, we didn't do anything, so there's nothing to worry about." Still, my heart continued to race.

"Let them tell you what they have on us before you lay down your info, okay? It's strategic. You need to know what they're working with so you can see if there's anything we need to worry about." Spider glowered at the two young cops in the front seat, then stuck his middle finger up at them so that only I could see. "This had better not fuck with my parole, that's all I have to say."

And then I was alone in a warm, windowless interrogation room with a cup of watery coffee, a one-way mirror, and my frayed nerves. My hand had bled through its paper-towel bandage. Not exactly a look that screamed innocence.

I waited a long time before Arlene and Bill finally appeared. I wondered if they were interrogating Spider first, or just making both of us sweat. Either way, I hated them for it. And it was working. I was sweating. I didn't smell good, my stomach had gone sour, and my feet, stuck inside my sneakers without any socks because I'd rushed to do what the officers told me, itched.

"Hi, Sydney. Sorry about the wait," Arlene said when she finally showed up. She was wearing the exact same suit as the other day. The only change was that tonight she had no makeup on. Her gaze flicked to the blood-soaked paper towel around my hand and then back to my eyes. "I just really needed to get to the bottom of things tonight. There's some new evidence that has been kind of bugging us."

I made my face into stone and stared at her across the table. Then I thought of Rain and swallowed down a wave of grief.

"We appreciate you and your brother coming down here on such short notice," Bill said when he waltzed in a moment later. He shut the door behind him. *Like we had any choice,* I thought as I nodded hello to him.

"I didn't have anything to do with the fire," I whispered. "And neither did my brother."

"Well, see," Bill said. "We figured you were going to say that."

"Because it's true!"

"You had no issue with Brianna, then? No reason at all to be upset with her?" Sitting across from me, Bill's bald head gleamed. His double chin was soft and it made him look almost kind, but I didn't like the way he stared at me. Skeptical, like he was about to snare me in a trap.

I opened my mouth, then shut it. What did he know that he was dangling over me like a guillotine? "We didn't get along. But—"

"When you say you didn't get along . . ." Bill tented his hands in front of his thin lips.

"We didn't like each other, Bill. She wasn't my favorite." I glared, not wanting to say any more. I opened my mouth to tell them what I knew, but Spider's words came back to me, and maybe he was right. They needed to show their hand before I showed mine.

"The tip line was sent a voice recording earlier today," Arlene said. "But it got sent to a transcription service instead of going straight to me. I only just got the tape and the transcript back tonight after I got off the phone with you. You can imagine, a lot of people have been using the tip line, the community is very invested in this case. So there's a lot of stuff on there we have to sort through."

I smiled tightly and folded a clean edge of my paper towel bandage over the blood-soaked part. If I wasn't so curious about their new information, I would have already begun to explain about Brie and Rain and what I'd figured out. How dumb were Arlene and Bill going to feel when I told them I'd cracked the case wide open? If I wasn't so destroyed inside, I would have taken some satisfaction in it.

"We made a transcript of the recording. I've highlighted the important parts for you, Sydney. Bill and I both agree that one of people in the recording was you."

Arlene slid the transcript over and I read the first line:

I have some things to say, actually. To both of you.

I put my hand over my mouth and looked up at Bill and Arlene, who were watching me closely. I read on, the words swimming on the page.

Brie had recorded the whole fight we'd had in Candice's house and sent it to the cops. The perfect student, the perfect manipulator had struck again. Yet another psychotic move to frame me.

I skimmed the rest of the fight and found the lines Arlene had highlighted.

You burn down people's lives for fun. Just because you can.

He's out now. Home today. Maybe you heard? He's actually here at this party. Said he wanted to talk to you.

You turned him in, didn't you?

One day someone's going to do that to you, and you won't even see it coming.

When I finished, I looked back up at Bill and Arlene. "You can see here that she's not a nice person." I said, trying to keep my voice calm. What if this could be used against me somehow, even if it was Rain who'd been killed? I took a deep breath through my nose and out through my mouth and tried to calm my racing heart.

"Unfortunately, Sydney, the other thing we see is that some of your statements sound an awful lot like threats," Bill said.

"And motive," Arlene added. "For you, and for your brother."

"Good thing Brie isn't dead then," I burst out, smacking the table in anger. "Because I guess we'd be in big trouble."

I let my words sink in, watched a few beads of sweat form on Bill's waxy forehead. Arlene sat back and looked at me with raised eyebrows but didn't say anything.

"I actually wish she was, because if she were dead—if I'd killed her, then maybe my friend Rain would still be alive. That's the other girl in the conversation Brie sent you."

Arlene and Bill glanced at each other. They both kept quiet, but I could tell Rain had been a part of this puzzle for them.

"But yeah, I didn't hurt Brie," I added. "And neither did my brother. Brie's fine. You should find her and ask her about the fire."

"Back up, Sydney." Arlene spoke up at last, her voice infuriatingly calm. "You're saying Brianna Walsh is alive? And you believe Rain Santangelo to be the victim?"

"Yes." I began to explain everything. I showed them the long string of Rain's texts, how they'd changed after the fire. I explained about the Peoria joke. I even explained how Brie's verbal tic of an insult was a tip-off.

"You need to test the body. I'm positive you'll find out it's Rain who died," I said, holding back tears, thinking all over again of Rain trapped in Brie's room, somehow unable to get free. "Now can me and my brother go home? We've been through a lot."

Arlene cleared her throat and turned to Bill. Whatever communication passed silently between them, I could tell the night hadn't gone the way they expected. "We'll need to subpoena your phone records," Bill said, turning back to me. "Because if you're right, they will be key evidence. And they might help us locate the suspect."

"Whatever it takes for you to find Brie and make her pay for this, I'm here to help," I said. "But can you at least send my brother home? He had nothing to do with this."

Bill and Arlene nodded. "We just want to ask him a few more questions," Arlene said. "And then I think we can send him home."

"Good." I remembered what Arlene had dismissively called all this when I'd first met her. "Because this is girl drama."

36

I stayed home for the next several days, just me, Mom, Spider, and the TV. We kept the lights low and our voices hushed, all three of us stunned and grieving. Mom and Spider made all my favorites, but I could barely eat. They watched me push food around on my plate and would not stop hassling me until they saw me choke down a few bites.

On the third day, I got a call from Arlene. The dental records had come in. "You were right," she said simply. "I'm so sorry about your friend. We'll find the person that did this."

"You mean Brie?" I needed to hear from Arlene that she was their main suspect now.

"Sure is looking that way, yes."

"Okay." I let out a relieved breath. I'd come so close to taking the fall, but at least now the police were looking in the right direction. "One more question."

"Shoot."

"Does Joan know?" I'd been too cowardly to call Joan, telling myself that we didn't know for sure. "Rain's mother, I mean?"

"We visited her this morning," Arlene said.

I hung my head and pictured Joan getting the news. I could almost hear the scream erupting from her throat. I hung up with Arlene and sat there crying. Mom hovered behind me and rubbed my back, whispering "Sshhhh" until my sobs died out into numb quiet.

There was still one more week of school, but nothing that happened there could bring my grades down low enough to risk my scholarship. There was, as I saw it, no reason to return to school at all. I wasn't interested in people watching me grieve.

I emailed my teachers and explained. Two of them let me turn in projects via email and two others told me they would excuse me from final exams considering the situation and how hard I'd worked up until now. I was surprised how nice everyone was, and even more surprised by the nice things they said about Rain. "She was one in a million," Mr. Sanders said. Ms. Martin called her "spirited, charismatic, a born debater." Ms. Wu said she had a wonderfully dry sense of humor. "Rain Santangelo had gravitas," Principal Stokes wrote in a Facebook post. "She carried with her a wisdom and healthy skepticism that far surpassed her years."

Rain had touched people in her short life, even teachers. Even as disconnected as she'd always felt from school, she'd made an impression.

I told Mom I wasn't going back, that I was making up what little work I still owed from home. She chewed her lip and nodded. "That's okay, honey. You don't have to." I could feel her watching me closely, though, concern radiating from every pore. I told myself I couldn't break down and give up forever, even though I desperately wanted to. That I needed to return to myself and my future, for Mom. And for Rain. I needed to live as big a life as I could muster for the both of us.

The more days that ticked by, the more I felt I needed to get away from here. Everywhere I turned in my house was another reminder of Rain. Every inch of this place was somewhere she used to be. "Maybe I could go to Aunt Debbie's a little early," I said after a week had gone by, too afraid to look at Mom. "I could get a summer job in Oxford before school starts."

When I dared to look up, Mom was already dialing her phone. She had always trusted that I knew what was best for me. Me, her golden child. The one who until recently had never fallen apart, who until recently she'd never needed to worry about. She'd always believed in my bright future, and now she would do whatever it took to pull me away from the trouble that had found me.

The day the news broke about Rain, I got a text from Chase.

I can't believe this. I'm so sorry. Can I come over?

Thank you. Me neither. Maybe in a few days, I wrote back, touched that he asked but knowing I couldn't handle seeing him, or anyone. I'm too much of a mess right now.

Pictures of Brie and Rain began to run on a continual loop every half hour, having moved from the local news to CNN. The story was disturbing enough to go national. The tabloids Mom brought home from the grocery store each had their pictures on the front page: HIGH SCHOOL TRACK STAR KILLS BEST FRIEND AND FAKES HER OWN DEATH, FUGITIVE STILL AT LARGE; WINNING, "TWINNING," AND SINNING—MURDER SUSPECT SOUGHT AFTER ASSUMING HER VIC-TIM'S IDENTITY, STEALING LOTTERY WINNINGS. None of them got Rain or Brie quite right, but I hoped all the attention would at least help the police find Brie.

After the news broke on TV that a national manhunt was under way for Brie, I finally called Joan. Poor Joan. She didn't pick up. I left a message.

"I'm so sorry. I loved her so much. She is with me every day." I hung up then, having begun to cry.

Two days after the manhunt began, Ed made the rounds in a too-tight suit on cable news, begging Brie to turn herself in and "clear her name," certain that it had "all been a misunderstanding and a horrible mistake."

"My daughter could not have done anything like that," he said to the camera, still red-faced, his tone as angry as ever. Beneath his bluster, though, there was a flicker of pain, the expression of a man who knew he'd lost everything. I turned it off, unable to watch him insinuate that maybe the girl who had died in his home was the one who had set the fire.

When Joan called back and asked me to meet her at the diner by school, it was the first time I'd left the house in almost two weeks. The clattering of plates and smells of food were more stimulation than I was used to—I jumped when the hostess asked me to follow her to a booth in the back.

Even here, I couldn't escape the coverage. Pictures of Rain and Brie flashed on the silenced TVs above the diner's counter. *Murdered girl's car found in El Paso,* the chyron said, and sure enough the video was of Rain's black maxi Mini being hoisted onto a tow truck. *Brianna Walsh is believed to have crossed U.S. border.* I tried to avert my eyes. I didn't want to cry before I even found Joan. Brie must have been long gone by now. For all I knew, she'd driven through all of Mexico, had made it past El Salvador, Guatemala, Honduras, Panama. Or maybe she'd faked everyone out and gone north to Oregon, Washington, and then Canada, or east, like I was about to. She could have been anywhere. In any country. Who knew what she'd have access to, how she might blow through Rain's money? Brie had always been so shrewd in our econ class, so quick to plan out how an economy could get back on its feet. She was like that when it came to war strategies, too, in all our history classes over the years where people had needed to swerve a different way than they'd thought. Napoleon, Robespierre, the Romanovs. Anyone who'd ever felt cornered, Brie had always been drawn to. She'd been cornered all her life, in a way, living with Ed. Maybe she was used to it.

In the very last booth, Joan looked like she was barely hanging on. Her cheeks were sunken in. Her gray was growing in at her roots, the red fading away, like she'd literally lost her color.

"Hi, baby doll." She stood up, put her arms around me. I breathed in the same Joan smell I'd known since childhood, Trésor perfume and Newports. Soon we were both weeping, hugging and awkwardly settling into the same side of the booth, our hands clasped as if we were clinging to the sides of a building and trying not to fall.

"You were always like my daughter. Always there with us. I was so mad at Rainey when you stopped coming over. I knew she must have done something to push you away. I said 'Rainey, you don't just trade one friend for another,' and she said she knew, that she was going to fix everything with you, but it was like she was obsessed with Brianna for a while there. Brianna kept her too busy to remember you. I was pissed, Sydney. Truly I was."

I nodded. *I was pissed, too.* But there was no point in saying that now, not with everything that had happened. "It's okay. I'll always remember Rain as my best friend."

"You were everything to her." Joan broke down for a second and I squeezed her hand tighter. "I know she died knowing you loved her."

This sent me into another fit of crying.

After a while, we both regained our composure. I sat in silence a few minutes before I was able to continue talking.

"Do they have any leads on Brie other than the car?" I wondered if Joan was in better touch with the police than I was.

Joan shook her head. "I only know what we see on TV. But even if they do find her, it won't bring Rainey back. That girl—*that* girl is suffering either way. She'll suffer running, and she'll suffer when she's caught. Ed, that bastard, when he's not on TV being a blowhard, he walks around like he's seen a ghost. I saw him at Trader Joe's putting frozen food in his cart. I couldn't resist going up to him." Joan shook her head as if to chide herself.

"'How are you holding up?' I said to him. You know, parent to parent? Somehow I thought I owed him that. But he just stared right through me. That's when I realized how angry I was."

The waitress arrived with steaming mugs of hot water and two paper-wrapped Lipton tea bags. "Thanks, hon," Joan said.

"So anyway," Joan resumed her story. "I started shouting at him 'Where's your daughter, Ed?' I got up into his face in the middle of the frozen foods aisle. I was shaking, screaming, the works. 'Because *my* daughter's dead.'" Joan unwrapped her tea bag and dunked it three times in her hot water. "It was awful." She looked up at me, her eyes full of remorse. "I shouldn't have done it. Didn't help anything and he just stormed out of there. Left his food and everything right there."

"I'm glad you did that." I cupped my mug of tea and let the steam float up and warm my closed eyes. I could almost see Ed wandering through his days, haunted by what Brie had done. "He needs to hear it."

"I always knew I should have done more for that girl when she was little. She wasn't strong like you. She didn't have a mother and Ed was . . . well, you remember how he was. I should have acted back then." Joan craned her neck and looked around her as if checking that nobody was listening. "In my gut, I knew something was off.

"By the time I really understood Rain and Brianna were close again, I still had that bad feeling about Brianna. But you all were so close to grown. I couldn't interfere except to be nice to her, show her some hospitality, same as I would do for any of you kids. And now look what's happened. Every day I think I could've been more involved. I knew she was troubled. Underneath all her . . . *achievement.*" Joan wrinkled her nose at this word like it smelled. She broke down again and turned to press her face to the vinyl backing of the booth.

Oh, Joan. You didn't deserve any of this, I wanted to say.

"You were a great mom to Rain. And to me," I said instead.

"Nobody could've predicted this. Rain always had the best bullshit detector. If she couldn't see it, how could we?"

Joan took a few shaky breaths. She put her thumb to my cheek and wiped a tear away. "I'd like it if you kept in touch with me. You're my daughter now more than ever."

I nodded. "I want you in my life, too."

You're my only link to Rain. We both felt it. It didn't need to be said. It just *was.*

Joan rummaged through her purse and pulled out a wrinkled envelope. "Listen, I know you won't want to take this, but I am insisting. It's an order, not an offer, okay?"

I shook my head, knowing already that it was going to be too generous. "I don't need anything—"

"I'm not asking what you need, baby doll. I know you don't need a damn thing and I know you've always worked a job and are perfectly capable of earning for yourself, as is your mom, as is your brother. Still, I am insisting you take it." She pressed the envelope into my hands. "Rain would've wanted you to have it."

"No. Joan, I can't." I laid the envelope back down on the table.

"You can and you will. My sister made me put the money in the bank after everything that happened. This is a cashier's check. You have to cash it at the bank, and you can't lose it. Because if you do," Joan whispered now, "if you do, whoever finds it can cash it. Put it away for now. It's going to look like a lot of money when you see it, but I'm getting pretty good at making money and I won't miss it. As you may have heard, in this country the rich get richer." Joan shook her head as if she almost couldn't believe the way her funds were expanding. "Everything, every law and every rule, is set up for me to increase my wealth and for your family to never get the littlest leg up, and it's not fair. Never was, never will be. So you can just put this in the bank and figure out what you want to do with it, maybe give some to your mom, or do whatever you want. It's yours now."

I nodded stupidly, wanting to object again louder, to be that proud girl she knew I would try to be. Instead, I thanked her. Threw my arms around her and pulled her to me and tried not to cry again.

"Don't thank me. I'm just doing what my daughter would want."

I sipped my tea, put a lemon wedge in my mouth and for a split second, I was back to my childhood in Termico, in the AstroTurf yard behind Rain's house, sucking on lemons we'd picked from the tree behind Panchitos after we'd applied the juice to strips of our hair so they would lighten in the sun. For a minute I was there again with her, the buzz of heat and hunger making me shiver, already longing to remember this moment even as it was happening, Rain in her stars-and-stripes plastic sunglasses, grousing about something, stretching out in the heat of the afternoon, in the heat of our adolescence, too cool for it all but also vulnerable, searching, scanning the horizon for clues about what would happen next.

My hand found the corner of the envelope. I folded it in half and tucked it into my back pocket, made sure it was safe. I didn't want to think about the money yet. There would be time for that later. Right now, I wanted to remember my friend.

EPILOGUE

SEVEN MONTHS LATER

You think money will make you happy, but it doesn't. It didn't even make Rain happy when all that money fell like magic from the sky for her and Joan. Sharing it made her happy, but the money itself, when she was all alone? It didn't change a thing. Not really.

But I'm doing my best to live the way I think Rain would have wanted me to. It's January, winter break at Miami of Ohio, and I'm home, back in the desert for the first time since June. Spider and I are about to take a road trip up the 101. He's on break from culinary school. I'm paying for it, so he owes me this weekend. We're going to drive north and listen to his collection of early-2000s rap CDs and try to relax.

I'm pumping gas into the sensible car I've bought him, a Honda CR-V. I wave at Rafid's son, Amir, home for the holidays and glumly manning the register. He looks up from where he's scrolling on his phone, waves back. I'll stop in and find Rafid when Spider and I come back. For now, we need to get a move on. We're headed to a full moon party up in the central valley past Oxnard, in California's breadbasket, where everything is grown. Spider's idea. After Whit was arrested as an accessory to Rain's murder over the summer, Spider threw away all the pills he'd brought home from Pine Grove and declared he was done with substances forever. He's into

EDM now, says dancing sober late into the night is his new drug. That it's better than getting high.

I put Joan's ridiculously large check into a bank account and didn't think about it again except to replace the family cars, encourage Spider to start culinary school, and give Mom enough money to buy a condo down in the valley. She's still going to open houses, emailing me listings all the time. Taking her time in picking something out, constantly texting me, Honey, this will be your nest egg and things like that. I write back, Thank Joan and Rain, I'm just the delivery girl.

My first semester at college, I got all As except for a B-plus in astronomy. Guess I'm just not ready to think about stars. They feel too close to Rain. To where she is now. Even though I've never believed in a literal heaven, I can't help thinking of her returning to stardust.

Every two months like clockwork, Arlene calls me and asks if anyone I know has heard from Brie. And every time, I'm destroyed all over again when I have to tell her no. Even though the case has become federal and a different unit is working on finding her, I can tell it haunts Arlene that Brie's trail has run dry. It haunts all of us. I'm on a group chat with all her old besties now, suddenly absorbed into their scattered communications in her and Rain's absence as we all try to make sense of what's happened.

Where could she be?? Deirdre wrote in the middle of the night back in September. I had a dream she was in my dorm. It felt so real.

Does anyone else still feel panic whenever they smell smoke? Min wrote in November.

It's cold comfort knowing we're all traumatized by what Brie did, that we're all grieving Rain in our own ways, but it does make me feel a little less alone.

I'm getting ready to pump the gas as I've done a million times before at this spot, putting the nozzle in place and pressing the big yellow button. When I look up, a familiar blue hatchback Cabriolet is pulling in. The door opens and something buzzes in my head, the tiniest frisson of longing and pain.

It's Chase. All the way up here in Termico.

I squeeze the pump and feel the gas start moving into the car. I wave. My sunglasses hide whatever I'm feeling, or so I hope.

He looks exactly the same. Same puffy brown hair I used to wind around my fingers. Same full lips. His chin has a little more stubble than I've seen before, but other than that, he's exactly the boy I remember.

"Hi." Chase smiles.

"What are the odds? In all the gas stations in all the towns," I joke.

"I come up this way on school breaks. You don't answer my texts."

That's true. I've received them in the college cafeteria, in my dorm room, in class. It never feels like the right time to answer, or like I know the right thing to say. They make me smile, though. I imagine him typing them from someplace in Santa Cruz, a skate park or the beach or even from one of the carnival rides on the boardwalk, though I don't really think he spends much time there.

"What are you up to?" He smiles again and there's that gap between his teeth that always made me melt.

"Just going to a full moon thing with my brother," I say. "Spider's into EDM now." I shrug and feel my face grow warm.

"How are you doing?" Chase's eyes search mine. He looks underslept, dark circles sitting where there used to just be sunburn.

"Oh, fine. I mean, not great. But fine, considering." I still have nightmares a few times a week. I still feel a pit in my stomach most days, and my heart races when I smell a fireplace. But I don't need to get into that with him.

"Totally," he says. Then we stand there in silence. "Same."

"How's college?" I say at last.

"Good, pretty good." His hand wraps around mine then. "Kind of overwhelming."

"It's intense, right?" My voice catches in my throat. My palm buzzes with the familiar sensation of his fingers around it.

"I miss you." That crooked smile. He looks at me, all earnestness. "I miss hearing your voice."

"Me too. But . . . I've been . . . taking a break from all that." From all what, though? Where has this expression even come from? All that intimacy? Closeness? Risk of rejection? Maybe all of it. Yes, I decide. It's the truth. I am indeed taking a break from all that.

I think of Sam Stillman, who has my same work study job at Miami. We both swipe dining hall cards at the south entrance three mornings a week. Sam, who is in Miami's art program and is always covered in flecks of paint. Who lets me cry and doesn't try to fix it. Who seems to be satisfied just stroking my hair. I think of how desperate I'd been when I was with Chase. Desperate to bet my whole heart on him, and then later, desperate to assume the worst, to watch it all explode into flames. Desperate to believe he'd hurt me, maybe. How easy it was for Brie to drive a wedge between us, because maybe I'd been looking for an excuse to blow it all up and feel used. And why? For what? He was just a person. Probably trying his best.

The gas shuts off, done pumping. I put it back in its holster, hug Chase goodbye, and feel tears loosen in my throat when his arms tighten around me. For a moment I'm safe, protected, innocent again in a world where everyone I love hasn't left me, where someone cares about me. It's enough to tether me to this spot a little longer, where the world is a steady, safe place where good things will keep on happening. I close my eyes and let myself grow dizzy with touching him again. Unconsciously, my eyes still closed, I find his lips and kiss him, not more than a moment of contact but it's like finding something I lost forever ago and didn't even know how much I still missed. Neither of us pulls away until the car horn honks.

"Yo," Spider yells from the car, annoyed. "We gotta set up the tent before it's dark."

"He's right," I whisper in Chase's ear and sadly pull away from him. "We have absolutely no idea what we're doing."

Chase laughs. "Well, good luck with that, then. See you later, Syd." Chase leans in, his voice low. The intimacy is almost too much to bear, but in a good way.

The smile Chase gives me when the car roars to life and we pull away will make my heart thrum for the rest of tonight. We'll see what happens there, I tell myself.

For now, it feels good to leave this place in the rearview again, to escape everything that has happened, if only temporarily. It feels right to turn onto the little dusty highway that will feed into larger highways, five lanes in a row stretching away from here, to points cooler and gentler and more hospitable to human life. Toward a future where everything isn't singed and roasting, where girls aren't hothouse flowers about to wilt or burst into flame.

Spider is already rapping along to vintage Eminem. I turn up the volume and get ready to belt the chorus. I roll down my window, gulp the January air, and squint against the winter sun that blasts the desert with a yellow haze that if you didn't know better, you could almost mistake for some kind of grace.

We take on speed and I feel Rain all around me, propelling me down the mountain, urging me onward to someplace new and green. To someplace better.

ACKNOWLEDGMENTS

With thanks:

To Joelle Hobeika, Josh Bank, and Sara Shandler, for your unshakeable belief in the Termico three. Fathomless appreciation especially to the brilliant Lanie Davis, who knows what it took to get here.

To Sarah Barley, for your expert editorial guidance and enthusiasm in shaping this story. It has been a joy to work with you. To the entire Flatiron team, especially Cat Kenney, Jordan Forney, Malati Chavali, Megan Lynch, and Sydney Jeon, for all your work on behalf of this book, and to Keith Hayes and Henry Sene Yee for the beautiful cover.

To Faye Bender, for always knowing the right thing to do.

To Cathrin Wirtz and Laura Sims, whose early support of the book has meant more than I can say.

To Rachel Sherman, for knowing what these characters would wear. To Alana Sherman, who took a trip with me several years ago to the Salton Sea that inspired much of my early thinking about the world of the book.

To Aria Chiodo, Corrie Hulse, Katherine Willis, Nusrat Hossain, and Sarah O'Hare, for your grace and good humor through difficult days spent in windowless rooms. My ability to write this in our off hours was due entirely to you.

To writer pals and confidants Anne Ray, David Ellis, Elizabeth Logan Harris, Elliott Holt, Helen Phillips, Marie-Helene Bertino, and Tom Grattan. The writing life may be solitary, but because of you it's never been lonely.

To Emily Jackson, Jen Stone, Jessea Hankins, Julia Landau, Lauren Flower, Mehernaz Farsi, Naomi Schultz, Shasta Lockwood, and Thaïs Jones. Everything I know about life-altering friendships formed at a tender age I learned from you.

To my family, especially Agnes and Ivan Sanders, Lizzy and Neil Postrygacz, Cory Kahaney, Ken Misrok, Ariel Cristini, Jeannie Kahaney, and Phyllis Kahaney. To the next generation: Rufus, Asher, Meka, Sofia, and Magnus. You all inspire me.

To Ezra, who, in the course of my writing this book, somehow became old enough to read it.

To Gabriel Sanders, always, for everything.

ABOUT THE AUTHOR

Amelia Kahaney is the author of the Brokenhearted series. Her short fiction has appeared in *The Best American Nonrequired Reading*, *One Story*, and *Crazyhorse*, among other publications. She teaches writing in New York City, where she lives with her husband and son. Visit her online at www.ameliakahaney.net.